Here, There Be Monsters

"WATERBEARER"

Edited by Lily Ingersoll
Cover Illustration by Martina Fichera
Cover Layout by Erica Lynn Evans
Spanish Translation by Casey L. Guyer

ISBN: 978-1-963266-16-0

Visit the author on the internet
http://www.therunespring.com

Foreword

Hello, Dear Reader! Know first that I couldn't have done this all on my own. My deepest thanks to my beta readers, John and JW, for making sure I had something worth sharing. Thanks also to my amazing cover artist, Martina, and my equally amazing graphic designer, Fidget, for making all my covers into truly professional works. Casey for adding an authentic touch en Español. Most of all, thanks to my best friend and editor, Lily, who puts up with my commasplosions and is never afraid to give it to me straight when something sucks.

This is what I feel to be my best work to date. I have always tried to put as much effort as I can into every aspect of my novels, but this is the first one where I feel like I have reached the proper distribution. I can't wait to get back to working on my other novels with the knowledge I have gained while writing this book.

An important word on authenticity. In this novel, multiple characters speak more than one language. One of those characters, though, is much younger and less adapted to his language set due to his upbringing and daily environment. To add a touch of authenticity to his character, I asked a friend who speaks fluent Spanish to translate parts of this character's speech at points where we felt the character would be stressed into switching languages without realizing.

In places where what was being said to the characters in the scene was ambiguous only to the reader, I have added a small translation key at the bottom of the page. Translations are shown in the order in which they appear on the page. Where those in the scene do not understand, they may ask for a translation themselves. I hope I have kept everything smooth for everyone while adding authenticity!

Without further ado, welcome to one of my favorite Earths. Be wary, Reader! Here, there be monsters!

BEFORE ALL THAT FOLLOWS, REMEMBER FIRST. THEY KNEW.

1
"ONE"

Footsteps sounded across the adjacent rooftop, stirring echoes from the brick buildings surrounding the tenement where Elenor sat, frozen.

Remaining still was her only defense, maintaining the ruse that she was just a large dog. It didn't explain her presence on the roof, but it was better than anyone actually seeing her for what she was.

Her ears twitched with each light step. *Not the heavy footsteps of an adult*, she thought. Elenor risked turning her head with extreme care. If she moved too quickly, the spines above her shoulders would stand and reveal her ruse.

On the next roof, a small figure crept through the mishmash of colorful nylon-strapped chairs, faded metal tables, and wooden loungers with a hesitant step.

"Elly?"

The light Spanish accent in the young man's voice came from the rooftop next door in a whisper only she would hear. The boy she had come here to see. Her friend of two entire days and, quite possibly, the only person in the entire city who thought of Elly as anything but a monster. She opened one of the shimmering golden eyes on her back. The extra visual input from behind was confusing for Elenor. Their armored lids also kept them protected and invisible. She didn't use them often.

She could see him crouching on the roof of his building, peering through hazel eyes widened to penetrate the gloom. The moment she saw him, she realized she could feel the water in his body pressing against her supernatural senses. *Idiot, you have to pay better attention.* It was her best early warning system for knowing when someone was nearby.

"Hey, Mateo. This is, unfortunately, me."

The darling girlish voice that issued forth from Elenor was an utter discordant contrast to her monstrous appearance. The shape of her tongue and the double row of razor-sharp triangles that served as her teeth caused her voice hiss with a slight lisp. It had just begun to change when the mutations began, and it then became clear that it never would. She had been that little girl, once.

She turned and felt her spines standing from where they hid beneath her fur. When she saw Mateo, she paused at the edge of the rooftop, standing stock still between the two buildings. His thin, muscular body tensed, his round face wearing a look of apprehension. He wore a navy jacket of thin fleece, blue jeans, and beat up black sneakers. He looked around at the small piles of snow at the edges of the rooftop and shivered a little from the cold.

"Mateo?"

She had met Mateo under strained circumstances a few days earlier. She knew he had not gotten a good look at her. The startle was understandable. Elenor had seen her reflection before, and it was not a good sight.

Her face mildly resembled the otters she had seen at the zoo, at least if they were the size of a large black bear. Then she opened her maw to reveal the dozens of obsidian razors that had long ago replaced her human teeth, removing all resemblance to any normal animal. The twisted ribbon-like horns of black blue and purple that curved back to wicked points past her rounded ears further advertised just how alien she had become.

That was only the beginning of her oddities. She had discovered that if she sat very still, people would often mistake her for a large dog if the lighting was poor. Especially if they couldn't see her eyes. Mismatched like some dogs, one blue, one purple. They would luminesce in contact with the slightest light. Even in broad daylight, her eyes glowed slightly blue and purple. Not that she got to see much daylight these days.

"Está bien, Elly. Just didn't see you at first."

"Sorry."

The gap between the buildings was about eight feet, but unlike when she was human, her body had no trouble leaping the distance. She bunched her hindquarters and made the jump to Mateo's roof. The black flexible spines running down her back and peppering her thick tail allowed her to judge the wind, adjusting so she made a clean landing. Her talons clicked on the concrete of the short wall and she hopped down gently to the rooftop.

Elenor looked around the well-lit rooftop with some paranoia. She'd not had a friend since whatever had happened that had turned her into a creature that Hollywood would kill to cast in horror movies. Mateo had been the first person to not run away screaming when he had seen what she was. *Besides Mom and Dad.*

"It's ok." Mateo brought out a small soft-sided lunchbox he had hidden behind his back. "¡Sorpresa! I brought you some tacos from dinner tonight. Mi Mamá makes the best!"

Elenor paused a few feet away. She sat down on her haunches keeping back from Mateo. "Thanks, Mateo, but I can't eat that." It was a small lie, but everything about her seemed to terrify everyone she met. She wouldn't risk Mateo seeing what happened when she ate something.

"Why not?" He took one of the tortillas out, and began to eat it. Siren scents rose up from the bag to taunt her nose. Fried beef, lettuce, tomato, cheese, sour cream, and some spices that she didn't immediately

- Está bien – It's okay
- ¡Sorpresa! – Surprise!
- Mi Mamá – My Mom

recognize. Her stomach growled at her.

"You seem hungry."

She cursed her body. She hadn't eaten anything fresh in some time. None of her dumpster diving ever made her sick, which was a plus, but none of it ever smelled as good as that taco. She knew if he saw what happened when she took a bite, he might bolt and never talk to her again. He took out another taco, and held it out to her like she was some sort of skittish animal that might run away if he moved too fast.

"Promise you won't freak?" She'd only had this one friend in the world, even if he was younger than her.

Mateo shrugged. "Pretty sure I would have run off already if you scared me. I mean, don't get it wrong. You're super scary, and I'm pretty sure you could bite my hand off in a split second with all those teeth, but you could have easily killed me the other night in the park. I never even saw you until you said something. Plus, those guys would have beaten the crap out of me if you hadn't scared them off." Mateo shook the taco at her. "What could get creepier about you anyway?" He laughed.

"You're a little weird," Elenor said, but she padded closer, careful not to let her talons make too much noise on the rooftop. If she had to pick one thing to complain about with her body, it was the talons. Her front paws still had opposable thumbs. Unfortunately, the digits on her front paws were tipped with a thick claw almost two inches long. The claws were beyond razor sharp, made of the same shimmering black material as her teeth.

Oddly, they wouldn't cut her own body, but they would go through anything else they touched like a knife through hot butter. She could sink them into solid stone, or even steel. She took great care not to let them touch Mateo as she held out her front paw pads up.

"I'm a lot weird, but I'm also not wrong." He paused as he held out the taco, looking at the obsidian black claws.

"Be careful not to touch them. They're super sharp." Elenor warned.

Mateo carefully put the taco on the palm of her paw. "Why are you so worried about me watching you eat?"

Elenor sighed. "Just, keep it together?" Above everything else that had somehow magically happened to her when she turned sixteen, this was the most unnatural part.

She took a bite out of the taco. For one long moment, she could taste the food. The tortillas had been homemade, fried in oil until crispy. The oil in them burst on her tongue. The salsa was fresh, and she enjoyed it for that one perfect second before she felt the heat. As she chewed the bite, carefully moving her teeth only up and down to break up the food, it began to burn. The heat inside of her mouth felt to her like eating a little bit of jalapeno. It lasted only for a moment, but steam and smoke poured out of her mouth and nose. By the time she was ready to swallow the bite of food, it had burned completely to ash.

She didn't understand that part at all, but she could only consume ash. Even if she tried to bolt down the food as fast as she could, it never made it past the back of her throat before it had burned away to ash.

"¡Híjole!" Mateo's eyes went wide as he stared at the smoke and steam leaking from between her razor teeth.

Elenor was amazed he didn't actually freak out. But even her brief time in high school Spanish was enough to recognize a curse.

"¿Qué estás tú?" he asked.

Elenor's demon face scrunched into an agonized cringe and she leaned slightly away from Mateo.

He seemed to realize what he had said right away. "Elly, I didn't mean it like that. I just mean, you know

- ¡Híjole! – Holy crap!
- ¿Qué estás tú? – What are you?

what, I mean a lot of things. ¿Qué te pasó?"

Elenor took another bite of the taco, and then another, savoring that one second of flavor before it burned. She made a little shrug, the spinelike blades across her shoulders fluttering up for a moment. She put the last of the taco in her mouth, chewed, and swallowed.

"I haven't the slightest idea. A few weeks after my sixteenth birthday, this started. The fur came first and then I got the horns." She reached up to touch the curving black ribbons with highlights of blue and purple.

"My parents tried to get me help, but after a few weeks, I couldn't stand up like a person anymore. My legs changed and my talons grew in. That's when doctors started to get really interested in me. I'd probably be all over the internet, The Baltimore Monster Girl or whatever, but my parents never let anyone take any pictures. My dad's a lawyer, and he was careful to make everyone sign papers saying they wouldn't talk about it. After I couldn't seem human anymore, they made doctors come to our house, but no one knew what to do." Elenor let out a short soft sniffle, but she held in any tears.

"Anyway, the doctors and some other alphabet soup guys showed up at the door one day, saying they didn't think my parents could take care of me anymore, which was bullshit. I ran. I'm not ending up as some lab experiment. This is already weird enough." She gestured to herself.

"Alphabet Soup guys?"

"You know, they're part of organizations that have a bunch of letters as the name? The ones that showed up at our house were supposedly from the CDC. They said they were worried I had caught some sort of disease, which is stupid because if I had, my parents would have caught it ten times over."

• ¿Qué te pasó? – What happened to you?

Mateo sat up straighter, and set aside the lunchbox.

"Elly, there have been guys in suits asking questions around here the last few weeks. Asking if we have seen any weird animals around town. I think they're looking for you."

2
"ALARM"

Crimson light swelled from the crack of a partially opened door followed by a gentle but penetrating chime of sound. As the chime faded, so did the light. The door swung open out of the small space to reveal a slight young woman with a heart-shaped face. Amythia rubbed her eyes irritably, finally pulling her hands away when the next chime sounded. White light swelled this time, lighting her vibrant green irises. Her eyes locked onto the orb producing the light. Fizzing white sparkles floated up from the orb before fading away like the dying bits of a burning firework.

Eyes widening with realization, Thia rushed into the room and slapped her palm onto the orb. The white light immediately vanished and the surface of the orb resolved. An image of the Earth appeared on the surface turning the sphere into a globe. Flashing repeatedly above the east coast of North America, the vibrant blue dot was something she thought she would never see.

"Holy shit," she mumbled. She dropped into the plush leather office chair. Amythia pulled herself up to the desk holding the orb and a number of computer screens. She fumbled the phone out of her pocket without taking her eyes off the crystal ball. She looked away only long enough to hit the first speed dial on the touchscreen. It rang three times before the call went through.

The muzzy voice rose from the phone. "Mm'ello?"

"The Oracle is showing a Bearer."

There was a clattering noise followed by muffled cursing and then a click. The phone screen showed a red disconnect icon. It took only a minute for pounding feet to sound on the stairs down the hall. A second woman appeared in the door, panting. She wore a long black t-shirt with the words "A Wizard Did It" emblazoned across her modest chest. The young woman sitting in the chair spun herself to reveal the oracle sphere, blue dot pulsating on its surface.

"How did you know? It's been…" Thia trailed off.

"Fourteen hundred years. It was inevitable, Thia."

Helen came into the tiny office and sat heavily in a large leather recliner that barely fit in the room. "It is time to pay for the mistakes."

"What do you mean? You didn't do this." Thia's concern was evident.

"No, Thia, I did not do this."

"Then, how's it your responsibility?"

"Because I did not stop it, either. I could have, and at the time, I had a thousand reasons to do it. But it only took one reason for me not to. I trusted Myrridin Wyllt."

"But why? He's almost gotten us killed three times in the last twenty years. He'll cross any line to get what he wants," Thia accused.

"He was not trying to get us killed, he was just trying to get the Relics back."

Thia narrowed her eyes. "That's bullshit."

Helen shook her head. "I am not in denial, Thia. I know he is not my friend anymore. I did not let him get away with what he did, now did I?"

Thia grunted. "You know that if I get the chance, I will absolutely force feed him a bullet."

Helen held up her hands in surrender. "After what he did to you in Korea, I would not even think of trying to stop you. He's certainly earned it."

Thia grunted an affirmative.

Helen sighed. "The point is when I knew him back then, he was determined, intelligent. He saved my life on more than one occasion. After Osiris, he changed. I think that he blamed himself for hesitating and decided he should not hesitate again."

"That's no excuse for doing the kinds of things I've seen him do," Thia asserted.

"I agree. He doesn't adjust to failure well, and he has lost his ability to judge when he has gone too far. He is, at this, about to go much too far."

Thia narrowed her eyes. "But you still won't stop him?"

"I do not trust him anymore, Thia, and I never will again. I just don't want to hurt him unless I'm forced. We were friends once."

"He isn't your friend anymore," Thia growled.

"No, he is not. If he manages to get himself killed trying to stop us from fixing this problem we created, I will not save him. I will do the deed myself only if it becomes necessary."

"So, he just gets to keep doing," Thia began to argue, but Helen cut her off.

"If it becomes necessary, Thia!"

Thia rolled her eyes and pointed at the Oracle Stone. "Does this also mean Surges will work again?"

"I cannot say for certain," Helen replied. Thia's face fell. Helen smiled reassurance. "This is the beginning, Thia. Eventually, you'll be able to put your training to the test."

"How much time do we have?" Thia asked, looking back to the oracle stone.

"Not much. Myrridin will be hunting these people as soon as he knows. The Relic he is using isn't nearly as accurate or sensitive as the oracle stone. We have a little time."

"Do we call up the network?" Thia asked.

Helen shook her head. "Not yet. We do not know what we are dealing with yet. We will go first, ourselves."

Helen held out her hand. Thia picked up the oracle stone from its pedestal and deposited it in her mother's hand. She touched the blue dot and the image blurred.

It seemed as if the image projected on the stone were from a bird diving toward the ground. It slowed to a stop, still at a high altitude, but close enough to see the buildings clearly.

"Somewhere in Maryland, looks like city," Helen said, and Thia tapped the computer keyboard in front of her. The screens came to life and displayed blank desktops with a few scattered icons. She chose one and a moment later, a map of the United States was displayed on the screen. She looked from the oracle stone to the screen, comparing the images.

"Baltimore, near Johns Hopkins. Can we get closer?" Thia asked.

Helen shook her head. "Not from here. We need physical proximity to increase the accuracy."

"I'll call the hangar and get the jet spun up."

Thia powered down the computers and stood up. Helen stood as well and held out the oracle stone. Thia held up a finger. She yanked one of the desk drawers open and dug through it for a moment. She came up a moment later with a square leather messenger bag. Attached to the end of the bag was a small square case filled with dense grey fur. She took the shotput sized stone, slipping it into the square case. A magnetic snap clicked when she shut the lid.

"Will you at least tell me the whole story now?" Thia asked.

"I promised that if we ever reached this point I would, did I not?"

Thia looked expectant.

Helen began speaking as they left the office. "It began back when they still called me the Iðunn,"

NC 17, EPOCH 18426.283

"We warned him that divination was a dangerous field. I thought his curiosity merely academic," Myrridin said as he watched the image play on the oracle stone.

"You, thought? You know what divination does to people. Do not derogate him because he trained beside you. He was told it was a banned field of study. He was told only madness awaits those who trod that path."

"He has only been Osiris for…" Myrridin began.

"Four months!" Iðunn shouted. "Are you watching this?" Iðunn stabbed a finger at the image on the oracle stone.

Myrridin grimaced. "If we do as the law prescribes, who will take over as Osiris?"

"Get one of the Morrigan's apprentices to do it. They are ready."

"You know that none of them will live in a desert."

"One of them will," Iðunn growled.

Myrridin shook his head. "You cannot kill him, Iðunn."

"You cannot stop me. The law is clear. Can you not see where this is going?" Iðunn stepped away from the marble plinth that supported the oracle stone.

"We can contain the spread and place dampers on his power," Myrridin began, but Iðunn cut him off, her hand striking through the air like the blade of a sword.

"I know the last Osiris was one of your mentors but this man is not going to get away with that!"

She gestured violently at the oracle stone again. The image on the stone was of a man with bronze skin. He wore a pair of loose cotton pants with a belt made of gold links. His toned chest was bare and a large golden torque encircled his neck. His face was narrow and his sandy brown eyes were wide with manic glee.

Extending from his fist was an object familiar to all Callers. The Striker was a collection of fluted crystal rods. The rod in the center was a straight line of deepest black, about foot and a half in length. Spiraled tightly around the black rod were nine other rods of various colors. The Master's instrument.

The Iðunn growled at the image. "He is testing empowering Surges! Our law is there for a reason. If he continues, eventually his power will turn and we will spend centuries hunting down the twisted power-mad spawn he creates."

Myrridin sighed. "We don't know what he's done. If you kill him, we will have no chance to extract that information."

Iðunn shook her head, sending her platinum locks dancing. She began to pace around the aisles of the massive stonewalled workshop. Each table contained some collection of mystical curios and Iðunn perused them as she passed, trying to pacify her rage.

"I'll not be swayed, Myrridin. There is too much risk in letting this continue. That path has been walked."

"You can't know that it will spread that far," Myrridin said.

Iðunn slammed her fist into the wall, chips of stone flying from the impact. Cracks spread through the stone wall, and she spun on him. "I have seen it with my own two eyes! How do you think I became Iðunn?" She roared. "My predecessor gave her life to kill the last cursed Caller who tried to force supernatural powers upon normal humans! Thousands died." She shook a finger underneath his aquiline nose. "You were not here for the last. There will not be another!" Iðunn's venomous hiss seemed to be an invisible force that pushed Myrridin back a step.

"Fine, but at least give me a chance to find out what we need from him," Myrridin requested.

"We don't need to know,"

It was Myrridin's turn to cut her off.

"Then what are those?" Myrridin pointed a long finger at another part of the oracle stone. In the image, the ground surrounding Osiris was a perfectly circular sheet of obsidian. At the compass points stood four crystals embedded in the glass. Like Osiris' Striker, the crystals were emitting a bubbling froth of malachite illumination. Streams of the putrid light were flowing away into the village he stood on the edge of.

"Clearly, he is using them as an amplifier for his Surge," Iðunn said.

Myrridin shook his head. "If you continue the recollection, you will see that they support his Surge for many hours after *he departs. This is a test, Iðunn. He is creating a way to make his Surges outlast his presence."*

"Impossible."

"Everything is impossible, until it is not."

Iðunn's anger cooled as her endless curiosity drew her to the oracle stone. She examined the images moving across its surface. She bit her knuckle in thought before she began to mumble.

"Resonance without the Caller is impossible to achieve. You and I both know that."

"Without a doubt, and yet the evidence suggests that somehow, Osiris has been able to leave his presence behind here. He has done the impossible."

"Find out what he is doing and how he is doing it. After that, I will enforce our laws," Iðunn pronounced, and then she disappeared through the shimmering galactic portal that served as a door to Myrridin's workshop.

3
"HOME"

Elenor entered the subway tunnel through a maintenance hatch that she had to regularly slice the padlock off of. They kept replacing the stupid lock, and she'd even had to wreck a camera they had put up to try to watch what was happening. Occasionally, she would have to wait out a cop sent up there to watch the hatch, but no one had seen her.

She let her body twist as she flipped upside-down, a trick she had discovered not long after the transformation. As long as she gave it a little concentration, her paws would adhere to almost any surface. She walked down the ceiling of the subway tunnel and into the darkness.

Finding that hatch in the first place had been a real chore, but it was worth the trouble. Before she found it, she had to walk miles across the city to where the subway tracks came up to street level. Entering the tunnels from there would let her avoid the stations, where she certainly would have been seen. She would have to crouch down if a train came along, of course, but she had never been clobbered by one.

Mateo had explained that he and his brother had seen men in suits offering money for information about strange animals in the neighborhood. She hadn't wanted to leave Mateo. Not only was he the only person she knew besides her parents that didn't look at her like a monster, they actually liked a lot of the same things. Still, people looking for her was not a good sign.

She thought for a long moment of dropping to the tracks and waiting for the train. She just wanted all of this to be over. With some effort, she shrugged off the thought. She would not put her parents through that. She kept walking towards her favorite hideaway.

There was one possibly more important reason not to wait for the train. She wasn't sure that it would kill her. She knew for a fact that bullets just bounced off of her spines and skin since, in the second most pants-shitting incident in her entire life, a Baltimore police officer had shot her several times a few weeks after she had first left home.

"I guess there had to be some advantages to being a freaking Cthulhu monster," she mumbled to herself.

She had been on alert through the entire jaunt to get across the city. Her head twitched at every sound that was not completely familiar. Even if she had to be stuck in this stupid impossible body, she was damn well not going to end up as someone's science experiment.

She had never once used the well of ready power that resided somewhere in the center of her chest. Somehow, she knew what it did. It was knowledge that she had simply awoken with one day after her body had stopped mutating. She suspected the instinctual knowledge was only the bare minimum of what the power could do.

She could reach out and take control of the water inside of anything living. Trees, animals, people. Every time she thought about doing that to someone it made her a little sick. Still, this power, whatever it was, was how she had survived on the streets. She could feel the living things all around her. Inside her head, there was some sort of new input that explained how close each living thing was to her, what direction it was in, and how large it was. It was sometimes extremely distracting when she was surrounded by a lot of tiny things. The power seemed to detect things even as tiny as insects, and she had yet to find a way to make it leave her in silence on the subject. She wasn't sure she wanted to. It had kept her safe and hidden on numerous occasions when someone from the transit authority had been getting too close to where she was sleeping in the maintenance tunnels.

This was one of the better places in the city she had
found to safely sleep. Not many people came into the
tunnels and she could hide from the ones who did. She
had gotten lucky on the way back from Mateo's house
and found a heavy leather bag in one of the dumpsters
near the tenements. It might have been a purse because
of its small size, but the heavy leather made her think it
was something else.

She had been looking for something like it since her
claws had sliced apart the purple backpack she had
brought from home. One errant twitch had turned it
into tatters. The leather bag, with some care, could be
fastened around her neck so it would sit on her chest
between her front legs - the only area of her body not
burdened with razor sharp spines.

She had managed to scavenge some completely fresh
steaks from a restaurant that had clearly thrown out an
order that someone hadn't picked up. They were in
blue-green Styrofoam containers with a logo embossed
on the corner. It was one of the other things that she had
learned about this nightmare. To feel satisfied, she had
to eat several meals in a day. Three just was not enough.

It began to get warmer as she went further into the
night-blackened tunnels. The scratchy concrete surface
made her pause. The concrete had never been scratchy
before. The ceiling was always kept in good repair. It
was still a little too dark to see the floor well, even with
her night vision, which was much better than it had been
when she was human. It would get even better if she
focused on it. Something about the power of, whatever
it was, in the center of her chest let her make her eyes
much better at seeing in even the darkest areas.

She concentrated and the environment brightened
around her, revealing some things she hadn't noticed
before. First, the concrete was rough because a small
part of the roof had cracked and collapsed. The pieces
had been swept to one side of the tunnel to be removed

later, she supposed. There was caution tape stretched across the tunnel on two poles. She skirted around the hole in the ceiling and headed towards her hidey hole.

It was at the station end of the tunnel, where a large heavy steel door hid the room that contained the heating equipment for the nearby subway station. Elenor didn't get nearly as cold as she did when she was human, but she still hated feeling cold.

Finding warm places to sleep when she couldn't go inside, where people might see her, had been a challenge. For almost two months, she had been breaking into the basement of a tenement near to where Mateo lived to sleep near their furnace, having left home just as winter was setting in. That had resulted in too many close calls, so she had started searching the city for someplace more secluded. Not exactly easy to find in the dead of a northeastern winter. She had found it in the heating maintenance room for the Baltimore subway station at Charles Center.

That station, unlike most of the others, had a convenient maintenance hatch nearby and was closest to the area of the city where her parents lived. Shot Tower or Johns Hopkins station would have been better, but both were far more crowded and traveled than Charles Center. The maintenance hatches were farther walks in the tunnels to reach the dingy maintenance rooms where the heating equipment was housed as well.

Elenor reached down with a paw, careful not to punch her claws into the door, and tried to shove it open. She rolled her luminescent eyes when it didn't budge. Then she looked around carefully for any new features in the tunnel. Cameras were a real concern. She didn't want anyone watching her. When she found nothing, she just assumed that maintenance had replaced the stupid lock again.

Carefully, in perfect silence, she crept down the wall. She hopped to the floor and turned around to sit in front of the door. She held up a paw and jammed one of her shining black claws into the keyhole. She wiggled it around, careful not to pull the freakishly sharp substance through the door knob entirely. A moment later, she had scrambled the inner workings of the lock. She put her paw on the door knob, twisted, and it clicked open.

It would be a while before she found it locked again. They only came down when something was wrong with the furnace, or whatever that large boxy machine that gave off heat was, was broken. At one end of the large room was home sweet home, an enormous vent grate sunk into one wall. She pulled it open and walked in. Inside was a small tunnel that ran all the way over to the subway station. Another slightly smaller tunnel ran off to the left, towards one of the ticketing rooms. This smaller tunnel was where she had made her den. A small pile of stolen blankets and a pillow sat on one side of the large duct.

Nestled into the blankets on the floor of the duct was a small picture frame. It held three pictures. One was of her and her parents when she was still human, standing in front of Cinderella's castle at Disney World. Her mom and dad were wearing Minnie and Mickey ear hats, and she had been dressed as Alice from Alice in Wonderland. Her parents loved that picture, as ever the tomboy, Elenor rarely let them dress her in anything that resembled truly girly clothing. But it was Disney, and she had taken full advantage of being able to be dressed up like a princess that day. She had been ten.

The second was a picture of her when she was six. In it, she was holding a tiny dachshund puppy that she had named Scraps because he was a merle and his fur looked like scraps of cloth all sewn together to her.

The third was the most recent, and one of the only pictures ever taken of her post-transformation. It was taken only a few weeks before she decided staying at home was too dangerous for her parents. Before living in an air duct beneath the Baltimore streets had become her life. She was sitting on the couch in careful stillness, smiling her Cheshire smile full of sharp teeth as her parents had insisted she do. She was book-ended by her parents, mom on the left, dad on the right. They had managed to very carefully smooth down her spines so they could sit close enough to be in the picture next to her.

With care, she pulled the small bag over her head. It had been just big enough to carry the two small food containers and a single bottle of water that Mateo had given her. Water was the only thing she could drink. Though if they were the tiny ones, she could still add the little flavor packets to it and get the taste going down. Too much of anything besides water, she had discovered, would trigger whatever function of her body that burned things in her mouth. Soda turned to steam and left behind only the surgery syrup which would immediately burn to a tiny amount of ash that she would have to drink something to swallow down.

Carefully, she took the plastic bottle of water out, making sure not to puncture it. She put it down next to her blankets. She would stick it outside in a snowbank when she wanted it cold again. She unpacked the food containers, and set them aside too. She was just about to lie down when a scratchy sound came through the ductwork. It was from the other end of the duct that emptied into a heating vent for the offices.

She carefully made her way down to the opposite end of the large duct and turned right. She approached the office grate carefully to make sure the lights were off. They were sometimes on at all hours of the day and night, though usually by two in the morning everything was shut down.

There, standing on the other side of the large grate, was her only other friend in the world, a large orange and cream tabby cat. Elenor had named the stray Bottlecaps on account that the cat kept bringing them in from somewhere. Bottlecaps meowed at her again. She pushed the bottom of the heating grate and it swung open on a hinge. She pushed it until the opening was just wide enough for the cat to squeeze inside, and she let it carefully settle back into place, not making a single sound. Why this one animal among all the others did not flee in terror at the sight of her was beyond Elenor. Bottlecaps rubbed up against her side and purred.

"Hey, Caps."

She didn't dare try to pet the cat, and she waited until Bottlecaps was a few feet away before she began to move, lest one of her sharp barbs injure the cat. She would not risk visiting that horror on her tiny furry friend. She turned around carefully and followed the cat down the duct. Elenor looked over her shoulder and wondered for a minute how Bottlecaps got to that grate every night.

She always came to the one in the office even though it seemed like it might be easier to come to the one that emptied into the station. Elenor couldn't have let her in there, though, because the cameras would have seen it. Bottlecaps turned left of her own accord, and when she got to Elenor's pile of blankets, she opened her mouth and dropped a Joe's root beer cap onto the ever-growing pile on that side of the blankets.

"Why do you bring these things in here?" Elenor asked the cat. Bottlecaps just looked up and meowed at her. "Fine, furface."

She carefully poked open one of the styrofoam containers. Inside was a steak dinner with a baked potato and green beans. It had gone cold, but not too long ago. It would still taste good. Elenor used her claws to cut off a sizable chunk of the steak. She put it down for Bottlecaps and the cat began to eat.

Elenor sat down in her pile of blankets and speared the other piece of steak with her claws. She took her time eating it, enjoying the bare few seconds of taste before the steak turned to ash. When the first container was gone, she settled down carefully, curling herself in the blankets to make sure none of her spines shredded the fragile cloth.

"They're in here, Mom." The voice was female and sounded fairly young. Elenor perked up as soon as she heard it. It was nearing three am. The Metro didn't run past midnight on most days so no one should be in the station at this late hour. Still, it wasn't the first time someone had woken her up. Occasionally, maintenance people showed up in the station or even in the room she came in through.

"Keep your voice down, Thia. We do not want them to hear us straight off. They will run."

Elenor pushed herself to her paws and looked around. She caught sight of Bottlecaps, thankfully not sleeping right next to her. Very carefully, she prodded the cat with the very tip of her tail where there were no spines. Bottlecaps opened her green eyes and then yawned. She didn't want the cat to be trapped in here so she carefully shooed her down the ducts back towards the offices.

The voices were indistinct, and she didn't care to hear any more. They were clearly here to find Elenor. Her mind was frantic as she carefully pushed open the grate for Bottlecaps to get out into the office. The cat clearly was not happy to be shoved out into the office in the middle of the night, but she went when Elenor bared her teeth at the cat. It ran off with a tiny hiss of displeasure. Only one thought kept repeating in Elenor's frantic brain. *How did they find me?*

Carefully, silently, she made her way back out into the maintenance room. All she could think of were the men in suits that had come to her house and what Mateo had said. Men in suits looking for her. The sound of voices chased her through the vents as she pulled open the steel door.

"It's moving, heading into the tunnels somehow."

Elenor grimaced. *Could they see me on the station cameras somehow?* She was meticulous in checking to make sure no new cameras had been added to see her. She got the door open and turned to the wall of the tunnel. She ran up the wall, flipping over onto the ceiling a moment later. She could already feel the winter cold just outside of her cozy hideaway.

She paused, looking back down the tunnel into the darkness between her and the subway platform. For one long moment, she thought about using the mysterious waiting power floating in her chest. She did not want to lose this spot. But then she realized that even if she made them go away once, the spot was already lost. They knew she had been here. She turned and scuttled down the tunnel ceiling. She had backup places to sleep at each of the subway stations and that was just to start. Two years was a long time to find good hidey holes when you didn't have much else to do.

4
"FAST"

"Holy crap, it's fast, like muscle car fast." Thia's exclamation echoed off of the empty concrete walls of the subway station. She held the Oracle Stone in her hands as the dot streaked across the surface as if it were a GPS locator.

"Not it. This is not a thing. No matter what they look like, this is a very likely scared, young human being, Thia."

"Sorry, Mom. I only meant that I don't know what we're dealing with."

Helen signed, and nodded. "Which way?"

Thia pointed down the tunnel the way the Oracle indicated. Helen took step towards the edge of the platform but then paused. She turned back to Thia.

"There is no way to catch them on foot. I am fast, but not that fast. They are almost to the next station already."

"You said the Bearers would be powerful, but this is insane."

"If my guesses were correct, they have experienced a physical transformation. There is a high chance they are also now bound to the Writ. There is no telling how powerful they are."

They both turned to leave the subway, Thia carefully cradling the Oracle. They did not hurry, but they did not linger, either. The Relic they had used to keep themselves invisible in the closed Subway station would not last forever.

As they neared the top of the stairs, light boiled from the surface of the Oracle. The red light that they had initially gotten was a one-time warning that some new Writbound person had entered the world. The Oracle stone had never been truly meant for only the purpose of finding the Bearers. It had been meant to find any new living being bound directly to the Writ in some way. This new light was a putrid sickly green that Helen had never thought to see again.

"No," she whispered as Thia froze.

"What is it?"

Helen's face twisted in anger and revulsion. "The curse of Osiris. The Bane."

Thia stared, almost uncomprehending. Her mother never spoke of what had ended the use of the Writ in the world. Once considered a goddess by those without an Arbiter's gifts, she still blamed herself for not being able to do more to stop what the Bane had done.

"What does this mean?" Thia asked.

Her mother started to run up the stairs back towards the street. She didn't hesitate for one moment when she got out onto the street. She turned toward where they had parked their rented car, and sprinted out into the street. Horns honked as cars streaking towards Helen slammed on their brakes. The driver of one car, a bright red Corvette, was far too slow. Helen jumped over the hood with the fluid grace of an expert parkour traceur. Thia, right behind her, paused for a bare second to let the corvette screech by before resuming her sprint.

"Mom! Have you lost your mind?!"

Her mother did not answer, she just ran to the car. It was everything Thia could do to keep up and not drop the Oracle stone. Her mother yanked open the door of the silver Camry they had rented and waited just long enough for Thia to click her safety belt into place before she screeched out into traffic.

"Call in everyone, Thia," her mother said.

"I can call Hap and his team in from Philadelphia," Thia started to say, but Helen shook her head.

"No, activate every contact, Thia. If this is the Bane come again, we have to contain it before it can spread. It is not like any disease the world has ever known. Only death contains this infection. No quarantine in the world will stop the spread of the Bane. It infects the very soul." Helen kept her eyes on the road, darting nervous glances to the Oracle every few seconds to make sure she was still headed in the right direction.

"Can't it infect us?" Thia asked.

Helen shook her head. "Even though I no longer have access to the Writ, the power still flows through me. It also extends to everyone nearby to me. We have no choice, Thia. We have to find and kill the one touched by the Bane."

Helen screeched to a stop outside of an office building. Stories of concrete and tinted glass windows stretched for a block in both directions. The building had no sign that Thia could see, but she took out her phone. A quick peak at a mapping application told her that the drab façade contained a government office building.

Horns honked at her dead stop in the middle of the street. She dug in the pocket of her white jacket and came out with metal disc twice the size of a fifty-cent piece. She held it up by the edge and then flicked the side of it with her index finger, as if it were a tiny drum. Incongruently, the coin began to vibrate, and a moment later, a halo of bubbling yellow light effervesced from the surface of the coin. The Relic would hide the car from anyone seeing it, but it would also make people avoid it without really knowing why. It wasn't a perfect defense to anyone finding the car because it clearly made a strange hole in the traffic. Helen had little care for the rules of modern men. She pushed open her door and swung out, slamming it closed behind her.

Yanking open the trunk revealed what appeared at first to be a large duffel bag. She grabbed the handles and yanked out the massive bag. Once it was clear, it was obvious that it was rolled like a sleeping bag. She closed the trunk and unrolled the carrier to reveal dozens of pockets and sheaths holding dozens of odd objects. Long-fingered hands ran over the pockets. A moment later, she flipped open one about the size of her hand.

Thia slipped the Oracle stone into a fur-lined bag sized just for the object, twice the size of a softball. Her mother shoved the object from the pocket into Thia's hands. It was a small steel box with a hinge on one side. She flipped it open, revealing ancient patinaed compass. At the points of the needle were two glowing stones. One was a tiny emerald with glowing green script etched into the needle below it. The other was a sapphire stone with glowing blue script. The sapphire though was not glowing at all.

"What's this?" Thia had seen an impressive number of her mother's magical Relics, and used almost as many of them. She had never seen this compass.

"Bane Sensor. You haven't used it before because there was no need, and because it's one of the handful of Relics that will only work if I am present to feed it power. You can't keep an eye on the Oracle and be ready to defend yourself. You need a simpler tool."

Helen pulled a hard sided case out of the trunk. She flipped it open to reveal a pair of pistols. The black Glock G21SF pistols came out and were placed into holsters. Chambered in forty-five caliber, they would be more than enough to stop any human that came at them.

She handed one of the holsters to Thia. She took it without hesitation, and, sliding the compass into another pocket of her bag next to the oracle stone, she fitted it onto her belt. Though it seemed a little at odds with the pleated blue skirt and white tights Thia was wearing, she was an expert with the firearm and wore it with confidence.

"We're just going to run into a government office building and gun someone down?" Thia asked, a little uncomfortable.

Helen shook her head. "No, *I* am going to go in there and cut someone down. Thia, you have no idea what is going to happen if the Bane begins to spread. It will expose this world to powers that they are not at all prepared to deal with. It does not just kill. I will explain more later."

Helen pulled a pair of hair ornaments out of another of the roll's pockets. Bows with steel clips, one pink, one blue. She handed the blue one to Thia. She repeated the process with the steel clips she had with the coin. Each began to bubble with bright blue light.

Thia recognized the bows, which looked nearly new. The steel clip underneath, though, looked ancient. The imperfections made it clear the clip had been hand made. Thia quickly slid it into her hair on the right side, knowing the resonance flowing off of it would make her impossible to recognize even to cameras.

"They only work for about an hour before they will need to be left to recharge."

"What about cameras?"

Helen shook her head. "They will not be able to make out your face or any area of your body. These ones warp the air. I would kill to be able to Surge the Precept's Rest and cover all the possibilities for people seeing us, but this will do fine for now."

She belted on her pistol, and reached into the trunk one last time, pulling out a black wood and leather scabbard. It was a short blade, about two feet long. The scabbard showed the triangular blade within was thinner at the point than where the blade met the hilt. The hilt was a simple round bar with an acorn pommel, wrapped in black ray skin held in place with silver wire. It offered an excellent grip. It had double spade-shaped shell guards above the hilt.

She pulled the sword from the scabbard, revealing a mirrored blade of that appeared to be made of a sapphire blue metal to check that it was clear. She slammed it back into the scabbard and then swung the baldric over her head. It settled the sword so the hilt rose above her right shoulder. She took a moment to clip the bow into her platinum blonde locks behind one ear.

"We can't do this," Thia protested, but Helen shook her head. She put her hand on her daughter's shoulder.

"This is your last chance, Thia. This is, unfortunately, the right thing to do. I am going to do it, but you do not have to. I have given you every opportunity to go your own way. But if you do this, there is no turning back. Whoever is Infected is not trying to kill us yet, and they are likely entirely innocent. Still, if I do not kill them, it will cause tragedy the likes of which the modern world has never known. You have to decide if this is what is right for you. I absolutely refuse to force you. Decide for yourself." Helen turned and jogged towards the doors of the office building.

Thia knew her mother. Having trained beneath her for over ninety years, she knew Helen only ever tried to do what was right, no more, no less. Her mother had never failed to answer any question Thia had to ask. Though she didn't always agree with everything her mother did, she had never once been able to come up with a better solution to any problem that Helen had solved.

Decision made, Thia drew her Glock, racked the slide to chamber a round, examined it, and slid it back into the holster. She sprinted to catch up with her mother before she could disappear into the building. She was done with her mother trying to turn her aside. She had known and trained with numerous people over the years. None were better than her mother.

"Let's go," she said. "At least there shouldn't be too many people in here at ass-crack-of-dawn'o'clock."

She took her cell phone out of her bag and started to send messages, calling in the network of people her mother had built for when the Bearers emerged. The network was not like the company that Joshua had built. He had built his empire on money, and power. Her mother had built her network on people who she had helped in times when no one else would. Thia hoped that it would be enough.

5

"PULL"

NC 17, EPOCH 19914.326

Elenor ran faster than she ever thought possible. Each stride was a leap of amazing proportions, turning her body into a streak as she flew down the ceiling of the tunnel. All she could think of was getting away, and the fact that they clearly knew about her only pushed her to run faster.

Suddenly, something tugged against her chest. It was as if someone had thrown a rope around her and yanked. She almost tripped, skidding along the ceiling. Her talons left deep furrows scored into the concrete, and she cringed when she saw they were at least twenty feet long. She didn't think she had skidded that far. Before she could lament the damage, the tug came again. Something was pulling her in a different direction.

She had never felt anything like it. The pull went sort of in the direction she had just come, but not exactly. When it came a third time, the direction was definite - towards the street somewhere above her. She shook her head, turned around, and then began to run again, heading towards State Center station. She blew past the station so fast that she was certain that not a single camera would have seen her, even if they were pointed directly at her path.

Just as she was about to turn left to head towards her bolt hole at Upton station, the tugging sensation became far more insistent. This time, she was physically spun around, and she lost whatever grip she had on the ceiling. She flipped towards the ground as gravity asserted itself. Frantically, she flung out her tail back towards the ceiling. The spines sprouting in rings around her tail slammed into the concrete, piercing the stone like it was soft putty. It yanked her to a painful stop and for a moment, she thought she had broken her spine where her tail connected to her body. She swung from the ceiling like the oversized pendulum of Satan's nightmarish grandfather clock.

A few deep breaths later, the pain in her tail faded. She considered her predicament for a moment. She had slammed the spines on her tail deep into the concrete of the tunnel roof. She silently thanked the city planners that the trains did not run twenty-four hours a day. She curled her body and bounced a little against her tail. When the pain did not return, she curled up her body and straightened as hard as she could, bouncing her body on her tail, trying to yank her spines free. They didn't budge.

"Oh, <u>come on</u>!" she groaned, swinging limply back and forth. Then she realized that her gentle swinging was bringing her closer to the ceiling. She started to wiggle her body rhythmically back and forth. A moment later, she swung herself far enough that her paws touched the ceiling. She clutched her front paws, and her claws sunk into the concrete, stopping her swing. Once she had a good grip, she concentrated until the sensation of her paws clinging to the ceiling returned. One paw at a time, she pulled her talons out of the ceiling. She tried to pull her tail free again but it still wouldn't budge.

"You have <u>got</u> to be shitting me!" Elenor cried out in frustration and anger. She spent a full ten minutes yanking at her tail, but it remained stubbornly stuck in the concrete.

Finally, in pure frustration, she bent all four legs and threw herself towards the ground as hard as she could. All of her weight slammed against her thick tail and her spines finally gave up, sliding free of the ceiling, sending her streaking towards the rails. On instinct, she twisted her body violently so that her paws hit the floor instead of her spine.

The gravelly floor of the tunnel could not penetrate her paws, but that did not mean that hitting the sharp stones didn't sting. Elenor let out a very catlike hiss and danced from paw to paw.

"Son of a…" She howled as she felt the tug in her chest yet again. She walked over to the wall of the tunnel, put her front paws onto it, and then pulled herself up. She got back to the ceiling and, with a snarl, she started to stomp in the direction she had been going.

I am not going anywhere but to Upton station to get some freaking sleep! The tugging in her chest became a constant pull against her as she forced herself forward. Determination snarled her face as she continued to stomp down the tunnel against the resistance in her chest. When her paws started to slip against the concrete, she dug her claws into the stone.

"I," she stomped a few more steps, "am," she dragged herself forward a few more inches before the pull became overwhelming, "going to bed!" She screeched in fury and yanked herself forward with all of her strength.

Suddenly, the resistance snapped as if it were an overtaxed rope. Once again, she was thrown from the ceiling toward the floor of the tunnel. This time, there was no way for her to twist in time and she landed with a thud, sprawled on her back. It wasn't terribly painful, but she still screeched a stream of every single curse word she could remember hearing in her life.

"What the actual hell?!" She turned over, and then growled. She could walk on the damn floor for a while. *Let the cameras get an eyeful. I don't give a damn anymore.* She continued to stomp angrily down the tunnel, but the further she went, the more an uneasy feeling grew in the pit of her stomach. She bared her teeth and kept walking. "I swear, I will throw up and keep walking. Stupid body," she groused.

But it did not fade, it just got worse. Her stomach churned more violently with every step she took towards Upton station. Finally, she stopped. She threw her head back and screamed in frustration.

"Isn't it enough that I have to walk around looking like weapons grade nightmare fuel?!" The sob of rage echoed back to her a dozen times as it scoured the tunnel walls. She had been pushing down tears for hours now, but today had been over the top. Hot tears streaked through the fur on either side of her muzzle. Elenor hated crying. She barely ever cried, so it infuriated her that enough had happened to push the tears to the surface. The girls she used to call friends said they felt better after they cried. It never felt better to Elenor. It just made her anger flare and upset her that much more. Clearly, it mattered not one bit to the feeling in her chest. As soon as she turned around and started walking in the opposite direction, the feeling in her stomach faded. The tugging sensation in her chest returned, but much gentler this time.

"Now I have to chase my stupid Spidey sense across town? Great!" She continued to swear and mumble to herself as she turned to walk up the wall of the tunnel again. She had to pick her way around the claw gouges she had left in the ceiling, and the sizeable hole left when she yanked her tail free would definitely draw the attention of everyone who worked in the tunnels.

Those concerns were niggling voices among the cacophony of thoughts about what was happening to her. She had accepted that there was no scientific explanation for what she had gone through. She had stepped firmly into the supernatural the day she had woken up with a pair of horns sprouting from her skull. The fur could have possibly had some bizarre scientific explanation, but the horns made it undeniable. They had grown in overnight.

The rest of her transformation had proceeded at a preposterous pace. Each time something new happened, it had been a shock. Waking up each morning with some new change to her body had been bad enough. Those things, though, had been a pleasant dream compared to the transformation of her legs. The memory of the revolting feeling of her ankles twisting of their own accord flew through her mind. She had been standing at the top of the stairs.

The dizzying feeling of tilting forward and the painful tumble as she bounced down the stairs toward the floor. Crashing to the living room floor as her legs reshaped themselves into something more canine than human. She shook herself like a dog throwing off water as the memory slipped away. That had been the last transformation. The next morning, the power had appeared in her chest with the knowledge of how to use it on instinctive level somehow crammed into her brain. She thought it had been over at least, but now more things were changing. *It's not fair!*

She paused as she got closer to State Center station. The sense of pulling had changed direction. If she wanted to follow it, she was going to have to go up to the street level. That meant that if she wanted to get past the cameras she would have to use the maintenance hatch that came up next to Eutaw Street. She could do it, but doing so risked someone noticing her. There really wasn't a better option, though, if she was going to follow the feeling. She turned into the access nook on the side of the tunnel and walked to the grate. It was heavy. She looked up through it and saw the padlock keeping the hatch shut.

She snarled as the tugging sensation became more insistent. She pulled back her paw and swiped her talons at the heavy steel grate. Sparks flew, and her claws sliced through the steel with almost no resistance. She swiped again, and a piece of the grate fell away into

the nook. She reached through and hooked her claw on
the hasp the padlock was through. She yanked and the
hasp sheered away. Pressing a paw against the grate,
she lifted it as slowly as she could manage. It was hard
because it weighed almost as much as she did, but
whatever supernatural strength had filled her body did
not come up short.

The grate lifted on a well-greased hinge. She looked
around. At this late hour, there were few people on the
street. Some cars whisked by, but she really wasn't
worried about the drivers seeing her with their eyes on
the road. She waited for a couple to pass by the grate.
She needed to move fast. She couldn't possibly take the
time to lower the grate silently. When it slammed back
into place, she needed to be gone.

She shoved the grate hard. It flew up out of the well.
She hooked her claws into the stone and yanked herself
out of the hole in a blur. Yanking her tail out of the way
of the grate, she bolted to the left, leaping up onto a
short fence set into a brick wall separating the sidewalk
from a parking lot. She scrambled over the fence and
turned left to head for the corner of the brick wall.

Elenor squeezed past a dumpster sitting in the corner
of the parking lot, ignoring the awful smell of the trash
receptacle. She pushed her back into the corner of the
brick wall and hunched down to make certain that none
of her body poked up over the wall. In her brief glimpse
of the parking lot, she had seen car headlights on one of
the cars. A moment later, she was rewarded by the
sound of an engine revving.

Lights illuminated either side of the dumpster as a
car turned toward the exit. The driver never saw her.
The moment the car was gone, she ran diagonally across
the parking lot towards the building. As soon as she
was close enough, she leapt with all of her strength. She
flew almost twenty feet into the air and her paws hit the
windows of the building with a crack. The windows

were extremely thick so they did not shatter, and Elenor didn't take the time to see if she cracked the window. She needed to get out of sight. She ran up the side of the building as fast as she could make her body go.

She paused at the edge of the roof, peering over the edge and looking around. She saw no cameras, and it was very unlikely there were any. Most cameras had lights on them that were invisible to humans, but to her eyes, the infrared light was like a blinding spotlight. To her, most cameras stood out in the night like a lighthouse. There were none here, so she scrambled over the edge of the roof. She took a moment to judge the direction of the tug in her chest. She turned toward West Preston Street. It was in that direction. She stared across the street. She couldn't cross without anyone seeing her.

Can I jump to that other building? She stared at the building in the direction the tug was going. It was so far, at least the distance from one end of her high school soccer field to the other. She knew that she could jump tremendous distances now. Further than any animal or human she had ever read about, but a soccer field was three hundred feet long.

Can I possibly jump that far? She had jumped to the roof of a three-story building without straining at all. She had been shit-all terrified at the time. That was the night she had been shot by the police. She didn't know she was so… bullet resistant until after that.

How far will I go if I put everything I have into it? Will I hurt myself if I fall all the way to the ground? The worst pain she had felt since her transformation was stinging like her hand had been slapped with a ruler, but she also hadn't fallen the seventy-five or so feet to the sidewalk before. The tugging sensation became almost violent in her chest. She spun around in frustration and ran to the opposite end of the building. She turned around and bolted towards the edge of the building. She would

have to jump at an angle to clear the street. She ran
faster, her body stretching out as she crossed the roof in
a blur.

Ten feet from the short wall surrounding the end of
the building, she jumped. Three hundred plus pounds
moving at that speed seemed to be more than the
materials of the roof could handle. She heard a crack as
she thrust her legs with all of her power. She launched
into the air over Preston, and within a single split
second, she realized she was going immensely too fast
and high. She cleared Preston Street effortlessly and
shot towards the building she had been aiming for. She
was going to miss it completely.

6

"CROWN"

NC 17, EPOCH 19914.326

"Oooooh shhhhit!" Elenor screeched as she blasted past the roof she had wanted to land on. This was why her power terrified her. Her limits were completely nebulous to her. While she knew that the power in her chest allowed her to take control of the water inside of living things, she strongly suspected that was the bare minimum of what the power did. The thought passed from her mind as she streaked towards the windows of the adjacent building.

"Shhhhhiiiiittt!" She screamed again as her paws smashed into the fifth-floor windows. These windows were also extremely tough, but simply not up to the task of resisting the force of her smashing into them claws first at far past a hundred miles per hour. The window exploded into the room, causing her to tumble end over end. Flipping over and over, Elenor desperately tried to hook her claws into something to slow her. Her claws sliced through everything they grabbed onto, barely slowing.

She smashed into a cube wall and instinctually, she curled her body into a ball, grabbing the end of her tail in her front paws. She tucked her head down between her front legs, beginning to roll. The sound of sheering metal and ripping fabric roared through the room as her spines, now standing all over her body, obliterated the cubes between her and the opposite wall of the room. Her spines cleaved through the cubes, desks, and computers as if they were made of wet cardboard.

She slammed into the wall of the room and barely slowed. Her spines slid through the drywall and steel studs with near zero resistance. Finally, she smashed into the next wall across a central hallway. Behind this wall's façade was thick cement, and she grunted as she came to an abrupt stop. She opened her eyes and then uncurled her body slightly. The tugging sensation in her chest was now pointing upwards and slightly to the right. She uncurled the rest of the way. Her face scrunched up in annoyance when she realized that her paws were hanging a few inches from the floor. Once again, her spines were lodged in the cement. She spit, snarled, and wiggled her body furiously until her talons finally scraped the carpet. They left furrows cut through the industrial stuff and she stretched even harder until she could sink her claws into the floor.

"This, is, bullshit!" She grunted and snarled until she was able to yank herself free of the wall. "Some freaking monster you are." She mumbled to herself. Then she turned and looked at the swath of destruction she had left behind. She shivered. If anyone had been between that window, and the wall they would undoubtedly be a corpse. *No question at all that I'm a monster. What else could do this?* She trotted to one end of the hallway, quickly looking for the stairs. She saw the light of a security camera shining around a corner and sped up. She had reached an extremely high speed by the time she skidded around the corner, her claws biting into the floor to help her turn.

Her eyes locked on the camera and she launched herself at it in a blur of speed and fury. Her talons sliced through the camera lens and the glass fell out in four pieces. By the time they bounced across the carpet, she was into the stairwell. There were no infrared spotlights here so she went up to the next floor. She crouched down to look for light beneath the door, but there was something blocking the gap. Elenor clicked her tongue.

Well, screw it. I left a disaster downstairs already. Broke all my rules about staying hidden. Who cares about one more door? She sat back on her haunches to free both front paws and stuck a talon through the steel. Then she used her other paw to cut a circle around that claw. When she pulled back her claw, the circle of door came with it, giving her a view of the other side. No light from a camera just outside of this door. She pushed open the bar. As soon as she walked out into the hallway, she heard two women whispering.

"The Sensor is spinning. They must still be further up." The first voice said. "Wait, the blue stone is glowing now. It's shaking back and forth."

"The Bearer is here. How did they find us?" The second voice was a little more mature sounding, but had similar tone and pitch to the first, with some accent Elenor couldn't place. She stopped when she realized the tug in her chest was still trying to pull her up.

"Bane first, Bearer later?" The first voice spoke again and Elenor recognized it from earlier. It was the woman who found her at Charles Center station.

Elenor backed up and turned to head up the stairs. She didn't want to meet those women. She just wanted to do whatever her stupid body wanted her to do, and get back to her cozy spot in the subway. She reached the next landing up and cut a hole in this door as well. None of the odd infrared light, but here, a normal light was coming from somewhere in the cube farm. Elenor silently pushed open the door and slipped inside.

Instead of letting the door close and make a sound, she grabbed a square waste basket carefully between her front paws and stuck it in the door so it wouldn't close. Elenor crept slowly in the direction that the pull was taking her. The light glowed from one of the cubes - someone was working awfully late in this building. Elenor crept slowly towards the cube but she didn't turn towards it. She looked around the room for cameras but didn't see any. It seemed that they were only on some entrances and exits.

Elenor padded silently to the other end of the room, careful to keep her claws from clicking against anything. It was always difficult since she could not retract them into her paws. She knew which way the cubes faced, so if she wanted to see into that cube without the person seeing her, she needed to go this way. She crept past the cube and turned, putting her paws up onto the wall. She pulled herself up, whatever strange gravity defying power she held taking effect.

She slunk up the wall and then turned to creep across the ceiling. When she could finally see into the cube, she paused. It was not what she had expected. There sitting at the computer was a man. It was just a man, but the longer she watched, the more she realized that something was very wrong. She couldn't put a claw on it.

His shoulder length brown ponytail swayed as he looked down at some papers. Then he went back to typing on his computer. That was when it hit her. His breathing was bizarre. He would take a huge breath, let it out, take another, and then his breathing would stop. As she watched, the pull in her chest began to fade away. Abruptly her vision changed. Colors faded away until her environment fell into shades of grey. Except for the man.

Shimmering into view around the crown of the man's head was another crown, one of sickly green light. The longer she watched, the more the crown resolved into a band of sharp light that passed within an inch of the man's skull. Shards of light like broken glass facing inwards from the band seemed to penetrate the man's skull.

Inexplicably, she knew that if she did not destroy that band of light, somehow, that this man would die. But worse, that was not where it would stop. She had no idea what that worse was going to be, she just knew it would be. She crouched and prepared to spring at the man. The door to the stairwell burst open, and two women came through, both holding handguns.

The man immediately stood up, his head popped up above the cube. As soon as he did, the woman with the lighter hair raised her gun without hesitation. Every instinct Elenor had gained since her transformation screamed that she had to stop this from happening.

"Stop!" She hissed and sprang at the man. The gun cracked, but Elenor's body came between the man and the gunfire. She hooked her claws onto the green crown at the same time she felt the bullets pancake against her spine. She might be sore, but nothing penetrated her skin.

The green band resisted her claws in a way that nothing else had since she had gained them. She dragged the man headfirst across his desk, smashing apart his computer monitor. By the simple impetuous of her motion her spines flared, and sliced apart the cube wall between his cube and the opposite one. Elenor did not let go of the crown, even as she dragged the man through the ruin of his cube.

"What the hell is that?!" Elenor heard the younger sounding of the two women shout.

"The Bearer!" The older sounding woman shouted.

Elenor yanked again, attempting to destroy the band of viridian light. The man, having put his hands on either side of the partially destroyed cube wall, was pulling back against her. He screamed wildly and yanked frantically against her to try to get away. That was of little consequence to Elenor. Anything to help her break the damned crown and get out of there before she had to deal with the two women. She put her hind paws against the edge of the opposite desk and wrenched with all of her might.

The crown of green light shattered.

It exploded into a million sharp shards of solid emerald light, and a shockwave of force threw Elenor away from the man. He slammed back into his office chair, which shot across the carpet and slammed into the chair in the cube behind him. It all tipped over into an impressive pile of human and chair limbs. Elenor was blasted away, tumbling through two more cubes as the blades standing up from her body sliced apart everything in their path.

"Catch the Bearer, Thia!" There was a startled sound.

"Mom, the green light went out."

Helen froze statue rigid at the words. "That's impossible."

Elenor pushed herself up to her feet. She shook her head. That had hurt more than anything she had felt since before she had grown horns and a tail. Her vision was fuzzy at the edges, but the colors had come back. She could tell from the pink blob of disgusting gum she could see on the underside of the desk she was looking up at. She tried to scramble to her paws, but tumbled dizzily over onto her side once again.

She heard footsteps at the end of the row, and just as a pair of blue round-toed shoes appeared at the end of the aisle, her vision cleared. She dragged herself drunkenly to her feet and stumbled slightly. She felt like it was the day after she had first been forced to start walking on all fours. She started to trot down the aisle towards the other end of the room. The windows were high up on the walls, but that did not slow her. She picked up speed, and leapt onto the wall. She darted up the wall to the window. Two quick slashes to the glass, and it crumbled.

"Wait!" The younger woman yelled, but Elenor did not look back. She launched herself through the window and into the night.

Thia turned back to her mother. Helen was crouching over the office drone that the Bearer had attacked. She stared poleaxed at the man.

"The Bearer sliced through one of those windows like tissue paper."

"Is everything ok? Are you still going to…" Thia looked at the office worker with some concern.

Helen held out her hand. "Oracle."

Thia nodded and dug the stone out of its protective case. She handed it over and her mother lowered herself to the floor. She sat cross-legged and cupped the oracle stone in one hand. She held up her other hand and a moment later, a black liquid gathered in her palm.

In a display of true magic, the liquid elongated into an opaque black bar of what appeared to be glass. Thin tendrils then burst from the sides of the black rod and spiraled around it until it was surrounded in ten thinner rods of opaque crystal. Each rod was a different color. A brass band circled the bottom of the black rod where it emerged from the others, expanding until it formed a handle similar to a set of brass knuckles. Finally, the colored rods circled the bottom of the rod and arched until the ends rested beneath her fingers. Each finger was near two of the rods.

"Mom? What are you doing?"

"Trying to find out what in the bloody hell Osiris has done to our world."

"I thought you said you couldn't use your Striker anymore."

"I cannot use it to play Surges, but the Relics have their own self-sustaining ones. Most of them can only do simple things, but the Oracle stone has a few abilities I haven't needed to show you before. To activate them, I need to use my Striker to trigger them."

She struck the instrument against the side of the oracle stone. All other sounds of the city seemed to be pushed away by the pure tones coming from the collection of rods. Helen's fingers moved, gently touching some of the rods to mute their vibrations. They continued to move as music formed from the instrument. Oddly, when she took her fingers away from the rods she had muted, their sounds seemed to return just as strongly even though she had not struck them again.

The music was nothing Thia could identify. In a hundred years of life, it was the first time she had seen her mother actually play her Striker. Thia had learned how to play the instrument by memorization only, but her mother's Striker never produced a sound when she used it as a training instrument.

The oracle stone effervesced bright veridian light for a moment. Helen's Striker melted once again, and was absorbed back into her skin. She held up the oracle stone between herself and the office worker.

"This will show us if he is still infected." Looking through the orb was like looking through a slate of green glass. The man, though, was limbed in a cascade of sunshine yellow light. The aura of a sleeping human. The edges were just starting to bleed to a bright aqua color that indicated he would wake soon.

"Mom?"

Helen stood up and stepped back abruptly. Her expression was haunted and confused. She turned away from the man and strode towards the exit. She held out the oracle stone as she passed and Thia rammed her pistol into the holster so she could catch the glowing stone.

She opened the case, and the green aura surrounding the stone faded. A chime sounded and Helen froze. Thia looked down and saw red light bubbling like fireworks from the surface of the oracle stone. It flowed out of the sides of the case before fading away.

"He is here," Helen hissed. "We have to find that Bearer."

7

"DEFECT"

NC 17, EPOCH 19914.322

A knock sounded on the thick ebony door. Joshua looked up from the ancient tome laid open on his wide oak desk. Joshua's eyes darted around, checking what was visible in the office. Not everyone in the company could be allowed to see the things he might be working with. The strict policy about knocking on any door before entering had prevented numerous mishaps. Though several people had been fired in the past when they had not followed the policy and a point had to be made. Seeing nothing questionable on display, he called out.

"Come in."

The door swung open, admitting a dark-skinned man of average height. He had a runner's build over a wide-shouldered frame. Sweat beaded on the arc of his perfectly shaved head. He was wearing a tight black compression shirt and matching pants that fit him like a second skin. He was not out of breath, but had clearly come straight from his morning run.

"Sir, the Catalog has registered a Defect." His voice was slightly monotone, with an accent so faint that only someone who knew him would know he carried it.

Joshua waved him inside. "Where is it, Alex?"

Alex shook his head. "Not enough data yet. Eastern seaboard somewhere between Richmond and Philadelphia."

Joshua stood and moved to a cabinet on the wall. To wiry to be truly imposing, Joshua was still tall enough to dwarf Alex's average height. The carved oak case hung on the wall just above the floor but was as tall as Joshua. Snow white hair brushed his shoulders as he turned his head to Alex.

"Put the strike team on standby. Find Randal and send him in here."

"Yes, sir." Alex left the room.

Joshua unlocked the carved oak door and swung it wide, revealing a number of objects. From them he took a sword. The black leather-covered scabbard was simple with no ornamentation. The hilt was covered in black scales that gave the slight cushioned feel of a leather grip, but it glittered like steel. It was long enough to allow two hands to be placed upon it, but could still be wielded one handed if necessary. It had a simple crossbeam guard.

He slid the sword from the scabbard revealing a three-foot blade of a pure white material. It glowed softly with internal light. He slid the blade back into the scabbard, veiling its light. He took a second item from the cabinet, a staff of dark wood that appeared to be made of three thick roots twisted together. At the top of the staff, wrapped in the roots, was a sapphire crystal.

Another man entered the office. His skin was so dark he might have been invisible in a darked room. Randal's pitch-black hair was pleated into a multitude of braids tight to his skull. His black fatigues marked him as a soldier, or at least a mercenary. Joshua held out the sword to him, hilt first.

"Have you been keeping up your sword drills, Randal?"

"Daily, Sir." Randal took the sword. He pulled a bit of the blade free to make sure it was clear in the scabbard and then held it at his side.

"Good. I get the feeling guns will be of little use on this job."

"This is more Caller business?" Randal asked, holding up the sword as the subject of the question. Randal had seen unbelievable things in Joshua's employ. Things that he would have called magic in the impossible sense.

Joshua nodded. "It is, but make no mistake, this is not a Relic hunt. We will be going after something truly dangerous."

Randal raised a brow. "Are we equipped to handle something more dangerous than a Relic hunt?"

"Do you want the truth or a lie?"

Randal chuckled sardonically. "Doesn't really matter, does it? We're the only ones equipped at all."

Joshua nodded. "Get the chopper spun up would you Randal? Well take the team to the Virginia office for prep."

"Yes, sir." Randal put the scabbarded sword over his shoulder like a baseball player headed for an at-bat and headed out through the offices. A young blonde woman in similar black fatigues to Randal's came out of an office. Her voice held a lingering hint of an irish brogue.

"Where we headed, sir?"

"Home office," Joshua said, and the woman's face pulled a frown.

"Operating on US soil? We get hazard pay on this one?"

"Lena, would you please call and brief our police contacts in every major city from Richmond to New York. We aren't sure where the Catalog will point us, so just let them know we might be entering their city with the strike team."

"You got it, chief." Lena pulled her cell from a pocket, and put in a Bluetooth earpiece. She broke off from them and headed down the stairs. Randal and Joshua continued down the wide hallway towards the elevator. A moment later, they were riding it towards the roof.

"Gather the rest of the team, Randal, and one other thing. Put Pierce on searching for private flights coming into all the major airports. Small planes, no more than ten seats. It will be carrying two women."

"It's been almost a decade since we last saw them," Randal interjected.

Joshua shook his head. "They will be there."

"I'll make sure Pierce gets a full description. Anything else that needs to be done?"

Joshua shook his head. "I'll take care of the rest. Only people who have hunted Relics before, Randal. I need people on this mission who know what we are up against."

The elevator dinged, and the stainless-steel door slid open to reveal a blank concrete hallway with overhead fluorescent lights. Randal stuck the sword into the elevator doors.

"What loadout?"

"Structure the loadout around capture, but bring live ammunition as backup."

"Been a long time since we ran a mission like that." Randal lifted a brow in question.

"I would rather this issue disappear quietly, Randal, but best to be prepared for what we are about to go into. Capture first. This thing should never see the light of day."

Finally, Randal let out a put-upon sigh. "And, what are we going into, sir?"

"We're going to hunt down a monster."

8
"CHASE"

Her mother started swearing in Old Norse under her breath as she turned back toward the stairwell. Thia was already holding the door open. They jogged down the stairs and burst out onto the street. Running to the car, they both started stripping off their gear. Helen dropped the magazine out of her Glock and racked the slide, popping out the round in the chamber. She did this all with the efficiency of a trained soldier, a glimpse of her past. She added the round back to the magazine and put the three mags and pistol back into the hard case.

"Shouldn't we keep the gear on?" Thia asked.

Helen shook her head. "Did you really see that creature? These toys wouldn't even slow them down. We'll need to use the Relics when we catch up if they attack us."

Thia handed over her pistol, which had been similarly unloaded and checked. Helen did a quick chamber check on Thia's pistol before putting it back into the case next to hers. She added the Relics back into the equipment roll and shoved it all back into the trunk. Thia had already belted herself in. She was holding the Oracle in her lap when Helen got in beside her. She took the coin from the dash and dropped it back into her pocket.

"Which way?" she asked.

Thia turned the Oracle stone until she could see the blue dot streaking across its surface. "She's running south by southeast towards the water. How is she moving so fast? She's going way faster than a car."

"She?"

"I heard her yell back there. Definitely a girl's voice." Thia shivered a little. "A creepily young girls voice."

Thia turned the Oracle. At a mental command, the view of the city from above pulled back to show more of the area. "I'm losing resolution here. She's getting too far away."

"I will get us closer, just keep an eye on it. We are losing our lead, Thia. Joshua's Catalog will have told him that something odd was happening near here before the Oracle ever triggered. He would not have come until he was certain, which is the only reason we got ahead at all," Helen said.

"Still think he hasn't changed, even after Korea?" Thia asked a little skeptically.

Her mother snorted. "Not a chance. He may have changed his name, but underneath, he is still the Merlin. He does knows not how to change."

Helen stomped the accelerator to the floor. She went as fast as the streets would allow her at four AM. Turns out that speed was somewhere between terrifying and ludicrous. Thia held on for dear life as they skidded around corners and raced down streets at speeds they were never meant to allow for.

Both she and her mother had superhuman reflexes and even superhuman strength. It was part of the Surge her mother had invested into herself before the Writ had broken fully, though that wasn't to say that they were immensely beyond human limits. Still, it allowed her mother to drive in relative safety at much higher speeds than almost any human on earth. As fast as that was, though, they were crawling across the city in comparison to the Bearer. The blue dot streaked across the map on the surface of the Oracle.

"How fast could she possibly run?" Thia wondered.

Her mother glanced at the Oracle for a moment, but then her eyes went right back to the road.

"We have no idea what her limits might be, Thia. Something has changed drastically, and I no longer have a frame of reference for predicting what we are dealing with. We are in uncharted waters. Here, there be monsters." They screeched around a corner, and Thia saw the police car out of the corner of her eye.

"Police."

"Do not worry about them. Where is she?"

"Turning East."

Her mother swung a hard left, and Thia saw the sign for East Pratt Street. There was little traffic at that time of night, and her mother pushed the accelerator to the floor. The lights flashing behind them were beginning to concern Thia, no matter what her mother said. Her mother reached into her pocket and pulled out the coin she had used to make the car invisible earlier. Helen clinked it against the dash and it began to hum with low vibrations. She dropped it on the dashboard. A moment later, the flashing lights speeding up behind them fell away.

Thia let out a breath she didn't know she'd been holding. "How long will that last?"

"Not long when we are moving. Just long enough to get the police off our backs. The good news is that with it in my pocket drawing off my own power, it regains power quickly." She moved the coin back to her pocket and focused on her driving.

"Where could she be going?" Thia wondered.

"We chased her out of her home, but if she avoided using any Surges, she could have been here for years. She could have a hundred places to hide out."

Thia turned the Oracle sphere. "If she keeps going the way she is, she'll hit a park." There were no convenient labels on the Oracle. Thia kept her phone out and scrolled the map to keep pace with the Oracle. "Patterson Park. She's headed straight for the northwest corner of the park. Now turning slightly north. Still headed straight for the park."

Helen felt something she hadn't experienced in decades. Beneath the skin of her right arm there began a tingling sensation. Not enough for it to itch or truly distract her, just enough to let her know it was there. For this, though, she did not need to call out her Striker. It was an indication that it had detected the presence of another Caller.

"Joshua has caught up," Helen whispered in annoyance.

Thia clicked her tongue in shared annoyance. Thia had only ever met the man once. After the Second World War, Helen and Thia spent almost two decades collecting Relics from China, Japan, and Korea. The entire region had been hit hard in terms of people who had untapped potential as Callers.

Callers were still occasionally born into the world. Because of the damage to the Writ, most never knew they had magical abilities. With the massive increase in population in the last two centuries, Helen wasn't sure that was a bad thing. Having millions of Callers without any of the relationships that helped them to learn how to use their powers responsibly could have dire consequences for their world.

That was almost exactly what had happened in Asia. Even though Callers could not exercise their craft, they still served a role as keepers of dangerous Writbound artifacts. Asia, though, hadn't had a new Caller born in over a century. All knowledge in the region had been lost. When new Callers were born, and then inevitably drawn to the Relics, they had no idea what the consequences of using them would be.

That was how Thia had met Joshua and learned to hate him. They had discovered that after the war, a North Korean black ops team lead by a man with the untapped potential of a Caller had gotten their hands on a very dangerous Relic. Both Helen and Joshua had gone after the Relic because having any government in possession of a such power was not going to turn out well for anyone. He had almost gotten them killed trying to take back the Relic when Helen and Thia had already gotten it away from the Koreans. Thia thought that she could quite happily shoot the man in the face and lose very little sleep over it for the grief he had caused them getting out of North Korea.

"She stopped somewhere in the Park close to the northeast corner." Thia swiped fingers over her phone screen. "It looks like there is some sort of observatory tower there." Thia looked at her mother with some trepidation.

Helen shot through the intersection of Pratt and Patterson Park and locked the brakes. She spun the wheel and the rented sedan slid up to the curb, still sticking partially out into the street. Again, she flicked the coin and set it onto the dash. She leapt out of the car in a flurry of motion.

"He has no idea what he is dealing with. I have no idea what we are dealing with, either, but I know that if he tries to take on the Bearer, it will not end well for any of us. Get everything out of the trunk."

"How do you know?" Thia asked

Helen shook her head. "I cannot explain. Just a feeling."

She held her right hand out to the side and her Striker grew from her hand until she was holding the brass handle. Helen could no longer play Surges, but each of the eleven rods had been invested with a single fixed effect. She held it up, pointed it down the street, and then turned in a slow circle, pointing the instrument like the needle of a compass. The vibration running through her fingers from the Striker intensified as the center rod lined up with the center of the park.

Thia rummaged through the trunk and came up a minute later with the roll of relics. She had a bullet proof vest over her blouse and she held out one to her mother too. Her mother raised a brow.

"Joshua being here means a team. And guns."

Her mother took it and took a moment to pull open the Velcro straps before wrapping it around her torso. She slung her sword across her body so it stood up behind her shoulder.

"Are you sure I can't just..." Thia put her hand on the grip of her Glock.

"If it comes to him or the Bearer, I will kill him," her mother replied, her eyes hard.

Thia scowled. She had no attachment to Joshua Trent, but her mother had known him when he was different. It would hurt her mother to have to kill him in ways that would not bother Thia at all. Not that killing another human was something Thia found to be easy. However, Joshua Trent didn't qualify as human to her after the way he had acted in Korea.

When Thia saw two men in tactical gear approaching from down one of the trails wending its way through the park, she wished they had called in help sooner. Her mother, though, simply raised her Striker and swung it in a graceful arc.

The central rod struck a light post. The instrument rang with a pure note. Helen's fingers acted as dampers on the rods producing a short repetitive tune. A moment later, one of the twisted rods began to glow brightly. Its lavender color was soothing to look at. The two men collapsed mid-step and tumbled a few more steps down the asphalt path. Her mother let out an unhappy, weary breath.

"I am using too much energy today," she complained. She held out the Striker to Thia. "Do you remember how to use this?"

It had been at least thirty years since Thia had seen the Relic. Helen rarely used it. Without being bound to the Writ, the Relic used a tremendous amount of energy directly from their bodies. Thia rolled her eyes. She had trained day in, day out with the instrument for over twenty years to master it. She knew how to trigger its inherent powers just as well as her mother.

"I think I can handle it." She took the instrument from her mother's hand and they both started to jog into the park.

9
"LEFT ALONE"

NC 17, EPOCH 19914.326

Elenor perched on top of the Observatory tower, her eyes dimly shining in the last few hours of the night. The Observatory had been closed for some time due to damage on one of the lower floors that had been done by vandals. Repairing the century-old structure apparently took a lot of work. It meant that the Observatory, for the time being, was a great place to keep warm. That was how Elenor had met Mateo. The park was more or less empty at night aside from the occasional jogger. It was usually pretty safe in the park, even in the middle of the night.

Mateo hadn't been in the park. He'd been on a street nearby. She'd seen him from the very spot where she perched at that moment. Her mind turned back to the men walking through the park. It was getting close to dawn. While she had flaunted so many of her own rules about staying hidden in the past few hours, running around in daylight was not at all advisable.

She lost all of her advantages in daylight. She couldn't easily see cameras, and they recorded movement better in the day than at night, so just moving too fast for them to pick her up was also out. Elenor had known that it was only a matter of time before she either had to leave the city or be seen. She had done her research about cameras before she left home, knowing she would need to hide in the city.

That was when she could still use a computer. The problem was it'd been two years and technology didn't stop advancing. Eventually, she knew that she would need to get to someplace with a lot less cameras if she wanted to stay hidden. She hadn't been able to make herself leave yet, but now she knew it was past time.

Before she could, though, she had to buy herself one more day so she could get out in the night.

The men were advancing towards the tower. All of them glowed slightly in her sight from whatever power had altered her vision. It was a power that seemed to kick in all on its own when she needed it. One of them glowed in her sight as if he were wearing a suit made entirely out of LED lights. The roiling cloud of light around him glittered in all of the colors of the rainbow.

The others had more subtle auras, with only a single color each. She wondered what that meant, but it was a small worry inside of her mind. The larger worry was that these people clearly had some way to track her movements. Out of the corner of her eye, she saw two other people coming into the park from the west.

They, too, glowed, both of them brightly with roiling rainbow clouds. She wished that she had had this type of vision for her entire two years of scrambling around the city. It would have made it a lot easier to make sure no one was sneaking up on her. Still, she hoped it would go back to normal, because seeing almost exclusively in black and white was kind of depressing. She watched as the two women broke into a run. They raced up the path towards the Observatory tower.

"Now or never, Elly," she whispered, giving motivation to herself. She had desperately avoided using the well of… whatever it was floating in her chest. She had a little bit of knowledge of how to use it, but even that little bit of knowledge terrified her. She closed her eyes and began to think a very deliberate series of thoughts.

The first part was targeting what she wanted to affect. *I want to control the water inside of these people.* Elenor opened her eyes and looked at each and every person in turn. She concentrated on fixing each one in her mind as an individual. The second part was laying out the effect. Elenor riffled through her memories of anatomy and biology from high school with frantic urgency. *I want to stop the movement of their blood for twenty seconds. Then create a film of water in their lungs to block breathing.* This was the part that scared her the most. It was abstract. She wondered how whatever mystical power hovered in her chest understood what she was asking. She felt she was doing this as safely as she could, but really how did she know? The third was the termination for the power. She had to tell it how long she wanted the effect to last. She knew that she couldn't hold on for more than four minutes without killing someone. That was a figure that stood out from her textbooks as the average amount of time a person could hold their breath. *The effect will halt in four minutes.*

She knew from whatever had been crammed into her head that if any of the three parts was incomprehensible to the power, there would be some feedback, some sensation to let her know she had used a condition that was not clear. It was the only small safety valve for her power. That did not mean it was, in any way, actually safe. The power would do whatever she wanted within its limits as long as it understood her instructions. It would let her yank every drop of water out of their bodies like wringing out a dish towel, instantly killing them, if she told it to.

The power had no moral lines. It would not stop her from committing mind-rending atrocities.

She waited a long moment, but no feedback came. What she had constructed was an acceptable set of instructions for the power to activate. She held it in for a moment as the two women placed themselves between the observatory and the men moving in from the south. She tried to listen as the men stopped. The taller of the two women was clearly shouting something at the men.

Unfortunately, the sound was lost to the wind whipping past her at the top of the observatory tower. Elenor paused her attack. She didn't want to hurt anyone. She would not become the monster that her body appeared to be if there was any way to stop it. She just wanted to go back to her normal life. To be left alone.

Elenor continued to watch. As long as they didn't advance on the tower, she had no reason to stop them. She didn't understand what was happening. *Are they fighting over who gets to kill me?*

It didn't make any sense to her. Even with her powerful hearing, she couldn't overcome the sound of the wind. *Can I get closer?* She almost didn't dare, but with her power primed and ready, she had little to fear from them. If they tried to attack her, it would take only a single thought to unleash the power on them. She narrowed her eyes. They clearly hadn't seen her yet, which was likely only due to the angle. Her glowing eyes stood out in the night like beacons, but people very often mistook her for a normal animal, specifically because of their glow. By the time they figured out that the glow was happening without them shining any sort of light in her eyes, she had already had enough time to get away.

Before she could jump down into the small copse of trees to one side of the tower, though, something changed. The older woman reached over her shoulder and pulled at something. When she freed it, Elenor had to turn away from the brightness of the light coming off of the item or risk her eyes glowing so brightly that they would be seen from space.

She squinted through the corners of her tear-filled eyes at the bar of searing white light the woman seemed to be holding casually in one hand. She pointed it at the man, who seemed unphased. Elenor had not taken so much as a scratch since her transformation had completed. Something about her skin was armored, and extremely tough. Despite that, Elenor somehow knew that whatever the woman was holding would cut her to ribbons just fine. She realized that she could feel the thing somehow. Like the tug she had felt in her chest earlier that night. It wasn't the same sensation, but it was similar.

Once again, Elenor sighed, once again she had no idea what was going on. It was becoming far too regular an occurrence for her taste. She longed to go down there and pry some answers out of these people, because they clearly knew something from the way they were following her. However, looking at whatever that woman was holding made her think that it would be a very bad idea to get into the middle of this fight.

Elenor almost scrambled back when the woman swiped the white bar of light through the air to point directly at Elenor. For a moment, she thought it might just be an accident, but as she moved away, the bar of light tracked her movement as it were an automated gun locked onto her body.

Somehow, despite her care in keeping her eyes from reflecting any light sources, the woman knew exactly where she was. She almost turned and ran again, but it was getting very close to daylight. They could easily move in daylight where she could not. That was when she caught a snippet of the shouted conversation below.

"…cannot kill her, Myrridin! This is far too important to let you foul the job again! You have no idea what you're dealing with! I am the only one with the knowledge…" The wind howled past her again cutting off the conversation.

Elenor had heard enough. This was just a group of people who wanted her dead. She needed to find out what they had that let them track her and take or destroy it. That bar of light couldn't hurt her if the woman couldn't swing it. Elenor focused and released the power she had been holding back in her chest.

In her sight, a slightly transparent arc of blue light flashed away from her body toward the figures below.

Oddly, it didn't strike the figures like light. When it hit them, it reacted more like smoke. It wafted around them, curling and twisting. For most of them, it took only a moment for the smoke to be sucked into their bodies as if it were pulled in by a vacuum. The figures who had rainbow hues cascading around them seemed to realize what was happening. That didn't last more than a few pregnant seconds before the blue light sucked into their bodies. They collapsed, twitching.

Elenor leapt off the top of the tower. She didn't make it all the way to the ground, but that wasn't what she had been trying to do. She had aimed for a large tree about fifty feet from the base of the tower. Shooting between the branches, she got slapped in the face with some leaves, but a moment later, her paws hit the trunk of the tree. She flexed her paws, sinking her claws into the trunk. This did not completely arrest her momentum. Her claws sliced through the tree bark with almost no resistance. She slammed her hind paws into the tree, digging the claws in there, too. With all four sets of claws dragging through the tree bark, she slowed herself enough to come to a stop before her rear could smash into any large tree branches. That would have stopped her much more effectively, but it would have been uncomfortable at the very least.

Elenor jumped from the tree a moment later, landing lightly in the frosted grass. Almost immediately, she experienced an overwhelming reflex to shake the freezing water from her paws. Gritting her teeth, she ruthlessly suppressed the reflex. She would not walk up to these people ridiculously shaking her paws with each step. She quickly examined the people she had subdued. The larger group of men and women looked like soldiers, dressed in tactical equipment with gear on belts around their waists. Elenor wished she knew more about everything they were carrying on those belts. She wasted no time because she knew that what she had done to them was painful.

Using her claws, she sliced open pockets and pouches, destroying whatever she found inside. Phones went first. She didn't want them calling in more help before she could get clear of the city. She examined some boxy electronics on their belts and decided those might be radios for communicating. Some of them let out satisfying shrieking sounds when she raked her claws through them. Next were the guns. Elenor didn't know much at all about guns, but she figured if they were cut into several pieces, they wouldn't work anymore. She approached the man still glowing with a cascade of rainbow hues carefully.

It had taken longer for him to go down than the others so Elenor was wary of him. He was wearing far less gear than the others. No phone, just the boxy little contraption on his belt, which she destroyed. Lying on the ground next to his outstretched hand was a long staff. It appeared to be made of twisted roots that had grown together that way. Gripped in fingers of gnarled wood at one end of the staff was a fist sized sapphire. It glowed softly with internal light. Elenor reached towards it with her talons. Sparks flew the split second the black material touched the wood. A shower of rainbow light reminiscent of fourth of July celebrations splashed around her and she yanked her still-smoking claws away.

"What the hell was that?!" she growled, all of her spines standing up like the fur of a scalded cat. She backed away from the staff and made a wide circle around it. She hurried to the women. The clock was ticking. They would be waking up in a minute or two. Elenor really had no idea if what she had done would make any difference, but she had to try.

She went through the women's things. When the larger of the two women had dropped the bar of white light she had been holding, it stopped glowing. In her greyscale vision, she could see that it was a sword with an oddly shaped blade. It had an edge on both sides and was much wider at the hilt than the tip. She reached out towards it but paused. If it was like the staff, for all she knew, it would explode if she touched it.

She walked around it towards the smaller of the two women. There she saw a square pouch with white light bleeding through the edge of the flap covering it. Elenor tried to open the flap carefully but her claw slid right through the material as if it were wet toilet tissue. Elenor let out a sigh and simply sliced away the flap. When it fell open, Elenor took an involuntary step backward as she was blinded by the light coming from within. She blinked rapidly but could not banish the purple shadows across her vision. Finally, between one blink and the next, her vision faded back to normal.

Colors bled in from the edges of her vision and the light from within the pouch faded to a very dim level. It was a perfect glassy sphere the size of a cantaloupe. Unthinkingly, Elenor pushed her claws into the pouch to roll out the sphere. She tried to yank her claws back the instant the thing started to move, realizing that it would probably react like the staff had.

To her surprise, it didn't. The sphere rolled out and clinked against the talons of her other paw. There, in vivid color, was a perfect depiction of the park she was standing in as if seen from above. It was not like looking at Google Earth. If anything, it was even clearer than that, but there were no lines or delineations to indicate what she was looking at. The only reason she knew it was the park was because she could see the figures lying on the ground around her. Where she was standing there was a blue dot.

"Great," Elenor growled.

She didn't dare try to claw the thing apart after what had happened with the staff. She only had about a minute before they would start to wake up unless she was willing to kill them. She wasn't.

She turned and bolted toward the tower. She scrambled up a tree, bounced on a large limb, and leapt off it like a springboard. She had done this a dozen times so she knew the limb would hold. It launched her onto the exterior balcony of the second floor. She turned and walked up the side of the building, upside down to the balcony above, and then scrambled over the railing of the third floor. Carelessly, she went too fast and her claws sliced through the railing. The piece of metal fell away, peeling down the metal mesh below it. It clanged loudly, which startled Elenor for a moment.

She turned to look at it and saw something that made her cringe. Not far away, coming towards the tower, were a pair of people. Considering the flashlights they were shining around the path, they were likely police officers. She was out of time to be careful.

She ran to the glass windows that made up the walls of the second floor of the observatory. She slashed her claws through the window in four quick swipes, sending the piece of glass falling into the building to shatter. Elenor cringed again, but there was no time. She dashed through the hole and bolted up the central spiral staircase.

She managed to wiggle through the strap of her bag without slicing it to pieces. She turned and dashed out the door. She didn't bother with the tree this time and launched herself off the balcony. She bent her legs slightly, ready to absorb the impact at the ground. *This is going to hurt.*

A small amount of dirt and grass blasted away from her paws when she slammed into the ground next to the smaller woman. She hissed at the stinging sensation in her paws but didn't pause for long.

Carefully using the side of her paw, she held open her bag. Using her other paw, she rolled the orb within.

Almost simultaneously, all of the people on the ground around her let out a gasp followed by a cough. They all began to move, groan, and generally attempt to recover from a very unpleasant lack of oxygen.

Elenor turned slowly in a circle. She didn't know which way to run at that point. Her only other place to hide was a long way off. It wasn't a sure thing, though. She had found that place in the cemetery by accident, and she knew that it was used for funerals with fair regularity. Hiding there for a night would be fine, but it could backfire on her. Her mind turned to her new friend Mateo.

Would he help? She had saved him from a beating but when they had talked, she had gotten the idea that he had at least one sibling. She really didn't have a choice at this point. She could make it to Mateo's house in Canton while it was still dark. She turned southeast and leapt over the men, vanishing into the night.

10

"UNEASE"

Helen clawed her way up from unconsciousness. She sat bolt upright, and started to choke and cough. She looked around wildly, trying to figure out what exactly had happened to her. She spotted Thia, who was gasping spastically as she twitched on the ground. She checked her body for wounds but found none. She picked up her sword and slid it into the scabbard over her shoulder with practiced ease. She didn't bother to check on Joshua's men.

Whatever had happened to them had been the power of the Writ in some form. It was the only explanation that she had, and knowing that the Bearer had power made it all make sense. Something they had done must have made her feel threatened enough to take action.

"Thia, are you ok?" Helen asked. She eyed Joshua, who was coughing himself awake.

"Yes, just a little dizzy. What happened?"

Helen held out her hand. Her Striker materialized in her hand a moment later. "I am about to find out. Keep an eye on Joshua." Helen raised her voice enough to make sure everyone with Joshua heard her.

"If he or any of his men even seem to be reaching for their weapons, feel free to shoot them. Also, please put out the Displacer. Someone is approaching with flashlights from the south." Helen turned her attention to her Striker.

Thia reached into the bag at her side and then noticed the square pouch on one end was missing the top.

"Oh, fuck," Thia hissed. "She took the Oracle stone."

"Not surprising she figured out that we are tracking her." Helen wasn't even paying true attention at this point. Her focus was entirely on her Striker.

Thia pulled a small black box, one a bit bigger than her fist, out of her bag. She flipped open the lid. Turning it over, she poured out a cube that just fit within. From a pouch on the side opposite from the one missing the Oracle stone she pulled out a bottle of water, filled the box with it, and then placed it on the ground in the middle of everyone.

That done, she held up the cube and flicked it with a fingernail. It began to vibrate. She set the cube down into the water, careful not to splash any out of the box. She closed the lid in one swift movement. Water sloshed out of all four sides of the box evenly. As the water washed over the sides, Thia felt her ears pop as the Relic activated. A moment later, the flashlights of the police officers passed over the space where they were standing. The officers saw nothing and moved along up the path.

The Displacer used the water as a representation of space. The cube, when pushed into the water, shoved space away from the box, putting everything inside fifty square feet slightly out of phase with reality. Not so much that it constituted being in another dimension, but enough that they couldn't be seen by normal means. That was one use of it, at least.

"We screwed this up," Helen hissed.

"Seems a motif for you. We can't let that creature run wild. Who knows how many people it will hurt!" Joshua growled.

"I have no time for you right now, Joshua. Shut your torrid hole. I can exclude you from displacement any time I want. You can have a conversation with those two police officers about your illegal weaponry. I have real work to do," Helen growled.

Joshua had no qualms about dealing with the police. They were not an obstacle for him. Still, it was easier to use her for his purposes for now. Besides, he had an idea of what she was about to do, and if he was quick, he could get the information she was chasing after. He reached for his staff. A gunshot rang out and dirt struck him in the face where the bullet hit the ground in front of him.

"I believe my mother was quite clear. You nearly got us killed in Korea. It may have been thirty years ago, but I find near death experiences tend to stick in my mind. My mother may feel conflicted about killing you, but let me be crystal clear. I am not," Thia said. Without taking her eyes off of Joshua, she spoke again. "That goes for the rest of you. Some of you may get to your weapons, but not all of you. Do not test me."

Helen ignored them and struck the wide steel band on her wrist with her Striker. The clear note that rang from the Striker reverberated around the park. Helen pressed her fingers across all of the rods except one. It began to glow.

The Striker had some fixed powers, as all Strikers did. Magic that could be called upon without Resonance. The dark purple rod that vibrated on the Striker continued its low, clear note, pushing away all the other sounds in the world. It could show her past events. It couldn't reach very far into the past, but up to a few hours was no trouble. Everything around her shimmered slightly as transparent images overlayed everything. Most things hadn't moved, so they just seemed to glow.

A moment later, as the image finished generating, she could see her body, Thia's, and then Joshua with his team. All of them were unconscious. A moment after that, as if it were a video running in reverse, the Bearer came into view, walking backwards towards Thia. She crouched down, and then the Oracle stone rolled out of her bag to lie on the ground next to Thia. Things proceeded in that backwards vein right up until the point where they all collapsed. Then the images began to run forwards.

Helen reached into a pouch on her belt and pulled out a deep green stone, about the size of the palm of her hand. It was sheered flat on one side and had a hole bored through the middle of it. She struck the stone against the steel bracelet on her wrist and it produced a different note. The stone effervesced bright blue light for a moment. She held it up to her eye, lamenting for the days she could do this unaided, while the scene played out.

When Elenor walked into frame, it was everything that Helen could do to hold in any sort of reaction. If Joshua saw what the adder stone had revealed to her, he would stop at nothing to kill the Bearer.

Hovering above Elenor's head was a glowing rune that Helen could not make out. To her eyes, each edge of the symbol was distorted until the boundaries blended into one another. She could tell there was a shape buried somewhere in that blur of light, but she could not reproduce it in her mind, no matter how hard she tried. She couldn't have written it down if her life depended on it. It quickly became clear that the Bearer had somehow used her power to knock them unconscious for a time. Helen had a suspicion as to how it had been done, but it was nothing that she would share with Joshua. Even the tiniest bit of information could be dangerous in Joshua's hands.

"What do you see?" Joshua asked.

"You seem to misunderstand this situation, Joshua," Helen said as the recall of the events finished playing. She slipped the adder stone back into the pouch. "In the past, I have forgiven your interference due to our shared history. I even foolishly ignored you nearly getting us killed by the Korean military police when you attempted to relieve us of the Relics we recovered from them. Heed me, he who was Myrddin Wyllt, for I will give no further warning."

Thia could feel power gathering around her mother. As if she were about to push all of her energy into some powerful Relic. Thia had never felt anything like it. Her mother was boiling over with cold rage.

Helen lifted her Striker and pointed it at Joshua's chest. Tears of fury and frustration filled Helen's eyes, though they did not fall.

"If I see you threatening that poor child again, I will dedicate my every waking moment to accomplishing your end until one of us is dead." Helen's voice rang with the air of ritual and absolute authority.

It was a vow if Thia had ever heard one. The terrible power that had gathered around Helen did something. It flowed away from her, but unlike when she poured it into a Relic, it didn't seem to go anywhere. Something had changed, though. Thia could see the fear and anger on Joshua's face. Helen had once loved this man like a brother, but he had willfully gone down a path that she had warned him would not end well.

The adder stone had shown Helen the truth. If they were to repair the Writ and bring the power of the Callers back into the world, the Bearers were the only way. She had seen the symbol above Elenor's head but also the Writband on her chest. The Bearers now held the power of the Writbound. They were the Callers now, and this one, at least, was something much more.

Joshua looked as if he was about to dive for his staff regardless of Thia. Helen reached down and plucked up the Displacer. She flipped open the lid to the box. With the displacement released, the air that had been trapped in the area rushed away from them in an explosive gust that made a sound like the air brakes on a tractor trailer. Helen held out the box to Thia. Thia grabbed it, and with both of them touching the box, Helen closed the lid again. When Joshua finally came up with his staff, Helen and Thia were gone.

Helen and Thia bolted toward their car. The look on her mother's face terrified Thia. Decades of working together to keep Caller Relics from being used to cause chaos in the world had never caused such unease on her face. She looked as if the world had somehow fundamentally changed, and it was possible that it would never be right again. They slowed to a jog as they neared the car.

"What did you do? Something changed at the end. Joshua went from angry to murderous. I saw it in his eyes," Thia asked.

"Something I hope you will never be fool enough to do. I made a Caller's Vow."

"How much haven't you told me?" Thia asked in frustration.

Helen shrugged in response. "Much of what I could not teach you directly because I no longer have access to my full abilities. There are only a handful of powers we can use without Resonance to play a Surge. I am stupid for allowing myself to lose control like that. That vow means that if I see Joshua menacing the Bearer again, I will be compelled to kill him. I am not sorry." Helen yanked open the trunk in a squeal of bending metal. She hadn't bothered to unlock it.

"Joshua has gone beyond reason and I can turn a blind eye no longer. He was once my friend. He is, no longer. But a vow like that one is an anchor around your neck, Thia. Do not ever make one unless you are willing to give your life to achieve the vow. I am. This is important, Thia, more important than our lives. Joshua must be stopped and we must help these new Bearers of the Writ understand their power."

"That's not all that's the matter," Thia stated. They stopped near the trunk of the car.

Helen just shook her head. She was quietly gasping in breath, trying to control her fear. Her hands shook as she pulled off her vest and threw it into the trunk.

"Not here. I will not even slightly risk Joshua finding out what I have just learned, Thia. I will say only that I was right. Everything I thought I knew about what we would be facing is irrelevant. I was so far off the mark that I do not know what kind of world we live in anymore. The only way forward is to first find a way to communicate with one terror-stricken young girl with near godlike power and very little idea of just how far that power reaches."

11
"HELP"

Elenor ran. She was moving far faster than she had even thought possible. She ping-ponged between buildings to keep herself hidden from the growing light of dawn. Bricks buckled as her paws struck each building. She tried not to cringe as she left a minor path of destruction behind her. She attempted to avoid hitting areas where people would notice the damage by keeping to alley sides of buildings. She couldn't slow down or she wouldn't make it before dawn.

She turned a corner and saw a street coming up. She wasn't one hundred percent certain exactly where she was, so she slowed down slightly as she approached the street. She needed to see the signs as she jumped the street. She twisted her body and slipped between the railings of a fire escape. Her paws hit the landing with a loud clang. Then she launched herself between the railings again, sailing over the street. She made the fifty-foot jump almost effortlessly.

As she crossed the street, she caught sight of the signs she needed. Now knowing where she was, she turned her body again. Her paws slammed into the wall of a building and she pushed off. Moving at these speeds, it was hard for whatever power made her paws stick to things to get a grip. She continued to bounce off the buildings like a rubber ball shot by a cannon, using what little grip she had.

She turned a corner and rushed down the alleyways between tenements until she reached Mateo's street. Slowing down, her paws finally got a grip on the side of the building. Then she leapt horizontally, away from the building she was clinging to. She flew across the street toward Mateo's building and, at the last moment, flipped herself so her paws landed on the brick façade.

She scampered around the front of the building into the alleyway and then dropped nearly silently onto the fire escape outside Mateo's window. She was careful to place her paws so she didn't leave gouges in the fire escape.

The only part of her talons that would not slice everything they touched to pieces was the blunt section on top where they met her paws. She carefully turned her paw over and tapped that part against the glass of Mateo's window. Her ears perked forward when the sound of movement came from inside. Still, no one came to the window.

She tapped her claw again. This time, the movement was louder, the thump of feet hitting the floor. A moment later, Mateo's tanned face appeared through the window. He worked the latch and then slid the window open.

"Elly? Es demasiado jodidamente temprano. ¿Por qué estas aquí?" His voice was groggy with sleep explaining his lack of ability to speak English.

"Two years of high school Spanish isn't gonna cut it for whatever that was." Elenor complained.

"I said, it's the ass-crack of dawn without the sun part." Mateo grumbled as he rubbed the sleep from his eyes.

"I need someplace to hide. People are chasing me and they found all the places I normally stay. I took the thing they were using to track me. I just need a place to stay until it's dark again so I can get out of the city."

Mateo blinked at the tidal wave of words. He opened his window all the way. "Can you get in here without cutting my room to pieces?"

She nodded, and he stepped back. Elenor made an odd dipping motion with her head and then flowed lithely through the window. All of the spines on her body laid totally flat while she was doing it. As soon as she got through the window, they sprang back up around her like a cage of obsidian death.

"I think your closet is big enough I can curl up in there without cutting up anything," she said, but Mateo shook his head. He opened the doors to his closet, and it was entirely full with a set of cubby shelves with dozens of baseball hats displayed inside.

"You can sleep aquí mismo. My parents are really big on privacy. They won't come in without knocking. Who's chasing you?"

"I don't know who they are. Two women at first, but then there were a whole bunch of men, too. It was at Patterson Park. I swear they were fighting over who got to try to kill me, Mateo." Elenor's shaky voice was filled with terror.

"Va, sólo respira." Mateo's eyes had gone wide, and he was watching her with wary respect.

Elenor realized she was scaring him. She took a deep breath and arranged herself into a sitting position. When she let out her breath, her spines fell lax into her fur. "Sorry, Mateo. I didn't want to come here, but I couldn't think of a better idea. I can't get through the city in daylight. At night, there are things I can do to stay off cameras, things that I can't do during the day," Elenor explained.

"Está bien. You can stay in here. My parents are taking off for work soon, and Sofia is gone to my grandparents until tomorrow night," Mateo explained.

Elenor lowered herself slowly to the floor to make sure her spines stayed flat to her body. She put her head on her front paws, and let out a sigh.

Mateo cracked a smile. "Didn't think I'd end up with a monster sleeping in my room when we met a few days ago."

- aquí mismo – right here
- Va, sólo respira – Ok, just take a breath
- Está bien – That's fine

"I didn't think I'd have to run away from a bunch of crazy people tonight."

"What did you think you were going to do?"

Elenor raised a single ear by reflex. "What do you mean?"

Mateo shrugged. "I mean, you couldn't have hidden forever."

"I did just fine for over two years."

"De veras, but someone is going to see you at some point."

"None of you saw me in the park until I wanted you to, but my plan was to leave," Elenor taunted. That made Mateo think of two nights previous, when he had first met Elenor.

NC 17, EPOCH 19914.323

Mateo jogged down the street. He had wanted to see a movie that night, but he hadn't anticipated the trains being shut down early. Some issue with the rails, they'd said. His parents didn't own a car, and he didn't have enough money for cab fare on him. He could have called his mother, and she likely would have called him an Uber.

While his family wasn't destitute, money was still snug, if not actually tight. Besides, he had walked home before plenty of times. He had decided to head past Patterson Park on the way home because it was the shortest way from the theater. It was still an hour's walk, and when he had passed the park entrance near the corner of East Baltimore and Patterson Park Ave, he knew he had made a mistake. A group of men not much older than him saw him go past and began to follow.

Mateo knew the park pretty well, so he turned into the park paths at the entrance across from Lombard. He immediately turned right and headed towards the Observatory. The pack of gang bangers had been far enough behind him that they lost sight of him when he turned into the park.

Mateo immediately took off at a sprint. He bolted towards the Observatory as fast as his legs would move.

 • De veras - Sure

It just wasn't fast enough. He heard shouts behind him
and then pounding footsteps as the bangers ran after him. He
ran faster, and about halfway down the path, he turned off
into the lawn. He darted through some trees, running flat
out. There were enough trees around the tower at the
Observatory that he might be able to hide from them.

Elenor heard the shouts of the young men below. She had
been sleeping on the top floor of the tower as she had for the
past week since repairs had paused for whatever reason. The
tower was warm inside, that was all she really cared about.

"Wonder what that's all about?" she mumbled to herself
and got up from where she had been curled up near the
stairwell that spiraled down the middle of the building. From
there, she would hear anyone coming up the stairs, so she
would have enough time to get out if anyone came up. She
shook herself as she padded onto the balcony. It was freezing,
and though she knew she would survive the cold from
experience, that didn't mean she liked it. She peered over the
edge of the balcony.

There, running across one of the lit paths, was a young
man. About a hundred feet through the woods she could see a
group of other men running after him. Suddenly, she had an
overwhelming desire to see why they were chasing him. She
pulled herself over the balcony railing and walked down the
side of the tower. When she reached the ground, she trotted off
into the trees, her ears twitching as she followed the sound of
the panting young man. When she finally spotted him
crouching behind one of the bigger trees near the Observatory,
it was clear that the pack of shouting idiots was going to find
him. There just wasn't enough cover to hide behind, even in
the dark.

Elenor put her front paws up on a tree, and then after a
moment to get a good grip, she walked up the trunk. She
jumped from her tree to a large branch in the tree he was
hiding under. She peered down at him. Her creepy glowing
eyes had to be good for something, she supposed. After a few
minutes, Elenor thought that maybe he had managed to hide,
but then a flashlight began to shine through the trees. Elenor

made certain not to look directly at it to keep her eyes from glowing like spotlights. The panting guy swore under his breath.

"Might as well come out," the man holding the flashlight said. "We're gonna find you, kid." That was when the beam of the flashlight struck the deeply tanned young man beneath her tree. "Got yo ass."

For one long second, it appeared he might try to run again. Then he saw that the gang had circled up around him. Elenor became unreasonably angry. She could not understand why. Maybe it was because she'd always hated bullies. Maybe it was just because she was a good person who didn't want to see someone get hurt. Whatever it was, the anger railed against her better judgement. She had survived by staying hidden, but right then that didn't matter.

Elenor walked down the trunk of the tree until she was just above where the beam of the flashlight hit the tree. Then she craned her neck backwards and let the flashlight hit her eyes.

"What the fuck is that?!" the man holding the flashlight screeched.

Elenor turned and scrambled back up the tree trunk. As soon as she was high enough, she jumped from one tree to another, closer to the man holding the flashlight. He and his compatriots were spinning about, trying to find her. It wouldn't take long with her eyes glowing like headlights. She skittered down the trunk of the tree until she was almost breathing on the back of the man's neck. Even in the dark, she could see the hairs raise on the back of his neck. She bared her bear-trap grin at him.

Slowly, the man turned around, sudden paleness showing even on his teak skin as he came face to meat-grinder with Elenor.

"I think you should leave my friend alone," she hissed.

The scream the man let out was strangely satisfying. At least her nightmare face was good for something.

In his mad scramble to get away from her, he dropped his flashlight and darkness descended when it stuck in churned up *earth.* He took off running through the small patch of trees back towards the park paths.

She looked around, her lamp-light eyes scanning for any of the gang members who were not smart enough to run away. There were none.

"Thank you." The shake in the young man's voice made his words unclear.

Elenor turned to crawl back up the tree.

"Wait." The young man's voice steadied.

Elenor paused. She looked back over her shoulder.

"Hablaste," the pause was as if he were trying to figure something out. "puedes hablar."

"Yes, I can talk, but you're testing the limits of my Spanish." she said in an incongruous little girl voice that he would have associated with one of his younger cousins. Then she turned to walk back up the tree. He wasn't going to be any different than anyone else who had seen her.

"¿Estás bien?"

Elenor halted. He had sounded genuinely concerned. She turned back again, and this time, she jumped off the tree. She landed on the ground in front of him with a heavy thump.

He had not gotten up from where he had been sitting, and surprisingly, he didn't scramble away when she stalked towards him. Only a bare handful of people had seen Elenor since she had started hiding, but none of them had talked to her. There had only been screams of fear. "Shouldn't I be asking you that?"

Mateo just shrugged. "Pareces muy triste," he replied.

"How can you tell?" Elenor's glowing eyes turned to the ground. "I barely have a face anymore."

"I just, can. Just because you're not human, doesn't mean you don't have a face."

"Shouldn't you be screaming and running like them?" Elenor asked, baring her teeth at him. The obsidian razors glinted in the moonlight, but he didn't flinch away.

- Hablaste – You talked
- Puedes hablar – you can talk
- ¿Estás bien? – Are you ok?
- Pareces muy triste – You look really sad

"Nah, You saved me at least from a beating. Probably saved mi vida. What's your name?"

Elenor was still focused on the not human part. "I used to be human," she mumbled, still looking at the ground.

"It doesn't really matter if you look like a monster if you are going to go around saving people from gangs. I'm Mateo."

There was a long pause as the creature's glowing eyes roved back up to him.

"I'm Elenor."

"That's a normal name for," Mateo paused his eyes rolling up in thought.

"For a monster?" Elenor sniped.

"Pues, I was trying to think of a nicer way to say it, pero sí."

"Told you, I didn't always look like this. You better get home before those tools come back looking for you." Elenor walked up the tree trunk, her spine-laden tail disappearing into the foliage a moment later.

Mateo watched wide-eyed. She disappeared so effectively that he questioned whether or not she had ever been there in the first place. He shook his head to clear it and then shouted.

"Hey, wait a minute!" No response came. Whatever it, she, was had disappeared completely.

It turned out that Elenor had followed him all the way home to make sure he had gotten there alright, even though he had never seen her. She had come back the next night and again tonight.

"Why didn't you scream and run away that night?" Elenor asked. "I know I scared those jerks off for you, but I still look like," she used a paw to gesture at her entire body. The spines above her shoulders sprang up and their razor edges vibrated aggressively. "This."

"You're gonna make fun of me if I tell you why," Mateo objected.

- mi vida – my life
- Pues – Well
- pero sí – but yes

Elly shook her paw at herself a little more wildly.

"Really?! Have you… looked this over?"

"Bien. It's your voice. If I hadn't heard you talk, I probably would have run faster than I have ever run in my life. You look like a freaking demonio. But, you did save me, and then tú es tan," Mateo sighed in frustration. "Precioso. Como mi primita. How was I supposed to be afraid of that?"

Elenor attempted to squash the laughter that was bubbling up inside of her. She managed it, but not without shaking violently enough to make all of her spines stand at terrifying attention. Mateo's eyes had gone round as saucers again. The sound of something clattering to the floor behind her made her look around.

"I think you just cut off the corner of my desk," Mateo said. She looked down to her left. There, still spinning slightly on the floor, was a triangle of wood. So clean was the cut that the edge sparkled as if polished.

"Oh my god, Mateo, I'm so sorry."

"Could you…" Mateo pointed to her quivering spines.

Elly took another deep breath and relaxed every muscle in her body. It was something that had taken weeks of practice to figure out when the spines had first grown in. Thankfully, that had been after she had left home, because if it had happened in her room, it would have been a total disaster. The blades had been the very last portion of her transformation.

"I'm sorry, they react to every little movement. I hate these stupid things." Elenor tilted her head and looked him over. "I don't mean to be rude or anything, but how did you get like this?"

- Bien – Fine
- demonio – demon
- tú es tan – your voice is so
- Precioso – Cute
- Como mi primita – Like my littlest cousins

Mateo got an odd look on his face. "What do you mean?"

"I'm an <u>actual</u> monster, Mateo. There is no way my stupid six-year-old voice explains why you even let me within a thousand feet of you. Much less let me in your house." Elenor scooched away from his desk with careful attention to her spines.

Mateo sighed. "No, that's not the whole truth. I've never seen anything like you of course, but before we moved here we lived in a very bad neighborhood near Los Angeles. That's why I wasn't really worried the other night. Those guys might have beaten the crap out of me, but I'd have probably survived. There were days in my old neighborhood where I might not have."

He reached up to his shirt collar and pulled it down and to the right. There on his chest was a puckered scar. It was faded with age, but clearly at some point, something had made a hole in his upper right chest.

"This happened when I was eleven. One of the gangs was trying to recruit me, but when I told them I wasn't interested, they tried to kill me. When they shot me, they thought I was dead, and I almost was."

Elly lifted her paw and held it out towards the old wound.

"I don't know who called the cops, but they found me and got me to the hospital. It still hurts sometimes."

"But…" Elly started. Then she trailed off. She wasn't sure what to say to that. Mateo, though, was remembering that train-tunnel-sized gun barrel expanding before him just before the shot. After certain death, even a nightmare like Elenor just didn't pack the same punch.

"Anyway, after that I guess there just isn't anything I can really be afraid of anymore. I gotta just do whatever I want because I'm out of second chances.

Esto es el fin," Mateo finished. He saw that she wasn't completely convinced.

"Also, I did mention that not biting my entire body off made it pretty clear that you're not pure evil."

Elenor giggled. "Okay, okay I'm convinced. You have giant brass ones." Elenor's maw opened wide in massive yawn.

"¡Híjole!, that looks like the thing that would eat the Sarlacc." Mateo laughed.

"I don't look at them that often." Elenor bared her double row of bear trap teeth at him in what could only be generously called a smile.

"I'm exhausted. I'm gonna get some sleep. If you need to wake me up, just say my name. Don't touch me because…" She wiggled her body a little, and her spines sprang up in a threat display worthy of an angry kraken.

"Got it. Looky, no touchy." Mateo slid carefully around to her right, but he still didn't look afraid. Just respectful of the fact that she was an actual walking, talking meat grinder. He closed the door quietly behind him.

- Esto es el fin – This is it
- ¡Híjole! – Holy Crap!

12

"CONFUSION"

NC 17, EPOCH 19914.327

Helen sat in the uncomfortable rust colored chair in their hotel room. She stared into the middle distance as she had for hours while Thia bustled around the room, putting all of the Relics and equipment they had brought with them into order. In her hands, she held her Striker. The instrument had been humming quietly for several hours. At irregular intervals, Helen would move her fingers on the rods to produce a small piece of music. It was complex and beautiful, but most of all, Thia found the haunting melody sinister.

At the end of each piece, Helen would take her fingers from the instrument and jot something down in one of her ubiquitous notebooks. Then she would return to staring into space as if the world around her no longer existed.

"So, it's been fourteen hours. Care to give me a clue?"

Helen did not respond immediately and Thia finally rolled her eyes. She snapped her fingers loudly in front of her mother. Helen narrowed her eyes.

"If I am not answering, it is likely because I do not have any answers."

"You have something."

"I have a very bad feeling."

"What's that Surge?" Thia gestured at Helen's Striker.

"Bits and pieces of the Bane Surge, the music that started all of this. At least the parts of it that we could find."

"And why are you playing it over and over again?"

"I am trying to find what I missed. What Osiris did was unprecedented. He found a way to maintain the Resonance of a Surge without the Caller present."

"You said it was something to do with crystals, like the ones you used to make your Striker."

Helen nodded. "Yes. Each crystal rod of a Striker is invested with a bit of our spiritual energy when it is shaped and added to the instrument. As far as we knew, it was impossible to make crystals that would sustain resonance on their own. Osiris found a way."

"How?"

"How is a Surge played?" Helen asked.

"The music you play through a Striker, or any other invested instrument, creates a Resonance with your Spirit. It shapes that energy, triggering the changes you want in reality around you."

Helen went on. "The reason you cannot just make an instrument that will create Surges on its own is the Resonance required. Objects, even invested ones, will not work without a Caller."

Thia was not sure she liked where the explanation was going. "So, how did he do it?"

Helen's eyes watered, and she swallowed down her regret. "At first, he tried to create a crystal that would contain the soul of a Caller, or a human."

"He, sacrificed, people?" Thia's horror was writ large on her face.

Helen nodded. "But, it got much worse."

NC 17, EPOCH 18430.52

"What is this place?" The cave had been clearly been carved from the mountain by man. It was a perfect cube, massive, with no natural formations to speak of. It had at least a hundred stone pits, each one about twelve feet square and six feet deep. Paths ran between the pits in a perfect grid. Each pit had two stone shelves jutting into the middle. The shelves had a single hole in the middle. The corners of the pits were occupied with stone posts that suspended a cross of metal about five feet above the lip of the pit. A circle of metal the same diameter as the holes in each stone shelf joined the bars.

"This is how Osiris made his Resonance crystals,"
Myrridin said, and then pointed down the rows to a pit at the
end. "We must have just missed him. It is still fresh."

Iðunn walked between the pits to the corner of the room
Myrridin indicated. When she drew close enough to make out
what was on the shelves in the pit, Iðunn froze. There, lying
on the shelves in the pit, were two bodies. The one on the top
shelf was human. The one below was an animal. Each body's
limbs had been shackled with chains and stretched to full
extension at the corners of the shelf. A long javelin of pitch-
black glass had been pushed down through the ring of metal
above the platforms. It had been brutally shoved all the way
through the man and the animal below him. Blood had begun
to coagulate in a small basin on the floor of the pit. Occasional
drops fell from the end of the spear like a nightmarish melting
icicle.

Myrridin Wyllt's observations were clinical as they always
were. "The apparatus is designed to kill those placed on the
tables in sequence. I have examined the killing implements
and they are constructed of Relic stone."

Iðunn did not hear the Merlin's recitation of what he had
found. She reached out and placed a single finger against the
black spear. The moment her skin contacted the surface of the
spear, her face twisted in fury and revulsion. She yanked her
hand back, and it was all she could do to keep her lunch where
it belonged.

The Merlin continued his recital of the facts. "The spear is
designed to generate a note when a spur at the top contacts the
metal frame. In this way, the Relic stone does not activate any
Surge activity until the animal is killed."

"This is how he did it," Iðunn whispered. In the absolute
silence of the cave, it might as well have been a shout. "At the
moment of the death of their Caller, Familiars are vulnerable."

Myrridin nodded. "Yes, at that moment, they
momentarily lose their sentience and will as the connection
between the Caller and the Familiar is severed. At that
moment, this spear of Relic stone draws in the spiritual
essence of the familiar."

"And he uses it as a core for the crystals that maintain his surges," Iðunn finished.

"Yes, the living soul of the familiar separated from its body, kept in a suspended state has no will of its own. It can be imprinted with the spiritual signature of anyone with the skills to do so. With enough such crystals, he could expand his Resonance to do almost anything."

"He could make permanent changes to the entire planet that way," Iðunn reasoned.

"Without a doubt. The only thing that limits our ability to make such widespread changes is the reach of our Resonance. With this, he has bypassed those limitations."

"How many has he made?"

The Merlin gestured around at all of the pits. "Enough. From just the residual imprints, I can account for several hundred."

Iðunn finally turned away from the horrific evidence of Osiris' transgressions. "What is he planning, Merlin?"

The Merlin hesitated, and Iðunn narrowed her eyes.

"Myrridin, I have let this go for far too long at your request. You have found what you wanted. It is time to end this."

The Merlin turned and walked towards the wall of the cave opposite of the entrance. He seemed to disappear through the wall, but when Iðunn followed him, she found an opening cut cleverly into the wall that made it almost invisible until you were right on top of it. Inside was another large room.

Dozens of long simple work tables carved from the floor of the cavern itself were arranged in a double ring in the middle of the room. Each table held instruments and tools specifically for working with glass and stone. Merlin ignored most of the room and turned to a small area with a tiny desk carved of dark wood. On it was a book.

"Osiris shielded this room from post cognition. I could not look into the past here because the residual imprints were scrambled. I instead constructed a minor temporal anomaly to retrieve this from the past timeline."

"Was it worth that risk?" Iðunn was unsettled by Merlin's ability to reach back through the timeline. It was small comfort that he could make no significant changes without severe consequences for himself, not to mention the timeline itself.

"The timeline displacement will be minimal as long as we destroy the book as soon as you are finished reading it. It would not go well if the secrets held within became widespread."

It did not take long for Iðunn to page through the book. Eidetic memory was a hard-earned skill that each Caller learned through necessity. Each page crumpled Iðunn's face into a mask of disgust. The moment she closed the small book, she stood from the leather cushioned chair and her Striker appeared in her right hand.

She struck it softly on the steel bracelet on her right wrist. The Merlin's eyes went a little wide when he could not hear the notes she played. Wider still when the desk, the book, the chair, and everything else in the small alcove turned to black dust. Then the dust swirled and dispersed entirely as if it had never existed at all. He had never seen anything destroyed so completely. He wondered if this was how she killed.

He had always known that Callers like Iðunn, those who enforced their laws, were terrifying in their power. This was leagues beyond what he had ever imagined. He had always been a powerful Caller. He had taken the name of his mentor, after all. But Iðunn was on a completely different scale.

Cold hazel eyes fixed on him and he swallowed.

"How long have you known?" Iðunn's voice had a cutting edge. An unspoken threat.

"I have had suspicions since we saw what he did at that village outside of Cairo. I could not find the evidence until now."

"Two years. He plans to attempt to change the very nature of reality. He is attempting to engineer the development of the human race. It is just what I said he would do!" Iðunn roared the last sentence.

Merlin, to his credit, did not flinch. "And if you had simply killed him and someone else had found that journal?"

"I would have been thorough."

"Spatial displacement has never been your area of expertise."

Iðunn paused for a long moment. Myrridin was not one for petty insults.

Realization took but a moment. "This is a port dimension," Iðunn concluded.

"That door cut into the rock did not exist before I got here. This space is displaced from reality."

Iðunn shook her head. "I would have been thorough, and he must be stopped."

"I agree, but finding this was important. I just hope I haven't taken to long."

Iðunn scowled in response. "Hope is not going to help us now, Myrridin. I know where he is, but it will take me several days to catch up to him."

"Be careful, Iðunn. I do not know what else he may have been researching. There was one other thing, though I do not know how important it is. There was a less, technical, journal here. It appeared to have been dropped by someone evacuating the facility. An assistant of some sort, unless I miss my guess."

"And?"

"It talked about Osiris and his work. It was not the ravings of a zealot. It did not contain enough details to be truly useful, but these were the words of someone who believed in the logic of what Osiris was doing. I mention this only to make sure you are wary. He may not be as insane as you think, and he may have more Callers with him."

"Each hunt is the same, Myrridin. I never let my guard down."

"That must be hard."

"Not if you want to live."

13
"STAND"

"Elenor…" The voice was quiet and a little hesitant. Elenor was about to shake herself when she remembered in a flash where she had been sleeping. Instead, she opened her mismatched eyes, remaining in complete stillness.

"Mateo?" Elenor mumbled.

"Don't wear it out," he joked. "Está oscuro."

She didn't move right away, only lifting her head to see where she was. Then, she carefully got her paws under her and, keeping her body as relaxed as she could, pushed herself up. Her spines bounced a little, but they didn't turn into vibrating murder springs. Elenor looked toward the window and her body turned slightly in that direction.

"Where are you going to go?" Mateo interrupted.

Elenor paused and shrugged in response, making her spines quiver menacingly. "Doesn't really matter, I can't stay here," she whispered.

"What happened, Elly?" Mateo asked.

"Two different groups of people came after me last night. They were talking about trying to kill me."

Mateo looked a little taken aback. Then his face slid back into a more normal expression. "That sounds like a pretty tall order though. Didn't you say that bullets just bounce off your skin? You're freaking Superman."

"Yeah, but I think they had some sort of magic weapons. It sounds so stupid to say it. How can any of this be real?" Elenor fought back the tears she hated so much.

Mateo shrugged. "Mí Papá says that imposible is just

- Está oscuro – It's dark out
- imposible - impossible

a word that people use to make themselves feel in control. It doesn't actually mean anything."

Elenor told Mateo everything about what had happened. She took out the glowing crystal sphere that she had taken from one of the women's bags.

"I think they were using this to track me somehow, but I have no idea how it works."

That was when she noticed there was a glowing green dot showing on the surface of the orb. The color caught her eye, as it was unmistakable. It was the exact shade of green that made up the band that she had seen around the man's head in that office building.

She reached out to turn the sphere with the intention of seeing the dot a little more clearly. As soon as her paw touched it, the opaque surface of the crystal cleared and an image of the city from above appeared on the surface. She pulled her paw back instantly, but the image did not go opaque again.

"¿Que hiciste?" Mateo asked.

Elenor shook her head. "I don't know. I just wanted to see the green dot better."

Elenor craned her neck over the orb. It was like looking at a real-time image from a satellite like you saw in the movies. She could see cars and people moving on the streets. The green dot was hovering over a building. She didn't recognize any of it besides the fact that it was in a city.

"That looks like GPS on steroids," Mateo commented as he looked over the orb. "Where do you think this is?"

"It doesn't matter," Elenor said. There was no tugging feeling in her chest this time, so she could ignore the stupid green dot. "I have to go, Mateo. Could you do one more thing for me?"

Mateo's raised eyebrows shifted his nonchalant shrug to affirmation.

• Que hiciste? – What did you do?

"I have a couple of cheap cell phones in my bag that I got to send my parents messages. I can do it but the claws make it hard not to wreck the phone. Could you come down the street with me and send my parents a message to let them know I'm ok, and that I am leaving?"

Even without a human expression to read, Mateo could tell that Elly was distraught. "Sure. But I still think you should stay. You have actual, honest to dog, super powers. Just bite their heads off or something."

"Ick. Hard pass. I bit a crazy guy once in the park because I caught him tormenting a dog with a stick. People taste awful."

"With those meat grinders? How did he get away with all his limbs?" Mateo chuckled a little.

"Nasty… turns out you can hobble pretty fast even with a bunch of holes in your leg." They both laughed.

"We should go. I don't want anyone else getting hurt because of me."

Elenor sat down and reached out to pick up the orb. When she lifted it between both front paws, she noticed there was another dot on the surface. This one was not a single color, though. It coruscated through all the colors of the rainbow. She turned the orb until she could see the dot on the foggy surface of the orb. When she focused on it, the image cleared again. The cityscape surrounding this dot was different from the previous one.

"¿Qué es eso?" Mateo asked.

Elenor shook her head. "I don't know. It's rainbow colored." The moment she said she didn't know, another dot appeared on the surface of the of the orb. This one was white, and it pulsed with a silver glow that repeated.

Considering the different behavior of this dot, Elenor

- Va – Sure
- ¿Qué es eso? – What's that?

had an idea of what it meant. To test her theory, she picked up the orb and balanced it in her single paw. She carried it across the room. As she did, the pulsing white dot moved with it. Elenor's eyes went wide with realization and she looked up at Mateo.

"I have to go, Mateo. They are right outside."

"¿Quien esta afuera?" Mateo asked.

"I don't know, but someone is, and I can't let them find me in here with you."

Elenor bent her neck and wiggled her snout beneath the strap of her bag. She got it around her neck and carefully adjusted it until it was at the base, beneath the reach of the spines on her shoulders. When she looked up, Mateo was standing between her and the window.

"You can't run away forever, Elly."

"I don't need to. I only need to run away long enough that no one else is going to get hurt." Elenor had never understood what had happened to her, but she knew that she didn't want to be responsible for everything falling on her landing on anyone else.

"¿Entonces qué?" Mateo asked. "Just going to lay down and die for them, all alone?" Mateo's feelings on the topic were made clear by his angry tone.

"What do you expect me to do, Mateo? I don't know how to fight. I don't even know much about how my powers work. I could have killed the shit out of those people last night if I had done a single thing wrong!" Elenor stared toward the window, but stopped short when Mateo didn't move.

"So, what if you did? Seems like they were trying to kill you. Self-defense is still a thing!" Mateo growled.

Elenor shook her head. "I can't kill people, Mateo. That's not going to lead anyplace good."

"You can't let them drive you out of your home. My parents and I had to leave everything we cared about

- ¿Quien esta afuera? – Who is right outside?
- ¿Entonces qué? – Then what?

because we couldn't do anything about it, but you can."

Elenor's anger almost made her cruel. She opened her mouth to say something truly damning, but then the bullet scar on Mateo's shoulder flashed through her mind. She couldn't do that either. He had every reason to not want to give up anything else, even if it was someone he had only known for a few days. She let out a sigh.

"Fine, Mateo, but I can't do this here. I don't think your poor house would survive a fight with me in it. I need to lead them away somewhere no one will see what happens. If I make it, I'll come back."

He nodded in response. "¿A donde vas?"

"English?" Elenor requested, he had spoken a little too quickly for her to catch it.

"Where are you going?" Mateo repeated.

Elenor scooped the Oracle Stone back into her bag. "I'm going to lead them to Hart-Miller Island. I don't know what's going to happen if I start using my power more. I haven't ever used it before yesterday, and it scares the shit out of me."

"¿Por qué alla?"

Elenor shook her head. She had no idea why she had chosen that spot. She knew it was the right place though. "Seems like a good idea. This time of year, no one should be in the park. My parents used to take me there sometimes," Elenor reasoned.

"Bueno. But you shouldn't go out of the window. I'll show you how to get up to the roof."

Elenor nodded and followed him out of the room. The bare concrete walls of the stairwell echoed slightly as Mateo ran up the stairs with Elenor hot on his heels. He held open the door for her.

"You better come back."

"I'll do my best, Mateo."

- ¿Por qué alla? – Why there?
- Bueno – All right

Mateo let the door close silently as she crept across the lawn furniture strewn rooftop. She put her paws up on the short brick wall around the roof and pulled herself up just far enough to see over the edge.

It took not even a single split second to spot the man just down the street. She narrowed her mismatched eyes and the colors faded from her vision. Against the aged brick façade of the tenement across the street, he leaned speaking into a cell phone. The tactical gear of the night before was gone, replaced with fairly standard street clothes. Black slacks and a grey hooded sweatshirt. None of that gave him away, though. Instead, a glowing rainbow aura surrounded him in Elenor's sight.

She watched him for a long moment as he looked up and down the street. He knew she was here, but not exactly what building she was in. Must be the thing she stole from the women wasn't the only way they had of tracking her. What Mateo had said had stirred anger in her. She didn't care what she looked like anymore. She wasn't some beast. Mateo was right.

What does it matter if they kill me here, or somewhere else? Elenor knew that looking at the light surrounding the man had brightened the glow of her eyes because the faded navy sky had brightened considerably in her vision. The stars were almost blinding, even here in the city. She hopped down from the edge of the roof and turned in the direction she had seen the man.

Elenor kept her eyes lidded and crept over the short wall that stood over the alleyway between the two buildings. The concrete scraped at her paws as she pulled herself over the wall and slunk down the side of the bricks. She pushed off one wall, flipping herself over so that her paws hit the wall of the opposite building.

The next building over was almost identical to Mateo's. Elenor wasted no time slinking across that roof. Unlike Mateo's rooftop, this one showed no signs of life. Several more rooftops brought her to the building directly across from her stalker. She narrowed her gleaming eyes at the man.

"Freaking jerk," she mumbled to herself. For a few short seconds, she entertained simply murdering the man. She could feel that ready well of power swirling in her chest. She could quite literally crush his heart while he was standing there. He would just drop dead with no explanation whatsoever. The thoughts didn't last. She couldn't just go around killing anyone she wanted. Even if they were a jerk. That had to be her last resort. Maybe she could convince him to just leave her alone.

Screw it.

Elenor backed up a few paces, and then bolted toward the short wall surrounding the roof. She leapt at the last second. She cleared the wall and the street streaked past beneath her. She landed in the alleyway adjacent to where the man was watching her from, making no attempt to be quiet.

The thud resounded off of the buildings much more loudly than she had anticipated. She had wanted the jerk's attention anyways. A minute later, he passed the alleyway looking impressively casual. She glared at him, and as soon as she caught his eye, he turned and bolted down the alleyway. The staff that had thrown off a rainbow of sparks when her claws hit it appeared in his hand. *That's right, chase me, idiot.*

Elenor turned and shot of between the buildings. She leapt and ran straight up the wall at the end of the alleyway. She tried not to wreck the building, but as fast as she was going, her claws left gouges in the brick exterior. She heard the man shouting, but he wasn't shouting at her. She started to slow down to let the guy catch up, but then the sound of a helicopter screamed overhead. A circle of light illuminated the bricks around her. She turned toward the bay and ran.

14
"FLIGHT"

Even the helicopter couldn't keep up with her as she catapulted from building to building. She had no idea how she moved so quickly. It almost felt like something had removed all of the effort it took to move her body. Just like when she had made that huge jump the day before yesterday. Truly, she felt like Mateo had said. Like she had super powers.

She slowed down just enough from time to time to let the helicopter catch up. She had one problem that she wasn't sure how to solve, getting across the water to the island. She figured she would just have to swim. She hated the idea because the water would be freezing, but the cold wouldn't really hurt her. It was just hateful.

Elenor ran out of buildings at the intersection of South Eaton and O'Donnell, turning onto O'Donnell Street. She kept to the shoulder and sped up as fast as she could go so that no one would really see her. She turned and leapt both lanes of traffic to land on the O'Donnell Street cut-off. She followed that until it turned into Boston Street and took that all the way to the end of the street. Cars zipped past her as the asphalt blurred beneath her paws. When she made it to the end of Boston Street, she leapt fences and made a b-line for the water.

She scrambled through manicured yards sparsely covered with the remnants of winter snow. Elenor weaved around colorful playground equipment that people kept for their children. She finally ran out of the housing developments at the intersection of Delvale and Holabird Avenue.

The intersection was momentarily quiet so she bolted directly across it and galloped down the street to Marshall Road. At the corner of Holabird and Marshall, she bunched her hind quarters and exploded into the air. She cleared the street but came up a little short of the first building in the row of tenement houses.

Her claws bit into the bricks as she scrambled up onto the roof. The spotlight from the helicopter hit her again and she didn't waste any time streaking towards the other end of the rooftops. A short leap between two stretches of adjacent square brick buildings got Elenor to the end of the row at Bayard Ave. She turned right when she saw a not quite road between two housing developments. The dirt track was just wide enough to fit a single car, but not wide enough to be a street. Houses were shadowed blurs in her vision as she threw up dirt from the path behind her.

She dodged between some large standing posts that separated the housing development from a large asphalt parking lot. A wide two-story brick building loomed above her, and she leapt onto the roof of a car in the parking lot closest to the doors. From there, she was able to clear the roof of the building without much trouble. She skidded to a halt at the edge of the building. Brick dust sprayed her in the face as bullet holes puckered the top of the wall just in front of her. Elenor stumbled back, shaking her head and wiping at her stinging eyes with her paws. The gritty stuff didn't seem to do any damage to her shining eyes, but the feeling made seeing anything impossible.

"Son of a…" she started to swear, then bullets pinged off of her spines, shattering into pieces that whizzed off wildly in all directions. She flattened herself to the roof to give herself a moment to get the grit out of her eyes. They didn't stop firing, even though the bullets had no effect. She realized they weren't trying to hurt her. They were trying to give that man time to catch up. She exploded up from the building roof and landed in the midst of the group of five firing at her.

She had to be extremely careful, but she could feel through her power exactly where every one of them was. Exactly how each one was standing. She spun her body and felt slight resistance against various spines.

Spines on her tail slid through the calves of the two behind her, hamstringing them. They collapsed with shouts of pain. Spines on her shoulders clipped the knee of the woman on the right, who spun to the ground clutching her leg with a scream. She swung the claws of her right paw in an arc that passed through the shins of the two men in front of her. They would all live, and better, it had happened so fast that they barely saw her before she tore off down the concrete path between houses. She streaked through a pharmacy parking lot, where she heard a couple of shouts of surprise and confusion from those who caught brief glimpses of her darting past.

She zipped across two larger lawns to the juncture of Merritt Boulevard and Wise Avenue. Knowing that Wise Avenue had a bridge across the creek, Elenor ran along the side of the road. Stretching out into her run, she shot through two sparsely inhabited strip mall parking lots on the south side of the road. The whup whup whup sound of the helicopter was further off, but still ever-present behind her as she reached the bridge.

Elenor squeezed onto a slim concrete walking path that ran along the south side of the bridge. The path opened up into another residential area. It went past a well-tended forested area that she was pretty sure was a country club. When she got to the end of Wise Avenue, she paused at the intersection. She was certain that if she continued straight, she would hit the water and eventually it would run into Hart-Miller Island. But that would be a lot of swimming. She hadn't been in the water since her transformation, but she was pretty sure she could dog paddle just fine.

She decided to swim it. At least if she was in the water, they wouldn't be able to do anything more than take a few pot shots at her. She took off through a dense patch of forest. As soon as she broke out of the trees, she realized that she couldn't run across the Beltway because it was packed with traffic. Instead, she leapt over the entire road.

She blurred through another patch of forest and jumped over the northbound lane. She crashed through a second stretch of trees and broke out into a razed area strewn with gravel. A set of train tracks crossed her path north to south.

Just as she was about to jump over them, an odd whistling sound came to her ears. Muscles bunched and she launched herself into the air on instinct. There was a deafening roar, and she was propelled forward by an enormous unseen force. She curled herself into a ball, grabbing the end of her tail in her front paws.

She smashed into the sparse treeline at a tremendous rate of speed. She hit a tree, but that barely slowed her as her spines cleaved through the trunk with almost no resistance. She hit the ground with a tremendous whomp of sound, skipping to a stop in the road. She uncurled herself and scrambled to her feet.

Elenor let out a near maddened screech at the helicopter. "Are you fucking crazy?!"

A massive cloud of dust and dirt muddled the lights of the city. The tree she had blasted through let out a crack like thunder and toppled to one side. The helicopter broke through it a moment later. They had shot some sort of explosive at her in the middle of the city! *What if they had missed and hit a house or something? What if there had been a train, and they had hit that?* It could have been a disaster.

Elenor had wanted to lead them away somewhere that no one would see anything, not wreck half the freaking city. *Screw it, no more sandbagging. They are obviously tracking me somehow. Let them track me.*

She took off towards the water once again. She didn't bother with slowing down anymore. House lighting stretched out into ribbons of illumination as she reached speeds that a drag racer would be jealous of. Her claws dug into the pavement of Cove Point Road, propelling her down the street in massive leaps. At the end of the street, she leapt over a fence and crashed through a few hundred feet of forest. She came to a glassy pond gleaming in the moonlight. She cleared it in a single leap, landing in the back yard of a house before smashing through a hedgerow and emerging on Sea Bay Court.

Bolting directly across the street, she heard a confused exclamation from someone getting out of their car when she went flying past. She knew she wasn't far from the water when she dodged between the trees and into the last patch of forest. She had left the helicopter behind long ago, but she could still hear it in the distance as she made it through the trees.

Then the bay yawned open before her. She leapt out into the water without hesitation. When no freezing splash came, Elenor froze in pure, stiff legged confusion. She had closed her eyes, anticipating the salt water would sting. She opened her luminescent orbs to find herself bobbing slowly up and down. Her paws were making contact with the surface of the water, but not sinking into it at all.

"Sure, <u>why not?!</u>" Elenor shrieked with confused frustration. She couldn't stop to figure out why she could now walk on water. Running across the water was such an odd sensation. She couldn't seem to go much faster than the running pace of the average canine her size. It was like running on glare ice with a fresh covering of snow. Just enough traction to get moving, but not enough to feel stable enough to really run.

Because of that, it took her another fifteen minutes to reach Drum Point.

By the time she had reached the island and made her way up the beach to the Park Observation Tower, the Helicopter had caught up. Just as she heard it coming up the beach, she stopped at the end of the dirt track she had been following.

She wriggled her bag over her head and hid it just off of the path in some scrub brush. She couldn't fight wearing the silly thing around her neck. Elenor had no idea what she was going to do. *Will I have no choice but to kill someone?*

As she approached the grey-sided buildings, she got an uneasy feeling in the pit of her stomach. She couldn't take the time to analyze it, though, because the helicopter swung into place over the beach. It landed a moment later and a team of at least twenty men piled out of it, carrying weapons. They must have been packed into the craft like sardines. Half of them took up positions around the helicopter while the other half came up the beach in a wedge formation.

Her vision faded to greyscale and each person stood out, surrounded by a soft glowing aura in various colors. Except for the one standing at their center. That man was outlined in a coruscating rainbow of colors. The man next to him was carrying what looked like a bar of brilliant red light in his right hand.

Elenor jumped to the peaked roof of the building that faced away from the beach, losing sight of the men momentarily. Her claws left gouges in the shingles as she crept up to the peak. Elenor peered over the edge. The guns they were carrying were like toys against her. She thought the explosive they shot at her earlier might have hurt her, but she just had no idea what she was capable of.

She knew one thing she was capable of that she couldn't do. She couldn't kill them. Maybe someday, that would be a step she would have to take in self-defense. She wasn't ready for that, though. She had to talk to them first, at least. Just in case, she prepared the same instructions for her power that had knocked them all out before and waited for them to come up the beach towards the observatory building. The shingles of the roof scraped at her paws as she backed down the peak so they wouldn't see her. She heard their footsteps coming up the wooden walkway towards the buildings.

"What do you people want from me?!" Elenor shouted at the top of her childlike voice. "I've never done anything to you!"

"You are Defective. You are a danger to all of humanity!" She recognized the voice of the man from the previous night.

"How? I haven't hurt anyone the entire time since this has happened to me. I didn't choose this!" Elenor yelled back. "I don't want to hurt anyone. I just want to be left alone."

"It doesn't matter what you want. You'll do it anyway just by your very presence in the world. What do you think is going to happen if people learn that what they call magic is a reality? Do you think they would do good things with it?" he yelled, and Elenor heard men moving up creaking planks below. They knew how to be quiet but they were no match for her hearing.

Magic? Is that what my powers are?

"You're willing to kill me just because of what might happen if people know about me?"

"Absolutely. You are one, balanced against the lives of billions." The man's voice was hard.

Elenor's breath of frustration hissed between the black razors she called teeth. "It's people like you that…" Elenor never got to finish the thought as the odd feeling in the pit of her stomach ratcheted up to the feeling of a thousand snakes squirming through her bowels. Every sense and feeling told her that something was coming towards her.

She jumped to her feet and rushed up the incline of the roof to the peak. The men raised their rifles as soon as they saw her, but Elenor did not even notice. Her eyes were locked on the water behind the place where the helicopter was powering down. Just below the surface, a faint circle of sickly viridian illumination shimmered into view.

She barely felt the bullet impacts as they ricocheted off of her spines and skin. She noticed that the man with the rainbow aura had turned to the water as well. As she watched with rapt attention, a wavering cloud of radiant threads lifted from the surface of the water in a slowly undulating cloud. The ethereal threads of light stretched out as spider silk might waft upon a breeze. They did not seem to have any substance as they passed through the helicopter without any resistance. Elenor watched in growing horror as the pilot began to scramble to get out of the helicopter. He never made it.

The helicopter exploded.

"Down!" Elenor screamed, but it was far too late. Debris from the helicopter blasted into the group of men and women who had been attacking her. The group protecting the helicopter simply vanished in a spray of blood and raggedly torn viscera. One of the blades of the main rotor screamed toward the buildings. It smashed into the group, slicing two of the ten people clean in half.

The remains of one of the helicopter doors slammed into the man who had been carrying the bar of red light that she suspected was some sort of magic sword. He didn't even have time to make a sound as the flying door blasted him off of his feet. His back smashed into the thick wooden stairs leading up to the observatory buildings from the beach. He vanished beneath the mass of the steel helicopter door.

The group had only five men and three women left when the man emerged from then water. He walked up and out of the lapping waves, water sluicing from his body as if his very existence were oleophobic. Water seemed to draw back as if it were being pushed away from him by some unseen force.

The questing threads of light reached out towards the men and women. Elenor stood frozen, trying to process what was happening. The man who had been chasing her, though, was not frozen. He leapt forward and slammed his staff into the ground. For a short moment, it felt as if the whole world was shaking around Elenor.

An enormous wall of stone rose from the ground at least a hundred feet wide and ten feet thick, cutting them off from the man. Elenor finally began to move. She could see from her vantage point that the wall would not stand long. The lambent threads passed into the wall and it crumbled, not even slowing the man. He ran through the gap, not even bothering with the group of men and women. He shot directly towards Elenor.

Unfortunately, she saw what he left in his wake. The searingly bright threads attached themselves to the tools of each of the remaining people. The guns exploded first, magazines ripping apart in showers of bullets. That, however, was the least of the problems. Light exploded from the staff held in the hand of the man with the rainbow aura.

Elenor knew without any doubt that she could do nothing more to help them. She turned and crouched. The roof crumpled beneath the force of her jump with a resounding crack, and her body shot away from the building. A moment later, a thunderous explosion came from behind her. The explosion from the missile earlier had been like a stiff breeze compared to the overwhelming force that hit Elenor from behind.

15
"FIGHT"

Sandy terrain sparsely dotted with scrub brush shot by beneath her, and she twisted her body on instinct. Her paws smashed into the grainy turf, tearing a wide furrow as she skidded. She felt her body smashing through brush before she finally came to rest. She blinked away purple blobs that had been burned into her vision from the exploding staff. She had not had that happen to her since her transformation. She had discovered she could stare into the brightest source of light without any sort of damage to her eyes. It must have been the flash of light from the exploding staff. Maybe whatever made the staff work was different from normal light.

Elenor looked around for any signs of the man surrounded by glowing filaments of light. He must have been caught in the blast. The only reason she hadn't been was because of her jump from the roof. If she had been any closer, she thought she would be dead.

Dust and debris still filled the air in an enormous spreading cloud. Suddenly, a massive wooden beam slammed into the ground a few feet away. Then more debris began to rain down around her. Massive chunks of shingled roof and other detritus began to fall from the sky where it had been thrown by the explosion. Elenor flattened herself to the ground, tucking herself into a tight ball. All of the spines covering her body stood to quivering attention.

A large section of stairs fell directly on top of her and was torn to shreds on contact. The weight of the pieces still slammed into her back and sides, causing her to wince in true pain for the first time in years. She would have bruises, that was for sure. A few moments later, she could hear that the deluge of wreckage had stopped.

She lifted herself, shaking off the remains of the shredded stairs. The cloud of dust was slowly beginning to settle, and impossibly, she saw the silhouette of a man forming within the cloud. A fog of vacillating threads formed in her vision as he emerged.

"It tells me that you must be destroyed if I want my family back," the man shouted.

Now that she had time to look at him, he was tall, with the lanky, wiry build of a runner. His clothing was amazingly clean considering that he slogged across the bottom of the bay from what Elenor had seen. A charcoal grey dress shirt with matching black slacks. His feet were adorned with a pair of leather loafers, also bone dry.

He had a square face with a wide, crooked nose. A well-trimmed beard covered his cheeks and chin, though his upper lip was shaved clean. His eyes were oddly dark, as if someone had poured dark grey paint into them. Elenor didn't think it was an effect of her special vision, but she couldn't be sure. A single point of verdigris light served as a pupil. They were fixed on Elenor.

"What are you talking about?" Elenor asked. The well of power in her chest thrummed as if it were a struck bell. It made her whole body vibrate, and it got worse the closer the man got to her.

"It makes perfect sense. A monster. Killing a monster is a good thing." His voice warbled with the gibber of madness. It certainly didn't make sense to Elenor as she strained to hear him. When he emerged from the cloud about fifty feet in front of her, she could see the jagged crown of bilious light swirling around his skull. Unlike the man in the office, though, the crown was considerably larger. Dozens of points like jagged glimmering glass disappeared into the man's skull.

Elenor shook herself more violently, dislodging the last of the debris from her spines. She started to back away when the floating threads quested out towards her, but not nearly fast enough. She cringed back when they shot forward. When they came within about a foot of her body, they slammed to a halt as if they had hit an invisible wall. They strained to reach her, the threads shaking and crumpling against whatever held them back.

"So, it cannot touch you, but what about what is around you?" the man mumbled.

The threads stretched away from her and up into the sky. They dove into the ground below her. A moment later, she found the ground crumbling beneath her as a massive pit yawned open beneath her paws. On instinct, Elenor whipped her body around and her tail smashed into the wall of the pit, her spines imbedding themselves deeply into the sandy earth.

She swung for only a moment before she scrabbled at the wall. Her claws found purchase, her paws a after that, and she yanked her tail free of the loose earth of the wall of the pit. Elenor bolted for the lip of the pit. Looking up towards the sky, she could see dark clouds churning in the sky above where none had been before. Flashes of lightning flickered through the clouds warning of strikes to come. She leapt over the edge of the pit, skidding to a halt on solid ground not twenty feet from the gleaming-eyed madman. Wind howled as the storm built above them.

"What do you want from me?!" Elenor screamed over the roar of the wind.

"Your life!" the man screamed back. He raised a hand to the sky, palm up. "Give me my family back!" Froth bubbled from the corners of his mouth.

Elenor thought back to how she had destroyed the crown above the man from the office. Her claws had cut through the band made of light that had been attached to his skull. This one, though, was much different. The instinctual knowledge that had guided her before was quiet now. She had no idea what to do other than try to break the crown.

The strike came in the next moment. Lightning lanced down from the sky and smashed into the ground not five feet from Elenor. Dirt and stones peppered her side, telling her she had received her only warning. Elenor launched herself at the man, flying directly toward the crown of glowing thorns that encircled his head. At the last moment, the man ducked. She flew past him, but her claws snagged on a large collection of the threads that had stretched into the sky. Her claws severed the filaments as if they were gossamer spider webs.

Showers of jade sparks rained down around her when she landed. The man screamed in rage, and what Elenor thought might be pain. He spun wildly, his face scrunched into a murderous rictus. The feeling of warmth and tension that usually hovered in the center of her chest had spread throughout her entire body. Muscles bunched with tremendous tension pushing her to move, but fear froze her in her tracks. Lightning streaked across the sky quickly, followed by a thunderous crack.

The gleeful madness sparkling in the man's eyes terrified Elenor. Some part of her hind brain was screaming at her to move to no avail. Thunder rumbled overhead and finally, the instincts that had been screaming at her managed to override her fear.

She slammed her tail into the ground on pure reflex. A split second later, the lightning smashed into her body. She felt it dance over her skin, making all of her fur stand on end. Then it shot down her tail and into the ground.

"I didn't do anything to your family!" Elenor shouted, but the man did not seem to hear her.

"If I kill you, they will come back. You are all that stands between me and them!"

Elenor knew what she had to do, but she couldn't force her body to move. Something inside of her still couldn't hurt this man. Lightning came down again, but this time, it inexplicably struck the man. The bolt had nowhere to go this time, and the man's body went rigid. He was blasted ten feet through the air when the lightning bolt vanished. He tumbled to the ground in a twisted heap of limbs.

"Stop screwing around with him!" The woman's voice had a slight accent, and Elenor recognized it instantly. It was the woman from the subway. She was racing up the dirt road from the opposite direction that Elenor had come onto the island now off to Elenor's left.

"I don't want to hurt him!" Elenor yelled back as the wind roared again. Unbelievably, the man began to untangle himself. He coughed but continued to rise to his feet.

"Pain is reserved for the living! The Bane is just working that body like a puppet!" Helen shouted over the roar of the storm. "I can't stop whatever this is, but you can! Destroy it now before this gets any worse!" Helen gestured around to the rapidly growing storm.

"He said something about his family!" Elenor roared back at her.

"Not **him**, fool girl, it! They are dead too. It kills everyone connected to the Infected. We will have to find them before they kill and infect more people!"

The man was on his feet now and he turned back to Elenor, his eyes blank orbs of putrid green light. More threads of light sprang up around him and stretched toward the sky. The roiling clouds became more violent, lightning springing between them in jagged arcs.

"I can't kill him," Elenor protested, and Helen shook her head in response.

"You can't kill him because it is no longer a he. It is already dead. You are only destroying a corpse. Look at what it is doing!"

Helen gestured to the sky again. A funnel cloud was beginning to form over the waters of the bay. It was of such size that, like looking at the night sky, it made her feel tiny. Miles wide at minimum, it seemed to cover the entire breadth of the sky. Lightning stuck the ground around them in wild bursts, but Helen just stood her ground. She said no more. She let Elenor make her choice.

A funnel descended from the sky, rotating winds whipping slashing gales of water from the bay as it moved toward the island. The remains of the observatory buildings became a shredded storm of wooden beams, shingles, and vinyl siding that was carried away into the storm wall. Elenor's choice had suddenly become quite clear.

Elenor dashed towards the man, but just as she got close enough to strike, lightning lanced down from the sky. Dozens of lightning strikes streamed around him, forming an unpassable cage of electricity. The storm wall moved towards them. Elenor stared at the lightning as dirt sprayed over her. She knew now that she could ground out the lightning without killing herself, but she would only have a second or less to do the idiotic thing she was considering. Again, she grounded the spines of her tail, and then, digging her claws into the earth, she pulled herself forward.

The creature's putrid eyes widened when she pushed through the bolts of lightning. Smoke rose from her spines, but Elenor sprang at the man. Her front paws slammed into his chest and blew him off his feet. She landed with all four paws on his chest. Unable to stop her claws, they sliced through grey flesh of his chest.

She couldn't worry about that. Instead, she drove forward, slamming her claws against the crown of viridian light. Emerald sparks flew from her claws, and she felt a jolt go through her body. She shook violently

with the effort of keeping her obsidian talons in contact
with the crown.

The man had gone rigid when her claws had bit into
the light. She took advantage of his momentary
paralysis to climb off his chest. She dug her hind claws
into the ground, smashed her tail into the sod, and
flexed her entire body, yanking her claws against the
thing. Her claws began to slide through the crown of
light. The man bucked and began to scream. His hands
flailed at her paws and he lurched toward her. She
rolled backwards onto her butt and she lost the grip she
had on the green light.

Suddenly, the woman from the subway appeared
next to the man. She slammed what looked like a rod
made of fragile crystal against a rock. Elenor cringed,
expecting the delicate thing to shatter. Instead, it gave
off a pure ringing tone. Thick brown roots snaked from
the ground and coiled around the man. The man
struggled violently, but it was no use. Then he stilled
and the thread began to rise from him again.

Elenor scrambled to her paws and rushed over,
slashing her claws through the threads. They dissipated
in a shower of decaying green sparkles. She wasted no
more time. She hooked her claws through the crown,
anchored herself once more, and began to methodically
pull her claws thorough the steel-hard luminescence.

His screams became fevered and spittle foamed at the
corners of his mouth once more. Elenor noticed the
woman was watching her. She was holding up
something to her eye with a hole bored through the
middle, almost like a monocle. Elenor could tell it
wasn't, but her greyscale vision didn't allow her to
discern precisely what it was.

Then Elenor yelped as the resistance fell away, and
her claws sheered through the crown. The light
shattered like broken glass. Pieces sprang away from
the man's head and then froze in a jagged cloud of

noxious shrapnel. Immediately, the tornado's storm wall fractured. Within moments, the entire funnel broke apart and scattered. Debris showered to the ground and splashed into the bay hundreds of feet away as it was released by the wind.

"Oh, shit!" the woman screamed. Then she was running past, towards the side of the island where Elenor had come up from the water. Elenor watched her go for a moment, then looked back towards the collection of shattered light. The pieces were twitching now like a person hit with a taser. Shards were dissolving and flowing in rapid streams towards a tiny pinpoint of light at the center of the floating ring.

Elenor's glowing eyes widened as she realized what that probably meant. She bolted in the same direction the woman had gone. She passed the woman a moment later, and realized she had no idea where she was going.

"The creek!" the woman screamed as she tried in vain to catch up to Elenor. Elenor saw it then. Just ahead, a dip in the terrain with water flowing at the bottom. She jumped into it, and the woman splashed into the water a moment later.

The world quaked.

If the explosion from the staff was a bomb, this was a nuclear strike. Shrubs and massive clods of dirt flew by overhead. It pelted down on them, turning the water muddy as the downpour of earth partially buried them. The world went green with blinding light, and Elenor squeezed her eyes shut. It took a few seconds for the raining dirt to come to a stop, and a cloud of dust billowed over them. The sound was unimaginable, and Elenor thought for sure that she would be deaf.

Elenor crawled out of the water. She tried to shake off all the mud and detritus from her fur, but she still felt filthy. Unbelievably, she could see the man lying at the center of a small crater in the land. Though unmoving, he appeared completely unharmed, and all of the green light had left him. Then she noticed the woman standing up with the collection of crystal rods in her hand.

"Holy shit, are you two ok?" The voice of the younger woman from observatory tower came from behind.

Elenor jumped away from both of them. "Get away from me!" she shouted, and the woman looked up through a mask of mud. She reached up with her free hand and wiped the mud away from her face as best she could. Elenor turned tail and started to leave.

"Wait! We just want to talk!" Thia shouted.

Elenor turned back and hissed, "Talk about what? Killing me, like you were yesterday at the observatory?"

What Elenor could see of the woman's expression went blank.

"What do you mean?" Helen asked.

Elenor nodded at Helen as she spoke. "You said that you couldn't let that man screw up killing me. That you would do it."

"You did not hear the whole conversation," Helen said, and took a few steps closer. She froze when Elenor's spines bristled threateningly. "I am not here to hurt you. I'm here to help."

"Prove it," Elenor snarled. Helen sighed, but Thia interrupted her.

"I thought we agreed I would do this," Thia whispered.

"Fine," Helen said a little grumpily. She took a few steps back and the delicate looking crystal object seemed to melt in her hand. It flowed up her arm and vanished.

"You didn't hear the whole conversation. My mother," Thia gestured at Helen, "was telling Joshua that he couldn't kill you at all because you are our only hope of repairing what has gone wrong with the Writ. What you would call magic."

Elenor's spines wilted and she stood up from her defensive crouch. "I'm not anyone's hope of anything. That guy you were talking to is dead, by the way." Elenor pointed with her tail towards the remnants of the destroyed buildings. "His staff exploded when that thing came up out of the water."

Thia and Helen exchanged a glance. Helen ran off towards the buildings a moment later.

"We can help you." Thia's pleading voice cut through the dying wind.

"No one can help me." Elenor turned to head off to where she had hidden her bag.

"You know you can control all of those barbs and claws, right?" Thia shouted the query. There was a hitch in Elenor's gait and she almost tripped. She turned back to look at Thia with narrowed eyes gleaming.

"You can't see the resonance waves, but they are on the inside of your skin. We can see it with this." She held up one of the round things that her mother had been using to look at the man earlier.

Elenor willed her vision to go back to normal and looked at what Thia held more closely. It was a flat piece of green stone with a hole bored through the middle. Thia flicked a finger against it and amazingly, the stone produced a musical vibration at an extreme low.

"I'll hold it for you so you can see if you let me," Thia offered, holding out the stone. Elenor raised her right ear and dropped the left, lending almost comical emphasis to her skeptical expression. "I would offer to just drop it, but I think you would have trouble using it with your paws," Thia coaxed.

Elenor's ears finally straightened up and she moved closer. It was dangerous, but if there was even the tiniest possibility to be able to not slice everything she owned to pieces, it was worth almost any risk.

Thia met her halfway and crouched down to eye level with her. She held up the stone horizontally, so Elenor could look down through it at her paws. Sure enough, as soon as she looked through the hole, glowing blue lines appeared. She squinted her eyes and the lines resolved into waves, like when her science teacher showed them sound waves on an oscilloscope.

"We can teach you how all of this works. I promise you can trust us, but you don't have to. If Joshua is dead, we can help you get home to your parents. I'm Thia, by the way."

"He and his entire team are gone. The infected did something to Heartwood and it exploded. There is nothing left to find," Helen said as she came back from inspecting the destroyed observatory. "I'm Helen, what's your name?"

"Elenor. Elenor Selinofoto." She turned her body and backed away, not wanting to be caught between the two women.

"We will not hurt you, Elenor, but we should all go. If we are going to teach you anything, we cannot be dealing with the police," Helen said.

"You don't have to go with us. We will come to your parents' house in a day or two if you want," Thia offered.

"How did you get here?"

"We have a boat. Walk and talk, though, if you are coming with us. The boat will keep anyone from seeing us." Helen suited her words by heading towards the southeast corner of the island.

"Can you really teach me how to control these things?" Elenor held up her claws for emphasis.

"Yes, and a lot more than just that, too," Thia responded, and followed her mother. Elenor paused for only a moment before following behind them both.

They had been gone for an hour when the people finally began to pull up to the island in boats. Park

Rangers had seen the brief but colossal tornado forming over Hart-Miller Island. As they picked through the remains of the observatory buildings, the sound of a man shouting for help caught one of the Ranger's ears.

He rushed off into the scrub brush toward the east side of the island. When he pushed through the scrub, he found the well-dressed man sitting in a small crater. Wrapped around his left leg was a coil of thick root as if one of the shrubs had grown around his leg. He quickly checked the man over, only to find that he was impossibly devoid of any injury, alive, and well.

16

"WHY ME?"

NC 17, EPOCH 19914.328

Elenor crouched at the back of the small single cabin cruiser that Helen and Thia had appropriated to make it out to the island.

"I can't get out here. There are cameras on those houses."

"Okay, that is the creepiest thing I've ever seen. Can you stop that?" Thia asked. Elenor paused in her nervous pacing.

"What?"

"Whatever it is that you're doing with your eyes. They look like two dark train tunnels with a train coming at me."

Elenor let her vision return to normal. "Sorry, it's how I see the lights on security cameras. This better?"

Thia shook her head. "Not really. You still look like you would make an Alien Queen shit its pants." Thia grinned to show she was joking.

"Yep, just dump on me because I asked for this nightmare," Elenor groused.

"Just having a little fun with you. Come on, Mom's got the cameras covered."

Elenor slunk off the boat and onto the weathered wooden dock. The sky was growing lighter on her left, and she saw the sign for Bay Drive as they walked through the empty lot the dock backed up onto. Thia watched her with some concern as she came back from the chain link fence surrounding the area.

"Elenor, you're safe with us, at least for tonight, but you don't have to go with us if you don't want to." Thia waited for a response from the crouching creature.

"Are you telling the truth about these?" Elenor sounded skeptical. She lifted her paw, showing the gleaming obsidian claws.

"Thia, what is the issue?" Helen called from the road just past the chain link fence. Thia turned and jogged over to the fence. Elenor watched as a short conversation ensued. She could just barely make out what was being said.

"What is it?" Helen asked.

"I have to teach her now, at least this one thing. She's not going to trust us just because we say we can help her. I wouldn't want her to. Would you?" Thia said.

Elenor saw Helen lean over to look past Thia toward her.

"No, I would not. Alright, Thia. Show her how to control her Relic." Helen turned and headed back to the car she had left idling near the entrance to the lot.

Thia walked back towards Elenor.

"What's a Relic?" Elenor asked, and Thia raised a brow.

"Eavesdropping on us?" Thia smiled.

Elenor wiggled her ears in response. "It's hard not to hear with these things."

"A Relic is an item invested with the ability to manipulate reality."

"Magic item?"

Thia rolled her eyes. "Sure, let's go with that massive over simplification."

"Magic isn't real."

"You transformed into a creature that would give a Cthulhu monster a heart attack and magic is the thing you are having trouble with?"

"This could just be some mutation." Elenor didn't sound confident, and Thia rolled her eyes.

"Yeah, you believe that."

"Alright, fine. But magic?"

"Again, magic is oversimplifying. I can't cram everything into one conversation. Your Relic. I can teach you how to control that right now. You can't hear the Chorus just yet, so just keep this in mind. What I am going to teach you won't work forever. You have a lot to learn."

"The Chorus?"

"The music of the world," Thia replied, and Elenor tilted her head, one ear folding down. It was so clearly a question. Thia looked back to her mother, but then shrugged. This was for her to do.

"Everything in the world gives off, for lack of a better word, vibrations. All those vibrations make a sort of music that we call the Chorus. Once you can hear it, you can play your own music that will cause the vibrations to Surge. It changes the vibrations, and so, changes the world."

"And, what? Someone did that to me?"

Thia shook her head. "Not what I'm implying. A Surge to perform a transformation like what has happened to you would require skill and power unlike anything I've ever heard of, and my mother knows almost everything there is to know."

Elenor sighed. "Then why me?"

"We don't know that, but I will tell you this. If anyone can find out, it's my mother."

"How?"

"No idea, but she's like eighteen hundred years old, and she used to be able to do things that would make you shit out your tiny little monster brains." Thia grinned.

Elenor opened her mouth to protest then closed it.

"Yeah, you were about to say that's impossible, and you, of all people, should have tossed impossible out of a window the day you turned into whatever you are." Thia said it gently.

Elenor took a deep breath. "Alright. I've got pretty much no choice but to believe you because I can't keep living like I am." Elenor's eyes went a little wide with realization. "Are there going to be more of those… people?"

"Yes." Helen didn't shout, but her voice cut through their conversation as if she were standing right next to them.

"Are they all going to come after me like that?"

Thia shot her mother a glare as if to tell her to shut it. "We don't know. We have a lot of questions ourselves. We're hoping you can help us with that."

"Show me," Elenor said, and Thia nodded. Then she squinted at Elenor. She tilted her head for a long moment.

"Alright. First, have you ever just tried just thinking at your Relic?" Thia asked.

"I'm not sure what you mean?"

"Like my mother's Striker, it is has somehow been integrated into your body. So, in theory, it should be like moving your leg or tail. You've probably been doing it unconsciously," Thia explained.

Elenor shook her head. "I don't think so. I've wanted my claws to stop slicing everything to pieces lots of times. Still sharp enough to cut diamonds like butter." She wiggled her digits, showing off claws that would be the envy of any bird of prey. The gleam of the wicked slicing edge flashed in the streetlights.

Thia blew out an exasperated breath. "I know you've been trying to figure this all out, but we are not so new as you. Just try to concentrate."

Elenor did just that. She focused on her claws and tried to think about them getting shorter and less sharp. Nothing happened. A few minutes passed and finally, Elenor looked up and shook her head.

"Interesting. It's almost like…" Thia trailed off as she fished in her pocket for something. She produced the stone with the hole through the middle. Thia looked back at her mother tentatively. Then she held up the stone and flicked it with a fingernail. It gave a soft chime and she held it up to her eye.

"I'm not sure how, but it looks like your Relic isn't completely bonded to your body yet. Can my mother take a look at this?"

Elenor eyed Helen suspiciously.

"You go back over there, by the boat where I can see you."

"But the boat is behind you," Thia said, then she saw it, a chatoyant golden glow coming from just below Elenor's shoulder blades. Thia stood from her crouch and crept around behind Elenor. There on Elenor's back, two large golden eyes turned to fix on her. The pupils were slit and glimmered like two lines of mercury spilled across a golden platter. The eyes tracked her unerringly as she walked uncomfortably towards the boat.

"You are, holy shit, creepy. It's kind of amazing," Thia said in a surprisingly encouraging tone.

Elenor looked up at Helen as she approached and narrowed her glowing, mismatched eyes.

"I do not blame you for not trusting us. I would be upset if you did. Trust like that gets people killed and I cannot imagine you would have stayed hidden this long if you had it," Helen said as she crouched. She looked through the adder stone at Elenor.

"I just want this all to be over."

"Then I have unfortunate news. Your Writband is the most powerful I have ever seen and you are going to live a very, very long life."

"Well, I didn't say I wanted to die," Elenor mumbled.

"No, but it was what you meant."

Elenor gave her a look, half incredulous, half angry.

"Elenor, I am over eighteen hundred years old. You may no longer be physically human, but you are still human on the inside. There are no human emotions I have not seen and understood in that time."

Elenor sniffed like a child on the verge of tears. "It's not fair."

Helen lowered the adder stone and her eyes softened. "I am sorry, Elenor, but the reality of the world is that there is no promise of fairness in life." Her voice was gentle, and Elenor's ears fell.

"I know why your Relic is not responding to you. Though I've never seen it happen before, I have heard of it. A Relic like yours must be attuned to your Resonance. Sometimes, when a Relic was passed from one Caller to another, this would happen. What is odd," Helen lifted the adder stone back to her eye, "is that it's clear that your Relic has never had another holder. You, dear girl, are a mystery inside of a mystery."

"Can you help me?"

Helen smiled. "Yes. What Thia said is true. Until you can hear the Chorus, we cannot make a permanent repair. But I can…" Helen trailed off as she panned the adder stone over the rest of Elenor's body. She stood up abruptly and took a long step back. The look on her face was surprise at first, but mutated into awe.

"Tiny gods, no wonder it is not attuned. It's a Striker. Your entire body is a Striker."

"What's a Striker?"

"A percussion instrument used by Callers to play Surges."

"And what's a Caller? And a Surge?" Elenor was genuinely confused. Helen let out an exasperated breath.

"Oh, figure it out. That is utterly unimportant at the moment. The bigger question is… how has the entire city of Baltimore not gone up in a fireball? Have you never banged your tail on anything?"

Elenor lifted her tail and looked at the pinecone-like spiral of spines surrounding the black tip. "Sure, all the time when I first got the stupid thing."

Helen was incredulous. "And there was no fiery death involved?"

"I'm so confused," Elenor said, and Helen shook her head in response.

"We do not have time to explain this now. I will let Thia teach you what we promised. Also, do not open the eyes on your back again until we have time to explain things. They are dangerous." Helen waved Thia back over.

Elenor snapped her rear eyes shut. "What do you mean dangerous?" Her concern was palpable. Helen ignored her, though, and exchanged a few words with Thia. Thia turned back to her.

"She'll explain if you go with us. To fix your Relic so it will respond to you for a while, I need to teach you a little music. Can you whistle?"

"Not any more. I used to whistle a lot." Elenor touched a paw to her face. "This stupid split upper lip makes it impossible."

"Well, you should be able to hum it then. You need to hum a tune to Resonate with the Relic so you can control it temporarily."

"Temporarily?"

"That's the complicated part. You need to learn how to play Surges before you can attune the Relic permanently. The tune first. Listen to this very carefully and hum these exact notes." Thia tilted her head, then, as if she were listening to something no one else could hear. Then she began to whistle softly. The tune at first repeated three notes. Then they merged together, almost as if Thia was somehow whistling three notes all at the same time.

It was only a few seconds long, but when Thia finished, Elenor's maw was hanging open with incredulity.

"You whistled three notes at the same time? How am I supposed to do that?"

Thia chuckled. "You have a Writband and even I don't have one of those. Everyone can technically learn to do what I just did. You, though, already have. Even if you don't know it yet. Just close your eyes and hum along with me."

Elenor did not look convinced, but she closed her glowing eyes and her ears swiveled towards Thia. When Thia started the tune, Elenor began to hum the three notes. When the three notes melted together into a three-note harmony, Elenor swallowed apprehensively and tried to hum along. For a moment, she could hear only one note, but then she felt an odd sensation in her throat. An odd vibration in whatever served as her vocal cords.

To her amazement, three notes flowed from her at the same time. They finished the tune together, and when it was done, a new sensation blossomed inside of Elenor's brain. Like when her tail had grown in, there was a new set of muscles she could sort of flex.

"Great, a new thing I need to learn how to control!" Elenor grumped.

Thia shrugged in response. "Better than those talons destroying everything you touch?"

Elenor did not open her eyes. She just concentrated on feeling the new appendage that was her Relic. Thia watched her.

"Might want to hurry it up. I am hearing some sirens here!" Helen called from where she had wandered back to the car. Elenor's ears swiveled as she picked up the sound as well.

"I'm going!" Elenor felt an unsettling sucking sensation at her paws as her claws became liquid and flowed back into the flesh. With a bit more concentration, all of the spines except the ones on her tail drew back into her body. She realized that even her teeth were part of the Relic, but she left them alone.

The spines and claws were a pain, but her teeth hadn't ever caused an issue beyond scaring people half to death. She paused for a long second and stared at her tail. She could feel it the same way she could feel the rest of the Relic, but it didn't respond to her thoughts about the spines retracting. After a long moment of concentration, the spines rounded off until they were left safely dull.

Then she trotted over to where a tan Toyota Camry with rental plates was sitting with the back door open. Lights were coming on in the surrounding houses. A silhouette appeared in a second story window directly across from their position in the street. She eyed Thia, and then Helen, eyes glowing balefully.

"I swear, if either one of you tries to kill me in my sleep, I will bite your heads off."

Thia shivered but her mother rolled her eyes.

"If I was going to try to kill you, I would have let that infected devour you to save me the trouble," Helen grumbled.

"I heard that," Elenor said, and then hopped up into the car.

"I meant you too," Helen responded. Thia closed the door behind Elenor and squinted at her mother meaningfully.

"Where are we going?" Elenor asked.

"We can take you home if you tell us where that is." Thia turned in her seat. Elenor had curled herself into a tight ball with her tail over her nose and eyes.

"I don't have a home. They came looking for me at my parents' house. I had to leave."

"Who is they?"

Elenor's shoulders went up and down in a shrug. "Guys in suits. I didn't stick around long enough to find out who they were."

"How long ago was that?" Helen asked.

"Two years."

"Well, whoever it was might show up again in a few days, but you can go home for a night or two while we

figure out someplace where I can teach you how to be a
Caller without burning down half of Baltimore."

"You weren't kidding about the fire?"

"No, I was not."

"Alright." Elenor rattled off her parent's address.
"Take me home before someone else tries to blow my
face off with a rocket launcher."

"Wait, what?!" Thia stared at her with incredulity.

17

"NEVER AGAIN"

NC 17, EPOCH 19914.329

Mateo jerked awake at the soft clicking sound reverberating through his room. He knuckled sleep from his eyes before sitting up. The clock told him it was three twenty-eight in the morning.

"Elly? Do you know what time it is?" He squinted at her through his window and then scrambled out of bed.

"¡No eres Elly!" He didn't shout, but his voice was no longer a whisper. The creature outside of his window was similar to Elenor, but there were no twisting horns curving back from its forehead, and not a single spine vibrated anywhere on its body.

"Ssssh! I met some people and learned some things about my crazy body. Is this better?"

Mateo eyes went wide with incredulity as streams of black liquid flowed into lines all over the creature's body. Two of the streams gathered at its forehead and began to solidify into horns spiraling in a curve that followed the lines of its skull. A long moment later, spines sprang up out of its fur and prickled down its tail into an explosion of murderous razors at the tip like an obsidian morning star.

"Wow!" he exclaimed. He flung off his covers. Thankfully, he was wearing dark blue pajama bottoms that aped a pair of baggy jeans. He wasn't wearing a shirt, and Elenor stared for a moment, not expecting a physique including washboard abs and enough muscle to make Bruce Lee proud. *Damn, look at the body on this guy.* Then her brain caught up and she remembered he was two years younger than her. That wasn't even to mention the fact that they were two different species.

"Are you going to make a habit of showing up in the middle of the night?" Mateo complained, then carefully

• ¡No eres Elly! – You're not Elly!

opened his window. Elenor's spines melted back into her fur and she flowed silently through the window.

"I promise this will be the last time," Elenor whispered. Her hissing sibilance was more pronounced when she tried to keep her voice down.

Mateo paused. "¡Espere!" his eyes wandered around his room in furious thought. "You met people who know about what happened to you?"

"Yes!" she murmured excitedly.

"You don't have to whisper. Mamá, and Papá are stuck on an overnight so I'm alone again until tomorrow."

"What do your parents do?"

"They are both nurses at John's Hopkins so sometimes they have to stay for a long shift."

"That's cool. I just didn't want to come when anyone else was awake. I still look like I would eat a baby, if you hadn't noticed."

Mateo chuckled.

Elenor grinned a shark grin. "I came to give you a working phone number for me. My paws aren't great for texting, but I can get by now that I can control my claws."

"Awesome!" Mateo grabbed his phone from the small desk. She rummaged in the small bag hanging around her neck and took out a new smartphone. It was a relatively large rectangle of glass. She held it out, gripping it carefully in her paw. Her digits were short, making it difficult to hold onto the phone.

"Why did you get such a big one?"

Elenor wiggled the digits of one of her front paws at him. "Because it's easier to hit the buttons with the silly toe fingers on my sort-of hands." Elenor looked around his room with interest this time. Last time she was here, she had been so worked up that not a single detail of his

• ¡Espere! – Wait.

room lingered in her mind after she had left. It was as if she had never been there before.

He sat down on his disheveled twin bed, shoving aside his wadded blue quilt. Above the bed in a polished brass frame was a simple black poster with a green symbol in the middle that Elenor didn't immediately recognize until she read the text circled around it. As she peered at the Green Lantern symbol more closely, she realized that she could see pencil marks left to show through the marker-colored portions.

"Is this some sort of original?" She pointed at the poster with her tail.

"Sí, Mateo Rios el original."

Elenor eyed him skeptically. "You drew this?"

"So disbelieving!" He pushed off the bed and Elenor slid out of his way.

Mateo moved across the room to his desk. He lifted up the top like a lid, tilted it, and moved it down so that it sat at an angle. Mateo scooted up onto the comfortable looking stool that accompanied the desk and dug around inside. He reached up to a light hanging from a swinging arm and clicked it on, brightly illuminating the tilted surface of the drawing desk. In the middle of the desk was a circle of wood that would allow someone to attach a drawing and spin it, making it easier to draw from different angles. With practiced ease, he tacked a page to the drawing surface and then turned his chair so she could see it. It was a page from a comic book.

Only half of it was colored, but the drawings were rendered with amazing detail. It looked as if it would jump right off the page. On the page, a young man was using a spray can to paint something on a brick wall that took up most of the page. Elenor's glowing eyes spread to saucer-like dimensions when she saw what had been spray painted there. She didn't know at all what it

• Sí, Mateo Rios el original – Yep, a Mateo Rios original

meant, but the pattern was immediately recognizable to her. She had not been able to learn much in the short time she had with Helen and Thia, but what she had learned was how to recognize the wave forms that were inscribed on her own chest. The multiple waves woven together as if they were individual notes being played separately, but their visual representation had been laid atop one another. It wasn't. It was something only a Caller could play.

Two years of living on the streets flashed through her mind. Waking up each morning not knowing what parts of her body would have changed while she slept battered down her desire to tell him anything. *It's way too dangerous to tell him anything until I know more.* Elenor's teeth clicked together as she snapped her maw shut.

"That's amazing, Mateo." It was all she could do to keep it together.

"Es mi fuerte. I just have no clue if it's gonna go anywhere when I go to college next year."

Elenor tilted her head curiously and Mateo noticed. "What?"

"You said you were sixteen, right?" Elenor asked.

"Ah, Sí, I'm graduating a year early. I'm pretty good in math and science, and the other classes were a lot of boring work, but that's just my backup plan if art doesn't work out. I want to be a comic book artist and author. What are you going to do though?"

Elenor shrugged a little. "Find out more about what I can do. Try to get back to being human for as long as it's practical. They couldn't tell me much before they dropped me off at home. If I can't be human again, I honestly don't know what I'll do with myself."

She picked her phone from the side table of Mateo's bed where he had left it. She was just about to slide it

* Es mi fuerte – It's my thing
* Ah, Sí – Oh yeah

into the bag hanging around her neck when it began to
buzz. Elenor sat back on her haunches and carefully
held the phone in one of her front paws. Instead of
trying to balance on two paws to manipulate the phone,
she just bent her neck and pressed the screen with her
nose. Before she could even say hello, a loud woman's
voice came blaring out of the speaker.

"Elenor! Wherever you are, you have to leave!"
Helen's voice roared up from the device.

Elenor wasn't paying attention, though. The phone
tumbled from her paw and bounced on the floor, only
the case saving it from shattering. She could feel it, like
someone had tied a string around her rib cage and was
attempting to yank it out.

"Elenor?" Thia's concerned voice came through the
phone.

"One of them is coming."

"Yes. One of the Infected is heading your way. We
can't get there fast enough to try to intercept it. If you
fight something like that in the city, a lot of people are
going to die."

"No, it's too late to run. It's already here," Elenor
said and turned to the open window. A cloud of green
threads wafted into the air outside of the window. On
pure reflex, Elenor's body expelled her Relic. Wicked
claws emerged from her paws and spines sprang up all
over her body like an enchanted porcupine.

"Elly? ¿Qué es eso?" Mateo asked. He had spun in
his chair to stare out through the window.

"A <u>real</u> monster," Elenor said, and then her spines
tucked themselves tight to her body. She disappeared
out of the window in a blur.

Mateo darted to the window and saw Elenor land on
the street outside. To the west, about a football field
down the empty street, stood a woman. Mateo couldn't
make out many details at that distance. Just a short

• ¿Qué es eso? – What is that?

figure with long black hair standing in the pool of light generated by a street lamp. The one thing he could see clearly was her eyes. Two glowing orbs of putrid green that blotted out any facial features he might see. She screamed something that was a near inaudible tone of sound at the distance.

What was clear to Mateo was the danger. Threads of green luminescence floated in a twisting cloud around the woman. Anything they touched it began to degrade. Pavement sizzled where the wires of light touched it, then after a moment of contact, the heat waves subsided. Gouts of dust floated up as the pavement disintegrated, leaving gouges out of the street.

Most startling to Mateo was the lack of people on the street. Even in a residential neighborhood like his, the noise was constant, even in the night. But there were no cars, no people. Mateo picked up his phone and began to dial 911. Then he looked back down at the creature that Elenor was facing and realized the futility of calling emergency services. No mere human could deal with whatever he was seeing.

The threads whipped out to the sides of the street, cutting through anything they touched. Elenor had moved off down the street, closing the gap with the woman. She shouted something that was lost in the crashing sound of street signs. It lasted until some of the threads crashed into a large steel post at the end of the street. The light post, holding up the street lights blinking at the intersection, smashed to the ground in a cacophonous roar of crackling electricity. All of the street lights flickered and died. Mateo blinked, but there was nothing left to see. Just a pair of glowing eyes facing a cloud of virile green threads.

"Elenor!" A shout from Elenor's fallen phone caught Mateo's attention. He scrambled to pick it up.

"Hello?"

"Who is this? Where is Elenor?" The feminine voice from the other end was tense with worry.

"She's in the street. Facing off with that woman."

"What's your name?"

Mateo paused. He wasn't sure who he was talking to.

The woman's voice went on. "It doesn't matter. Tell Elenor that she needs to lead the Infected away from any people. Get to a park or someplace else in the open so she has plenty of room to fight."

"She can go to Patterson Park. It's only about a half mile away."

"That works. We'll meet her there and try to help. My name's Thia and my mother is Helen. In case we run into each other." The phone beeped when the call ended. Mateo could see Elenor's blazing eyes darting around in the darkness below. He couldn't shout to her, there was no way she would hear it. He had to get closer.

He grabbed the dark brown bomber jacket hanging next to his door and swung it around his body. Yanking on his sneakers, he stuffed Elenor's phone in a pocket and pulled his door open before bolting down the stairs. A massive crashing sound, more felt than heard, caused Mateo to stumble on the stairs. The stair railing bit into his hand when he caught himself. A moment later, he was pounding down the stairs again. He was panting by the time he hit the bottom of the stairwell at a dead run.

He burst out of the door onto a scene of utter destruction. The intersection four streets away was no longer visible from the ground. In the time it had taken him to run down the stairs, an entire building had collapsed. Rubble was spread in a wave that had washed up against the building opposite from the one that had collapsed.

Mateo froze when he saw a mangled, blood-slick arm waving at him from the rubble. The woman on the phone had said people would die, but to be presented with the bald evidence of the fact was jarring even for someone as stolid as Mateo. He tore his eyes away from the horror before him.

He couldn't do anything to help the people that had been caught in the collapse. Still, that bloody arm flashed through his thoughts, an old fear rearing from the depths of his mind. Something he had not felt since he stared down that cavernous gun barrel. He had only known Elenor for a few days, and the fearful kid inside of him said that she would be fine. He shouldn't get involved.

He forced his gaze back to the rubble, eyes narrowed in fury. He hadn't been ready to tell Elenor that if he had just been brave enough to tell his parents about the gang, he would have never gotten shot. *Never again.* He turned and ran towards the alleyway between his building and the next. He had to get to Elenor. If he could get her out of there, no one else would have to get hurt.

18

"MATEO"

Elenor scrambled up the side of the brick building. Everything had faded to sepia tones in her vision, giving her excellent dark vision. The only color that stood out was the vibrant green of the woman's eyes and the strands that twisted in manic waves about her form.

When the woman had slashed dozens of those cords of light through a building's façade, it had been all Elenor could do to get out of the way of the collapsing structure. She had wanted to run, but when she had tried, the tug in her chest yanked her back toward the woman. It seemed that she had no choice but to fight. The problem was that without the woman's crown, she had no idea what to do.

She had tried talking to the woman, just as she had with the man the day before, but none of her responses made any sense. It was like they were having two different conversations. Elenor landed atop the piles of broken bricks that had once made up the toppled apartment building. She shoved her paws off of the bricks, cracks spreading through them from the force. She soared through the air, curling herself into a ball and smashing into as many of the floating filaments as she could.

Jade sparks exploded around her as her spines tore apart the tendrils. Before she hit the ground, she used what Thia had taught her to plaster her spines to her body. They protected her when she bounced off the street. She unrolled herself on instinct and came to her feet at a run. She had quickly discovered that the smoke was poisonous, even to her. As long as she didn't stay still, the burning bits kicked up by the virulent wires was useless against her. Still, if she didn't do something soon, a lot more people were going to die.

"Elly!" Mateo's panting voice came from an alleyway not far off.

Elenor's head whipped around, but it was already too late. Verdigris snakes of illumination shot towards Mateo. They scorched the bricks of the buildings surrounding him. Elenor bolted across the street faster than she had ever moved before. She slashed her claws through the threads and then shot down the alleyway.

She blew through the cloud of smoke without inhaling any and skidded to a halt next to Mateo. Lying in the alleyway, he was coughing, but what drew her attention much faster was the black slash across his stomach. It had burned through his shirt and blood was oozing from the wound.

"Mateo, oh god, what do I do?"

Mateo pointed towards the street. The fur of Elenor's neck crawled, and she spun just in time to slice her claws through a column of threads that were attempting to smash at the buildings around them. She had to help Mateo, but she couldn't do that until the woman was dealt with. Elenor let out a roar at the top of her lungs that would have given a bear pause and dug her claws into the concrete, launching herself forward.

She blasted into the street, and the woman had no time to react before Elenor's shoulder smashed into her sternum. There was a crack like a gunshot and the woman was launched from her feet. The threads streamed behind her as she flew. She bounced once, then smashed into a dumpster about halfway down an alleyway across the street. The steel of the dumpster staved in as if it had been smashed by a battering ram. It crumpled around the woman and she slumped, seemingly unconscious. The woman tumbled to the ground and did not rise, but Elenor was unconvinced that she had killed the woman. Considering the amount of punishment the man had taken before she had destroyed his crown, she was certainly still alive.

She had no time for that. She spun and darted back towards Mateo. He was breathing hard by the time she got back to him, and she crouched over him. She knew what she had to do to fix him. She had to reach into that well of power in her chest and use it to knit him back together. She could feel the blood pounding through his body the moment she focused on that power. *What the hell am I doing, what the hell am I doing? This is so stupid. I could kill him if I do it wrong.*

"You have to run to Patterson Park. The women on the phone said they would help if you could get there." Mateo hissed through the pain.

"Alright, but I have to help you first."

Elenor gathered up her thoughts and began to construct the instructions for that well of power in her chest. Then she stopped. She had no idea what to do. She knew that the power could heal people. Whatever instinctual knowledge she had been given of the power told her that much, but there was no explanation of how to actually do it. The same instincts that had told her how to use the power in the first place left no room for uncertainty. She had to know exactly how to do what she wanted before she could do anything safely. In relative terms, making the water in someone's blood stop moving was simple to conceptualize. There was only one step to the process.

Some quick mental attempts at putting together instructions for healing made it very clear that it would not be as simple as *heal up this wound.* She needed help from Thia or Helen.

"Mateo, I need to go get…" She trailed off when Mateo groaned. Necrotic black lines, like macabre horror movie makeup, radiated away from the wound in Mateo's stomach. She had to take him with her. She flattened her spines to her body. She clutched his wrist in her paw, and then leaned to one side to drag him up onto her back.

"Can you hold on, Mateo?" He wrapped his arms around her neck. She worried for a moment about making the wound in his stomach worse. However, after seeing the black veins crawling across Mateo's skin, she was somehow certain no hospital would be able to save him.

"Your horns are really sharp and really close to my face," he advised.

Elenor focused, and her horns melted into her head. "Hold on as tight as you can, I am going to go fast."

"Will she follow you?" Mateo wondered.

"I think they're drawn to me for some reason. I can feel something pulling me back towards her. It wouldn't let me run away before, but I think that's because I was just planning to run."

Elenor's muscles bunched, and she tore down the street, her claws leaving gouges in the pavement. Mateo struggled to hold on through the pain. She turned right onto South Lakewood Avenue and stretched out into her run. She would have gone faster, but she felt Mateo's warm blood trickling through her fur. If she went faster, she might make the gash in his stomach worse.

If not for her night vision, she would have run into a car parked at the corner of Lakewood and Fleet. She leapt over the car, dodged someone sitting on the side of the road on a bicycle, and then skidded between a mailbox and light post to get onto the sidewalk. Thankfully, the lack of electricity meant that most of the people had fled the pitch-black streets.

That changed when she reached the corner of Lakewood and Eastern and ran into the bright electric lights. Here, there were many cars, but she didn't hesitate. Elenor dodged between two of them and then almost paused when she saw a small crowd of people gathered on the sidewalk between her and the park. Instead, she sped up. Mateo yelped in pain and fear when he saw how fast she was coming up on the people.

She streaked between them in a blur, just missing the light post at the edge of the sidewalk.

She leapt to the top of the small concrete stairs and took the path to the left. She turned harder to skirt the sports fields, heading directly for the wooded area around the boat lake. She slowed, panting, as she made it into the twilight woods. The lights in the park provided very little illumination, but Elenor did not need that to see that Mateo was not doing well. She carefully turned her body to let him slide to the ground and he let out a grunt of pain when his back bumped into a tree.

"Don't worry, Mateo. I can help you. I just don't know how. Wait here."

"No tengo otra opcion," Mateo said through clenched teeth.

Elenor turned and ran back out to the path. She looked around for the telltale protective rainbow shrouds of Helen or Thia. She didn't have much time before the thing that used to be a woman caught up to her. She couldn't go back out to the street. Bolting through at breakneck speeds only left people wondering what they had seen. Stumbling around in the open, though, would remove all doubt.

The sound of footsteps pounding up the path caused Elenor to shrink back into the trees, but when she saw the rainbow cascade surrounding the two people approaching, she ran towards them again. She blinked away the trick of her vision, and while she didn't have much trouble seeing in the near dark, it was definitely obscured compared to what it had been a moment earlier.

"Thia, Helen!" she hissed. They both skidded to a halt and whipped around, looking for her. A moment later, they were rushing into the woods following the flashes of Elenor's glowing eyes. In less than two

• No tengo otra opcion – Not like I have much of a choice

minutes, they were standing over Mateo. His normally bronze complexion had gone a pallid grey and the black veins had spread across his stomach.

"That is, not great," Helen said, and then crouched over Mateo. "Okay, if you want to keep your friend from melting into a puddle of black sludge, you do exactly what I say."

Mateo came to sudden alertness. "¿¡Espere!? ¿¡Qué!?"

Elenor's reaction was identical.

"In stereo, no less," Helen mumbled. She pulled a permanent marker from her pocket, pulled up Mateo's jacket, and began to scrawl on his bronze skin with it. She drew perfect sound waves in a circle on his stomach. One, two, three, four separate, overlapping waves. She didn't lift the tip of the marker until the scrawl was complete. Irrationally, Elenor could tell each individual wave apart from the others. "Elenor, use one of your claws to carve this into his skin."

"What?!" Elenor hissed.

"There is that word again. I will explain when your friend is not dying. I am not playing this Surge, so I cannot do it for you. You need to use your claws, your Relic, to carve over this Surge, and you cannot stop once you start. It has to be a single complete stroke, just like I wrote it. If you fail to do it right this instant, Mateo will die. Grit your teeth, young man, this is going to hurt."

Mateo simply shrugged in response. "Pretty sure it won't hurt worse than a gunshot wound."

Elenor's paw shook as she formed a single claw. She reached out, but her paw would not stay steady.

"Stop. Take a breath. You cannot miss a stroke. You must follow the waveform with precision."

Elenor followed her instructions, taking several deep breaths before she lifted her paw once more. *I have to help Mateo.* Her paw became as still as deep winter

• ¿¡Espere!? ¿¡Qué!? – Wait what?!

morning. With a single perfect motion, she stuck the barest tip of her claw into Mateo's skin and began to carve.

Mateo let out a hiss of pain. Elenor did her best to ignore the sound as she kept her paw at the exact same height. She did not want to cut him any worse than was necessary. Blood welled from the cut behind the tip of her claws as she moved it through his skin, but oddly, it did not run. It spread to the edges of the marks of the marker, but not a bit further. She matched each zigzag and gentle wave with precision. With a final flourish as if she were penning her name into his skin, she swiped her claw away, throwing off a couple of lingering droplets of Mateo's bright blood.

"Why is the blood doing that?" Elenor asked.

"Because it is trapped within the Surge. It's acting as a conduit for what you are going to do next," Helen responded.

"What now?"

"This is the part I cannot help you with. You have to play that Surge, and you have to do it now."

Elenor opened her mouth, but Helen immediately shushed her.

"Listen to me very carefully. Do not hum a single note out of tune with this. We told you not to make any sort of music, but now we have come to it. Anything that you do that risks your Resonance Surging into the world could be catastrophic."

"How am I supposed to do that? What do I do? Do I sing? Hum it? That looks really hard." The questions tumbled out of Elenor so quickly that they were barely intelligible.

"Calm down. Tell yourself whatever you need to focus, and then, Surge." Helen made a calming gesture with her hands.

Elenor took a deep breath and let it out. She watched Mateo breathing heavily and her eyes traced over the bleeding markings on his stomach.

Oh please, let this make me something more than just a monster. Then she began. At first, it was just a hum. A single note, rising then falling, only to rise again. The hum seemed to push away all the other sounds, to fill the entire world. Then she opened her mouth and began to sing. There were no words, just pure tones. The blood on Mateo's stomach began to bubble. The deep red of blood slowly gave way to a glowing golden light. The light effervesced into a riot of golden bubbles, swimming into the air above Mateo.

A second note joined the first as Elenor's song forced reality to move to her music, and another of the waves drawn in blood burst into golden light. The third and fourth note burst from her at the same moment, and so too did the remaining waves scrawled into Mateo's skin.

Elenor felt as if her insides were pouring out of her maw as she howled the notes into the night. All at once, she reached the end of the Surge. She was left panting when the music fled. The cloud of golden bubbles spun into a circle of blindingly bright light. Threads of gold spun away from the circle, reaching down to the wound in Mateo's stomach. Each thread flowed into wound until the hole was a pool of molten gold. It spread up the black lines that wormed across Mateo's skin.

When it vanished, the wound in Mateo's stomach was gone, and so were the black lines. Elenor let out a sigh of relief and Mateo blinked his eyes open. He reached down to touch his stomach. His mouth fell open with wonder.

"Gracias Elly!"

"You're welco…" Her words trailed off as her eyes fixed on the opening at the top of his shirt. There, at the top of his shirt, was a curved line of glowing citrine dots.

 • Gracias – Thanks

Each small dot was misshapen, but Elenor knew exactly what she was seeing. It was etched into her memory with such stark clarity that it might as well have been gouged across her eyeballs. She spun to Helen, and hissed. "What did you do?"

Helen's eyes went wide with surprise. "It was just a Healing Surge! What is the problem?"

Elenor spun back to Mateo, but she saw the look in his eyes. The worried concern. She turned her head and speared Helen with her glare. She jerked her head towards the trees. The thought of the Infected woman was still at the back of her mind, but she didn't have any idea how to deal with that. When they got far enough away that Elenor could no longer hear Mateo's breathing, she spun on Helen. She pointed towards her own chest with a razor-sharp claw.

"He has marks on his chest just like mine! What did you do?!"

"I cannot do __anything__!" Helen growled. "You sang that Surge! I just showed you how and had you carve a guide to make sure you couldn't screw it up. And none of it was __anything__ that would cause a Writband to form."

Elenor sat down heavily as the implications crashed into her mind like a speeding train.

"Is he going to turn into a creature like me?" Elenor asked.

Helen paused for a long moment and then nodded.

"Yes. I lack a good idea as to why the Writband is causing this transformation. I have had one for over a thousand years. It does not work anymore, though, and I can only imagine that your transformation is part of the explanation as to why."

Elenor shook her head. "We don't have time for this now. That woman is coming."

"Did you fight her?"

Elenor nodded. "But I couldn't stop her. She doesn't have one of those crowns like the other guy did."

"Crown?" Helen asked.

Elenor realized that Helen hadn't seen what had happened when she had been fighting the man on Hart-Miller Island. She was about to explain when Helen spoke again.

Helen's tone had changed to a reasoned whisper. "That is what you were doing when you were yanking at his head. There was something there that I could not see that you were trying to destroy."

Elenor launched into a quick explanation of what she had done to defeat the man on Hart-Miller Island.

"If it is a Relic of some sort, she might be hiding it inside of her body."

"It's bright green, just like the strings they use. It looks like it's made of green glass."

Helen looked thoughtful for a moment, but then shook her head. "It is possible that it is a Relic, but your description makes me think it is more likely some corrupted version of a Writband."

Helen's phone rang. Elenor's ears folded back at the annoying high pitched tone. She got both sides of the conversation. A baritone voice came out of the phone.

"We just got into the airport. Where do you need us?"

"Perfect timing, Hap. Who have you brought?" Helen replied.

"Everyone I could pull together in time."

A rapid-fire list of names came out of the phone speaker. Apparently, a dozen people had come along with him.

"Get to Patterson Park as fast as you can. You brought the Shrouds, right?" Helen asked.

"Just like you told us. We should be there in thirty minutes or less."

Helen swiped her finger on the phone screen and slid it into her pocket.

"What was that about?" Elenor piped up.

"We called some people for help."

"More people like you?"

Helen shook her head. "No, not like us." Helen reached into her pocket and took out a small metal box. It was shaking in her palm, and she flipped open the lid. "It is coming. Are you ready to fight?"

"No!" Elenor hissed. "None of you seem to understand I have no idea what I am doing! And we aren't done talking about Mateo!" She wasn't quite shouting, but she wasn't far from it.

Helen shushed her. "There will be more people in the park soon. We need to stop the Infected."

"We aren't done talking about Mateo," Elenor growled.

Helen sighed in clear annoyance. "This is nothing you or I did. This was going to happen to him either way."

Elenor noticed the green glow coming from the small box in Helen's hand was moving. Then the pull in her chest began to tug at her. She looked around at the trees surrounding them. There were not many areas of thick trees in the park, but the other side of the boat lake had one of them.

"It's after me. I'm going to run around the Boat Lake and lead it into the thick trees on the other side. I'm not great at fighting, but I am pretty good at sneaking around. If I have something to sneak through, I might be able to do something to stop her."

"Alright. I will watch her with my adder stone and see if I can figure out what you were talking about."

"The crown?" Elenor asked.

Helen nodded. "If I can see it, I will tell you where it is."

"What about Mateo?"

"He will be fine now. We will take him home."

Elenor sighed in relief. She turned around to head towards the opposite side of the Boat Lake. She paused a moment later. "Why didn't you tell me there were going to be more like me?"

"When have we had time for something like that?" Helen asked a little annoyed.

Elenor growled in an animalistic way that she didn't often indulge in. Helen held up a placating hand in response.

"I will answer every question I can once we have time for it," Helen promised.

Elenor's voice was resigned. "It knocked down an entire tenement and probably killed a dozen people or more. There is no way we're going to hide this."

Surprisingly, Helen shook her head. "You are going to be absolutely destroyed when you find out just how much supernatural nonsense people will ignore just to make themselves feel secure." The light of the Bane Sensor moved across Helen's face.

"I think she'll come right to me. Don't breathe in the dust she makes." Elenor sighed. "If something happens to me make sure you tell Mateo what is happening to him, **before** he winds up in a living nightmare." Elenor's voice dropped almost to a whisper. Clearly she didn't mean for Helen to hear. "We're never going to have time for questions."

Helen opened her mouth to try to cheer Elenor. It was clear that being on the verge of understanding what had happened to her was not enough of an improvement in outlook to help the damage done to her by her transformation. Before she could say a single word, Elenor's tail was disappearing into the trees without a trace.

Helen's face hardened. She would make time for those questions even if it killed her.

19

"ABANDON"

Cloaked by the park shrubs as she waited, Elenor discovered that she was beyond angry. Not only had her only friend in the world been hurt, this Infected thing was strangling the only small flame of hope that she had built up in two long years. Now, she just felt tired. Nothing was going to change, and the unfairness infuriated her.

Viridian light played over the morass of leaves and branches. Elenor looked up. At her mental command, her vision shifted until everything but the threads of energy shifted to shades of grey. The threads whipped about, ripping through the trunks of oak trees like a razor through rice paper. Bushes were sheared to the ground and a massive cacophony boomed from the small patch of forest as trees fell.

"This will not hide you! Give me back my family!" The woman's eyes glittered with vitriol as they whipped back and forth, searching for Elenor.

Elenor scrambled up a nearby tree trunk and then jumped to the next. There was no conscious thought in what she was doing. She moved purely on instinct. She jumped to another tree, her paws fastening to it like a fly to flypaper. She repeated the jump several times until she had managed to circle around behind the Infected.

A moment of concentration and the barbs on the end of her tail became a single hooked shape covering the tip of her tail. She set the hook over a branch and uncurled her body until she was hanging just behind the raging creature. Sharp teeth gleamed in the corrupted light of the deadly wires floating around the Infected. Elenor found an inexplicable grin on her muzzle.

She saw the downy hairs on the woman's arm lift in sudden fear, and Elenor knew she was the cause. The woman stood frozen, only the light from her eyes moving across the surrounding trees and shrubs. Elenor noticed the malevolent glow increase as the woman's eyes went wide. Elenor curled her body, her thick tail pulling her back up to the branch. She prayed the woman would not look up and see her eyes gleaming amongst the branches. She still couldn't see the halo of green light that she would need to destroy. *Where is she hiding it?*

In a blur of motion, the woman spun around. Threads snapped into a razor line that whipped towards Elenor. There was no time to react, but when the blurring lines slammed into her, they shattered like glass against stone. The parts that missed careened into the tree trunk, cutting cleanly through it. Ashy powder rose into the air around her, and Elenor jumped away to another nearby branch. Through the gap cut into the trees, she could see flashing lights. Strobes of blue and red at the edge of the park. *Oh no.* The police would have no chance of surviving a fight with this monstrosity. Bullets would not stop this woman any more than they would Elenor.

Spines rose across Elenor's body. Her talons lengthened, gleaming with killing edges. She did not want to be the monster that she looked like, but she refused to let someone else get hurt for her. A high-pitched screech of rage bubbled up from somewhere inside of her and she launched herself from the tree directly at the Infected's back.

The woman's body locked up in fear and Elenor smashed into her like a wrecking ball. She yanked her claws through one of the woman's shoulders as if it were soft putty. The devastating cut sheered away one arm and the woman screamed with such ferocity that it froze Elenor for a critical moment.

The Infected rolled, leaving behind her arm and knocking Elenor off balance. Webs of green whipped around her, cutting through everything in their path. Elenor tried to tackle her once again, but a massive tree trunk nearly smashed her flat. She stopped short, turned, and then noticed the clouds of ash swirling around them. Holding her breath, Elenor bolted up the trunk of a still-upright tree.

Once she was clear of the burning clouds of murder dust, she looked around frantically, trying to find the woman. Only venomous green reflections appeared through the billowing smoke. Of the Infected there was no sign. She realized something at that moment. When she had cut through the Infected's body, there was no blood.

Helen had not been lying. The Infected were no longer human. They might not be dead, but they had definitely been changed. A hard wind slammed into Elenor's back and she stiffened to keep herself from being blown out of the tree. The wind blew away the billowing clouds of poisonous ash. She looked around quickly, spotting Helen holding the crystal rod that grew from her hand. It was radiating blinding white light, and it was clear it was generating the wind.

When Elenor turned back, she saw the Infected holding the arm she had sheared away to her shoulder. The arm sealed back into place. Elenor watched with wide eyes as the wound healed almost instantaneously. A grim smile crept onto the Infected's face. Elenor's ears pricked forward as she caught the sound of men running toward them. She realized her mistake a moment later when the Infected saw her looking towards the tree line.

The Infected spun towards the tree line and Elenor did the one thing she feared more than fighting this thing. Mentally, she reached into the well of ready power in her chest. The woman did not bleed, but she still had water in her body. Elenor could feel it. She constructed the instructions in her head in a split second.

She abandoned her worries of hurting the woman, because that was exactly what she intended. Then she reached out one of her front paws and curled the short digits into a fist. The woman froze as if she were a statue.

"I won't let you hurt anyone else." Elenor's whisper echoed hopeless resignation that would haunt her nightmares for years to come. Elenor squeezed her paw tighter and the Infected's body collapsed in on itself like an empty beer can in a trash compactor. Sharp shards of bone exploded from the skin, snapping like brittle twigs under the tremendous pressure. She crumpled into a gruesome facsimile of the fetal position. Even after all of that, Elenor could still feel her attempting to move. The luminous green threads rose in clouds around her, whipping madly at the trees. Elenor closed her eyes, and forced down her gorge. She clenched her paw as hard as she could. There came a sound like wet canvas being torn.

Then silence.

Elenor did not look at what she had done. She still heard Thia's horrified whisper from the direction where Elenor had heard the police.

"Tiny gods, what did you do?"

"Stopped it." She walked down the side of the tree and turned back in the direction she had come. She passed through the destruction left in the wake of the Infected, leaves still fluttering to the ground as she passed.

Thia looked at the ruin that had been the Infected. It, for what was left was not anything recognizable as once alive, gave a final twitch as its nervous system ceased to function. She closed her eyes and shivered. She wanted to find fault with what Elenor had done, but that was only fear of what Elenor could do. She had eliminated a threat that could not be reasoned with or negotiated with. It had been done in defense of herself and others.

There were no reasons to kill more acceptable than those. Thia just hoped it would not break the poor girl. She hurried after Elenor as quickly as she could.

She caught up just as Elenor made it back to where they had saved Mateo. He was just starting to stir.

"How is he?" Elenor's voice was so soft and somber Thia could barely hear.

"He is fine. Your Surge cleared up the necrotic degeneration, but we need to get out of here before the police see us." Helen's phone chimed softly. She pulled it from her pocket and scanned the screen. "Hap will be waiting on the East Baltimore Street side of the park. Elenor, can you carry Mateo?"

"As long as he can hold on," Elenor said flatly.

"Take him and go on ahead. We will slow down the police," Helen said.

"Is… this guy going to be expecting me?" Elenor's skeptical tone made Helen pause.

"Oh, I see. Yes, he knows that you are not human. We will be right behind you. We are just going to leave a brief illusion behind to confuse the police temporarily."

"Come on, Mateo." Elenor laid down next to him, and let him climb onto her back. He was half her size, but he felt like he weighed nothing at all as she stood back up. She wondered if her power was doing something about his weight. She couldn't be sure, but she was starting to get the idea that some things it did happened entirely outside of her conscious control.

As soon as she was gone, Thia pulled Helen through the trees to the spot of the final confrontation. "Do you know what she can do?"

"I suspect a lot of things. She bears control over at least a small piece of a fundamental element of reality."

Thia pushed through a stand of bushy vegetation and froze. Helen almost bumped into her. There, where once had lain a barely recognizable lump of flesh and shattered bone, Thia found nothing. She turned to her mother, hazel eyes wide with disbelief.

"It was dead. There's no way," Thia whispered in disbelief.

"What?"

"The Infected. Elenor… crushed it." Thia shivered again. "Like someone had thrown a human body into a car crusher. Nothing could have survived that."

"Unless it was not alive. There are things that have obviously changed about the Bane, but I do not think that is one of them. Regardless, even if it has survived, it will take some time for it to recover from damage like that, if it can at all. We have to talk to Hap and find a place in the city that isn't a hotel. We are going to be here for some time, Thia. There is so much to unravel. I will lay down the illusion to slow the police. Go on ahead."

Helen gave her a gentle push towards the other side of the park. She lifted her Striker and lamented the time when she wouldn't be completely wiped out after just three minor expenditures of power.

Thia took a single step, then stopped to stare at the place where the Infected had been. She shook her head and then jogged off in the direction Elenor had gone.

20
"TEACH ME"

NC 17, EPOCH 19914.329

Elenor made it to the street just as a large black panel van pulled up to the curb. The door slid open and four large men wearing tactical gear piled out into the street. Elenor was startled by the weapons all of these people were toting around with such nonchalance. The largest of the men froze when she approached and then shook his head.

"Holy shit, Helen wasn't lyin'. You aren't human."

Elenor flattened her ears and tried hard not to bare her face razors at him. "Can you take him?" Elenor stretched her hind legs, lifting her back to show Mateo clinging to her. The man hesitated for one moment to long, and Elenor rolled her glowing eyes. She hissed angrily, "Look, big man. I can bite off a finger if that would make you feel justified in being scared of me. Otherwise, help me out already?" The huge man shuddered a little.

"Your voice is creepy. What're you, six years old? Where'd you learn to talk like that?"

"I'm nineteen, idiot. The voice is from whatever turned me into this. Are you going to help me out or not?"

He lurched forward, lifted Mateo off of her back, and put him into the van. Elenor sat anxiously, waiting for Helen and Thia. She was about to stand up and pace when Thia appeared on the park path. She ran to the white panel van, and got into one of the two rows of seats. Elenor climbed in behind her and attempted to draw her Relic back into her body. Unhappily, it did not respond.

"I can't control my spines. What's happening?"

"Remember what I said?" Thia asked.

Thia's warning came back to Elenor and she groaned.

"You said I can learn how to play Surges," Elenor affirmed.

Helen's voice came from the sidewalk outside. "We said we could teach you to Surge, but it is going to be difficult, because you cannot actually play the way you are." She climbed into the van, squeezing past Elenor's quivering spines.

"Why not?" Elenor asked.

"Because you already have a Writband. That marking on your chest is a brand upon your very soul that ties you to the Writ. It is a confirmation that your Resonance is recognized by the world and you are allowed to make changes as you will." Helen turned so she was kneeling on the seat to look over Mateo. "He'll be fine when he wakes up. Hap, take Jans and snag our rental, would you? It's the tan Camry parked near the corner of Eastern and South Luzerne."

"Keys?" Hap asked, holding out a scarred hand.

Helen fished them out of her jacket pocket and tossed them to the huge soldier.

"Where we meetin'?" he asked.

"At the hotel address I gave you. We will figure it out from there. Lupo, take the rest of the guys. Canvas the park and the surrounding area. You are looking for a woman. Five-five, shoulder length black hair, eyes that look like they have green LEDs in them, and grey skin that will make you certain she is dead, because she is. Do not engage with her, at all, on any level. Follow and report if you find her. If any of you even think for a single split second you have been made, you leave immediately."

"Yes, ma'am."

Helen had met him a decade earlier waging a guerrilla war against a cartel in Mexico. The cartel had gotten their hands on a Relic that they had been misusing to assassinate people who displeased them. He wasn't as massive as Hap, but he knew how to get the job done. He gathered up the rest of the men and took off into the park.

"Thia, call the broker. It is finally time to break open our piggy bank," Helen said.

A tiny throat clearing noise came from the cargo space behind the seats, and Helen looked up to see Elenor sitting very carefully in the back of the Van.

"Oh, right. Your Relic." Helen squinted at her. She then whistled a quick tune. It was similar to the previous one, but not precisely the same. Elenor hummed it quickly, and then sighed in relief.

After a few long moments of concentrating, her spines relaxed and flopped down into her fur as if they were made of soft rubber. Her claws did not retract, but the sharp edges blunted themselves down to the point that they wouldn't damage anything they touched. When she finally pulled her eyes open, Mateo was watching her over the back seat. The van was in motion.

"How are you feeling?" Elenor asked.

"Bien. Second, second chance. Eso es muy padre," Mateo replied.

"About that. Mateo, I have to tell you something," Elenor started, but the van pulled to a halt.

"We are here." Helen turned to look at them.

"Where?" Elenor asked.

"Mateo's house. I assumed this is where he would want to go," Helen said.

"Yeah, I need to be here when my parents get home from work. With that building being smashed and all the damage around here, if they show up and I am not here they'll kill me to death," Mateo joked.

Elenor narrowed her eyes at Helen.

Helen just shook her head.

Elenor almost said something anyway, but uncertainty filled her and she stopped herself. *What do I*

- Bien – Good
- Eso es muy padre – That's pretty awesome

really know about the situation?

Mateo slid open the van door and jumped out. The faint sound of sirens and shouting filtered into the Van from down the street.

"I'll call you after I get some sleep. Elly," he said.

"Are you sure you're okay? It was a lot." Elenor struggled to keep her worry out of her voice and failed.

Mateo shrugged. "I'm sure I'll be a mess for an hour or two once I am back in my own room. I'll be fine, though."

"Alright." Elenor was reluctant, but she wasn't sure what else she could do.

"Young man?" Helen asked, and Mateo looked up at her where she was looking at him out of the side window.

"Yes?"

"I assume you know you cannot tell anyone about all of this?" she asked.

Mateo nodded. "Sí señora. Pero I will need to tell mis padres eventualmente."

Helen nodded in understanding. "For now, though, not telling them will be safer."

Mateo waved acknowledgement and slid the van door closed.

As soon as they pulled away from the curb, Elenor bristled and hissed, "Why did you stop me from telling him?"

Helen held up her hands placatingly. "Because he cannot see it yet, and there are weeks at least before he will start to see the marks and the transformation will begin."

"What does that matter?"

"Because maybe by then, we can figure out how to do something to stop it."

- Sí señora – Yes ma'am
- Pero – But
- mis padres eventualmente – my parents eventually

Elenor's ears fell and her eyes went a little wide with hopeful shimmer.

Helen looked pensive and shook her head. "I do not think what I have in mind would help you, Elenor. Nothing is impossible, but I cannot see how we would reverse the transformative process now that it is complete."

Elenor deflated.

Helen sighed. "I am sorry, Elenor. I wish I had better news. There is some good news. If you learn, you will at least be able to trick everyone into thinking you are human with some clever illusions?" Helen's voice turned up at the end, making it a question.

Elenor let out a long-suffering sigh and flopped onto the floor of the van. "Better than nothing, I guess," she mumbled.

Helen narrowed her eyes. "I get that you have had it rough. This is not something I would wish on an unknowing person like yourself." Helen took a deep breath and held it for a second as if preparing for a Herculean task. "But I do not get why you are so angry about it, either."

Elenor opened her mouth to shout that her life turned to shit when this happened to her.

Helen held up a hand to forestall her shout. "Hear me out for just a second. You are on the verge of having a real, true blue magical adventure. I am offering to teach you how to do things that people literally dream of. Yes, the price of admission to this has been a small hell, but you made it through."

"And what about what I did tonight?" Elenor snarled, her sibilance becoming more pronounced as she angered. "You weren't there. You didn't see what I had to do to that thing to stop it."

"I have been alive for eighteen hundred years, Elenor. I have fought in wars and done things you cannot even begin to imagine. Some of it was easy, some of it nearly killed me in more ways than one, but I will tell you one thing my life has never been. Boring."

Elenor looked down at the floor for a long moment and then up to one of the van windows. It threw back the reflection of the monster she had become. "Maybe I'd like a boring life," she mumbled.

"You know, I have never particularly believed in coincidence. Humans like to use that word because they are so limited they cannot understand that it is possible that everything happens for a reason. What happened to you was not coincidence. Maybe this happened to <u>you</u> because it fits you. Maybe you just do not see it yet because you cannot see how amazing your life can be."

Elenor jumped to her paws, blades all over her body springing up angrily. "Amazing?!" Elenor spluttered in fury. "How can this ever be anything good?" Elenor hissed, enraged almost to tears.

Helen stared at her with absolute calm. "Answer me one question, Elenor. What would you do as a human that you cannot do now?"

"How about walk around in public? Enjoy my food?" Elenor spat.

"With what I will teach you, both of those things can be achieved. No, Elenor, tell me what you wanted in life that you cannot have now? There are, I admit, some important things that might make such a list, but it would be a short list indeed," Helen instructed.

Elenor opened her mouth to shout about, something, but her anger faded as she began to process what Helen was saying. *Kids, and meeting someone to share my life with?* Even that second one might be possible if more people were going to end up in her situation.

The more she thought about it, though, what Helen was offering could be wonderous. She looked down at herself. Dark brown fur and two paws with long glittering black claws. *Would this really be so bad if everyone didn't treat me like a monster?* The things she could do were beyond anything she could have imagined before. She had accepted this was her life a long time ago. *Am I just so used to it being awful that I can't accept that it could get better?*

A final sigh escaped and Elenor looked up to Helen. "Teach Me."

21

"SURGE"

Elenor roared in frustration. "This is impossible!"

Helen shook her head. "I wish I had a better answer for you. This situation is far from ideal. I cannot imagine why the Writ would subject you to a Writband without training."

Elenor was sitting on her haunches in the middle of a tiny clearing, surrounded by a small but dense patch of forest. The carpet of snow was freezing beneath her paws, but she couldn't deny that the silence of the forest in winter helped her concentrate. Clutched between her front paws was Helen's striker. She couldn't hold it well despite the fact that her paws had most of the features of a human hand. Her digits were just too thick for the finger holes in the grip.

"You cannot Surge the connections to your Relic into place with just singing. It takes all ten source notes to make that sort of connection, and no Caller has ever been able to sing more than five notes at a time. Try again," Helen encouraged, but Elenor tossed the striker back. Helen caught it without effort

"I can't play that thing with these stupid, stupid paws. We've been doing this every day for weeks. It's not working!" Elenor snarled.

Helen just shook her head. "Weeks, you think that weeks is a sufficient period of time to succeed at this? Do you know how many years I trained before I was even allowed to touch my master's Striker? Surging the music of the world is not a feat meant for the impatient, Elenor. Impatience kills Callers just as surely as a bullet to the head."

"You know, you sound like one of my boring ass teachers from high school," Elenor grumbled.

"You are not a child anymore. Do not act like one,"
Helen said sternly. "Do you want to be able to control
your life or not?"

Elenor's ears flattened and her scowl was so full of
gleaming razor teeth that even Helen was impressed.

"You should do something about that face." Helen
grinned as Elenor's scowl mutated into something far
more terrifying.

"She's baiting you again." Exasperation radiated
from Thia as she narrowed her eyes at her mother. "You
are the worst teacher, you know?"

"Save it, peanut gallery. I do not see you training any
apprentices," Helen grumbled.

"That would be impractical since I have never
actually played a Surge in my life, mostly due to the fact
that you, in all your ancient wisdom, destroyed our
connection to the Writ somehow," Thia said as she
strummed a guitar idly.

"Can everyone who does magic play an instrument?"

Thia shook her head. "Everyone who does, magic,
can play _any_ instrument. Haven't you ever tried?"

Elenor shook her head. "I like music but I was never
interested in playing it."

"Well, you could."

"Are people born Callers or something?"

"Yes and no. Some are born with a talent for Surging,
and by association, music. Like you. Others have to be
taught. It makes no difference in power, only training
time."

"Why do you think I have that?"

Helen held up a single finger. "One, your voice. I
know you think you just sound like a child, but what
you actually have is something that only the talented
start out with. Perfect pitch."

Elenor narrowed her eyes skeptically.

"You do not believe me?" Helen lifted her Striker and struck it against her bracelet. A moment later, a pure note was ringing from the instrument. "Sing this."

"I don't think," Elenor trailed off under Helen's hard stare. She opened her maw and was immediately able to produce the exact same note with only her voice.

"And follow." Helen began to play an intricate melody consisting of five notes. Without even trying, Elenor belted out the five notes in perfect rhythm. Her pitch was so perfect a match to the Striker it almost hurt to listen to. Helen squeezed the damper on her Striker and the notes abruptly stopped. Elenor's high soprano continued the gentle, complex melody for a few moments.

Helen held up a second finger. "Two, perfect note recognition. This, too, is a skill that can be trained, but you simply have it. Otherwise, you could not do precisely what you are doing right now."

"There's also the point that your entire body's a musical instrument," Thia put in helpfully.

"Not helping," Elenor ground out.

"All we are doing is helping," Thia said.

Elenor's ears fell and she squinted suspiciously. "What do you mean?"

"I mean, you're operating under the idea that we are trying to make this hard for you. I know that movies and stories have given people the false idea that magic," Thia made quotes with her fingers, "is both easy and that it can do anything."

Helen picked the explanation back up. "The fact of the matter is, it is neither of those things. You have found yourself in a very dangerous situation and you are not even aware. Most Callers sing, play, and study for years before they are ever even considered for the first investment of their Writband that allows them to actually Surge." She tapped her fingers on the rods of her Striker.

"We do this so that they are not off pitch or play the wrong notes. If they make mistakes when playing a Surge, they can very easily kill themselves and others."

Elenor touched a paw to her chest where her Writband pulsed gentle power beneath her fur.

"Right. I do not know how you managed it besides the fact that there must be some instinctive safety measure built into your Relic, but you, should be dead. At some point, you should have struck your tail on something without knowing how this works and the discordant notes should have created a deadly Resonance," Helen finished, and a horrified look came over Elenor's face. It was sometimes hard to tell what her expression meant, but this one was clear.

Trembling, she lifted her tail to look at the collection of spikes that swirled around the tip as if it had a mind of its own. She stared for a long moment and her eyes crinkled in concentration. Tears welled in the corners of her mismatched eyes.

"I can't make it go away!" Elenor sniffed.

"Elenor," Helen said, and Elenor looked up. "You will not be able to control all the aspects of your Relic until you can play the proper Surge. The only way I can help you control your Surges until you can do so yourself is if you play them on my Striker."

Elenor sighed, held out her paw, and took back the Striker. She sat back on her haunches and fed her short digits through the brass grip at the bottom of the collection of rods. She had been at this for months now. Between trips to her parents' house for the holidays, she had spent all of her time trying to learn to play this impossibly frustrating instrument.

The grip was made for human fingers, and despite the fact that it seemed to turn into black liquid when Helen absorbed it back into her body, she couldn't adjust any of its dimensions to make it easier for Elenor to play. The good news was that it was the only thing she had ever found that her claws wouldn't slice to pieces. She flexed her claws and carefully tapped out the ten note scale. Each digit tapped at two of the rods, and she continued to practice the scale for more than a minute before it fell apart.

"I can't hold onto the stupid thing. It keeps turning in my stupid paws," Elenor cried in frustration. Surprisingly, it was Helen, not Thia, who sat down in the snow next to her.

"I understand your impatience, but you are progressing at an amazing rate. You will get this," Helen assured her. "You need to stop squeezing the Striker so hard. It twists in your paw because you are partially engaging the damper, which causes much higher vibration when you strike the notes."

Elenor looked down through tear filled eyes. She sniffled once more, and then lifted the Striker again. She began to play, slowly at first. The scale of notes rang from the Striker. As the scale of notes continued to flow from the chiming instrument, a look of calm concentration smoothed Elenor's eyes and muzzle. Her paws began to shake, and Elenor's glowing eyes popped open. Helen was breathless, shaking her paws to stop her from playing. She looked around the clearing and her eyes went wide. The clearing was absolutely destroyed. Dozens of trees were burning. Craters had been scooped out of the ground like ice cream from a bowl.

"Stop!" Helen was shouting, but Elenor could still barely hear her. Elenor dropped the Striker and stared at what she had done. She put her paws up to her muzzle in terrified astonishment. Elenor backed away from the Striker in a blur of motion and she crouched with her back against the tree line. Helen left the Striker where it lay and came closer to Elenor, who was panting madly.

"Calm down, this is why we bought this property and came out here."

"I thought you said using your Striker would stop this from happening!" Elenor shouted.

"I was not lying. I underestimated the power of your Writband. I thought the third Surge in your Writband was only to support your transformation. I was incorrect."

"How am I supposed to practice like this?!" Elenor gestured around, not rising from her terrified crouch.

Helen smiled. "It will not happen again. I promise."

"But..." Elenor's posture slowly metamorphosed into something slightly more relaxed.

"Elenor, I warned you this might happen. Did you think that I was joking when I said something might blow up?"

"Well, yeah, sorta."

Helen shook her head. "Come on, one more try." She bent down and picked up her Striker. She tapped it against her steel bracelet and it began to hum. Then she slid her fingers through the grip and began to play. "This is the Surge to connect your mind to your Relic."

The music was complex beyond anything that Elenor had heard before. Interwoven notes that Elenor could hear both individually and all at the same time. The beauty of it was almost painful. Helen finished playing and then held out the Striker to Elenor.

"I can't do that."

"You can. What you cannot do is believe in yourself. I told you before, you became you for a reason. It might not have been your reason at first. Something was seen in you that granted you this power, but it is your power now."

Elenor had accepted over the last few weeks that Helen had been right. She had been taught a few things that had greatly improved her ability to move around unseen, and with that freedom, she had been able to see her parents whenever she wanted. She took the Striker and thought of the music that Helen had just played. This was the one thing that made Elenor think that Helen and Thia might be right about her. The music came back to her perfectly. Every note of the tune stood out vibrantly in her memory.

She sat back on her haunches, held the instrument carefully, and then tapped it with the spines on her tail. It began to hum and what passed for her fingers began to move. The notes drifted up slowly at first, and she let her mind go blank as the Surge pushed away all the other sounds around her.

Vibration came up through her paws as each digit damped rods and then released them to sing once more. Then she was at the end of the music and the sounds of the world around her returned. A new feeling blossomed inside of her. She could hear Thia shouting, one bare second before the Striker flew out of her paws as Thia tackled her in a hug. Elenor froze as she was bowled over.

"You did it!" Thia shouted.

Elenor realized that all of her spines had drawn back into her body the moment Thia had hit her.

"Well done. You have forged a connection to your Relic. Now you can truly begin to learn."

22
"ALARM"

Hap laid on one side of the brick wall that divided Arlington National Cemetery from North Marshall Drive. They had spent weeks trying to track the woman Helen had told them about. It had not been easy, and Hap had called in favors to get some surveillance assets to help him do the tracking.

Once they had found her, though, they didn't know what to make of her movements. They had found her on her way out of the city. She walked, unerringly, towards Virginia, only turning when there was a building or other obstacle too large in her way. They had lost her for some time when she had simply walked into the Patapsco River.

She did not swim, and Hap had written her off for dead, but when he had called Helen and explained, she had told him to check the other side of the river. Sure as the sun, she had walked out of the water on the other side of the river about an hour and three miles later. She had walked out dry. She had continued to walk without sleep, without stopping.

They had followed her for some time, but when the direction she was heading had become clear, Hap had used his contacts to just track her with surveillance footage. Finally, after several days of weaving through the streets of towns and cities, the woman, if she could be called that, arrived at Arlington National Cemetery. Hap had watched her walk right past marine guards completely unnoticed.

Now he watched through a spotting scope as the woman made her way among the grave markers. She wove between perfectly aligned rows of simple white grave markers. Finally, she stopped in front of a stone.

She drew back her fist and threads of verdant light gathered around it.

Hap's eyes went wide with anger when she threw the punch. He had been a marine, and defacing a military grave enraged him. He breathed in a sharp breath of fury. Then, a flash of blue light blew the woman back. She tumbled between the stones and slammed into a thick oak tree.

Shock writ large on his face, Hap dug his phone out of a jacket pocket. Years of training and more in the field made him keep one eye on his target. He didn't miss it when she stood up from her tumble and looked straight at him. It was utterly impossible that she could see him at that distance, and yet she locked eyes with him through the spotting scope.

Hap laid perfectly still, not taking his eyes off of her. It had to be a coincidence. He watched the creature as her glowing green eyes narrowed, but she turned away and slunk further into the graves. He rose and dialed Helen's number. She picked up on the first ring.

"Hello, Hap. What have you found?"

"I was made."

"Are you clear?"

"I don't know yet. Helen, she tried to smash a grave in Arlington. Why would she do that?"

Hap checked the street and found it clear. He walked down North Marshall Drive toward the Richmond Highway. More than once, he checked his six but he never saw anyone following. He slid into his truck.

"When she punched the gravestone, it flashed like a grenade had gone off and it threw her like a ragdoll."

"Did she see you? Did she even look in your general direction?" Helen's urgent tone made him shove his keys into the ignition.

"Looked right at me from four hundred yards out. No way she saw me."

"Lucas, get out of there right now! She is on you even if you did not see her. Get out!" Helen shouted.

She never used his first name. Hap mashed the gas and his tires spun. The truck did not move. His eyes tracked up to the rear-view mirror. They locked with the pair of glowing green orbs glaring through his back window. Her fingers were dug into the tailgate of his truck and dozens of glowing threads of poisonous light were floating around her.

Hap drew his 1911 from his thigh holster and without a second of hesitation, he unloaded it straight through the back window. Several rounds struck the woman in the head and shoulders and she released her grip on the truck.

"Fuck me, what is that thing?!" His truck shot down the street and he slid around the on-ramp for the Richmond Highway. He kept the gas to the floor until he was well past the Pentagon. He slowed down when the building flashed by and he realized that there were probably a lot of police around the area. The last thing he needed was to get pulled over with a freshly fired forty-five in his holster.

Suddenly, the wheel of his truck was yanked hard to the right. In the last moment of clarity as the truck began to tilt, he saw her. The woman was, beyond all belief, standing on the door of his truck. Her feet were somehow glued to the door and she stood with her arms folded, looking at him through the passenger side window. She grinned madly at him, and then there was only the sound of shattering glass and the roar of twisting metal.

23

"HAMMERSPACE"

Helen was stacking up an absolutely massive pile of odd doodads and trinkets. The storage room off of the kitchen was about twenty feet square, with bare red-brick walls. Steel shelving units filled the room and every shelf was filled with bric-a-brac.

"I can help," Elenor said where she lurked in the door.

"Not a chance. You are not ready for this. You barely have control of your Relic. I do not know what we are getting into, and you are far too valuable to risk."

"Helen, you have to let me help. You can barely protect yourself from those things," Elenor pleaded.

Helen checked the crystal sword, pulling an inch of the crystalline blade from the scabbard before sliding it back into place.

"I do not plan on fighting it, but what Hap described before his truck flipped was something I have not seen in over a thousand years. I did not even think it was possible to maintain such a thing. That blue flash that Hap talked about is a protection created by warping reality, but it took a lot of energy to maintain. I cannot think of many ways one could still exist."

"And if it jumps you?"

"I will use this." Helen flipped a large golden coin, catching it in the same hand. Then she pulled a golden spike out of a sheath on her belt. It was about a foot long and square like a railroad spike. The end was mushroomed as if it had been hammered into a hard surface many times, doming the top. Around the barrel of the spike was a pattern of six separate waves.

"The last time you tried to use that, you were passed out for six days," Thia grumbled.

"The last time, I did not have a Caller to power it."

"What is it?" Elenor asked, looking at the golden spike.

"This is a Reference Spike. Drive this into the ground and it sets a reference point that you can return to instantly using the coin. It eats a lot more power than I have to spare, but it's a drop in the bucket for you."

"What do I do?"

"Just touch it. You will not even notice a thing."

Elenor put her paw on the spike and surging blue light rippled down the spike, filling in the wave patterns carved into its surface. True to what Helen said, she didn't feel a thing.

"It takes me an entire year to put enough power into this Relic to make it function. It used to be as easy for me as it was for you just now."

"So, what do you think the Infected was after in the Cemetery?"

"A pocket dimension where Callers used to hide their Relics and safe places to work, among other things." Helen slid the spike into a sheath on her belt.

"Wait, you can make a Hammerspace?" Elenor was incredulous.

"What is Hammerspace?"

Thia answered. "It's a thing from cartoons. Infinite invisible storage space that lets you pull things out of thin air."

"How do you know that?" Helen asked.

Thia shrugged in response. "I watch TV, you don't," she said matter-of-factly.

"Well, yes, Hammerspace works, I suppose. Not what we called it. Either way, we have to get there and see what lies inside before the Infected gets in."

"What about Hap?" Mention of going to the cemetery brought thoughts of the big man to Elenor's mind.

"He will be fine in the hospital. The Infected was not really after him. He just got in the way. As soon as he is

discharged, I will teach you how to heal his injuries."
Hellen pulled the duffel she had been filling closed and
swung it over her shoulder.

"I'm going with you," Elenor said.

Helen frowned at her. "You will only get in the
way."

"Then I'll stand behind you. I'm going with you.
Think you can stop me? I can run faster than your car."
Elenor narrowed glowing eyes at Helen.

"Why do you want to go so badly?" Helen asked.

"Because I can feel the pulling," Elenor mumbled.

Helen and Thia exchanged a look.

"What pulling?" Thia asked.

Elenor's ears fell and she backed up onto herself,
curling up tightly. She wrapped her tail around her feet
and the spikes pulled back into it so she could curl it as
close as possible.

"I don't understand it. Sometimes, though, I can feel
them. Like someone has tied a rope around my chest
and they're yanking on it."

Helen just stared at her. "Could you possibly stop
turning everything I think I know sideways?"

"Do you think I like not knowin' anything?"

"I suppose you do not. So, you can sometimes feel
the Infected?"

Elenor nodded.

"And now?"

"It's pulling me that way." Elenor pointed with her
tail without uncurling her body. Spines swirled back
into place around the point of the tail, which swayed
unerringly south.

"Can you control it?" Helen asked.

Elenor shrugged. "I've never tried. It just started all
on its own the day we met."

"I will help you learn more."

"How are you going to do that? This isn't…"

"Not what?" Helen interrupted. "The only power you exhibit that is beyond my knowledge is this." Helen put a finger in the fur on her chest, where Elenor had described feeling her power to control the water inside of living things. "Even that is something I understand, at least a little."

"I said I would learn, but I didn't really want to keep fighting those things. I just want my life back and to make sure this doesn't happen to anyone else."

Helen smiled. "I know, Elenor, and I will do whatever I can to make that happen for you. I just feel compelled to tell you that this, power, you have been given... It seems specifically designed to fight the Infected."

"What does that mean?" Elenor voice was overshadowed with unshed tears.

"It means that the Writ thinks that it needs people to fight the Infected."

"It doesn't make any sense. Why would it pick someone like me, though? Not when there are people like you." Elenor sniffed.

"You have to understand. The Writ is the foundation that our reality sits upon. It knows things that we cannot possibly piece together. That is why I said there is a reason for what is happening to you. You are important. Mateo is important. Anyone who is about to experience what you went through is needed. I do not know why, but I do know that it is true."

Elenor took a few steps back. "You're not going to help Mateo?"

"That is not what I meant. I do not know for sure if we can do with Mateo what we used to do with our apprentices, but passing our Writbands was a well-researched practice, so it should work. As soon as you have improved your interface with your Relic, I will teach you how to help Mateo transfer his Writband. If that is what he wants. Thia will take it, I am sure."

"I will," Thia put in as she went about organizing the mess left behind by her mother's preparation rampage.

"You're all insane. I need you alive, though, so I'm still going."

"Fine. The first thing you have to know about the Surge you are feeling is that it is called a Soul Tether. We used to use them to track down people. Once a tether is made, all you have to do to turn it on and off is Surge against the trigger. Try this." Helen whistled a quick tune. Elenor repeated it in a hum and suddenly the feeling of the rope tugging her south was gone.

"It worked."

Helen zipped up the bag she had filled and headed toward Elenor.

"Good, now just hum it backwards to turn it back on." Helen turned right and headed toward the door to the garage. Elenor concentrated on humming the tune and suddenly the tugging insisted she go south.

"What if you have more than one?"

"I would not advise trying it. Last time I tried holding two tethers, it drove me to distraction. Hold onto them for too long and the conflicting signals could make you quite insane."

"What?!" Elenor squeaked. Then she skittered to the garage door.

"Not all Surges are safe, Elenor. I thought you would have learned that from your first experiences."

"How long will it take for me to learn enough to be safe?" Elenor asked as Helen opened the back hatch of the recently purchased hunter green Jeep Cheroke. Elenor hopped into the back.

"A few months of study should see you to the point where you will not kill anyone or yourself. Years to reach true proficiency." Helen dropped the bag in the back seat and Elenor put her paws on top of the seat, looking into the passenger compartment.

"So, what makes you think we are so important?" Elenor asked as Helen backed the jeep out of the driveway and onto the street.

"I do not have the slightest idea right now. When I killed Osiris, the Merlin decided that we could not leave correcting what Osiris had done to chance. We disagreed. That was why I had not spoken to him in over a thousand years. I thought it was a mistake to try to correct something that we knew so few details about," Helen explained as she pulled onto the highway.

"Does that mean that what happened to me could have been something he did?"

"It certainly could have contributed. I was never comfortable with how little we were able to find out about what Osiris had done."

"So I'm stuck like this because you screwed up a thousand years ago?" Elenor grumbled.

"Do you think that I do not realize that I may be partially responsible for what happened to you?" The drive was quiet after that.

It took them almost an hour to arrive at the cemetery. By the time they arrived, it was well past closing time. It was starting to get dark outside when Helen parked the car on North Meade St.

"Alright, we are not supposed to be in the cemetery at this time of night so I am going to teach you the two Surges you want to know more than any others." Helen produced her Striker.

"The one that makes me look human again?"

Helen grinned. "Close, but not quite. While that would work for this, you are not ready for it. Making an illusion of a human body that will mask your current body shape in a useful way requires more experience than you have. You will practice this one first. This one will make you look like a canine similar in size to your current body."

"A dog. You want me to look like a dog?" Elenor seemed a little annoyed.

"Well, either people see a nice golden retriever or they run screaming from the multi-eyed hell creature you are right now."

Elenor rolled her glowing eyes. "Fine, but can I pick the dog?"

"You can pick the dog,"

"Great,"

"*If* you can pick the dog," Helen interrupted. "This Surge contains all of the pieces of the illusion that will make you look like a dog to everyone looking at you. If you can figure out which notes translate into the dog's appearance, you can look like whatever kind of dog you like." Helen began to play the Surge on her Striker as they walked down the street.

When she finished, they walked a few more yards and then Elenor waved her tail as they passed a street sign. Her tail whacked against the steel post of the sign, sending the spines on it into a musical vibration. With some concentration, she flexed muscles in her tail, damping the vibration of the spines until the music Helen had played flowed into the air around her. Elenor could feel the world warping around her as the Surge took effect.

"How do I look?" Elenor spun as she walked, trying to get a look at herself and failing.

"You will not be able to see the illusion. If you could, it would not be very useful because it acts like a shell around your body. If you could see it, it would be in the way of you seeing other things. You'll need a mirror," Helen explained.

"Oh." Elenor flinched when the tug in her chest changed. It pulled in a slightly different direction than it had on the way over.

"You look adorable. You can look in a mirror when we get home. For now,"

Elenor interrupted, "It moved. It's moving."

"Is it, now? Which way?" Helen asked, a truly terrifying grin spreading across her face.

"It's still far away," Elenor said, and then lifted her tail and pointed the tight spiral of spines at the tip to the west.

"Good, that means we have time to setup a surprise."

"Shouldn't we be worried she will bring more... Infected?"

"If we were dealing with the same thing that Osiris created back then, there would be thousands of Infected by now. That is why I had Hap and his team following the Infected after your fight in the park." Helen dug in her pocket and produced a pair of hair clips with bows on them.

"What are those for?"

"You will not need one, but they keep anyone from recognizing me."

Helen flicked the metal clip on the back with her fingernail, and then clipped it into her hair. They followed the sidewalk towards North Marshall Street and paused at the corner. Helen watched the gate for a few minutes. She turned left and crossed the street, staying on the sidewalk. Across the street between them and the cemetery was a tall black steel fence.

"How are you going to get over that?"

"We are not going over it. We are going to walk right through it, but we need to get away from the gate."

They followed the asphalt sidewalk lined with well-maintained trees a few hundred yards down the road. Helen produced her Striker and began to play a slow melody on it.

"When we cross the street, play this tune. Make sure you keep yourself pressed against my leg. If you don't stay in contact with me, it will only affect you."

"What does it do?"

"It will make us incorporeal as long as you keep up the tune."

"What happens if I stop while we are standing inside of something?" Elenor worried.

"Well, that depends on the object you are standing inside when it happens."

Elenor tapped her tail on the asphalt. After a moment, she began to play the music Helen had played for her. As the notes flowed from the spines around her tail, she felt the bottom fall out of the world. She suddenly felt hollow. She could feel wind blowing through her body.

"This is weird."

"Yeah, it will always feel like that. It is going to feel even stranger when we walk through that fence. Make sure you keep playing," Helen warned.

Elenor felt the tug in her chest change again. Somehow, she could tell it meant that the Infected was coming towards her. "It's coming this way."

"How long do we have?" Helen asked.

"I don't know. I can't," Elenor started, but then as she focused on the feeling in her chest, she could tell. Like the information was injected directly into her mind somehow. "It'll be here in about forty minutes."

"Gaining better comprehension on how the tether works, are we? That is plenty of time to get inside and prepare."

"Get inside where?" Elenor asked as they walked through the stone wall and into the cemetery proper. Elenor felt her stomach clench at the sensation of walking through the solid object. As soon as she stopped playing and her body slammed back into full corporeality, she heaved. Nothing came up, which was a plus, but the dry heaves were terribly unpleasant. Helen waited.

"The Hammerspace, as you called it. Look around at the graves. You should be able to see it with those headlamps you call eyes," Helen prodded.

Elenor stopped at the edge of Ord & Weitzel Drive and sat back on her haunches, using her tail to balance as she sat up like a meerkat. It took her only a moment to spot a glowing blue bubble covering one of the gravestones across the street.

"Over there." Elenor dropped back to all fours and trotted off towards it.

"If you do that looking like a dog again, literally anyone who sees you will know you are not a dog," Helen advised.

"Fine, next time I'll climb onto a gravestone," Elenor groused. "She's getting closer fast."

"It knows we are here. I am not certain why it is trying to get into this space."

"Why do I feel like you should know more about all of this after a thousand years?" Elenor's sardonic squeak voice irritated Helen.

"I cannot remember everything about everything. Our brains do have a limited capacity, even with eidetic memory like mine. I have caches of books and journals preserved that contain all of my notes concerning everything we found during our hunt for Osiris. They are being shipped here now, but they are scattered across half of Europe and northern Africa."

They stopped in front of the gravestone with the transparent blue bubble over it. Hellen spun around, her eyes roving over the well-maintained foliage surrounding them. Despite it being a graveyard, the twilight island of idyllic forest in the middle of the city was a beautiful sight. Elenor lifted a paw towards the humming azure bubble. Helen's fist closed around Elenor's paw, holding it still.

"Touch that and it will cook you like a Thanksgiving turkey. Your Relic can probably ground out the forces,

but I would not bet on it. I recognize the work. This is
one of the Merlin's hideaways. The question is, what is
powering the entrance?"

"She's going to be here in about twenty minutes,"
Elenor cautioned.

"That is fine. Play this Surge." Helen played a tune
of such complexity that Elenor blinked at the end.

"I… can't play that."

"It is the only way to open the Hammerspace,
Elenor." Helen smiled encouragingly. "You can do it."

"Play it again?" Elenor asked, and then she closed her
eyes, listening as Helen played the music again. Elenor
took a deep breath, let it out, and then lifted her tail. She
struck the spines gently against one of the grave markers
and the telltale hum of a Striker filled the air. Each of
the ten spines at the tip of her tail vibrated musically,
pushing away all of the sounds of the world around her.
Then she carefully flexed the muscles connected to the
spines at the tip.

The same beautiful music began. The first note slid
in volume, up then down, in a metronome perfect
rhythm. Two notes joined the first, flowing into the
rhythm. Those notes paused on opposite beats in the
transition between the high and low of the first note.
More notes layered themselves into the music until a
complex melody surrounded them. She felt reality warp
as the music took effect.

"How is this actually useful in combat?"

Elenor continued playing and the azure bubble faded
from around the grave. A moment later, round stones
pushed their way up out of the ground on either side of
the grave marker. Two more stones pushed their way
out of the ground outside of the first two, floated up
from the ground, and stacked themselves atop the first
ones. The process repeated itself with increasing speed
until the stones formed a doorway. The interior of the

doorway vanished into a flat plane of perfect darkness. It seemed to be the lightless void of outer space.

"Surges become more complex depending on the complexity of what you are trying to achieve. Flinging about fire, lightning, or other elemental forces is relatively simple. Compare that to adjusting the alignment of an interdimensional gateway protected by an interspersion of elemental and spatial forces designed to obliterate anything that attempted to force its way inside of the space. Pretty sure you can draw your own conclusions."

Helen walked through the doorway and vanished without any further preamble. Elenor darted inside behind her and the doorway deconstructed itself, leaving no trace it had ever been there.

24

"THE FIRST PIECE"

Elenor blinked her eyes but the world didn't emerge. She twisted her head left and right, and still nothing became visible. It was the first time since her transformation that she had been unable to see through darkness.

"What the hell?" Elenor wondered out loud.

"Hello, Elenor." The voice was immediately recognizable and Elenor bristled. Her spines stood up and vibrated in a threat display that would make any reasonable thinking being lose control of their waste management organs.

"You, are, dead," Elenor hissed.

"Indeed. The mortal lifespan of my original body has come to a close. I am not the Merlin, Elenor. I am a remnant that was left behind to pass along the truth in the event that you survived. A shadow of his past self."

"Why would I believe anything you have to say? You tried to kill me," Elenor snarled.

"I am unaware of that. I have not been in contact with my mortal body for centuries. I was left behind as a failsafe, to speak with whoever might open this port dimension."

"How do you know my name then?"

"I am aware of everything that happens within a few hundred yards of the entrance," the disembodied voice of Shadow responded. "You may wish to close your eyes. I have brought you to an area where we can speak."

"Yeah, like I'm gonna close my eyes around you," Elenor sniped.

"As you wish. This will be bright. I assure you this is not an attack."

Bright light flooded Elenor's vision, but her eyes were far from human and it lasted for only a single moment before the room came into view. The room was massive, at least a hundred feet long and forty feet wide. To Elenor's right was a large fireplace with a deep brown fur rug in front of it. Two large armchairs upholstered in leather that cracked at the corners flanked the carpet. The deep brown leather was grey in places, showing the age of the furniture. The walls were made of irregular stones mortared together with deep grey cement of some sort.

The rest of the space was taken up by large work tables that extended the length of the room. Six rows of them lined the room, including two pushed against opposite walls. Each table was covered with an organized variety of equipment and bric-a-brac of every description. Elenor started to walk down the aisles between the tables, but out of the corner of her eye, she caught sight of an older man sitting in one of the chairs.

He had a neatly trimmed beard and shoulder length hair, both stormy grey in color. He had deep green eyes flecked with hints of glowing gold. He wore dark blue robes made of a shimmering fabric that almost seemed like it was made of metal. The robes were belted with a simple rope of bright purple that Elenor thought might be silk as it lacked the metallic texture of the robes. His feet, poking out from the hem of the robe, were bare. He had a warm smile and he had tented his fingers in front of himself.

"Hello, Elenor. Please, come and sit down. I feel we need to talk."

"If you didn't know that he was trying to kill me, why did you say in the event that I survived?" Elenor asked and the man shrugged.

"You, as in new Callers."

"You look like a real person."

The man chuckled. It was warm and rich, a true sound of pleasure. "I was, once, he, but now I am only a shadow left behind just in case what has happened, happened. Have you seen any of the Infected yet?"

Elenor nodded. "I was there when you… your… I was there when it happened. One of the Infected did it."

"That seemed the most likely reason that my previous incarnation wasn't the being of superior skill to open this Port. How did you gain your skills?"

"I haven't yet. I'm still learning."

"Who could possibly be teaching you?"

"Her name is Helen. I don't know what she called herself a thousand years ago."

The man's eyes narrowed. "The Iðunn?" he whispered.

"I don't know."

"No, it is her. Her Relic keeps me from seeing her but her Aura is unmistakable." He watched her for another moment. "Elenor, I promise I am completely incapable of harming you. This place is real but I am not physical. Look." He held out his hand in front of the roaring fire, where see through it to the fire beyond.

After a moment, Elenor crept into the chair, slowly taking her eyes off of him for only a single moment to spin herself around so she could sit comfortably.

"Is Helen alright?" Elenor asked.

"I assure you, she is in no danger from me. I was never her match, even when I was alive, though you are most certainly in danger from her."

"I don't believe you," Elenor replied, and the ghost of the Merlin shrugged.

"I do not require you to. But, I think you misunderstand. I do not mean any sort of immediate danger. You do not know who she was before."

"What do you mean?"

"I cannot reveal that information to you yet," he said, and Elenor bared her teeth in what could only generously be referred to as a smile.

"I'm not some sort of genius wizard like you and Helen, but I know when I shouldn't trust someone."

"You shouldn't trust me." He was frank, and then he made an odd gesture, waving his hand over his shoulder. "If I were to tell you what you want to know, it could put you in even more danger."

"If you aren't going to tell me anything, then why did you bring me here?" Elenor's annoyance made her lisp far more pronounced.

"There is plenty that I can tell you. I am sure Helen has noticed there are drastic changes from our time. I have some small leads to the answers of that mystery."

"I think you should be talking to Helen," Elenor pipped.

The Merlin shook his head. "She would never trust me, not even a shadow of me."

"I decided when I came in here that I don't really want this. When Helen told me I could probably transfer my Writband,"

The Merlin was shaking his head. "Unfortunately, that is not going to work for you."

"Helen," Elenor started, but the Merlin interrupted again.

"I'm sorry to tell you this, Elenor, but Helen is being optimistic. She is incredibly skilled, but there are things even she does not understand. One of them is the nature of your Writband."

"And what do you know about it?" Elenor didn't mean to sound abrasive, but her words grated.

"Only what I see, but I will not ask you to take my word for it." He extended a long, cultured finger at her chest. "The innermost Surge of your writband tells the story. Your writband, unlike mine, Helen's, or any other

Caller that came before you, was imprinted directly onto your immortal soul."

"What does that mean?"

"We have not the time for me to give you the complete explanation. In simple terms, it means that your writband cannot be transferred to another Caller."

"Does it matter if the writband isn't finished yet?" Elenor asked, thinking immediately of Mateo.

"It does. The bonding process of your writband, or another like it, will not finish until the transformation is entirely complete. The adjustment of the body to receive the power intended is performed by the two anterior Surges of the band. The interior band formed last, did it not?"

Elenor nodded.

"As I said, do not take my word for it. Approach Helen with the information. The only thing I do ask is that you do not tell Helen about me right away. It would be dangerous for both of us if she finds out about my existence. Take this to explain your new knowledge of your writband." The remnant waved a hand over his shoulder and a small black leather notebook floated from a shelf behind his chair which held many books with no titles on the spine.

"What is it?"

"This is a comprehensive treatise on the form, structure, and nature of writbands, and extrapolations of writbands that might convey greater power. Once she reads it, she will confirm what I have told you. When she does, and I have built some small trust, you can come back and we can talk more openly," the remnant informed.

"What about the Infected?"

"Ah, I did promise leads, did I not? I assume Helen is baffled with their behavior?"

Elenor nodded in response. The remnant tilted his head back and looked up at the ceiling.

"Not much time before the Iðunn finds her way here. I'll give you one thing you can prove and one relief."

"Relief?"

"Yes. It will relieve you to know that the Infected will not spread like they did in our time. I was only able to make a small study of the Infected you fought, but I learned something important. The criteria for who can contract the Bane has changed quite drastically. It will now only pass to potential Callers who have not had any sort of contact with the Writ. This greatly limits how quickly it can spread."

"And the other thing?" Elenor prompted.

"The first piece of the puzzle." He held out his hand to her as if to shake. She drew back her claws and put her paw into his hand.

NC 17, EPOCH 18417.357

The sun slipped below the horizon, drawing closed the shortest day of the year. The Chorus hummed in Osiris' ears as he held his Striker loosely in shaking hands.

"And, into the past," he whispered. He struck the etched steel bracelet on his right wrist against the relic stone bar at the center of his Striker and the familiar melodic hum pushed away the Chorus until its hum was all that remained. Osiris had spent years preparing this Surge, and the complexity was such that even a single mistake would taint the result. He had to know why every other attempt had failed.

The world began to run backwards around him. At first, he could see things moving in opposition to the timeflow, but quickly it became only a blur as the Surge accelerated his perception of time. Within moments, years were passing in seconds, and the world around him became such a maddening blur of color and muted sound that he was forced to close his eyes.

When the light against his eyes waned to stability, he opened them. The haste with which time passed had mutated his vision into a singular grey plane of unrecognizable motion.

The sounds of the world, muted by his Surge, became a continuous roar of white noise.

Without warning, everything vanished. Osiris stared for a long moment as tiny streaks of white stretched across the blackened canvas of his vision. He slowed his playing until he could recognize the streaks of white as stars.

It, was, impossible.

His Surge had been designed to move his consciousness of reality not only through time, but space as well. It attached his consciousness to the Chorus of the Earth itself. Within the time-space his consciousness now inhabited, there was no Earth. There was no solar system. He turned, even as he continued his playing, until he recognized the burning orb of the sun. For a long moment, he thought he had gone too far into the past.

His hand dipped into a pouch hanging from his belt and came out holding a sphere of clearest glass. He could not stop his Surge for long or he would lose this vision, but there was time for this. He tapped the crystal sphere with his bracelet, producing a wavering melodic chime, and light effervesced from the surface.

When the bubbling light calmed, an image was projected in light into the air above the sphere. It was an image of the night sky. He held the sphere up to his view of the stars and it quickly flashed through star patterns until the image matched the stars he was looking at in the sky. A moment later, maintaining his Surge to view the past no longer mattered. The star stone revealed something he had already begun to fear. He was viewing not trillions of years into the past, but only a few thousand turns about the sun. A scant eighteen millennia ago, their Earth had not existed.

NC 17, EPOCH 19915.14

When Elenor emerged from the vision, the shadow of the Merlin was gone. In the middle of her paw was a tiny marble of the deepest black. She stared at it for a long moment, wondering how she would prove the vision he had shown her.

The door at the other end of the room burst open and Helen strode through, holding the blazing short sword in her fist.

"Finally! This place is a disjointed dimensional space. Definitely the Merlin's work. Are you alright?" Helen asked.

Elenor nodded. "I found some things." She looked too the bookshelf that had disgorged the journal sitting on the arm of the chair next to her, but it had vanished. She blinked, but then looked back to Helen. She thought for a second about telling Helen everything, but she remembered that she had not known Helen for very long. Helen, though, had been planning this for over a thousand years. She had earned some trust from Elenor by teaching her, but she had refused to explain why she was helping.

"The notebook looks like it has a bunch of information about writbands. When I picked up this marble, though, I saw a vision. I think it was about Osiris."

Helen stared for a long moment before she spoke. "This is definitely the work of the Merlin. I found several Relics here of his make, not to mention something even more odd." She reached out to take the marble.

"It showed me the vision as soon as I touched it," Elenor cautioned.

Helen picked it up and her eyes went out of focus. She stood there for three long breaths before she blinked. She stared at the marble. "This memory was taken directly from Osiris' mind. How did the Merlin get it?"

"No idea. So what did you find?"

In answer, Helen produced a square wooden box slightly larger than a standard sheet of paper. She flipped open the lid to reveal a single sheet of thick, creamy vellum. In beautiful calligraphy written with golden foil, a simple document was penned. Helen recited the document, which she had memorized as she did almost everything else.

"To the first Bearer of the Writ to imprint upon this document I, Myrridin Wyllt, the Merlin, in the event of my death, bequeath all possessions in my ownership at the time of my death. Let this document represent the absolute proof of ownership of those things I have left behind."

It was signed with a flourished signature in deep crimson ink the color of blood.

"Is that?"

"He signed it in his blood, imprinted with the absolute authority of his will. If you touch this, you will own everything he owned."

"Why not you?" Elenor asked.

Helen shook her head. "I am not a Bearer. It would not function for me. And while Myrridin Wyllt and I disagreed on many things, I will never deny his skill as a Caller. With what is here, you can learn a great deal that I cannot teach you, Elenor."

Elenor reached out tentatively towards the paper. Her paw dipped into the box. The ground shook, overturning the chair and dumping Elenor to the floor. Helen snapped the box shut, keeping her feet somehow. She swayed with the movement of the earth beneath her and Elenor watched in awe from her huddled position on the floor.

"What's going on and how are you doing that?" Elenor yelled.

"The Infected is trying to get in!" Helen laughed, sounding at least slightly unhinged.

"You're insane!" Elenor squeaked. The shaking slowly subsided and Elenor stood up.

"I just know some things that you do not. No amount of force will allow the creature to pass into this space. It could technically destroy the entrance. That, however, is a technicality only. Even with your ability, you could not destroy a construct like this one. Gates like the one that accesses this space are absolute reality. No one can destroy them by force because, by their very nature, they enforce their own reality."

"So why did the whole place shake?" Elenor got back to her paws.

"It disrupted the connection to this space. It will not be able to do that again. It can stand out there all night smashing itself against the gate and we are going to let it." Helen held out the document box again, lifting the lid.

"We gotta leave sometime," Elenor said.

"We do, but once you own this space, you can make new gateways to it and place them anywhere you want."

"I don't,"

Helen frowned. "I realize that you do not want to be involved. You *are* involved, though. So, at least for now, can we stop fighting over this?" Helen held open the box.

A pit formed in Elenor's stomach. The Merlin had told her that there was no end in sight for her. All she had left now was helping Mateo. She put her paw down on the paper, next to the Merlin's signature. Light flared from beneath the pads of her paw and a print was left behind on the paper. The world vanished and blackness closed around Elenor.

25

"PUSH"

Mateo sat at his desk, scribbling on the thick cardstock he used for comic pages. His pencil traced a wavy pattern onto the brick wall he had already drawn, like someone had painted a sound wave onto the bricks.

He tapped his pencil on the markings with irritation. He had no idea where the idea for the markings was coming from, and it was at least the tenth time he had doodled the same marking somewhere in his comics without really thinking about it.

Just at the edge of his vision, Mateo noticed illumination near the roof of his room and froze. A band of verdant light moved across the top of the wall. The color was unmistakable, and Mateo shook slightly as he turned his chair to face the window. He pushed himself slowly out of his chair and crept on shaking legs across his room to peer out of his window.

The street was empty. He looked at the clock. Even past midnight, the street had only ever been empty one other time in his memory. Down the street, crouching over the evidence of a shattered building in the process of being cleaned up, was a small figure. Long, straight hair brushed the ground where she crouched, though in the light of thousands of brilliant green wires, it was impossible to tell the color.

Mateo snatched his phone from his pocket and furiously typed a text message to Elenor. He was barely able to type it correctly as he could not peel his eyes from the girl. She stood up, dusted off the front of her simple jumper dress, and turned slowly in a circle. She couldn't have been more than ten years old.

She stopped turning the moment she faced his building. As she began to walk towards the building, the glowing threads vanished as they contracted around her body. She paused before crossing the street. When she reached his side of the street, she looked up and her burning green eyes locked onto his.

Mateo backed up and his chest burned as if someone were holding a hot pan against his shirt. He looked down and ran his hand over his chest, but nothing seemed amiss. The burning continued, and when he looked back, the little girl was gone. His phone rang. He almost dropped the slate of glass and aluminum in his rush to answer it.

"Hello?" He didn't take time to see who was calling.

"Mateo, are you all right?"

"Elly?"

"No, Elenor isn't awake right now. This is Thia."

Mateo paused, not sure how to proceed. "I think one of the Infected is outside. There was a little girl with glowing green wires floating around her looking at the wrecked building down the street, then she came towards my building."

"Okay, slow down. We can't wake up Elenor right now. We are working on it. My mother is listening now."

"No sé qué hacer," Mateo complained.

A new voice came through the phone. "Do nothing, Mateo. I will be there in ten minutes."

A booming sound blasted through his building and the floor shook, causing objects to spill from shelves. His collection of hats tipped from his closet to spread across the floor.

"Mierda, the whole building just shook." The burning in his chest grew and he pulled the neck of his shirt open. Despite seeing nothing amiss, he hissed at the very clear pain.

"Mateo?" The voice from the phone seemed far away, and Mateo realized he had let his hand fall to his side.

- No sé qué hacer – I don't know what to do
- Mierda – Holy shit

"Sí, estoy aquí, pero my chest is burning. What does that mean?"

"It means I have to hurry and you have to move. That thing must know you're connected to all of this, somehow. Is there a fire escape?" Helen asked. Sounds of running footsteps came from her side of the phone call.

"Yeah."

"Get down it and into the street. Head straight for the park. I'll meet you before you get there," Helen said, and the sound of a car starting came through the phone. Tires squealed and Mateo put the phone on speaker. He grabbed his jacket and yanked on his boots.

"Will she follow me? Mi hermana está en el apartamento."

"I do not know, but it is the best advice I can offer. I will get there as fast as I can. Stay on the phone."

He hurriedly pulled his jacket on and grabbed his headphones before he slid open the window to his fire escape. He sat on the sill and yanked on his boots, barely taking enough time to tie them. He slipped through the window with practiced ease and began to run down the stairs. When he passed the second floor hallway window, he saw her. She pushed open the stairwell door at the exact moment he stopped to peek inside. Glowing green threads exploded from her body and shot down the hallway.

"¡Que Chinga!" Mateo yelled and dove to the landing. Glass shattered, falling over him, but his leather jacket protected him. He scrambled to the stairs on hands and knees and swung his legs over. He slid down the stairs to the next floor, and when he turned to head down to the last landing, the girl burst through the window. He jumped the last flight of stairs and hit the

- Sí, estoy aquí, pero – Yeah, I'm still here, but
- Mi hermana está en el apartamento – My sister is still in the apartment
- ¡Que Chinga! – Shit!

ladder at top speed. The counter weights zipped past him as the ladder dropped to the street. He jumped off and bolted towards the mouth of the alley. He turned left, his boots slapping on the concrete as he panted in terror.

"How do these freaks keep clearing the street?" Mateo shouted angrily as he ran for all he was worth. A screech of metal came from behind and he spun without thinking. The girl had made it to the street and the wires floating around her body had stretched down the street after him. They had whipped around a large steel post holding up a collection of street lights. It had sheared off and was falling directly towards him.

He dove to one side, narrowly avoid the light post as it slammed into the ground. Mateo tried to scramble away, but the cables used to hold up the street lights whipped around, slashing into his leg and sending him to the ground clutching at it. He tried to get up, but his leg folded under him – something had been severed.

He rolled over just in time to see the girl looming over him. Clouds of green threads spun through the air around her. A collection of them whipped into a spiral until it resembled a massive spike of glowing green energy.

"Bearer, you will not stand in the way of the hunger," the girl hissed. The spike drew back.

A bar of azure light passed through the girl's neck.

Helen slid to a stop a few feet past the Infected and spun to face the girl, holding the shining blade at a high guard position. The green threads vanished and the girl's head tumbled to the street just ahead of her collapsing body.

"Holy shit, ¡Carajo!" Mateo exclaimed.

"Not hardly," Helen said. "Get up. She will not stay down for long."

- ¡Carajo! – you killed her!

"No puedo, mi pierna."

Helen did not drop her sword. She kept it pointed unerringly at the body slumped on the street as she made her way to Mateo. She crouched next to him and looked at his wound for only a moment.

"Hamstrung. Keep your eyes on that thing. If it so much as twitches, I expect screaming."

Helen slid the sword into a sheath over her shoulder. When she finally looked fully at him, she froze. It lasted only a moment before she was hefting him over her shoulder. She ran for a tan Camry idling in the middle of the street. She yanked open the passenger side door and slung Mateo into the seat. He yelped when his leg banged on the edge of the seat.

"Sorry, we will get you fixed up soon." Helen slammed the door and bolted around the car. A second later, they were roaring down the street. Mateo looked back and he saw the girl. She was standing in the middle of the street, her blazing green eyes fixed on their car.

"She's back up."

"Unsurprising. These Infected apparently cannot be killed without destroying whatever magic is Infecting them."

"¡Chido! Do you know anything about this burning in my chest?"

Helen didn't respond.

"¿Qué pasa con mis padres y mi hermana?"

"I think they will be okay, but as soon as you are safe, I will go back and set up protections around your building that should confuse anyone trying to find you or them in connection with us." Helen slowed down as they got out of the neighborhood.

"What if she goes back right now?"

- No puedo, mi pierna – I can't, my leg
- !Chido! – Great!
- ¿Qué pasa con mis padres y mi hermana? – What about my parents and sister?

"Mateo, I can only do so much. I do not think she will go back to your building tonight, though. We think that if they are dealt critical damage, they lose access to their powers for a while because they need to use them to heal their bodies." Helen picked up her cell and took her eyes off the road for only a moment to hit a speed dial.

"Hello?" A man's deep voice came from her phone.

"Ellio, pull two guys off of the house. Go to the address I am about to text you and watch the entire street. If you see any of the Infected, you light them up. Get their attention and lead them out of the neighborhood."

"You got it, but we aren't going to be much good to you if we get picked up with automatic weapons in the city," he warned.

"I will make it go away. You are protecting a family until we can figure out how to deal with this problem. You won't have to stay long. I just need to make sure some folks stay safe for now."

"Alright. We're on it."

Helen hung up the phone and then handed it to Mateo. "Text your address to Ellio."

Mateo followed her instructions and then bent over to look at his leg. "I'm still bleeding quite a bit."

Helen clicked on the lights in the car and leaned over just far enough to see into the seat well. There was a sizable puddle of blood soaking into the carpet.

"Damn it, that is too much blood. It must have nicked an artery." She swerved onto the shoulder of the road and slapped the button that set the warning lights flashing on the car. She screeched to a halt, slammed the car into park, and then spun in her seat. She yanked a small black bag out of the back seat. A moment later, she was pulling a brilliant white leather strap out of the bag.

"Wrap this around your chest. When you pull it tight, you will feel a pinch. You are going to pass out for a minute or two. It will stop the bleeding."

Feeling slightly woozy, Mateo realized there was no time to argue. Helen pulled the car back out into traffic onto Eastern Ave. He worked the strap around his chest and threaded the strap through the odd sliding buckle. He pulled, and the moment he felt the pinch, the world faded away. Helen reached over and flicked the metal buckle of the belt with a fingernail.

Mateo jerked awake and looked around wildly. The city was still speeding by outside the car window. Brick buildings blurred by as his senses returned. He came to the realization that he was not breathing.

An edge of panic crept into his voice. "¡No respiro!"

"You are fine, I promise. The belt is a medicinal device that, for a very short period of time, pauses your bodily functions and acts as a life support system. Be calm."

Helen turned onto Interstate 95, heading south out of the city. It took about twenty minutes to reach the house in the woods. Mateo had no idea where he was as the drive had been a blur of speeding feats of driving that he normally would have only attributed to wheelmen in heist movies.

"¿Donde estamos?"

"About half an hour outside of the city. I purchased a house to keep Elenor close to her parents but get her a quiet place to train. The Infected cannot come onto the grounds."

Helen pulled onto a long driveway that curved into the woods just off of Mayapple Drive. It was a large two-story house, painted bright white. It had peaked roofs with shingles that looked brand new. Helen pulled into a two-car garage. The left-hand wall was

* ¡No respiro! – I'm not breathing!
* ¿Donde estamos? – Where are we?

covered in gardening tools, and a large zero turn lawnmower painted bright red was parked in the corner. There was a door on the right-hand wall, and in the back corner, opposite the mower, was a large black toolbox like Mateo had seen in his uncle's autobody shop.

"Why can't you wake up Elenor?" Mateo asked.

"It's nothing dangerous. She took on a writbound contract. It is taking a while for her to adjust to it. We expect her to wake up any minute." Helen got out and helped Mateo stand up. "You are going to feel weak while you are wearing that. It is normal and nothing to worry about."

The door to the garage almost burst from its hinges as Elenor came roaring through it.

Helen immediately stepped between Elenor and Mateo.

"Whoa!" Helen held up her palm flat in a stopping gesture. Elenor's entire body scrunched up as she slammed on the brakes, skidding to a halt before she could slam into Helen. "He is fine, but he is going to need some healing." Helen leaned down to whisper into Elenor's ear. "And we are going to have to have that talk about his condition right now."

"Pensé que estabas durmiendo," Mateo mumbled tiredly.

"I was until a few minutes ago," Elenor squeaked. She slid around Helen and oddly, she sniffed him like a dog as she walked around him in a circle.

"Elly?"

"Sorry. Helen told me that I don't use my nose enough because I was human once. She's right. I can get a lot of information about someone by smelling them." Elenor sneezed once, and then looked up from her inspection. "There is a lot of blood in the car and I can smell something inside of his wound. Not just blood, something else."

 • Pensé que estabas durmiendo – I thought you were asleep

"You are not ready for a Surge complex enough to replace blood," Helen warned. She knelt down to examine his wound. She fished an adder stone out of a pocket and looked through the hole at his leg.

"It is a sliver of the cable that cut him. Thia!" Helen shouted, and a moment later, the door swung open.

"Holy shit, what did you do?"

Helen rolled her emerald eyes. "Medical kit, please."

Thia disappeared back into the house. Helen took a folding chair from a collection of them standing against the wall and helped Mateo sit down. Thia was back within a minute. She handed over a large white plastic suitcase.

"Shouldn't we go someplace a little more…limpio…" Mateo looked around, realizing the garage was not just clean, but beyond spotless.

Helen chuckled. "Not our first time, kid. We have some toys that keep most of the house sanitized just for times like this."

"You guys get a lot of sucking chest wounds or something?" Mateo joked.

Helen cracked a grin. "One or two. This is going to sting."

Mateo gritted his teeth and nodded. He felt the tweezers probing the wound and pain shot up his leg. He clenched his teeth over a scream and then the pain intensified as he felt her pulling something from inside of his leg. He did not scream, but a deep, unhappy groan rolled forth from him. A moment later, the pain receded and Helen was holding up a thin wire about an inch long. Mateo took long, deep breaths.

"You ok?" Helen asked.

Mateo nodded. "Just need a second. Not nearly as bad as getting shot."

Helen looked at Elenor. Elenor nodded. She knocked the spines on the end of her tail against the

 • limpio - clean

concrete floor and a sweet pure chord filled the garage, pushing away all other sounds. Several notes fell away as the tone changed into music. It changed quickly into a smooth melody, containing a trio of notes rising and falling in a descending pattern.

Mateo hissed as his leg began to burn, and then tensed as the horrendous itching of rapid healing broke out across it. He had to restrain himself from scratching his leg furiously. The flesh pulled itself together and a moment later, the wound was gone, as if it had never been.

Elenor smiled, and even though it looked like she had a bear trap in her mouth Loony Tunes style, Mateo still smiled back.

Elenor's eyes tracked down to Mateo's chest, and then they went a little wide. Her head whipped around to Helen.

"You told me we had a few months!" Elenor snarled.

"We did. Considering the progression you saw, we did have months. I think his contact with the Infected gave the process a little push."

"Um, what're we talking about here?" Mateo asked.

Elenor narrowed her eyes at Helen. Then her ears fell, tears gathering in the wide glowing orbs as they turned back to Mateo.

"Mateo, we have to talk."

26

"THE BEGINNING OF A THEORY"

NC 17, EPOCH 19915.17

"Tengo que regresar a mi casa antes de mis padres show up, or they are going to freak," Mateo complained.

"If we don't talk, they're going to freak a lot more than that." Elenor's voice quavered with nervousness.

"¿Qué quieres decir?, Elly?"

Elenor took a deep breath then lifted a paw and touched a single claw to his chest. She hummed a little bit. The burning in his chest vanished and Elenor pointed the single claw behind him. He turned in his chair until he was looking into a small half bath. On the open door to the bathroom was a mirror.

In a ring on his chest were glowing orange wave patterns, just like the ones he had been scribbling in his comics for months. They were broken up into little pieces, but it was clear that they were meant to make to make up circles. Three concentric circles in all.

Elenor hopped down off her chair and sat next to his. She touched her own chest and hummed the same tune she had for him. Three fully complete rings, glowing brightly in blue on her chest.

"¡Carajo! Do you mean?" Mateo whispered. Elenor nodded, but it was Helen that spoke.

"Judging with how far your Writband has progressed, you don't have long before the transformation will begin."

"How long have you known?"

Helen jumped in to explain. "A few weeks. I did not feel it was a good idea to alarm you until we had actual answers for you. I was planning to let Elenor tell you

- Tengo que regresar a mi casa antes de mi padres – I need to get home before my parents
- ¿Qué quieres decir? – What do you mean
- ¡Carajo! – Holy Shit

after this week, when we were certain how fast it would progress."

"And you screwed it up?" Mateo sounded a little angry.

"No. Your progression had been static for several weeks. That is why we were ready to tell you. Once we were sure we would have had the option to give you a way out."

The glowing ring on his chest and Elenor's faded away and Mateo turned in his chair again to face Helen and Thia. Elenor climbed back into the chair next to him.

"A way out?" Mateo asked curiously. He was watching Elenor but responded to Helen.

"Yes, we didn't want to scare you until we were sure precisely what was going to happen, and if we could help." Helen advised. Mateo's eyebrows climbed as his eyes opened from narrowed slits.

"Wait," Thia started. "did you think we were keeping it from you until it was too late?"

"I wouldn't ever do that. I wanted to tell you right away!" Elenor squeaked.

"For a second, that's sure what it sounded like," Mateo said. "I didn't think you would do that, Elenor, but…" Mateo looked back to Thia and Helen. He thought they would be angry, but Helen just raised a single brow curiously.

"Smarter than you look, I see?" Helen asked, brows arched with respect.

"I've had a lot go down in my life." Mateo said, then looked down at his hands spread on the tabletop.

"Well, there was more to my decision, as well. I cannot do what needs to be done to transfer your writband to someone else. The only one I know of who has that power now is Elenor."

"If I don't get rid of this," he touched his chest, "Yo seré un…" He paused and looked at Elenor. He would

• Yo seré un – I'll turn into

not call her a monster.

"Yes," Elenor answered.

"¿Y seré mágico como Elly?"

Helen nodded. "You will, though I suspect your powers and abilities might be slightly different than hers. However, considering the situation, it is possible you would become exactly the same kind of creature she has."

"What do you mean?"

"It is only a guess. I think you were likely drawn together by your shared power. Elenor transformed years ago, but considering the progress of your writband and when Elenor said you met, you were already well on your way to your transformation long before that. Likely months. The power you were already developing drew you together with her."

Mateo knew then. He knew the exact moment that it started. The moment he had started his latest comic book over the summer. The first time he had doodled the wave pattern on the cover page of the comic book.

"La última semana de Junio. The wave patterns." Mateo touched his chest. "I started drawing them in June and they look exactly like this."

"That seems about right, considering how you were progressing before the Infected showed up tonight," Helen said.

"That woman," Elenor hissed.

"No, it was not her. It was a child. A little girl, maybe ten years old," Helen replied. "We can deal with that later. This is more important. We do not have long now. I thought I would have months to prepare, Elenor."

Elenor nodded.

Helen went on. "Thia, are you still prepared to accept his writband?"

- Y seré mágico como – And I'll get magic like
- La última semana de Junio – The last week of June

"I am."

"Can I even play this Surge?" Elenor asked.

"¿Y si quiero quedármelo?" It came out as a whisper so at first, no one heard Mateo say it.

"That is all up to you, Elenor. I can't say if it is doable or not. It is a difficult composition, and you will have to adjust it on the fly for the Chorus here."

"What if I want to keep it?" Mateo's voice was louder this time, but they still didn't really hear him.

Elenor stared at him. "What did you say?" she squeaked.

Everyone went quiet as Mateo spoke again. "I said maybe I want to keep it."

"What?!" Elenor's voice went into ranges that were barely audible to the human ear.

"I know you might think I'm loco, pero Elly, you can do real mágico. Even if there weren't real monstruos that we are going to need powers like that to fight, do you know how many amazing things we can do with that?"

"Like what, Mateo? Do you think anyone is ever going to let you get near them again looking like this? What about your parents?" The questions poured out of Elenor so fast they tumbled over one another.

"Quiero a mi familia Elenor, but this is the kind of thing that only ever happens once. If I pass this up, maybe I can do some good things with my art. Inspire a few people. Pero con esto, I can do anything. Maybe I can't fix the world, but I can make sure that a whole lot of kids in LA never have to face down some pendejo with a gun again."

- ¿Y si quiero quedármelo? – What if I want to keep it?
- loco – crazy
- pero – but
- mágico – magic
- monstruos – monsters
- Quiero a mi familia – I love my family
- Pero con esto – But with this
- pendejo - fucker

"Am I the only sane thing left on this planet?" Elenor's exasperation punctuated each word.

"What dream did this make you give up, Elly?" Mateo's insightful tone brought tears to Elenor's eyes.

"All of them!" Elenor snarled.

"I didn't get to have dreams because of this! I didn't know what I wanted to do and I never got a chance to find out because of this fucking horror show!" Tears dripped through her fur as she yelled.

"Oh, Elly." Mateo got out of his chair and put his arms around her, holding her as she cried.

"I lost all my friends and I couldn't even see my parents for two years." She sounded lost, hopeless.

Thia leaned over and stage whispered to Helen. "I didn't even know she could curse."

Elenor snorted a sobbing laugh. "Screw you!" she squeaked. "I never had a chance. There was no one there besides my parents, and I was terrified what might happen to them if they kept trying to protect me." She looked up to Helen. "Why did this happen to us?"

"I said over Christmas that I had a theory, but I do not have even a fraction of the pieces to this puzzle to be sure. It is really only the beginning of a theory."

"¡Cuéntanos!," Mateo affirmed.

"I think what is happening to you is a reaction to the Infected becoming active again. That band on your chest is called a Writband. The Writ is like a blueprint for reality itself. When you, Elenor, or anyone calls a Surge, what you are doing is temporarily overwriting a small piece of that blueprint. A long time ago, a man devised a way to permanently overwrite part of the entire blueprint and killed a lot of people in the process. We stopped him, but I think the damage was already done. I knew that in time the Writ would fix itself if we just left it alone, but my partner at the time did not agree. I think that what he did trying to correct the

• ¡Cuéntanos! – Tell us!

problem might have caused the reaction in the Writ that you are experiencing now."

"No entiendo. What does this," Mateo touched his chest, "do?"

"It is what gives you the power to make music that changes reality. It is like an access key to the Writ."

"But it does more than that?" Mateo asked.

Helen nodded. "A long time ago, it did not. We earned these Writbands after many years of training back then." Helen pulled down the front of her shirt just far enough so that he could see the two rings of sound waves on her chest.

"¿Solo dos circulos?"

"The third Surge inside of your band is what causes the transformation. We didn't get bands like that from the Writ, and it appears that it is now a necessity for accessing the power, since my abilities have never returned."

Mateo turned his attention back to Elenor. She seemed to have cried herself out. "¿Estás bien, Elly?"

Elenor pulled away from Mateo reluctantly. She wiped her lantern eyes with the back of a paw. "No, I'm not okay. None of that explains why it picked someone like me. I've never had to fight anyone."

"Maybe that <u>is</u> why you were picked," Helen broke in, and Elenor's face scrunched up with confusion. "One of the most important things we used to look for in apprentice Callers was someone who had no bad habits. Someone who was something of a blank slate. Someone with wonder in their heart and nothing holding them back that they had to unlearn. Not quite ready to pick their path yet. Someone just like you."

"But," Elenor started, and Helen just shrugged.

- No entiendo. – I don't understand.
- ¿Solo dos circulos? – Only two circles?
- ¿Estás bien – You ok
- pero – but

"It is true. Lots of our apprentices did not know what they wanted to do. We helped them find out."

"I'm ok with four legs and a tail, pero I might need some help con mi familia," Mateo said. "How do I tell my parents I'm not going to be a comic book artist, I'm going to be a multi-eyed magic monster? Is that even a profession?"

"Well, I think it would be best to bring them here, let them meet Elenor, and explain to them what is going to happen. I think that we can accelerate your transformation so your family sees it happen. It might help them stay convinced that you are still you. It might be easier to tell them a small lie, but that is your choice."

Mateo narrowed his eyes. "¿Qué tipo de una mentira?" Mateo was still somewhat suspicious.

Helen held up placating hands in a calming gesture. "A very small white lie. It might be better if you do not tell them this is a choice. I do not know your family but I know people. It may be easier for them to understand if they think this will happen no matter what you do," Helen suggested.

Mateo thought about it for a minute. It was not completely a lie. If he hadn't met Elenor, Helen, and Thia, it would have happened anyway. Finally, Mateo shook his head.

"No, I'm not going to lie to mi familia. I'm asking a heck of a lot out of them. Can't start that with a lie."

Helen nodded. "Alright. Well, they already know something is going on with you. So, we will have to figure out how to break this too them gently."

"Gently?" Elenor blurted. "This," she gestured to herself, "is going to make them shit out their brains. Are you really sure about this, Mateo? You know that if you let this finish there's no way to go back."

- con mi familia – with my family
- ¿Qué tipo de una mentira? – What kind of lie?
- mi familia – my family

"Honestly, Elly, more than I have been about anything in my life," Mateo said, then to Helen, "Pero what do you mean they already know something is going on with me?"

Helen chuckled. "They are your parents, kid. They always know when something is going on, even if they do not tell you so."

"Va, pero I'm not sure having mis padres come out here es un buen idea."

"Elly <u>is</u> scary like a horror movie ate a baby made of LSD," Thia quipped. Elenor stuck her tongue out at Thia, who grinned and then went on. "Still, I'm sure we can talk your parents down off the ledge, Mateo, but there is going to be some screaming." She chuckled.

Elenor sniffed loudly, sneezed, and then actually giggled. "It's almost like you think I haven't figured out by now that if nightmares had nightmares, they would be of me," Elenor deadpanned. Mateo laughed and Elenor swiped a paw at his head.

"Bet you're scarier looking than me when it's all done. Girls are always prettier."

"Yeah, speaking of that, is there any way I can have at least a little say over what I look like?" Mateo asked.

Helen shrugged. "Maybe, but I highly doubt it. I recently came into possession of a book that might let me safely make some alterations to your Writband, but it would be extremely dangerous."

"Just sort of hoped I would still be able to do some kind of art. It's kind of my thing," Mateo said.

"I think you'll be fine. Elenor's paws are a lot more dexterous than they look when she's walking on them," Thia said.

Elenor lifted one of her front paws and wiggled the toes, showing off her opposable digit. "I can do most

- Pero - But
- Va, pero - Okay, but
- mis padres - my parents
- es un buen idea - is a great idea

things. Really small things are tougher than they used to be, but I wasn't planning brain surgery as a career path anyway."

"The Writ needs the help of powerful predators. I doubt it will leave you unable to function considering it will want you to be comfortable with your new body. It doesn't think like a person but it is intelligent."

"Predators, Elenor. Humans on our own are not nearly dangerous enough for whatever the Writ has in mind for you."

"You seemed to do ok with that sword you had," Mateo said.

"Someone can take that sword away. I'd love to see someone try to run off with Elenor's claws and spines, or whatever natural weapons you end up with, Mateo," Helen countered.

"How long do I have before this thing is done?" Mateo touched his chest.

"Considering that I can see the Surge forming literally as we speak, you might have a day. Probably less," Helen advised.

"Guess I better make a phone call. Can I get the address here?" Mateo fished his phone out of his jacket pocket. "And I should probably get a new pair of pants. Si mi Mamá sees all this blood, they won't listen to anything unless they take me to the hospital first."

 • Si mi Mamá – If my Mom

27
"ONE CHANCE"

NC I7, EPOCH 19915.17

Mateo put down the phone as they sat around the dining room table in Helen's house.

"They are coming but I think they are pretty freaked. That kid wrecked part of our building and then apparently mi hermanita saw me running off down the street." Mateo grumbled in a way only siblings would recognize.

"Stop scratching your chest," Thia said. She had told him to remove his shirt and then sat with a pencil, her hand racing across the page like the head of a printer as she drew the Surges of his writband.

"How are you doing that?" he asked as he pulled his hand away from his itching chest.

"When you learn to hear the Chorus, you get abilities that mundane folks don't have. Abilities like this," Thia explained as she scribbled on the large sheet of paper. "This is hard for me because I haven't had a lot of practice creating my own Surges. Mom says that if I do this, I might be able to use what I learn from your Writband to get one of my own."

Elenor had gone outside after Mateo had made the phone call to his parents, and now she returned through a door on the other end of the kitchen.

"¿Te sientes mejor?" Mateo asked.

Elenor climbed into one of the comfortable padded chairs around the table, her spines, claws, and horns retracting into her body so as not to damage the it. She turned herself around until she was sitting on her back with her tail trailing off front of the chair. Mateo noticed that the underside of her body was not fur, but rather dark slabs of what looked like black plastic. The bands

---

- mi hermanita – my little sister
- ¿Te sientes mejor? – Feeling better?

were like overlapping armor plates and ran from her chin all the way to the base of her tail. He turned away before he looked too closely at her underside, but realized he had already seen everything there was to see. There were no genitals on her body, which was probably why she felt so comfortable exposing her underside.

"I don't know. I thought I was getting more comfortable with this, but to think that this might actually be the thing I was looking for? It's weird," Elenor trilled. Mateo had so many questions, but he focused on what she said.

"I mean, that's sort of how I found art. After I got shot, it wasn't long before we got ready to move here, but I still had to ride through our neighborhood to get to school. The school bus stopped right next to the alleyway where I got shot," Mateo remembered.

"What does this have to do with your art?" Elenor didn't want him to have to relive any more of that than he had to. He had already told her once. Mateo held up a hand, telling her to wait for it.

"Pretty much everyone in the neighborhood knew I was a huge comic book nerd." Mateo paused and took a deep breath fighting back tears.

"You don't have to tell me."

"Está bien, this is a happy thing," Mateo said, then went on. "So, a couple of days before we moved to Baltimore, I was on the school bus on the way home. We stopped right next to the alleyway where it happened. I didn't want to look, but it's like a train wreck, ¿ya sabes?" Mateo swallowed as the memory went through him.

"On the wall of the apartment building, someone had painted a huge mural. It was the most amazing thing I had ever seen. It was me, in a Green Lantern uniform. They had painted gang bangers on the walls, shooting at

- Está bien – It's okay
- ¿ya sabes? – ya know?

me with bullets bouncing off me. I was wounded in the mural in the same spot I had been shot. Still, I was fighting and winning, and I knew. I knew that I could do that for other people too. That's when I knew that I wanted to be a comic book artist."

"That's amazing, Mateo. Did you ever find out who did it?" Elenor sniffed back the tears that were threatening to spill down her face.

Mateo shook his head. "I asked around in school a little, but no one would say who did it. We left two days later, but some of my friends still text me saying that someone kept repainting it whenever they cleaned it. Eventually, they just left it up."

Mateo took out his phone and swiped his finger across the screen, going through pictures of himself and his family. Finally, he came to a photo of an alleyway taken from the street. The buildings were brick and the painting on the wall was vibrant. Elenor didn't know much about comic books, but it was clear that the young man in the green uniform was Mateo.

"Okay, I think I have this as close as I can guess." She turned to call out, "Mom!" Mateo and Elenor both jumped. "Sorry, didn't want to interrupt, but I think from what I am reading of this Surge, a lot of your traits have been fixed already. There are probably a few things that can be changed." Thia looked up and smiled. "That was beautiful, Mateo."

"Gracias. So… how much am I going to scare the mierda out of everyone I know?" he half-joked.

"Well, I mean, probably a lot. But I think we are actually going to learn a lot from the fact that your Writband is still forming."

A moment later, Helen came in from the garage. "What have you found, Thia?"

"I think you were right about Elenor's writband

- Gracias - Thanks
- mierda - shit

having some sort of protection on it to keep us from deciphering how it works."

Helen sat down and started looking at the drawing that Thia had done. A few minutes of study later, Helen sat back and then stared at Mateo. She held up the adder stone to her eye and watched him for a few more minutes.

"I cannot fix my Writband with this, but for you, Thia, I can trigger the attachment of yours. You will transform. Are you still all right with that?"

"Stupid question," Thia said. "Do you see the trigger requirements, though? They're packed so tight. All those predatory characteristics are necessities. No wonder she looks like that." Thia gestured at Elenor.

"You can see the differences here, though. He will look much different from her." Helen pointed at various parts of the Surge drawn onto the page.

"Care to clue me in?" Mateo asked.

"I'm not sure how we can describe this. I don't think you understand just how much information is packed into that Surge on your chest," Thia noted.

"It looks like it begins with an animal, then modifies things from there. The animal it has chosen for you is some sort of mustelid," Helen speculated.

"¿Qué es un?," Mateo started, but Thia interrupted.

"In general, a weasel, but there is a pretty huge range in those animals and there are size modifiers here…" Helen began to mumble as she leaned closer to the paper that Thia had drawn on. "Extra limbs," Helen mumbled, and Mateo's face scrunched up with concern. "Ah, more surface area for Van Der Waals forces," Helen continued to mumble. "No eyes, that is odd." She started to trace the drawing with a finger. "Tentacles." She tapped her finger on the paper. "Oh, those will be your defense mechanism, like Elenor's spines." She glanced up and noticed the look on Mateo's face.

 • ¿Qué es un? – What is a

"What, kid? Did we not warn you what you were signing up for?" She gestured at Elenor, who stretched an ear-to-ear grin at him so full of razor sharp triangles that he shuddered.

"Okay, so you have some decisions you can make, but a lot of this is set already. I wouldn't be too concerned. From what I can see, this Surge is designed to perform extensive subconscious personality analysis to provide you with a form that you will adapt well to."

"Uh…" Mateo deadpanned.

"It reads your mind to see what you like to make sure you're comfortable with your new body," Thia simplified.

"Uh…" Elenor deadpanned the same way Mateo had, though much squeakier. She made a flailing gesture at herself.

"Are you physically uncomfortable?" Thia asked.

Elenor scrunched her face into annoyance. "No."

"And tell me, how long did it take for you to get used to that body?"

"Not long," Elenor ground out the squeak.

"Uh-huh," Thia sniped. "Obviously, going from one body to another is going to be a shock for anyone. The Writ is doing the best it can to give you what you need while also making you comfortable."

"Your human body would not have cut it for the amount of power I have seen you throw around on a whim," Helen impressed.

Elenor's head snapped around and she struggled momentarily to flip herself out of the chair.

"What is it?" Helen dropped the adder stone back into a pocket.

"The Infected are coming closer," Elenor said.

"I would not worry about it over much. The diffusion ring is twenty-five square miles. They are more likely to find an actual needle in a barn filled with needle stacks," Helen reassured.

"But what about Mateo's family?" Elenor inquired. That drew Helen up short.

"They couldn't possibly make that connection," Thia said, but Helen shook her head immediately.

"The girl knew what building he was in. She could make the connection," Helen hissed, and then she was up, running out of the door.

Fast as Helen was, Elenor was a blur that went past her as if she were motionless before she could even make it to the car. Mateo was still pulling on his shirt when the car peeled out of the garage, leaving acrid smoke in its wake.

"Think they even noticed we aren't with them?" Thia asked.

"Nel," Mateo said. "What are the chances we catch up with them?"

"Ever try building a snowman in Death Valley? It's like that," Thia jibed in response.

"Can you make my Writband go faster? Quiero ayuda."

"Mateo, even if I could, you wouldn't be ready. It would take time for you to adapt."

"I have one chance to get this right con mi familia."

"I can't. Only Elenor can do it," Thia said, and Mateo looked off in the direction Helen had speed away from the house. Thia got up and headed for the door. She took another set of keys off the door, and then went through a door into another room of the house. She came back a few minutes later carrying a small steel box in one hand and a set of keys in the other.

"Come on," Thia said. She flipped open the box and flicked the side of it with a fingernail. It vibrated with a low bass note that was almost inaudible. A green glow emitted from the crack in the box's lid. Thia went

- Nel – Nope
- Quiero ayuda – I need to help
- con mi familia – with my family

through a door at the opposite end of the kitchen, which turned out to lead into another garage. Here, there was another vehicle. It appeared brand new, and Mateo saw the Jeep logo on the back.

"Why doesn't Helen drive this? Es mucho más catrín como el auto."

"Because it's way nicer than the car," Thia chuckled. "My mother tends to destroy vehicles. A lot of vehicles. So, she usually drives something that won't be too expensive to replace. This Jeep is mine." Thia climbed into the Jeep, opened the garage door, and flipped open the small box in her hand. A green light like a flashing police warning whirred from the box.

Mateo could see that it was like a compass. The needle glowed green and pointed off to the east. Mateo noticed that the other side of the garage contained an industrial workshop of some sort. Many tools that he did not recognize littered the two car stalls past the Jeep.

Thia pulled out of the garage and sped off down the long, winding driveway from the house. She turned left onto Mayapple Drive and floored it. The Jeep's engine roared, and they tore off down the street.

"You know that getting too close to the infected might trigger your transformation, right? We might not even be needed," Thia said.

Mateo shrugged. "Gonna happen anyway, and I can't just sit by if those things are attacking mi familia."

"Alright, but I wouldn't suggest running in if my mother and Elenor have things under control." Thia spun the wheel to the left, turning onto Crows Foot Road. She went around a sharp curve and the glowing green needle spun to the south. Thia tapped the speed dial that said "Mom" on her phone. It rang several times before the line clicked open.

"Yes, Thia!" Helen shouted over a roar of sound like

* Es mucho más catrín como el auto. – It's way nicer than the car.

an explosion.

"Do you need us?"

"No! Do not bring Mateo any closer." Elenor caught the Infected before they could do anything. She has them on the run! Get back to the house so there is someone there when Mateo's parents show up!" The line clicked and the call ended.

Thia let out a relieved breath. "That's good." She slowed the Jeep, and pulled a U-turn. The sound of a gunshot caused Mateo to freeze out of reflex. Thia whipped the wheel around and the Jeep spun.

"Son of a bitch, who is that?!" Thia slammed the Jeep into park and slammed her door open. She grabbed Mateo and yanked him out of the Jeep, putting the vehicle between them and the shooter. Mateo banged his hip on the center console as he was dragged from the vehicle, letting out a sharp yelp. Thia dropped her phone in Mateo's lap.

"Call my mother. I'm going to take care of this puke." Thia ushered Mateo to the back of the Jeep to put the tires between Mateo and the shooter. Bullets pinged into the Jeep and one of the tires hissed as it was hit. Thia slammed the seat forward and a moment later, she was coming out with a sleek black pistol. She loaded it, racked the slide, and slunk towards the front of the Jeep.

Mateo was hitting the Mom contact on Thia's phone when she dropped to the ground. She laid on her side and aimed her gun beneath the Jeep. Two rapid shots cracked and there was a scream from the other side. The phone clicked.

"Thia, what is it?"

"Not Thia, someone shot up her Jeep. I think she just shot him in the feet. She's going to check on him now." Mateo relayed.

"Elenor is coming. She says she can hear the gunshots so you can't be too far away. I'll be along in a minute." Mateo looked up and saw Elenor barreling up the road. Her claws threw off bits and pieces of asphalt as she skidded to a halt next to him.

"You alright?" she pipped, and Mateo nodded.

"Did you get them?" he asked.

Elenor shook her head. "They ran as soon as I showed up."

Helen roared up in the tan Camry and jumped out. Thia came running back around her Jeep.

"Whoever I shot is gone. Has to be another Infected. There is no blood. How did they find us with the Diffusion Ring activated?" Thia asked.

Helen stared at Elenor for a long minute, her mouth turning down into a frown. "I am an idiot, that is how. I made a mistake. I will explain later. I will fix the Diffusion Ring as soon as we get back. We have to meet Mateo's parents. They'll be through here any minute."

Helen and Elenor helped Thia push her jeep off the road before they all piled into Helen's Camry. They just beat Mateo's family back to the house. They had been studying Thia's drawing for fifteen minutes when the sound of a car pulling up outside made them pause. The sound of a woman yelling Mateo's name rang out, and then a stream of angry Spanish.

Mateo took a deep breath and blew it out. "Nice knowing you all," he said as he pushed himself away from the table. "Yes Mamá!"

Helen got up at the same time and followed him out the door. There was a long stream of rapid-fire Spanish between Mateo, his mother, and Helen.

Elenor looked over at Thia. "Helen speaks Spanish?"

"And Japanese, Korean, French, Swahili, German, Hindi, Arabic, Tagalog, Polish, Russian, Dutch, Italian, Turkish, Tamil. I mean, I'm pretty sure she speaks every language in the world, but those are the ones I've heard her speak."

"That's actually cheating," Elenor said, and Thia

shrugged.

"Sure is. I only speak eight languages and I'm over a hundred years old. I think she even speaks a bunch of dead languages like Old High German, Old Norse, and Latin, though I've never caught her at it."

Elenor's ears perked up when she stared hearing English from outside.

"Elenor, can you come out here please?" Helen called.

Elenor eyes widened a little in apprehension. Every single bit of her exposed Relic retracted into her body. Even the spike-like rods that made up the Striker swirling around the point of her tail retracted back into the relic. Amazingly, the swirl of spikes itself did not vanish. Left behind were sparkling rods of crystal in ten colors, shimmering with iridescence.

Elenor stared at the crystal spikes swirling around the tip of her tail.

"You've never seen those before, have you?" Thia asked.

Elenor shook her head no. "They look so delicate. Should I worry about breaking them?"

Thia shook her head. "No, they are just as indestructible as your Relic, trust me, but I never expected them to look like an actual Striker. They're beautiful. Go on. Ears up, try to look friendly? This is your first shot to make people think of you as something other than a monster. Do good."

Elenor nodded and headed for the door. She reached up to the doorknob, hesitated for one long deep breath, turned the knob, and then pushed it open.

"Madre de Dios! ¿Qué demonios es eso?" The woman doing the screaming had long black hair in a perfect braid that she had pulled over one shoulder so it hung down her chest, almost to her waist. With deep

• Madre de Dios! ¿Qué demonios es eso? – Mother of God! What the hell is that?

chestnut eyes and a copper complexion that matched
Mateo's, it was very clear she was his mother. Short and
a little stocky, but not overweight, she wore a heavy
white down jacket over a knee-length dark blue jumper
dress with white leggings and sensible white boots.

Mateo confirmed it with his response. "Mamá! No
seas grosera a mi amiga!" Mateo hissed angrily.

His mother clucked her tongue sarcastically. "Tu
Amigo?! Eso no es un amigo, no es humano!" Her
husband seemed to be frozen in astonishment.

"But I used to be," Elenor pipped, and did her best
not to flatten her ears in displeasure when the insulting
woman screamed.

"¡Mierda! ¡Puede hablar!" Mateo's mother yelled and
jumped back towards their car, dragging her husband
with her. That was when Elenor did flatten her ears.
Mateo's mother tried to reach out and grab Mateo, but
he pulled away.

"Madre, esto es mi amiga Elenor, and she has saved
my life three times this week. Deberías ser amable con
ella."

His mother looked at him, and barked rapid fire
Spanish. "What do you mean? Saved your life from
what?"

"Maybe if you stop treating her like some kind of
monster, we'll tell you." Mateo spat back.

Finally, Mateo's father spoke up. "You do not
disrespect your mother like that," he said sternly. With
buzz cut hair and a wiry frame, it was clear that Mateo
took his build from his father, if not his hair cut. The
man looked somewhat military, wearing a dark blue

- Mamá! No seas grosera a mi amiga! – Mom! Don't be so rude to my friend!
- Tu Amigo?! Eso no es un amigo, no es humano! – Your friend?! That is not a friend, that is not even human!
- ¡Mierda! ¡Puede hablar! – Holy hell, it can talk!
- Madre, esto es mi amiga – Mother, this is my friend
- Deberías ser amable con ella. – You should be nicer to her.

polo shirt and black slacks with shiny leather shoes.

"It's only disrespect if isn't true. Elenor is my friend and Mamá is not being very nice to her," Mateo snapped.

"I'd like it if everyone could stop talking about me like I am not right here," Elenor sniped.

The back door of their dark green Subaru popped open and a young girl got out. She could not have been more than ten years old, with the same wiry build as their father. Unlike either parent, she had bright green eyes. Long chestnut bangs framed a heart-shaped face with the rest pulled back into two long pigtails. She shared their copper complexion, though, and her hair was a carbon copy of their father's.

"Why is everyone yelling?" she asked as she turned to push the door closed with both tiny hands.

"Sofia! Get back in the car! Right now!" Her mother ordered, but the little girl turned around.

"Why, Mamá?" Then her eyes hit Elenor, and she froze for a single moment. A broad smile spread across her face, and she squealed in delight.

"Wow! That doggie's eyes are all glowy! She's so pretty!" The girl ran towards Elenor, who sat still as a statue.

"¡Oye! Sofia, ¡vuelve aquí ahora mismo!" her mother snapped, and the little girl stopped.

"But Mamá! I just wanna pet the doggie!" Sofi stamped her foot angrily.

"¡Eso no es un perro! Vuelve en el auto ahora mismo!"

Elenor stood up and walked over to the upset little girl. "I'm not a dog, but you can pet me."

The girl's eyes went so wide when Elenor spoke that

- ¡Oye! - Hey
- ¡vuelve aquí ahora mismo! – get back here right this instant!
- ¡Eso no es un perro! Vuelve en el auto ahora mismo! – That is not a dog! Get back in the car now!

she feared the girl would hurt herself somehow. "She can talk!" the girl exclaimed with wonder. Elenor dwarfed the little girl as she padded closer, and for a moment, she thought the girl's mother would jump forward and grab Sofia. Elenor bent her head and pushed it under the girl's hand. The girl scratched behind her ears and it felt fantastic. "You're so soft!"

"Thank you," Elenor purred.

Mateo's parents exchanged a look and then stared at her and Sofia for a long time.

"Told you she was mi amiga," Mateo finally said.

Elenor narrowed her eyes at Mateo's mother. "But my name is not that, it, or monster. My name is Elenor." She stepped back from Sofia and Mateo stepped up next to her.

"And if you're going to think she is una monstruo, then pretty soon you'll have to think I'm one too." Mateo nodded to Elenor and she began to hum. Her writband appeared on her chest outlined in brilliant azure light. A moment later, as she kept humming, Mateo's writband brightened beneath his shirt until it was an almost finished ring of orange wave patterns.

* mi amiga – my friend
* una monstruo – a monster

28
"TWO"

NC I7, EPOCH 19915.17

Hours of explanation had made Mateo's parents no happier with what their son had chosen to do with his life. Even a deliberate demonstration of Surges from Elenor couldn't calm the argument.

"What about your scholarship?" his father asked.

"There are other people who need it more than I do," Mateo replied.

"If it is any consolation, your son will receive an education more thorough than any person in any college could ever expect to receive," Helen said.

"Like that is going to do him any good if he isn't..." The woman stared at the door to the back yard. Elenor had gone outside to play with Sofia and keep her occupied while the more serious discussion happened in the dining room.

"We are going in circles," Thia interjected. She had been sitting quiet contemplation while the argument had fired back and forth across the dark cherrywood dining table.

Mateo's mother narrowed her eyes at Thia. "Esto no le concierne."

Thia opened her mouth to produce a crushing retort, but Helen stood with fury. She snarled, "No, this is between you and your son. But let me be crystal clear. He told you the truth, that with Elenor's help, we can transfer his Writband to another, but make absolutely no mistake. That is not our decision." Mateo's mother opened her mouth, no doubt to spit some acerbation that it was her decision.

"Enough!" Helen shouted, her voice mutating into a roar that could never be produced by a human throat.

 • Esto no le concierne – This is none of your business

The glasses in the kitchen cabinets rattled and the windows shook, almost to breaking. It stunned everyone to complete silence. "It is not your decision either! You are acting like a child. Mateo is of sufficient age, and clearly of sufficient intelligence to make this decision for himself. He has made it plain that this is what he wants, and regardless of your anger and fear, neither I nor Elenor can change that. So, you are both left with but one decision."

"And what is that?" Mateo's father asked, far more evenly that his wife. Mateo's mother seemed almost ready to boil over in anger.

"Either you will choose to accept your son or you will not," Helen hissed. Then she shoved her chair out of the way and walked toward the kitchen door that led into the back yard.

"Sorry, Mateo," Thia apologized, and then she left the room behind her mother as they went into the backyard.

Mateo shook his head angrily. "I know what you want me to do, Mamá, but I've played it safe for five years now."

"No te loco. No puedes hacer esto. Ella es una monstruo y you want to be one too?!"

"You aren't listening to me at all." Mateo seethed.

"I'll start listening when you start making sense."

"Sense? You saw what she could do," Mateo said. His mother shook her head.

"We are not discussing this any more. Tienes dieciséis años and you are coming home with us." His mother slammed her hand down on the table. She stood up from the table, knocking over her chair, and swept out the door leading to the garage opposite Mateo.

His father watched him for a long moment. This was

- No te loco. No puedes hacer esto. Ella es una monstruo y – Don't be crazy. You can't do this. She's a monster and
- Tienes dieciséis años – You are sixteen years old

his father's way. He did not speak much, usually following their mother's lead, but when he needed to speak, he always seemed to know just what to say.

"Tu Mamá worries for you always, Mateo."

"Ya sé, Papá. Pero this thing,"

His father grinned in response. "It's crazy."

"Mamá doesn't believe in things like this," Mateo said. "But you always said, 'There is magic in the world if you just look for it.'"

"Sí, pues, no pensé que fuera literal." His father chuckled. "Mateo, you know how hard this is going to be, my hero maker?"

"Harder than anything, everything."

His father watched him for another long moment. He saw the resolve in his son. Strong like his Mother. "Then I will help your Mamá understand."

"Gracias, viejo." Mateo grinned.

"Old man, am I?" His father chuckled darkly in mock anger, shaking a fist at Mateo in jest. "No sé si tu Mamá will see this. You know she is like a fire, she will burn down eventually. I suspect I'll be sleeping rough for a while. But, I will come see, and if you end up anything like the size of that girl, you can expect tu hermana to want to ride you like a pony," his father joked.

Mateo groaned. "Worse things have happened."

"Don't be too mad at your Mamá, she never understood what you standing up to those punks meant. I, on the other hand, always knew that you would be standing up to bad people again someday." His father smiled in support.

- Tu Mamá – Your Mom
- Ya sé, Papá. Pero – I know Dad. But
- Sí, pues, no pensé que fuera literal – Well, I didn't think it would be quite so literal
- Gracias, viejo – Thanks Old Man
- No sé si tu Mamá - I don't know if your Mom
- tu hermana – your sister

"No estoy enojado, Papá, I just want her to understand."

"She will, it just might take her a while to get there."

"Gracias, Papá." Mateo came around the table and his father met him, putting his large hands on Mateo's shoulders.

"¡Anda!, go be a hero again." His father gave him a little push towards the door.

Mateo passed the kitchen and stopped at the door to the back yard. He slipped his feet into his sneakers, but didn't bother to tie them. He didn't think he would need them much longer. He pushed open the back door to find Elenor carrying his little sister around the yard on her back, fulfilling his father's prediction. His sister was giggling madly as Elenor ran across the yard so quickly that it could not possibly be safe. Then he saw that Elenor had somehow shaped her Relic so that a thick black strap that was clamped around his sister's waist. There was no way she could possibly fall off.

Elenor leapt into the trees in a blur of speed and his sister screeched in glee as Elenor flew through the air, bouncing from tree trunk to tree trunk. When she took a sharp turn, she caught sight of Mateo. She dropped to the ground and ran back to the yard, coming to a skidding halt beside him. She crouched down and her Relic contracted, melting away from Sofia so she could climb down.

"That was so fun! Can we do it again?" Sofia asked.

Elenor giggled. "If your mom and dad say it's ok."

Sofia laughed happily, replied "Thanks, Elly!" and then ran off toward the house. Her Father was coming out of the door.

"How much time do I have left?" Mateo asked and Elenor narrowed glowing eyes at him.

- No estoy enojado, Papá – I'm not mad Dad
- Gracias, Papá – Thanks Dad
- ¡Anda! – Go on

"I would say a few more hours. The inner band is more than half done," Helen responded as she returned to the back yard.

"Are there still things I can pick?" Mateo asked.

Helen nodded. "Not a lot, though. Your physical form is pretty fixed from what I can read of it." Helen and Thia were each peering through an adder stone at his chest. Helen continued, "Take your shirt off. We are going to need to see this better if you want to make any choices."

Mateo stripped off his shirt with a bit of a shiver. "Está bien, pero está maldito frío afuera."

"It won't be for long. Okay, so there are a few features that aren't fixed yet," Helen said. "Sensory organs," Helen mumbled as she traced her finger along the wave of the Surge.

"That's odd, no eyes?" Thia asked, and her mother nodded.

"Extra ears, too. His entire sensory profile is going to change if we leave this the way it is."

"Wait, look at this." Thia pointed to a different section of the glowing band.

Helen stared at it for a long time and Mateo started to get a little uncomfortable.

"Uh, I would like to have eyes, please?" Mateo said a little hesitantly.

"What we are seeing here are the beginnings of changes to your brain structure for a different kind of sensory input. I honestly think that if we leave this be, you will see better than any of us."

"But what does that mean?" Mateo asked.

"Give me a moment to trace this. Okay, so you'll have at least one extra set of ears, but possibly two. Either you'll have a combined sensory organ that is sensitive to both sound and electromagnetic energy,

- Está bien, pero está maldito frío afuera. – All right, but it's damn freezing out here.

or…" Helen trailed off.

"So, would I still be able to see things?"

"Oh sure. If this progresses as is. That's what my mother means. You'll have vision both based on both light and echolocation. The neural structure we're seeing forming on the leading edge here," Thia pointed to the still forming portion of the band, "shows a combination of neural input."

"Which means you'll be able to see everything around you at all times," Helen finished.

"Pero, no ojos?"

"I do not think you will notice, frankly, but we can reshape the neural structure to promote more human optic vision if you really want." Helen paused as she studied the band more closely. "Wait, that is…" she trailed off.

"What is it?" Thia asked.

"Elenor, come over here, will you?" Helen said, and Elenor quickly moved to her side. Helen put her fingers against Elenor's chest and traced her Writband. "I can't make it out completely through the twisting, but look here."

"It adapted from her Writband?" Thia wondered in amazement.

Helen nodded. "The Writ made adaptations because Elenor had trouble with her extra eyes."

"How can you tell?" Mateo asked. Helen held out the adder stone to Mateo, and he held it up to his eye. He could feel the stone vibrating in his fingers.

"See this section here?" Helen pointed to a spot where the wave pattern twisted like it was a string that had been tied into a knot. Right before that was a densely packed set of lines scribbled back and forth. Mateo could almost see what it meant.

"Yeah, what does it mean?"

"It's a lead-in that explains how Elenor's brain should

• Pero, no ojos? – Yeah but, no eyes?

handle the input from her extra eyes." Helen brought out the drawing of his Writband from a few minutes earlier and pointed at a section that was almost identical to the one in Elenor's.

"So, it's the same. Why won't it work the same way?" Mateo wondered.

"Because it doesn't look like this now. I can see where this form has faded, and a new one has replaced it. By the time your band is finished, this will be gone and the new form will be there. It's not an improvement so much as it has altered to give you the same advantages as Elenor, but in a way that it is easier for you to adapt to."

"How is having no eyes going to be easier to adapt to?"

"Because this way, the sensory input will be merged. There is no independent eye movement. I think you might end up a little near sighted in some instances, because I don't see any means of focusing like the eye does, but this is complex and I don't have time to decipher it all. It will be much less confusing for you."

"But you can change it?"

"We can, I am just not sure it is a good idea. This is millions of years of evolutionary biology adapted in an instant by the Writ," Helen warned.

"I'm, not going to be cute without any eyes," Mateo joked.

"It won't be as bad as you think. Still, your call. It's your life, kid. At least this'll be a lot less dangerous than Elenor's creepy ass gorgon eyes in her back," Thia teased.

"Thank you, so much," Elenor quipped.

"Look, having gorgon eyes that you barely know how to control freaks me right out. You could have literally killed me that first night with those murder orbs," Thia chuckled.

Elenor rolled her eyes. "Your aura would have protected you. Don't be a drama queen."

"For the record, I think not having any eyes is no creepier than Elenor's glowing demon eyes. I think you are all meant to be scary in some ways. Fear is one of the weapons of a predator, after all," Thia comforted.

"Those things didn't seem too afraid of Elenor," Mateo said.

Helen chuckled. "You didn't see them running from her earlier. Alright, so you want to leave the sensory input the way it is?"

Mateo thought for a long moment, then nodded. "¿Qué más?"

"Well, you can change your fur color, if you like. It seems set at a sort of dark brown with some hints of red, with a white patch on your chest."

"Can I pick any colors?" Mateo wondered.

"Sure, but I wouldn't suggest making your fur hot pink," Helen said.

Elenor giggled and Mateo flipped her the bird. "Nah, was thinking of going with black, with some hints of blue and green."

"Your body, kid." They talked it over a bit more. When they got to the part about tentacles and his tail, the discussion got a little more heated.

"Tentacles? Like an octopus?" Mateo was skeptical.

"It looks like these are supposed to act as your hands. Your paws won't be designed like Elenor's. You need bigger paws for more surface area to allow you to safely cling to things."

"Am I gonna have a tail?"

"Yep, and it'll be similar to the tentacles your relic will produce. But your tail is also where your Striker will be, like Elenor."

"So, is everything that is different just some upgrade from what Elenor got?"

 • ¿Qué más? – What else?

"No, I think some traits will be common to everyone who receives a Writband and some will be based on their personality. In the case of both of you, your tail is the best place to put a Striker," Helen explained.

"Also, your sight is not an upgrade. There are serious advantages to what Elenor has. Her extra set of eyes are a weapon unto themselves. You're different, that's all," Thia added.

"Va, Soy un poco nervioso." He noticed Helen was scribbling on a pad of paper. She held it up to show him the sound wave she'd drawn.

"Your Writband is far enough along for you to understand this. Is this what you want your fur to look like?" Helen asked, and Mateo opened his mouth to protest, but realized the Surge was perfectly readable to him. He held out his hand for the pencil and flipped it around. He erased part of the Surge, and purely on instinct, he scribbled a new piece into its place. Helen looked it over for a second and then nodded.

"Alright." She held it up for Elenor to see and she took a long moment to respond.

"Is he going to feel this?"

"Of course he is going to feel it. It is going burn like fire for a few seconds. Just call the Surge already. He will be fine," Helen urged.

Elenor looked at Mateo, but he just shrugged. "I gotta look like this for the rest of my life. I'll take a little burn."

Elenor looked around for a moment. She blinked, then nodded. Two spikes rose from her back and she lifted her tail like a scorpion ready to strike.

"Whoa, is mine going to look like that?" Mateo pointed at the glittering rainbow of spikes swirling around Elenor's tail tip.

Elenor swung her tail and it chimed against the

* Va, Soy un poco nervioso – Okay, I'm just a little nervous

spikes protruding from her shoulder blades. All of the sounds faded around them. Then, music was flowing around them in a complex weave of notes that sounded odd to Mateo. It was almost like he could hear every note individually, along with all of the notes at the same time as with normal music. Then his chest was burning as if he had been lit on fire.

"¡Hijo de puta!" Mateo hissed, but as Elenor's Surge faded away, the pain vanished.

"That better not have been mi hijo," Mateo's mother said, and he spun to see her angry face.

"No, Mamá. No era yo." Mateo lied quickly. She came closer, his Father trailing behind her.

"Are you sure about this, mijo?" his mother asked.

Mateo shook his head. "No, Mamá, I'm not sure." His mother's face scrunched into dissatisfaction. Mateo laughed a little. "Come on, Mamá, it's my whole life. I've never been sure about anything. I've always felt like I needed a backup plan ever since that day. At least until now."

"It's almost done," Elenor said, and Helen looked at him through the adder stone.

"She's right. If you don't want to wait for the transformation to happen over time, we have to accelerate the process now," Helen said.

She flipped the page in her sketch pad and began to scribble furiously again. What she held up after a few long moments of her hand zipping over the page were eight interlocking wave forms, each one drawn in a circle. Amazingly, as Mateo looked at it, he could see each piece of the Surge individually, even where the pencil scribbles overlapped.

"How are you doing that?"

"Which part?" Helen asked with a mischievous grin.

- ¡Hijo de puta! – Son of a bitch!
- No era yo. – Not at all
- mi hijo – my son
- mijo – darling

"The part where I can see the pencil marks underneath the other pencil marks?"

"I'm not, you are. I'll explain it all later, I promise." She held up the drawing to Elenor. "This, though, is an important part, so listen to me, both of you. Do you remember when I drew that Surge on Mateo's stomach to heal his wound?" They both nodded, and Mateo's mother opened her mouth to speak.

"Ah-ah! This is not time for interruptions," Helen said, and Mateo's mother snapped her mouth shut angrily. Helen turned back to her two charges. "Do not, ever, do what I did there unless you have absolutely no other choice. Written spell forms are only for research purposes. The way I used the wave form and Mateo's blood to guide your Surge is dangerous beyond all reason. I used the method because at the time, there was no other choice to prevent mistakes. Do you both understand?" Helen's stern question made the answer a foregone conclusion.

"Good. Now Elenor, call this Surge." Helen tapped the paper with a finger and Elenor squinted at it.

"Uh," Elenor said.

"You are going to catch flies with your mouth hanging open like that. At least act like you spent the last two months learning to be a Caller," Helen groused.

"Right," Elenor squeaked, and she squinted at the paper again, her brilliant glowing irises scanning back and forth. Elenor reached up and tapped a dull claw on the page. "This part means I need to be in contact with him while calling the Surge, but what's this scrunched up part of the wave?"

"Thia?" Helen held up the page as a learning opportunity.

"It's a modifier that indicates how much contact is necessary. You call that part differently depending on how much contact is needed to make the Surge function.

This one just means you have to be touching him in any way," Thia illuminated.

"Okay, the rest is pretty clear." Elenor padded over to where Mateo was. "Sit down. I suspect you're going to fall down if you stay standing. You're probably going to feel pretty weird when this is done. I know I did," Elenor pipped as she sat on her haunches in front of Mateo. Mateo sat down cross-legged in front of Elenor.

She reached out tentatively and put a claw on his chest. "Okay, here it goes."

She pulled the same trick with the spikes on her back. The pure tone of her Striker rolled out silence over everything. The voices around her faded as all eyes tracked the motion of her tail. Elenor played each of the eight notes of the Surge, the tones rising and falling in volume in a stately march. The glow of the rings on Mateo's chest intensified until it was blinding, in clear reaction to her Surge. Her continued playing and the rhythm of the notes intensified into a frantic melody that felt as if it were pressing everyone away from Elenor and Mateo with physical blows.

Each person surrounding them was forced to take a few steps away under the force of Elenor's calling. Elenor could still see the Surge forming on his chest. The two outer rings finished joining together as the speed of the music increased. The third Surge formed far more rapidly, as if whatever cosmic machine was printing it onto Mateo's chest had been charged with an overwhelming outpouring of electricity. Her Surge trailed off as she finished calling, and the moment the last note of the Surge died, the ends of the inner circle snapped together.

Brilliance exploded from Mateo, transmuting his body into a roughly human shaped silhouette of golden light. The light contracted until it was no longer shaped like a human. It slowly converged into a rough blob.

"Mateo?" His mother started forward, but Elenor turned, barring her way. She bared her teeth and the woman stepped back. Helen took Mateo's mother by the arm and gently pulled her back.

"He is fine. A shape change like this one is disconcerting and he won't be able to hear you or speak until it is completed. Don't rush right in as soon as it is finished. He will need instruction and he could inadvertently hurt anyone too near to him," Helen warned.

The shapeless golden silhouette did not last, soon elongating into a new shape. Changes sped up legs sliding out from the body, and a long whiplike tail extruded from one end. The skull expanded, then metamorphosed from a roundish human shape to an elongated one, giving the shape of his head a more predatory appearance. A short, powerful muzzle formed. Elenor blinked when massive, triangular ears popped out from the top of the head with what appeared to be wispy fur roughs around the edges.

Then she thought she had it wrong when the delicate waving filaments folded around the edges of the ears, like squares of delicate lace, creating a boxier shape. Then, a second, smaller set of ears emerged from the sides of the head below the first. These were folded and had a more ovular shape, with tuffs of iridescent fur at the tips. The left was green and the right, blue. Smaller than the first set, these did not change shape, but simply resolved as the light began to fade. Just as everything seemed to be stabilizing with the tail end of his body thickening a bit to support the strength of his rear legs, a third set of legs sprang from the body, forming halfway between the first and second pair.

Three pairs of legs folded neatly beneath his long body, and just as the brightness of his silhouette became bearable, two long tentacles slid out of his back, just between his first and second pair of legs. Then, the golden light began to fizz as if someone had pulled the tab on a shaken soda.

It flowed away from his body in bubbles of sunlight radiance, revealing a sleek form with midnight black fur. His paws were covered in what appeared to be socks of iridescent color so dark it could be mistaken for black. Elenor tilted her head and saw that oddly, the socks on his paws alternated, blue on some, green on others. The curve in his face where his eyes should have been was just a racoon-like mask of the iridescent verdant shading.

The pair of ears closer to the top of his skull were, as she had thought, large, sleek triangles with woven filaments of what appeared to be delicate fishing line waving around the edges. When he stirred, though, she realized the truth. The clear filaments folded around the edges of his ears, changing their shape to a boxy, rounded shape. They began to glow as the light hit them, and he lifted his head, twisting it left and right.

"Ok, eso es muy chido y muy raro al mismo tiempo," he mumbled. His voice was not precisely the same as it had been. It had gone up in pitch slightly, though not nearly as much as Elenor's had when she changed. Something about the quality of his voice had changed, however, and he sounded every bit as young as Elenor's did. "Oh man, is that my voice? Wait, is my voice bouncing off stuff?" His voice had started to sound slightly panicked.

"If you do not relax, you are going to cut holes in the house with those tentacles. I know you do not understand, but your tail and tentacles have bladed edges that I can only guess are every bit as sharp as Elenors spines and claws," Helen warned.

"Ay, lo siento," Mateo said, and his tentacles which

- eso es muy chido y muy raro al mismo tiempo – this is amazingly weird
- Ay, lo siento – Oh, sorry

had been waving about uncontrolled settled down.

"Elenor, can you give you some quick instruction on how to control them and his Relic? Should be the first thing we do," Helen advised.

"Can he?" Elenor asked. Helen nodded in response.

"One of the modifications to his Writband was that it properly linked his Relic to him from the start."

Elenor walked around Mateo's prone form. Like his tentacles, his tail was devoid of fur and glittered as if it were made of obsidian. It was segmented like a rat or mouse. Two of the segments shared the same coloration as the highlights in his fur, one dark, glittering blue, and one dark, iridescent green. Each was separated by a single black segment.

Mateo was picking up each of his legs and moving them around while lying on his stomach. "How am I supposed to walk with all of these things?" he complained.

"Okay, that's not fair. Your fur looks so cool and mine looks so stupid and plain," Elenor complained.

"You know you can use a Surge to change your fur colors, right? I mean, it's not quite as permanent as his, but no one else is going to know that," Thia stage whispered to Elenor as she passed.

"No, I didn't know that!" Elenor hissed.

"The task at hand, perhaps?" Helen huffed. "You know, before he cuts someone in half with those decapitator flails?"

Elenor spent a few minutes explaining what she had figured out about controlling her Relic. By the time she was done, he could reliably retract his claws and tentacles, and his Striker was well under his control. Oddly, his Striker hadn't been extended after his transformation, but once he had learned how, the rainbow crystals seemed to be impossible to retract.

"Matta?" The little girl's voice came from somewhere behind Mateo's parents. Sofia was holding onto her mother's jacket, looking around her parents.

"Matta?" Elenor whispered, but to Mateo's new ears, it might as well have been a shout. He got the sense he could actually control how loud things sounded with concentration, but it would take practice.

"When she first learned how to talk, she couldn't say my name. That's how it came out. It stuck," Mateo whispered back. He, too, had developed a lisp, which was not helped by his slight Spanish accent. Elenor suspected it was a function of their teeth, as Mateo had a similar double row of triangular razors in his mouth.

"It's me, Sofi." Mateo finally arranged all six paws beneath him and pushed himself up his feet. He was easily three and a half feet at the shoulder, which made him slightly smaller than Elenor's four feet. He toddled around for a minute, picking up each foot and moving around slowly in a circle.

"This is going to take a while," Mateo said, but he finally seemed to get the trick of which paws to move at what point. It seemed his natural gait, much like Elenor's, was a direct register - moving all of the paws on one side of the body, and then the other. Then he paced over to where his parents and sister were standing. He posed for a moment with his tail arching over his back and his ears up.

"So, do I look cool?" he asked his head tilted towards his little sister.

"Yes!" his sister exclaimed, and she nearly knocked him from his paws, throwing her arms around his neck. His father, more the scientist than his mother, looked at him critically.

"How do you see?"

"Con estos," Mateo said, and wiggled his upper set of ears. "I can see sounds with them. When we talk, the

 • Con estos – With these

sound bounces off stuff and I can tell where everything is," Mateo said. "And with these." The woven pattern of clear filaments crawled over his ears, changing the shape from triangular to a rounded off square. "This is just like seeing with my eyes was, but I can't see as well when things are far away. Things get really fuzzy at about the tree line, but I can see everything around me like… I have eyes in the back of my head. I don't know how to explain."

"Dios mio," his mother finally whispered, but this one was a reverent sound, not an exclamation. "¿Es que tú, hijo, ahí dentro?"

Mateo nodded. "Yeah, Mamá, soy yo."

She reached out. "¿Puedo?"

"Sí," Mateo said, and stood very still. She touched his large ear.

"Isn't this like poking you in the eye?" his father asked.

"Uh, sort of." Mateo responded, and his mother yanked her hand away. He laughed. "It doesn't hurt, Mamá. They are sturdier than an eye. I just can't see anything in part of my vision when you touch them." The filaments peeled back from the tops of his upper ears, seeming to blend in with his fur somehow.

"Is that like closing your eyes?" His father's curiosity was obviously piqued. His sister, on the other hand, was attempting to climb onto his back. Her mother hauled her away.

"No climbing on your brother," she grumbled.

Mateo answered his father. "Also sort of. I can still see with the sounds."

"¿Ecolocalización?"

- Dios mio – My god
- ¿Es que tú, hijo, ahí dentro? – Is it really you in there?
- Soy yo – it's really me
- ¿Puedo? – Can I?
- Sí – Sure
- Ecolocalización - Echolocation

"I think so. The sounds and sights sort of blend together when I am using both."

"Alright, that's enough questions for now or we are going to be here all night, and we need to get to work." Helen said, and Mateo nodded. "Go take a walk with Elenor to try to get used to your new body while I talk to your parents. You can take Sofia with you. Thia, if you would go ahead with them?"

Mateo turned around and trotted off next to Elenor, his gait already improving. Elenor dropped down and encouraged Sofia onto her back. Thia trailed them into the woods.

"What do you need to talk to us about?" Mateo's mother asked.

"There are a number of things, but most important is your safety. Mateo will be able to take care of himself shortly, but you are not safe." Helen led them back into the house.

29
"THE NEXT PIECE"

NC 17, EPOCH 19915.25

The week passed in blur as Elenor tried to teach Mateo as much as she could about how his Relic worked. Helen worked with him on learning to play his Striker, but most of what they had gone through was just Elenor teaching him how to move around in his new body.

Today's lesson had involved Mateo falling off the side of a huge tree at least three dozen times. His paws had tiny hairs on them that Helen had explained were like a spider's feet. They should allow him to climb and move across almost any surface. She had theorized that was why he had been given six paws, so that he could easily maintain contact with a surface without falling.

The trouble came when he tried to walk upside-down. They quickly discovered that he had to change his gait because if he didn't, when he lifted his paws on either, side he ended up swinging by his opposite paws. As soon as that happened, he would lose concentration and drop like a stone. Helen had explained that he would have to change his gait to a two by two gait that most dogs ran in.

Mateo laid on his back with all of his paws spread and his tongue hanging out of his mouth. "Esto, es, imposible," he panted.

"I'm cheating, so don't think that this should be easy for you. Keep in mind it took me months to figure out how to walk on all fours, and you figured out all those paws in like two days, so I kinda hate you," Elenor said from where she stood upside-down forty feet above him. She was standing against a huge branch extending from a massive oak tree.

 • Esto, es, imposible – This, is, imposible

"What do you mean?" he asked.

Elenor showed him. She walked out away from the branch into mid-air.

"Qué carajo." Mateo growled. He clicked his tongue, a habit that he had developed because the loud popping sound helped him see more easily with his echolocation. "Are you seriously flying? Eso es injusto."

"Well, sort of, yes?" Elenor's uncertainty gave Mateo a little chuckle. Elenor went on, "I'm using my power to lift all the water in my body. It's how almost all of my super strength works. The Relic does some of it, but when you see me do those huge jumps and run at super speeds, that's how it works."

"How come I haven't gotten a power like that yet?"

"Helen thinks you will. It took a few weeks after I shape shifted before it showed up." Elenor jumped down to the ground next to Mateo and he rolled to his paws. His huge ears twitched back and forth. "Have you figured out how to quiet things down?"

"Not yet. I know I should be able to turn these things off, but I can't figure it out yet." Mateo had had trouble sleeping since his change because of how his vision worked. He said it was like trying to sleep with his eyes open on a bright sunny day. He couldn't stop seeing because every sound mapped out the world around him in his sight.

"Mateo, are you serious about wanting to help sick people?" Elenor asked. It was something they had talked about. Mateo had asked her to teach him how to be stealthy like she had for two entire years. He told her he wanted to be able to sneak into hospitals and use Surges to heal sick people.

"Soy yo." His nod held unshakable purpose.

"We could spend our whole lives doing that and still

• Qué carajo – What, the, hell.
• Eso es injusto – That is so unfair
• Soy yo – I am

never help everyone," Elenor worried. Mateo made an odd shrugging motion with his first pair of legs.

"No soy estúpido, Elly. I know I can't save everyone. That doesn't mean I can't do a lot of good secretly clearing out cancer wards, and emergency rooms."

Elenor nodded. "Alright. I'll help you, but I need your help too."

"Va. Con que?"

"I'll show you, but you gotta promise, Mateo. This has to be between you and me. We can't tell Helen or Thia about this yet."

"Elly, you've saved my life three times. I've got your back, always."

Elenor nodded, then looked around at the quiet forest. They had both noticed that whenever they came out into the woods for Mateo to spend some time figuring out his body, all the animals fled from them. Elenor slapped her tail against a nearby tree and her Striker rang, blowing away all other sounds. A complex tune made up of three notes wove between the trees. Rocks the size of cantaloupes began to push their way up out of the snow. They stacked themselves up until there was a double row of them in the shape of a doorway. The interior of the doorway vanished until it was filled with what appeared to be the night sky.

"¿Qué es eso?"

"Hammerspace," Elenor giggled.

"¿No chingues? Like from cartoons?" Mateo goggled.

"Sort of. Helen calls it a port dimension. It's a space outside of reality. This one is mine, now, but it belonged to Merlin."

Elenor had come to recognize that Mateo's two pairs of ears had different purposes. The larger, triangular

- Va. Con que? – Sure. With what?
- ¿Qué es eso? – What is that?
- ¿No chingues? – No shit?

pair she had started calling his sight ears were responsible for letting him see while the smaller, lower pair were responsible for him hearing. She thought of them like eyes for anyone else, part of his facial expression. Mateo's sight ears stood up and shivered like eyes darting back and forth. "Merlin? Merlin, Merlin? Like King Arthur Merlin?" Mateo asked.

"Is that surprising?" Elenor had started asking questions like this immediately after this transformation. At first, Mateo's new instincts had told him he shouldn't give away that information. To anyone else, he wouldn't answer, but Elenor had pointed out that if at least one person didn't know how he was feeling, it could get really lonely.

"Yeah. I mean Merlin? Guy is an actual legend."

"Same guy, I guess. I, kinda, saw him explode. It wasn't a good day. For some reason, he left this thing to me. Come on."

Elenor walked through the doorway before Mateo could ask any more questions. His ears twitched back and forth as he tried to judge where the door was, but the sound seemed to bend around the doorway somehow, so it was just a featureless blob in Mateo's echolocation. A moment later, the light filaments wrapped over the edges of his ears and the image cleared as the echolocation was overlayed with visual images. He froze, staring into the deep black cosmos within the doorway.

"Ya comin'?" Elenor's voice came from the doorway.

"Elly, that door leads into freaking space."

"Yeesh, you should have gotten chicken feathers with that new body," Elenor taunted.

"Augh! Fine!" Mateo growled before jumping through the door. For a moment, he could not see anything. Even his echolocation didn't return any sort of image. Then, he was stumbling into a warm room with a stone floor. He tapped the back of a claw on the floor to make the image of the room resolve.

A moment later, as the pulses of sound mapped the room for him, he saw Elenor to his left, shaking the snow out of her fur. The room was spartan, with stone walls constructed of irregular stones, as if someone had turned a cobblestone road into a wall. The furnishings were not. In the corner on the left was a large carpeted area with plush armchairs surrounding a massive, roaring fireplace. Three chairs in all, from the smell of them, upholstered with old, well cared for leather. Long, carved wooden tables were set up in rows throughout the rest of the room. No two tables were alike in their carving. Some had legs carved into animal shapes while others were embellished with Victorian scrollwork.

Each table shared two similarities. One, a thick band of bronze that ran around the edge of the entire tabletop. Each band had the waveform of a Surge carved into it. The second was a humming collection of bric-a-brac that had been placed atop each table. Each piece seemed to be a Relic of some sort, but Mateo had no idea what they all did. He only knew from the resonant hum that they were magical.

The crackling fire was of extreme interest, as each pop created a constantly resolving picture of the inside of the fireplace, with dozens of points of sound that his brain translated into a perfect image of the stones. The flames themselves, however, were almost invisible to his echolocation.

Over the few days since his transformation, he had realized that using only echolocation to navigate the world was faster and safer. He only used light-based vision when his echolocation lacked precision, or trying to perceive something that was not evident from bouncing sounds off of it. Mateo went through the process he thought of as opening his eyes. When the filaments were finally in place and the visual image resolved, Mateo jumped a little.

"Eh, es eso un fantasma?"

"I am not a ghost. Ghosts, as most people conceptualize them, are myths. The living spirit cannot be destroyed, shattered, or even slightly splintered. It goes on to whatever comes next after death. A spirit could be trapped here for a time, but that is against our laws, and is not what I am. I am a remnant. The easiest way to think of me is like a video recording of a person, but smarter."

Mateo could tell he was not solid because sounds passed right through him to bounce off the chair he was sitting in. They deflected from him slightly, though, creating a nebulous, human-shaped blob in his echolocation. He kept his optical sight open, which overlayed solid images on the wispy edges of his pulsing echolocation. The man appeared to be in his mid-forties with salt and pepper hair and a long beard to match. He had a middling build with long sharp facial features and an aquiline nose.

Mateo shook the snow from his own fur and then climbed into the chair next to Elenor's, careful to blunt his claws to keep from destroying the fine dark brown leather.

"Why did you try to kill me before?" Elenor asked. The remnant shook his head.

"I cannot say. I am several hundred years removed from my living counterpart. While I have learned of the outside world through people and devices that passed near to this place, I had no contact with my living body in all that time. At the time of my creation, I cannot see any reason that I would try to kill you."

"When I was here before, you said Helen was dangerous to me. Explain." Elenor knew that she could force him to tell her now that she owned this place.

• Eh, es eso un fantasma? – Uh, is that a ghost?

What was odd to her was, why would the Merlin leave his remnant in that position? **Could he really have been trying to help somehow?**

"I can only show you what you want to know in a certain way. You need to understand how we arrived at this point." The remnant held up his fist and uncurled long elegant fingers to reveal two marbles filled with twisting stars. As Elenor reached for one of them, the remnant spoke. "Keep in mind, I do not have all of the pieces of this story. Helen holds some of them, and others are out in the world where I am unable to access them directly. You will need to chase down all the pieces to assemble the puzzle."

It was Mateo who came to the realization first. "This is what those things are after, isn't it?"

The remnant nodded. "They have only made token attempts to kill you both because you are not their main goal. The suppression of this information is what is most important to their master."

NC 17, EPOCH 18429.197

The Merlin moved through the facility that Osiris had created. He had thought that the horrors he had found in the relic stone foundry had been the worst he would see of his old friend, but this went far beyond. The massive room was carved from the stone of the mountains, and the massive stone doors swung closed behind him in silence. For a moment, he stood in total darkness, then tapped Heartwood on the floor. The sound issued forth throughout the room. Emitter relics across the ceiling sparked to life, lighting the space as brightly as daylight.

"Black silence," Iðunn whispered the curse from where she stood behind him.

Spreading light revealed hundreds of round grey granite pedestals, two feet around and two feet in high. Each one was topped with a glass tube of the same width and six feet in height. Embedded into the glass near the top was a fine web of metal threads. None of that was what drew the curse from

Iðunn. Within each tube was the partially formed spiritual essence of a familiar. Soundlessly, they screamed, they howled, they clawed ineffectually at the glass. Merlin knew they had done so every moment since they were placed within their confinement.

He walked through the aisles of contained spiritual essence. No spirit could be broken, but the torture of being held in this world beyond their deaths was beyond conception. If any of these souls were reborn, they would be utterly unhinged for lifetimes to come.

Experimentally, he tapped the glass of one of the few empty containers with Heartwood. He gripped the Relic and focused on one of the stones within, invisible beneath the woven bark of the living staff. As the vibrations from the glass activated the stone, he focused on it, and the fist-sized sapphire gripped in the roots at the top of the staff glowed with incandescent vibrance. A boom echoed through the hall as a massive battering ram of pressurized air slammed into the glass of the container. This would have normally been enough to obliterate solid steel. Yet, the glass withstood the blast, which flowed around the container to dissipate harmlessly beyond.

"Hmm, it seems we will need to use harmonic imbalance to destroy these," Merlin mumbled to himself. The feeling of power gathering caused him to turn.

"I will erase this." Iðunn's voice was not quite her own. It was cold in ways that Merlin had seen her before, but it was not until this very moment that he understood what he was seeing. Perhaps he had willfully ignored it because he could not imagine anything interfering with the will of someone like the Iðunn. Perhaps he had just not noticed it, for it was there and gone in a split second. There was still no mistaking the subtle pulsing Surge that briefly touched his senses.

He made it past Iðunn just as she began to play those terrifying, unheard notes. Swirling gouts of black smoke flowed into the space, disintegrating everything it touched. He watched Iðunn, his face crumpled into a mask of disbelief as she annihilated the contents of the room. When her Striker *flowed back into her skin, she looked at Merlin, but he had already smoothed his expression.*

Inside, his mind churned as he tried to understand what he had just seen, but more importantly, how he had never seen it before.

"Finally. He made a mistake," Iðunn said before moving forward into the room.

Merlin watched as she moved through the room ahead of him, but he had lost interest in whatever the Iðunn had found. Instead, he looked up at the Surge emitters providing them with light and realized the truth. He had not seen the pulse of the mental Surge coming from the Iðunn by accident. Osiris had known that Iðunn was under some form of compulsion, and he had laid this trap to show it to the Merlin.

NC 17, EPOCH 19915.25

Elenor blinked and then looked over to Mateo, who was shaking his sight ears back and forth.

"Someone else made her do that?" Elenor doubted.

The remnant nodded. "It took me two years of observation to fully understand a small piece of what you just saw. It wasn't until much later that I fully grasped the issue at hand."

"What is the full issue?" Elenor asked.

"We aren't there yet. What I can tell you is that the Iðunn is compelled to destroy things related to certain specific areas of study with regard to Calling. It isn't her fault, and she has no control over it. I cannot tell you what compels her, as no matter how much I researched or how many times I tried to replicate it, I could never attach compulsion to another Caller."

"And what areas of Calling?" Mateo asked, his sight ears twitching with nervousness.

"I cannot tell you everything. I was never able to decipher the specific areas. I know only that the subjects that Osiris was interested in seemed to trigger her compulsion. Deep range post-cognition, evolutionary advancement, spiritual manipulation. Whenever we encountered notes or research on any of those subjects, the compulsion was triggered." The remnant got up from the chair, and despite his lack of apparent corporeality, he picked up a poker and adjusted the logs in the fireplace.

"Are you saying that Osiris wasn't the bad guy back then?" Elenor asked, and the remnant dropped the poker back into the cast iron tool rack next to the fire with a clang.

"No. The Iðunn was fully correct to hunt and kill him. The things he did were unconscionable. As I have told you, this is only part of the story that led to creation of your circumstances." The Remnant retook his place in the chair across from them.

"Estoy confundido. We aren't just trying to get rid of the Infection?" Mateo asked.

The remnant shook his head. "No, you are needed for something far more important than redressing the issue of the Infected. They are the smallest part of the threat."

"How can we possibly do this? There are only two of us," Elenor worried.

"It will not be two forever, but you are underestimating just how powerful the Writ has made you. You were made for this purpose. The next piece of the puzzle comes from Osiris, and you can find it somewhere here in the United States."

"How is that possible if he died over a thousand years ago? No one from that area had even traveled to America at that point," Mateo wondered.

"They dug it up and brought it here," Elenor said, and the remnant put a finger aside his nose and then pointed it at Elenor.

"She has the right of it. Look in Museums. Be careful, both of you. The longer this goes on, the more Infected will appear. They will try to stop you. You will

• Estoy confundido – I'm confused

need to figure out how to defeat them or you will eventually be overwhelmed," the remnant warned.

"About that, what do we do with the ones who don't have any crowns? Do you have any ideas?" Elenor asked as she climbed down out of the chair.

The Remnant paused and then shook his head. "I have, no idea what you are speaking of."

"Of course you don't. Helen is coming in later to catalog all the Relics," Elenor warned as she headed for the door.

"Why is that? Can you not just give her a list? Your ownership should have informed you of the contents."

"I tried that, but she doesn't recognize all the names of things I gave her. She wants to see them for herself," Elenor advised.

"I will see to it that I am scarce." The Remnant vanished behind them as the door to the field of stars appeared on the wall they had come from. They both emerged back into the snowy forest they had left.

"Elly, how can you stay with them knowing that?" Mateo asked.

"I didn't know that. He only told me that Helen was dangerous, and considering that his living counterpart tried to kill me, I didn't have any reason to believe him until now. I'm still not sure I do. How do I know how these things work?" Elenor held up the marble, pinched against the side of her paw with her thumb. She dropped it into the small bag hanging around her neck.

"That's why you are always sleeping in the weirdest spots, isn't it?"

"I didn't think anyone had noticed."

"I don't think Helen and Thia have any idea where you sleep, but these things make it hard to not see where everyone is." Mateo wiggled his sight ears. "After that little show, I think I will join you in the attic for now." Elenor turned around back towards the house. They had been out all morning practicing Mateo's climbing, but now she was starving.

"Let's get lunch and then figure out how far you can run before you get tired," Elenor said. She trudged through the snowy trees back towards the house.

"¿Qué? ¿Por Qué?" Mateo asked as he trotted to catch up with her.

"Because we have some museums to sneak into, and I don't want to spend hours riding in the car."

"Well let's start now!" Mateo yelled the last word and bolted for the house, his churning paws throwing snow all over Elenor. She shook her head, rolled her eyes, and stepped up into the air out of the snow. She took off after him, easily passing him without the hinderance of running through the snow drifts.

Mateo howled. "Tramposa!"

Elenor stuck her tongue out at him as she disappeared into the trees. When they burst into the house a few minutes later, the place seemed empty. The sound of a television news broadcast playing drew them both into the living room, where Helen was sitting on the plush black leather couch staring at the television in stunned silence.

On the television the headline read "Unidentified coma patient found on Hart-Miller Island identified." The story went on to explain that the man had been identified as a father of two, but when police investigated his home, they found it abandoned. Subsequent investigation had not turned up any evidence of foul play. His family remained missing. None of that was what drew Elenor's attention though.

"Holy shit, that's the guy I killed!" Elenor squeaked.

- ¿Qué? ¿Por Qué? – What, why?
- Tramposa – Cheater

30

"TETHER"

Elenor crept up the side of the building in complete silence. The sounds of the city were loud around her despite the low hum of her Striker pushing back the sounds as she called the Surge that kept them invisible. Mateo moved next to her, his paws clinging to the concrete of the building. Even in the darkest part of the night, the world brightened from the lights of the city.

"Are you ready?" Elenor whispered to him.

"Aren't you worried someone will see us?" Mateo asked.

Elenor shook her head. "The Surge I'm playing keeps us invisible as long as you are in my line of sight. So just make sure..." Elenor trailed off, then continued, "make sure there is nothing solid between you and me since you can see around corners now."

Mateo chuckled a little and wiggled his sight ears. "I'm really glad I didn't change these to eyes."

"And you call me a cheater."

"You can fffffllllllyyyy." Mateo drew out the word, tilting both of his sight ears to the right and then to the left, his equivalent of an eyeroll.

"Are you sure about this? I only need to see this guy to see if there is still anything weird about him. But sneaking in to try to heal people..." Elenor cautioned.

"If I don't, what did I do this for?" Mateo spread his front two paws wide, clinging with his rear four as if to say look at all this.

"Well, being able to call Surges is kind of a plus," Elenor argued.

"I guess, but this is important to me, Elly. Besides, my parents will be freaking out about this for the rest of the year. We can keep it to just hospitals around here for now. You were right, we can't save everyone," Mateo said.

"Alright. I'll keep this Surge going so no one can see us. You have to call the one to get us inside."

Mateo nodded and lifted his long tail. His tail was not as thick or powerful as Elenor's and his Striker was correspondingly smaller, but it didn't seem to make a difference to how well he could call Surges. He tapped it against the side of the building and the pure note pushed against the world. Only Elenor's Surge, already in progress, was still audible.

After a moment of hesitation, Mateo began to call the Surge. Over the last two weeks since his transformation, he had practiced for almost three hundred hours, barely sleeping, to try to catch up to Elenor. He still had a long way to go to catch up to two solid months of practice, but Elenor was amazed how well he had done. The ghost Surge, as Elenor had dubbed it, allowed them to float through the wall. They landed in a patient room that was momentarily empty.

Mateo ceased his Surge and their paws touched the floor silently. Elenor looked up and saw that there was a drop ceiling.

"Well, we can't walk across the ceiling unless I lift you," she whispered.

"¿Por Qué no?"

"That kind of ceiling won't hold weight. I almost got caught because I tried to cling to one once when I first ran away from home. Before I realized I could eat out of dumpsters without getting sick, I broke into a few places to get food."

Mateo paused. "You didn't tell me you ate out of dumpsters."

Elenor shrugged her shoulders a little. "It's not as bad as it sounds if you know where to look for food and never, ever dig to get it."

 • ¿Por Qué no? – Why not?

Mateo shuddered and then scurried to catch up with Elenor as she peeked into the hallway. There were few people to see at this hour of the night, but the hospital was never truly idle. A nurse was wandering down the hall with a clipboard in hand.

Keeping her voice at a whisper, she turned back to Mateo. "How much can you see?"

"Everything on this floor. The floors are pretty thick, so I'm only getting a little bit of the floors above and below."

"Can you see him?" Elenor asked.

"It gets fuzzy after the first couple of rooms. Too many walls. He's not in the next room, or the room after that," Mateo replied.

"You lead and be careful not to bump into anyone. Remember, they can't see us," Elenor warned.

They passed two nurses in the hall who looked right through them before going about their business. Elenor had spent the night before poking her head through on every floor, trying to find the man she thought she had killed by scent, but she had only found out which floor he was on before it got too late to do anything about it. She could have trailed the man's scent back to his room, but that could have had her chasing it all over the place if they moved him a lot. Instead, she had enlisted Mateo's help. His sight ears shifted from left to right as he searched for the likeness of the man.

"Found him. Two more rooms down the hall on the right. He is alone in the room," Mateo whispered. They crept through the white institutional hallways amidst the beeping of monitors and sleepy breathing of patients. They were careful to pause at doors and intersections to insure that they did not bump into anyone on accident. Finally, they came to a room where Elenor scented the man strongly. They slipped inside and Elenor stood up on her hind legs to ease the door closed. Using a dulled claw tip, she pressed the button to lock it.

Mateo opened his visual sight and looked around the dimly lit room. When he turned to Elenor, he did his blinking ear wiggle. "Why are your eyes a different color?"

"I can," Elenor paused, not sure how to explain. She continued, "change the way I see things. I can see Auras and Surges this way."

"Well, your eyes have a super bright green ring around them right now and it is freaking me out a little."

"Sorry not sorry?" Elenor mumbled at him as she stepped up into the air. She took another step up until she was hovering a few feet off the ground, where she could get a full look at the man lying in the bed. There was a name on a folder in a bin just to the side of the bed, Anton Stands.

In Elenor's sight, the man's aura was normal for a human. It was a line of mostly white light with hints of various other colors, surrounded by a wafer-thin line of midnight blue light that indicated deep sleep. One of the many things that Helen had tried to forcefully cram into Elenor's head over the last several weeks was the meaning of auras.

While trying to read someone's mind was completely out of the question even with Surges, being able to watch their aura was the next best thing. Callers could control their auras with practice, but with the average human, changing emotions and intentions would show up as various colors bleeding through their Aura. Elenor ceased her Surge and leaned down from her position in the air next to the man's bed.

"Wake up," she hissed into his ear.

A flash of light blue pulsed through his Aura and then a band of yellow fear flowed through it as he sat bolt upright. He opened his mouth to shout, and Elenor tapped her Striker against the pole holding the various pieces of equipment next to his bed. The note blew away all other sounds and Elenor called a simple two note Surge. The smoothly flowing notes came intertwined from her Striker, rising and flowing in long regular peels aside one another.

"Don't bother shouting again. No one outside of this room will know anything is amiss," Elenor warned.

Anton did not take her at her word and began to shout for help. She sat down on her haunches, floating several feet off the ground next to his bed.

"Can you make him stop? Those big stupid pulses of sound coming out of his mouth are really hard to look at," Mateo complained. His sight ears folded all the way down against his skull, his equivalent to squeezing his eyes shut.

Finally, Anton stopped shouting and Elenor rolled her glittering eyes at him. "Are you done?" she asked, and the man swallowed, looking like he might start screaming again. He opened his mouth but nothing came out.

"You were there," his baritone quavered and almost cracked.

Elenor nodded. Her vision changed again and she looked him over. There were no hints of that brilliant green crown she had shattered, but as he turned his head to look at Mateo, who had put his first paws up on the end of the bed, she saw something waving from the back of his neck.

It was faint, almost completely transparent, and a dark, shadowed version of the green that she had seen blazing around and through his skull the night they had fought so many weeks ago. It had the appearance of a braided rope.

"What the hell are you?" Anton asked as he leaned away from Mateo's searching eyeless gaze.

"I'm not going to hurt you," Mateo said as he pulled himself a little higher up to get a better look at the man.

"Rude much? That is none of your concern, anyway. What do you remember?" Elenor asked.

"I'm not insane, am I?" the man asked. "They keep telling me I suffered some trauma when I tell them I could hear a voice in my head, but they are wrong."

Elenor kept staring at the spectral rope trailing from the back of his neck and she was sure he was not. "No, you are not insane. What did the voice tell you?"

"I woke up to go to work just like any other day. When I came downstairs from the shower, the kids were gone, which was normal. Their mother got them ready and sent them to school almost every morning." Anton swallowed.

"It's okay, I know you're not insane. Tell us, maybe we can help." Elenor had a feeling she knew where this was going, and it was true that maybe she could help.

"So, I went back upstairs to get my phone so I could call her, thinking that maybe the kids missed the bus and she had to drive them in to school. But just when I picked up the phone, there was a voice. It scared the shit out of me." Anton shivered and wiped a hand over his face. He had begun to sweat.

"It wasn't human. It sounded like it had feedback from a bad radio in it. It told me that it had taken my family, and that if I wanted them back, I would do what it told me to. I agreed, what else could I do? After that, it was like I was a passenger in my own body. The thing took control of me. It gave me powers and I could feel a pulling in my chest that led me to you. I thought I had died because I didn't breathe anymore." He stopped, then, and put his face in his hands. He didn't cry, but it took him a few minutes to compose himself. Elenor and Mateo waited as he pulled himself back together.

"The last thing I remember was walking across the bottom of the bay and coming up on Hart-Miller Island. As soon as I saw the helicopter on the beach, everything went black until the EMTs were shaking me awake in the sand. They have no idea what happened to my family."

"We do," Mateo said, thinking of the Infected that they had watched trying to find their way to the house over the past two weeks. The device Helen used to keep them away worked but they kept searching. Elenor and Mateo had watched them trying to learn more about them.

Anton looked up, hopeful tears building in his eyes. "What," he started, but then his face crumpled into pain and terror. He already knew.

It suddenly started to make sense to Elenor, if only a little. "We'll try to help your family, but it's going to be a fight, and I can't make any promises."

"You've seen them?"

Elenor nodded.

"They are, like, what happened to me?"

Elenor nodded.

"Can you do for them, what you did for me?"

Elenor hesitated and looked to Mateo. "I don't know. They're, different, somehow. I think," Elenor hesitated because she wasn't sure, it was only a feeling, "that whatever was controlling you got smarter after I broke whatever it was using on you."

"But we will try," Mateo said, and Elenor nodded affirmation.

"We will. I promise we will."

"That is better than what I have now, which is nothing." Anton laid back down in his bed. He looked up at Elenor looming over him and then down at Mateo, whose eyeless face peeked over the bed, his sight ears turning slightly to face Anton.

"What are you?" he asked again.

"We used to be human. All we really know now, though, is that we are here to help," Mateo said.

"Please don't tell anyone we were here."

Anton looked up as Elenor hopped down off of the thin air she was seemingly standing upon.

"How will I know?"

"We'll make sure they get back to you, either way," Elenor said, "but, we can't help at all if you start screaming again or if you tell everyone about the monsters."

Anton nodded and Elenor ceased her Surge, releasing the room back to normal. She tapped her tail against the pole again.

"I'm going to put you back to sleep, and when you wake up, you will feel much better," Elenor said as she began to call a new Surge. This one had a similar tranquil melody, but had two more notes twined into what sounded like a beautiful lullaby. Anton fell asleep straight away and even Mateo felt refreshed after listening to it for a few moments. When the music trailed off, Mateo sighed and pushed himself away from the bed. He padded towards the door.

"Can we help them?" Mateo asked.

"I think we can, but I'm concerned about what he said about being controlled. There is some kind of spiritual tether left behind on him. We need to talk to Helen about what might be able to give them powers like that. Those aren't Surges or even the other power that I have," Elenor worried. "There is so much we don't know."

"Then we'll learn," Mateo reassured. "Ahorita, though. there are a lot of sick people here that we can help."

Elenor sighed. "Fine, but if we get caught, you are telling your parents about it. You're calling the invisibility Surge. My tail is tired and so am I."

"Helen said that you have to build your, whatever it is, to do Surges one after another," Mateo reminded.

"Well, if you want me to have enough energy left to

 • Ahorita – Right now

do all the healing you want and not pass out, then you play the Surge that keeps people from seeing us."

Mateo let out a put-upon sigh and tapped his tail against the floor. "It's not invisibility, it's confusion. That's what Helen said," Mateo sniped.

"Can people see us when you're playing it?" Elenor asked.

"No," Mateo ground out.

"Invisibility," Elenor squeaked, and then she used her tail to push down the lever handle of the door, popping it open. "Come on, Fuzzears. If we are in here any longer, I'm gonna start eating the furniture."

"Speaking of eating, how are we ever going to go El Taquito again? Someone will shit a pollo if they see us."

"What's El Taquito?" Elenor dropped an ear in puzzlement.

"El mejor camión de tacos en la ciudad, duh?" Mateo twitched both sight ears to one side, the equivalent of rolling his eyes at her. He mumbled something that he clearly didn't mean for her to hear, but her sharp ears caught it. "The only place I can get tacos better than the ones Mamá makes."

"Oh, I'm so telling her you said that!" Elenor taunted.

"¡¿Qué?!" Mateo yelped.

"Mateo thinks El Taquito has better tacos. You're toast buddy. Your mother will make tacos out of your ears for that little quip," Elenor prodded.

"I'll bite your ears off while you're sleeping if you tell her I said any such thing!" Mateo snapped his teeth at her.

"Give it your best shot, fur tube," Elenor dared as she led the way towards the glaring red exit sign above the stairwell.

- pollo – chicken
- El mejor camión de tacos en la ciudad – The best taco truck in the city
- ¡¿Qué?! – What?!

31
"RECOVER"

"Helen said that they checked Boston, Philadelphia, and New York. Nothing at any of them," Elenor yelled over the sound of rushing wind.

"So, where are we going?!" Mateo yelled, his voice cracking slightly as he tried to get over the sound of the wind blasting.

"Toronto! The next closest museum with a big Egyptian collection is Chicago!"

Mateo tried not to look down. He just kept running.

"How high up are we?"

"About a thousand feet. You won't die if you fall!"

Mateo's sight ears swiveled wildly. "Easy for you to say, I can't see anything without my light webs out. We are too far from anything that sound will bounce off, and I don't want to look down."

"Just keep running!"

"How are you doing this, anyway? This isn't a Surge."

They had spent so much time learning over the past couple of weeks that he'd had no time to ask any questions.

"It's the power that lets me control water in your body. I don't know how I got it. I've been practicing a lot with it."

"Where are we?"

Elenor looked over at him and the webwork of filaments around the edges of his sight ears,were glowing brightly. He was slowing down slightly because to see the ground, he had to tilt his head to expose the filaments to it. She assumed the glow was some sort of low-light vision like her glowing eyes gave her. She looked down too.

Far below, the bright lights of a city twinkled back at her. It was smaller than Baltimore had been when she had lifted them into the sky above the slumbering city. She slowed down until they bobbed in gentle waves in the general direction they had been heading. She reached up to the strap of the bag hanging from the harness wrapped around her neck and chest.

Thia had made and remade the harness at least a dozen times. She was adept at working with leather and, since there was no way to reinforce against Elenor's slicing spines, she had been extremely careful to fit it so that it was inches away where the spines instinctively sprung from her body. She pressed a button on the heavy steel clasp and the bag swung loose from her chest harness.

Strapped to the inside of the bag was her phone. She tapped the screen and it came to life. Carefully, she tapped in the code to unlock it. There were only a few icons on the screen since each had to be enlarged to allow her to easily touch them without hitting more than one. She hit the GPS icon and a map expanded to fill the screen. A moment later, her dot showed them as east of Harrisburg, Pennsylvania. She carefully hit the power button and then affixed the strap around her neck again. It was a bit of a struggle because her paws didn't quite bend the right way, but after a few moments, she managed it.

"This has been hard for you, harder than I thought," Mateo said. "Harder than it is for me."

Elenor lifted her shoulders in a shrug. "It's been two years. I've gotten used to it. I wish my paws were a little more like my hands used to be, but hey, you don't even have thumbs anymore. You're having to figure out how use those tentacles as hands. Maybe it was a little harder for me, but it's getting better now that I have a friend who actually knows what this is like," she said as she tugged at the bag to make sure it was tightly fastened around her neck.

"I had near death experiences and gangs to dodge to prepare me for this nonsense, but I get the feeling that wasn't you," Mateo said.

Elenor shook her head. "Not me at all. I was a bit of a girly girl, but I played soccer, did cheerleading. I meant what I said. I didn't know what I wanted to do. I was smart enough to do a lot of things. I kinda liked computers and I was good at science. I wasn't a fighter, but I guess I'll get used to that too."

"Sometimes, it's good to fight for things you believe in," Mateo assured her.

"I know, but violence wasn't really part of my life before, and I'm not sure I can ever feel good about it. Anyway, that's Harrisburg. We're in Pennsylvania, about a third of the way there," Elenor said, and then began to run off across the sky. Mateo bounded after and caught up quickly.

"How far have we come?" Mateo shouted.

"About seventy miles!"

They had been running for less than ten minutes. Mateo realized that Helen had been right. They were moving almost as fast as a commercial jet.

"How come we aren't getting hit in the face with every bug in the universe? And how come it isn't louder?" Mateo asked.

"Less bugs this high up, and I'm using the power to push away anything living that is directly in front of us. Even bugs have water in them."

Just then, Mateo saw something approaching. At first, it was just a dot of light far in the distance. A vibrating, wavy disruption in his vision.

"Elly, there is something up ahead!"

"I don't see anything!"

Elenor started to slow them, but just then, it resolved and it was coming up way too fast. It wasn't very big,

some sort of tiny helicopter with a flashing light on top.
A moment later, it sharpened in his echolocation. It was
a drone. Then they were almost on top of it.

"Shit!" Elenor yelped, and Mateo was flung away
from her in one direction while Elenor flew off in the
other. The wind from their passing caused the drone to
tumble wildly out of control, spinning back towards the
earth. Like the drone, Mateo spun end over end, out of
control. He couldn't get his body to stop flipping and he
saw the ground coming up at him far too fast.

He started to scream out of pure instinct. Just when
he was certain he was about to smash into the flat
rooftop of a building, he jarred to a stop. His whole
body froze, and he was entirely unable to move even a
single muscle. A panting sigh of relief came from
behind him and Elenor walked around in front of him.
They began to rise into the air again.

"I'm sorry, Mateo. I had to react."

Mateo shook his head. "Está bien. It wouldn't have
felt good, but I would have survived. I just hope that
thing didn't get any pictures of us."

"It didn't." She held up her tail, and that was when
he realized the staccato rhythm of a Surge flowed from
her Striker. "But I don't know how long we can keep
this up before someone finds out about us." When they
finally got back to a reasonable altitude, Elenor paused.

"You should run ahead. I know that with your sight,
it's hard to see up here, but those ears are a much better
early warning system than my eyes," Elenor said, and
Mateo nodded.

"Va."

"And if you see anything else, I'll stop faster next
time."

"Confío en ti, Elly." Mateo reassured. He turned and

- Está bien – It's fine
- Va - Okay
- Confío en ti, - I trust you

bounded off in the direction they had been going.

Twenty minutes and two stops to correct their course later, they came to a city about half the size as Baltimore and Mateo slowed until he was bobbing in the air. Elenor stopped next to him.

"¿Cómo estás?" Mateo asked.

"Right on track, that's Buffalo. We should go the long way around." Elenor gestured off to the west with her left paw.

"¿Por qué?"

"I know you can't see it yet, but open your eyes and look over there." Elenor pointed off towards the city. A moment later, the webwork wrapped around Mateo's sight ears and he looked toward where Elenor pointed.

"Oh, that is a lot of planes."

"Yep, and if we get any closer, they will see us. It'll only take a few extra minutes to run out to the lake. Helen warned me about the airports and a whole lot of other things we have to worry about."

Elenor was right. It didn't take them long to reach the lake, and they slowed as they came up on the shore. She let out a little gasp as the vista consumed the horizon. Across the lake front and for almost a mile onto the wavering glass surface, twinkling lights rolled on the waves as boats worked into the night. The black water reflected back the lights of the boats into a cosmos of stars as breathtaking as any panorama of space.

"Ya sabes," Mateo whispered, "if we were still humanos, we would never get to see this."

"How does it look to you?" Elenor wondered, a note of concern in her voice.

"It's a little fuzzy, but if I am being honest, it might be even prettier this way. Elly, I don't regret this, even with all the things I still have to figure out. Only getting

- ¿Cómo estás? – How are we doing?
- ¿Por qué? – Why?
- Ya sabes – You know
- humanos – human

to taste my food for a second or two before it turns to magic ash is a bit of suck sprinkled on top of the awesome sundae. But Elly, look at what we are doing. This has to be at least in the top ten most amazing things that have happened to anyone, ever."

Elenor swiped a paw at her eyes and spun in the air until she was facing to the north over the lake. "Thanks, Mateo." Elenor smiled, full of teeth. She ran down to a couple of hundred feet off the water and bolted to the north. Ten minutes later, they came into the bay of Toronto. Elenor brought them down to the water.

"I think we can run in on the water without anyone seeing us, but when we get closer to the shore, we are going to have to go underwater."

"Uh, I don't know how to swim yet with all of these paws," Mateo complained.

"I didn't say anything about swimming, did I?" Elenor leveled off about thirty feet above the water and they streaked toward the city. When the lights of boats became numerous, Elenor slowed down.

"We can't hit the water going this fast or it will hurt, a lot," Elenor pipped.

"Va."

"Ready?"

Mateo nodded and folded all four of his ears flat against his head. Then they were splashing into the water. All he could do was trust that Elenor knew what she was doing, but as soon as the splashing sounds went away and the water filled his ears, his echolocation lit up with the most amazingly clear picture he had ever seen. Every sound refreshed the image, and he could see for miles in every direction. Thousands of fish were so clearly visible that he could have identified them by name, if he knew fish well enough.

He could see the beach coming up at an alarming rate and he tried to flail his limbs to catch up to her, but before he could get any closer, they slowed down in the water. He got his paws onto the sand and followed Elenor up until they came to a large retaining wall. He could see the posts of a pier wide to either side of them as they came up out of the water.

Mateo paused to wonder why he didn't feel like he needed to breath, but then he saw Elenor waving him forward. She pointed to his sight ears and then up with her paw. He understood, and slowly walked up the beach. He looked up at the retaining wall and then hopped off the sand and tried to dog paddle.

He began to twist in the water because he couldn't seem to get his paws to work together, despite how well he had been doing. A moment later, he felt himself lifting towards the surface until just his sight ears poked out of the water. It took a moment before for the crashing of the waves on the beach resolved the image. No one was around as far as he could see. He waved her forward with one of the tentacles that emerged from his back. A moment later, they were rising out of the water as Elenor lifted them with her power.

"Have you been practicing trying to see other kinds of light?" Elenor asked.

"Sure, but it still doesn't work the way it does for you."

"Alright, then, have you been working on that Surge with Helen?"

"The one that makes an EMP? Elly, that's dangerous in the city."

"Well, I can't call the Surge that keeps us invisible the whole time we are in here. We need to kill the cameras somehow." Elenor said as she set them down on the white sand of an artificial beach that ran right up to the edge of the retaining wall. Mateo paused, his ears twisting this way and that as he took in the lay of the land.

"I can see a lot further than in Baltimore. I wonder why that is." At the same time, both of their heads whipped around to the east. They could both feel their tethers to the Infected tugging them to the right.

"That is not a coincidence," Elenor said, and Mateo shook his head.

"Not a chance. We have to get to that Memory thing."

"Fragment. Helen called it a Memory Fragment."

"Whatever it is, they are after it too," Mateo urged.

She padded towards the building of glass and steel. A multicolored sign labeling the building "Chorus" glowed in the night. She detoured to the south side of the building to avoid the sweeping IR spotlights of cameras. Mateo followed when she crawled up the side of the building and looked to the south. He walked around the corner to the west side of the building, and Elenor followed him.

They ran along the side of the building towards Queens Quay East. Pushing off of the building, they launched across Queens Quay diagonally to a building with a glass and steel roof. They darted across the roof, dodging cameras that happened to point in their general direction, and made it to a flat-roofed building on the other side of the block.

She ran across the flat rooftop, picking up speed until it ran out. Remembering at the last moment, she used her power to lift Mateo as well. They went over the short wall surrounding the roof and ran across the sky forty feet above the highway. Using her power to propel them to blurring speeds, they crossed a train yard in moments. Elenor realized that continuing to follow rooftops was just going to make it more likely that they would be seen. They could still use the buildings for cover, though, so they continued to run on thin air as she blurred past the bricks of the building shielding her on the right of Market Place.

They kept following the street until it ended, a park
across their way. They turned left on Front Street, right
on Church, and then a left on King, enormous buildings
flying by on either side as they ran through the narrow
canyons of Toronto's streets.

Elenor landed on the side of a huge building with
lines of vertical windows from the ground to the roof.
She flipped down her bag and checked the GPS.

"How far do we have to go? I can feel that thing
moving." Mateo asked.

"Not far."

The next cross street was York, and the one after that
was University, which would lead all the way to the
museum. Knowing where she was going, she sped up,
taking them up University. Bolting up the street as fast
as she could manage got them across the city in a pair of
minutes. Then she was hovering above the Royal
Ontario Museum.

It was an odd-looking building that reminded her of
pictures of the Sydney Oprea House in Australia. A
white façade of enormous wooden planks and oddly
shaped windows made up its sides. Portions of the
building were built to pyramid-shaped points at odd
angles stretching into the Toronto sky. Standing on the
north side, Elenor watched Mateo tilting his head left
and then right as his sight ears twitched in various
directions.

"Elly, this is weird. The streets are empty for blocks
all around. City big as this, there should always be some
people on the streets."

"I know. It was like that in Baltimore too. When they
came anywhere near, people unconsciously avoided
them. I ran that one right through all those people into
Patterson Park and no one saw it."

"It's certainly a neat trick." They both looked at the
museum with some worry. Their tethers pointed
directly inside.

"You ready?" Elenor asked.

"Not even a little. But if we want answers about all of this, they're in there."

Mateo knocked his Striker against a nearby light post and began to call the Ghostwalker's Etude. A moment later, they were walking through the glass doors of the museum into a glittering hall of speckled tan granite, with beautiful carved columns and dozens of exhibits encased in glass, sparkling as if it were just installed minutes earlier.

Before moving any further, Elenor tapped the end of her tail against a couple of spines that sprang up from her haunches and began to call the Precept's Rest. The uneven notes of the slightly discordant melody would hide them from anyone and anything looking for them. Mateo ceased the matter phasing Surge and their paws touched down on the granite floors. They both looked up in the direction the Tether was leading them - towards the upper floors.

"Go up through the floor or take the stairs?"

"Stairs. If we go up through the floor, we might pop up right in front of whoever or whatever is in here looking for the Fragment," Elenor said.

Careful to retract her claws, she padded silently to a stand to one side of the entrance. The white painted metal display had dozens of pamphlets on all the various museum exhibits, but the one she was after took up most of the first two rows of the display. She put her front paws up on the stand and plucked a museum map out. Dropping back down to the floor, she carefully spread it open in front of herself and Mateo. He bent his neck and flattened his ears so that the visual webs outlining his sight ears could see the paper.

Elenor pointed to the stairwell that was down the hall directly in front of them and then to the map of the third floor, where the Egyptian exhibits were held. They were about to pad away when scorching white light illuminated the dark hall. They spun and immediately froze in place when they saw a figure of medium height with a slight build. Elenor's vision shifted to the infrared and the light became much less blinding. Instead, it was a simple point of red from the heat of the flashlight bulb itself.

A moment later, it was clear that she was looking at a security guard, considering the radio on their belt. She motioned a paw to Mateo to let him know to back up out of her way. Elenor wished she knew how to alter the Surge she was using so it would let them talk, but no matter how hard she listened to the Chorus, she couldn't understand which notes to add to her Surge to affect the sound. The guard walked by them and stopped where the map was spread on the ground.

"Now how did the cleaning crew miss you?" the woman mumbled to herself as she picked up the map off the floor. She shined her light around the darkened entryway. It passed right over Elenor and Mateo. They both felt it when the Infected moved. It came towards them from above until it was standing directly above the guard.

Oh no, Elenor thought. She bolted forward, slamming a shoulder into the guard a moment before a huge slab of concrete and granite smashed through the drop ceiling, crashing to the floor. Standing atop of it was an enormous man at least six and a half feet tall. His body was wrapped in thousands of venomous green threads like a suit of glowing armor. On his shoulder, he was carrying a small bust-sized statue that looked like sandstone with faded and degraded enamel paint.

It looked like the pictures of statues of Cleopatra that Elenor had seen before. The massive Infected turned like he hadn't seen them and dashed towards the entrance doors. Elenor scrambled to her feet and spun to check on the guard. The woman had slammed into

one of the granite pillars. A cut on the side of her head
was leaking blood onto the polished granite floor.

Elenor heard the Infected smash through the doors
onto the street. Mateo skidded to a halt on the other side
of the woman.

"Take over the Precept's Rest, I have to heal this
woman."

"We gotta catch that guy," Mateo hissed, but he
tapped his Striker against the ground and began calling
the Surge. Elenor ceased her Surge, and, just as she was
about to tap her tail against the floor to play the
Mender's Lament, she stopped. Helen's words about
the Surges she knew came back to her.

"The methods you have for healing right now are like
battlefield medicine. You don't have the experience to
heal anything complicated. If you don't know exactly
what you are dealing with, you had best not do it at all.
You can do more harm than good." Elenor stood there,
shaking with frustration.

"Elly, what are you doing? We have to go," Mateo
said

"I can't fix her. I could do more damage than good."

"Va, well then use one of the burner phones to call
for help, but we have to go," Mateo said, and turned to
the door.

Elenor took out one of the phones. "Go, I'll catch
up." She tapped her tail on the floor and took up
Precept's Rest once again. She pulled out one of the
burner phones, a simple flip phone that worked
internationally. Helen had bought an entire box of them
as just-in-case things. Elenor always kept a couple of
them on her, and Mateo would as well, as soon as Thia
finished a pack for him to carry things in. She dialed 911
and put the phone on speaker. She put it on the floor
next to the woman, and as soon as the line clicked open
and the operator identified herself as emergency

• Va - Okay

services, Elenor spoke.

"There is a guard hurt in the Royal Onatario Museum. Send help please." Elenor scooped up the phone and then ended the call. She hooked a claw into the back of the phone and popped out the battery. Taking it with her outside, she dropped it into a trash can on the street. She put her nose down and began to sniff around. It only took her a moment to find Mateo's scent, which led her to the south. She looked down the street, but they were already out of sight.

She lifted a paw to start after them, but her ears perked, twisting back towards the museum. Some noise that she heard had made her turn back. Bright verdant light exuded gently from one side of one of the hexagonal windows on the third floor.

She looked down the street in the direction that Mateo had gone. He had proven to be a much better fighter than her, even in his new body. He had told her his father had been teaching him jujitsu since he was eight. He had begun adapting all of that knowledge to his new body almost right away.

She turned back to the Museum and lifted her body with her power, and a moment later, she was watching another of the Infected prowl into the Egyptian exhibit. Her muzzle spread into a frown as she realized the truth. They had sensed she and Mateo coming and realized that they couldn't take time to search for the fragment. The other Infected was a decoy. She paused long enough to lower the pack from around her neck and type a text to Mateo.

That was the only thing that Thia had been able to work out, a waterproof case for Mateo to carry a cellphone in. He had to use his tail and tentacles to work the thing, but he would check it and come back to her soon enough. She ceased her Surge, tapped the glass of the window with her Striker, and called the Ghostwalker's Etude.

Once inside the exhibit, rather than landing on the floor, she flipped upside down to walk across the ceiling. She found the other Infected on the eastern side of the Egyptian exhibit. It was standing there staring at a large stone tablet, three feet tall by two feet wide, carved with hieroglyphs.

It was then that she realized something of interest. Each of the Infected seemed to shape their magic threads in a different way. This one had bands woven around the wrists, ankles, and about her neck. She was no bigger than five and a half feet with long black hair and a slight build. She reached up to the glass case and the band around her wrist expanded until it covered her hand in a tube of green light. As soon as it contacted the glass, it began to spin, and a moment later, she pulled a large circle of glass out of the case.

Elenor swung down from the ceiling, carefully testing the top of a large glass case holding a painted sarcophagus. When it easily held her weight, she settled down on top of it and crept to the edge. Gleaming eyes, purple and blue, tracked every movement of the Infected as she reached into the case to place a grey-skinned hand upon the black stone tablet. Instinct guided Elenor until she was crouching on the edge of the case, hot breath nearly brushing the back of the woman's neck.

Radio static crackled through the room, and a flashlight shined on both Elenor and the Infected.

"Stay right where…" The guard, a man by his voice, never finished the sentence. The Infected thrust her hand out toward the guard and a circle of menacing green snapped around his neck. It tightened instantly, squeezing off his air.

"Shhhh," the Infected hissed as if shushing a child. Elenor could wait no longer. Unconscious instincts raised her tail end for better agility and she pounced. The glass case beneath her shattered from the force of her jump, though the safety glass remained in one piece. She slammed into the Infected with the force a battering ram. She hooked her claws into the Infected and they skidded across the granite, smashing through another display case.

Even before they stopped tumbling, a band of green energy snapped around Elenor's neck and began to squeeze. Elenor smashed her Striker into the floor and she called the only other Surge that she could reliably conjure. Oddly patterned discordant notes began to shatter the air. Elenor folded her ears down at the sound of the notes, but she continued to claw viciously at the Infected. A moment later, the notes of the Surge took hold and the bands of green energy the Infected was using exploded into motes of inoffensive light.

Elenor took a deep breath through her newly released throat and then clawed her way up the Infected's tattered body. She put one paw on the woman's skull and bent down until her muzzle was almost touching the woman's face.

"You're going to give me answers," she whispered into the Infected's ear.

"What the hell are you?" The guard was rubbing his throat. Elenor just ignored him. It would take a moment, but the disruption Surge had two effects. One would disrupt any sort of warping of reality. The other would make anyone who was not a Caller forget anything they saw. A moment later, the security guard's eyes glazed over and he sat down peacefully on the ground.

"Now, where were we?" Elenor seethed. When she looked back, the Infected's eyes had drawn down to full grey orbs with pinpricks of poisonous green so bright that they seared Elenor's eyes, like looking at the sun did before her transformation.

"Speck." The voice that issued forth from the mouth of the Infected was deep, rumbling, and not at all meant to emerge from a human throat.

"Who are you?" Elenor demanded. The woman struggled, but Elenor's power gave her strength far beyond the human, and she pressed down on her skull with enough force to make it clear that there was no escape.

"Hunger. You are sustenance. I am inevitable. The drones are many and the answers will not save you. There is only the end, ever has it been." The pupils of the Infected's eyes expanded back to their normal size and she began to struggle more violently.

Elenor stepped back off of her and then concentrated on the power floating in her chest. She quickly constructed the instructions in her head and lifted her paw. The Infected was lifted helplessly from the floor and Elenor yanked her paw towards the huge window behind her. The Infected launched out of it at speed, shattering the glass and disappearing into the night. Elenor looked up to the black tablet that the Infected had been touching. In the distance, Elenor could faintly hear sirens.

Elenor sighed in resignation and turned her back to the tablet. While her normal eyes could see in a few different light spectra, the eyes in her back, Helen had told her, were just as special. Not only could they induce temporary or permanent paralysis if she concentrated on activating their Surge, but they could see warps in reality.

Helen had explained that they had the same effect that the adder stone Relics did. She closed her normal eyes so that she wouldn't get confused and opened the large golden orbs on her back. Sure enough, in the top left-hand corner of the tablet, a tiny white spot winked at her.

Elenor's phone vibrated. She flipped down her small pack and prodded the phone awake. She typed in her password and there was a text from Mateo. One word. "Help!"

32
"DANGER"

Elenor carefully listened to the Chorus for a long moment. She could hear the vibrations of the memory fragment in the resonance of the world. She quickly played her Surge and swiped her ghostly paw through the black stone tablet. She felt the Fragment hit her paw and she pulled it free. Her phone pinged again and she dropped the marble full of stars into her bag, zipping it closed. She flipped the bag down and saw that Mateo had shared his location.

She buckled the bag back around her neck and ran towards the window. Mateo was just down the street. Elenor leapt out, clipping her Striker against the edge of the building to call Precept's Rest once again. She took off running through the air, feeling the fatigue that calling so many Surges in quick succession brought to her form.

Down the street, standing quietly amongst all the modern buildings of glass and steel, was a beautiful cathedral. Bright red doors set into irregular tan brick walls gave a bit of color to the otherwise dour façade. The quaint appearance had been shattered, just like the center door of the church.

Sitting on the stairs was an older man wearing the outfit of a priest. Black suit, white collar, shiny black shoes. It was hard to tell how tall he was sitting down, but she guessed about five feet ten inches. Light brown skin behind a salt and pepper beard surrounded brown eyes. Slight of build with a bit of a paunch around his stomach, he was rubbing his head as if he had taken a blow. Bursts of green light were coming from inside. Far too many to account for just one of the Infected.

"Oh no," Elenor whimpered. The Priest looked up and his eyes went wide saucer wide.

"My God." The priest crossed himself.

"How can you see me?" Elenor asked, and the priest slid away from her a little. Elenor's ears flattened in displeasure. "He can't save you now, Father. Only we can do that."

Elenor bolted up the stairs and skidded to a halt in the door. She ceased her Surge, since it was clearly pointless if the priest could see her. Her eyes darted around and she counted three Infected in various parts of the Chapel. Expansive vaulted ceilings crowned a massive room that was being quickly torn apart by the three Infected. Her eyes roved quickly over the cathedral, and only after she didn't find Mateo did she remember to look up. He was there, clinging to the ceiling with all six paws. Elenor's eyes went wide when she saw something dripping from Mateo's fur.

They had not noticed her, so Elenor spent a moment composing instructions for her power in her head and then reached out to each of the Infected. She lifted a paw and curled the digits into a fist. The Infected were yanked from their feet and smashed together in the center of the massive room. Elenor held them with little trouble, but knew she couldn't hold them forever.

"Are you ok, Mateo?" Elenor called.

Mateo scurried across the ceiling and then dropped to the floor next to her.

"Ahora soy, but one of them hit me with a spear of that green light. It broke against my Relic, but when it hit me, it did something that hit me on the inside." Mateo's voice quavered a little. It had shaken him.

"We can't leave them here and I can't hold them forever. We have to figure out how to stop these things for good. Which one hurt you?"

Mateo steadied and his fur bristled. Tentacles sprung from his back and developed razor sharp serrated edges along their length. "The smallest one with the coils

• Ahora soy – I am now

around her arms. So, do we fight them?"

"No, we crush them."

Elenor yanked her paw to the left and two of them smashed off the walls like pinballs. "I'll take the little one. Mateo, they don't care about who they hurt so no more sandbagging. Tear them apart," Elenor growled.

Mateo tilted his head and one of his sight ears fell in question. "How did you," Mateo started, and Elenor gave him a little smile.

"Because I thought the same thing, until they tried to kill you for no other reason but that you were standing nearby. We can't kill them. We can only put them out of the fight for a while," Elenor warned.

She frowned at the smaller figure as Mateo bounded off, scrambling up the wall on the left-hand side towards where the other two figures had gone flying. She was a bit surprised when Mateo did something new, his tentacles shooting out to stick to the ceiling and sending him swinging off into the darkness. Elenor stalked forward toward the remaining infected. She was mentally exhausted from overusing both her bearer power and her Surges.

She gave a mental push against her Relic and her spines slithered out from her body and then sprang up with menace. She stepped forward tentatively. She was terrified to go into a fight with someone who might actually be able to hurt her or Mateo. One of the few things that Helen had been able to hammer into her in the short time she had was that even the best fighters were afraid. The best fighters overcame it.

Elenor had always hated fighting, but Helen and Thia had given her a different way to look at it. Thia had said it in their training sessions. It is always better to avoid a fight, but sometimes if you want to protect something, fighting is the only way. Her parents were pacifists by nature and believed in doing all their fighting with words. But her exchanges with the Infected so far had shown her clearly that words would not be enough. Her claws began to rake the floor as she prowled towards the Infected. She wove between and behind benches as the Infected spun towards Mateo.

Some instinct overtook Elenor and she bared her teeth. "Oh, you don't want to look at my friend," she pipped, and her unnaturally high-pitched voice seemed to echo off of the inside of the church as if it were filling the entire vaulted space. Elenor's body crouched as she crept through the obliterated pews with liquid grace, drawing closer to the Infected. The woman was turning this way and that, trying to locate Elenor. She seemed frantic, almost as terrified as Elenor herself. As she crept closer, she narrowed her eyes, examining the thick coils of woven putrid light wrapped around the woman's arms, legs, and torso. The coil around her right arm flowed forward, unspooling from it until it formed into a spear of light.

Elenor circled to her left, and that was when she noticed something odd about one of the bundles of green threads. There was one that stood out from the rest. It trailed away from the middle of her back, but instead of ending sharply like the rest of the undulating bundles, this one seemed to fade away. She focused on it, listening to the Chorus with as much attention as she could spare. It somehow sounded familiar to her, but she couldn't place how it was familiar.

Mateo let out a surprised roar, and Elenor saw him flying across the huge room to the west. He was clinging to one of the infected, tearing at them with claws and tentacles. They smashed into some pews and then tumbled to a stop. The enormous Infected was sprinting through the debris trying to reach Mateo, but before he could, Mateo released his grip on the limp body of the third Infected and slunk away into the darkness.

Elenor turned her attention back to the diminutive woman. She crept forward, following the instincts that told her to keep herself low and slow. The moment the woman turned away towards Mateo, Elenor darted forward. The Infected spun impossibly fast and jammed the tip of a spear of light at Elenor. Eyes going wide, Elenor leapt straight into the air like a scalded cat. A chunk of the stone floor was blasted out a few feet from the end of the spear, and Elenor realized the danger.

The woman's weapons were designed specifically to fight against Elenor and Mateo. Instead of hitting their relics, it somehow projected force beyond the end of the spear so it would hit them on the inside of their bodies.

Elenor snarled as the woman raised the spear of light towards her and lashed out with talons. Green sparks exploded as her claws sheered through the spear. The woman jumped back and her coils glided forward in an attempt to form another. Elenor did not give her a chance.

Her claws hooked in the stone floor and she launched herself forward, smashing a shoulder into the Infected. Her spines there slashed through the Infected's arm, shearing it away as if it were rice paper. The spines cut deeply into her side before sliding past her. The woman screamed, but not in pain but rage. Her irises drew down to glowing green pinpoints, just like the woman in the museum. Her scream cut off as if someone had flipped a switch. Elenor sprinted past her and disappeared into the rubble of the destroyed pews. The floor exploded behind her as the woman finished forming her second spear.

Elenor prowled through the broken debris, and when she came around, her eyes went wide. The priest she had left on the front steps of the church stood silhouetted in the door. The Infected did not hesitate. She drew back her spear and threw.

"No!" Elenor bolted, her power pushing her to speeds that caused a bow wave of air to blast away from her as she passed the spear. There was no time to do anything more than put her body between the spear and the man. It slammed into her side and she felt it shatter against her Relic. Then, whatever power the spear was holding smashed into her chest.

She plowed into the floor, her spines raking gouges into the stone. She coughed and tasted copper, but the gout of fluid that spilled onto the floor from her muzzle was a deep royal blue instead of red. She had not seen her blood since the transformation, but there was no mistake.

"So you can be killed," the Infected gloated as she raised yet another spear of light. Elenor slammed her tail against the floor, her Striker hitting the stone tiles so hard that they shattered. The peel of sound absolutely destroyed all other noise, and Elenor called the Chords of Chaos. The thick, verdant coils around the various parts of her body exploded into motes of poisonous light before disappearing.

"Not that easily," Elenor fumed. She pushed herself to her feet and stalked forward. She gestured toward the Priest. "He is not a part of this and you would have killed him!" Elenor shrieked. She leapt in a blur and slammed her paws into the woman, knocking her to the ground. She stood on her chest, teeth bared in the Infected's face.

The woman's eyes drew down to pinpricks of angry burning light. That awful voice crawled from her throat. "All are part of the feast. Meaningless." The grinding, noxious whisper issuing forth from her mouth was beyond inhuman. It was a queer facsimile of a human voice, as if something were only aping a human but did not really understand. Each word was spoken flatly as if it were recorded entirely out of context and just played back in the correct order to make a sentence. Even robotic computer voices had more life than whatever this was.

Elenor roared in anger, her claws elongating until they were obsidian daggers. She slammed her claws down on the skull of the infected, sheering it into several pieces. Elenor swayed and ceased her Surge.

She looked up and saw the Priest in the doorway again. She turned to see Mateo padding towards her. There was no sign of the other two Infected, and Mateo's tentacles slithered back into his shoulders, vanishing from sight.

"Elly!" Mateo shouted, and ran towards her. The Priest startled, but he knelt down over her. Mateo looked as if he might attack.

"No, Mateo. He is…" she trailed off as she passed out.

Mateo leaned down and sniffed her, but there was no scent of death. He put one of his sight ears down against her side. They didn't need to breath nearly as often as they did when they were human. Mateo had easily held his breath for over thirty minutes, and Elenor had told him that her power allowed her to go without breathing at all. Instead, he looked at the blood flow. Their circulatory system was not quite like a human one, but they had been able to learn a few things. They each had a heart, and as long as the blood was still pumping, she would recover.

He lifted his head away from her side. Her heart was still working, so she would be fine. His sight ears picked up another odd sound and he turned his head towards the small puddle of blood that Elenor had coughed up. He pushed out his light webs until they wrapped around his ears to let him see. That was when he noticed that Elenor's blood was evaporating into motes of blue light.

"¡Vamos! Elly, get up," Mateo whispered.

 • ¡Vamos! – Come on!

"Are you demons?" the priest asked.

"No, Padre. No somos demonios. Simplemente ya no son humanos. Not sure how you can see me, you shouldn't be able to." Mateo focused on his Striker, and the Percept's Rest was still issuing forth from the multicolored crystals.

"I don't speak Spanish, Son." The priest replied.

"Not demons, just not human anymore." Mateo repeated.

It had certainly worked on the Infected. They had only been able to see him when they were touching him.

"Sorry about the church, Padre."

"Pews are just things; they can be fixed. Your friend saved me, will they be alright?" the priest asked.

"She'll wake up in a second." Mateo looked around. They couldn't just leave the Infected in the Church. They would recover, and when they did, they might wreck the place even more. They might hurt the priest.

Elenor's eyes popped open, and their glow intensified for a moment as they darted around. "What happened?" she whined.

"Just think you over did it. From what I can see of your insides, you've healed up from the spear just fine. Elly, we have to go and take the Infected with us."

Elenor pushed herself to her paws and let out a little whimper. "I can get them out of the city for a while. I don't think they'll come back once they recover, as long as we take the Fragment with us." Elenor padded towards the entrance. The priest stood between her and the way out.

Elenor narrowed balefully glowing eyes at him. He watched her for a moment, then seemed to realize he was standing in her way. He stepped aside and Elenor headed for the door, but froze when the priest spoke.

"Thank you."

"You're taking this much better than the last ten people who ran screaming from me," Elenor said.

The priest gave a little shrug. "The God I know never told anyone that only humans deserved love and respect."

Elenor looked up at him, and gave a little smile, no teeth involved. "Thanks, Father. Sorry we wrecked the place."

"A small challenge in the grand scheme of things for one in my line of work," he said. "You don't sound like you are old enough to be out fighting… whatever those things are."

"Yeah, well I doubt you'll ever see us again, so not your problem," Elenor grumble-squeaked.

"I don't need to see you again to worry for you."

Elenor sighed. "Sorry, Father, I've been on my own a long time. I'm older than I sound. I don't need anyone's concern after the fact."

Mateo came out and her ears perked as she noticed he was already calling the Surge to keep them invisible. "You're going to want to stand, not in the door, Father."

Elenor began to construct the instructions for her power in her head. Then she realized she was missing an important component. She unbuckled her bag and fiddled with her phone for a moment.

"Wow, the lake is freaking huge," she mumbled to herself as she struggled to buckle her bag back into place.

"Elly, ¿Qué haces?" Mateo sounded apprehensive.

"This." She finished her instructions for her power and let it loose. The power surged in her chest and the bodies of the Infected rose into the air. The large man was stirring and appeared to have mostly healed, though his left arm was still twisted viciously out of shape. A moment later, the bodies shot out the door and then catapulted away into the night as if fired from a ballista the size of a building.

   • ¿Qué haces? – what are you doing?

"Dónde," Mateo began, but Elenor knew what he was going to ask.

"The middle of Lake Ontario," Elenor said, and then headed down the stairs.

Mateo hurried after her. "¡Eso fue muy padre!"

"No, it was not! That was terrifying!" Elenor complained, but then she grinned. "I guess it was a little awesome."

"Hostia, did little miss doom and gloom actually crack a smile?" Mateo prodded.

"Shut up!" Elenor swiped a paw at Mateo but he ducked it. She rubbed her side where the spear had hit her. It felt fine now, but the phantom of pain was still there. "We're going to have to be more careful from now on, though," Elenor complained.

"We knew we weren't invincible, just durable."

"Guess I should have expected them to figure it out. It only took Helen a couple of days," Elenor groused. She lifted them into the air and pointed them back to the south.

- Dónde – Where,
- ¡Eso fue muy padre! – That, was awesome!
- Hostia, - Holy crap,

33
"MEMORY"

"What did you find?" Helen asked as they landed in the back yard.

"Hey, Helen, we almost died, great to see you too," Elenor squeaked and narrowed her eyes.

"It's almost like no one warned you that it would be dangerous and you should wait until we could go with you. Oh, wait. I did," Helen snarked sardonically.

"Yeesh, you're such a know-it-all," Elenor complained.

"Sorry, just feel useless sitting here. If I have what you found, at least I can help," Helen said.

"We got the memory fragment, but we ran into four of the Infected. They were different than the first ones. More controlled," Mateo said.

Elenor fished the marble out of her bag and held it up. Helen bent to inspect it, but then she stood up again.

"That is not for me," Helen said, her face pulling a frown.

"What do you mean?" Elenor dropped the Fragment back into her bag.

"I mean I cannot use it. I think only you can. I don't understand how that is possible. Ten generations separate you from the making of that Fragment."

Helen walked back towards the house, leading the way onto the covered patio of patterned brown brickwork. She sat down in one of the padded wickerwork chairs. Elenor's spines and claws melted into her fur and she climbed onto the comfortable white cushions of the matching couch across from Helen. Mateo followed suit a moment later, curling himself into one of the chairs that barely managed to hold him.

"We need another couch," he grumbled.

"We'll get one soon. So, go on check the memory,"
Helen urged.

Elenor unzipped the pack and dug through the
pocket until she came up with the new marble. She
squeezed it in her paw but nothing happened.

"It's not working."

"It's dormant, then. Just tap it against something. It
needs your resonance," Helen explained.

Elenor extruded a claw and tapped the marble. A
moment later, the world faded away as the Fragment
projected the memory onto the vaults of her mind.

NC 17, EPOCH 18418.137

*Osiris gazed upon the Writ for only the second time in his
life. Not since the day he was given his Writband had he seen
the Writ in person. Further, it had taken him years to figure
out how to access the Writ again. When he finally discovered
the method, he realized that there was a reason no one ever
attempted it.*

*The personal cost to access the Writ for a second time had
almost killed him. To bring yourself into the port dimension
where the Writ could be viewed required you to pay the cost
for the Surge to open the dimension from your own life force.
To gain access, the need would have to be so dire that one was
willing to risk their life to achieve the goal.*

*The polished stone wall inscribed with thousands of
symbols appeared before him as he pushed into the dimension.
Osiris could understand but not keep the symbols in his mind,
as they faded the moment that he looked elsewhere. Still, it
was enough for him to do his research. The stone pillar was
ten feet wide and no taller than his height of five feet, seven
inches.*

*He stepped up to the wall and placed his hand upon the
stone. He had never touched it before, and his eyes widened
with wonder as the wall seemed to unroll to his left and right.
It disappeared into the infinity of the port dimension which he
had entered to view it.*

He concentrated on moving through the numerous layers of the Writ. Here, he could not change anything, but he could see all of their reality laid out, all of history in ways that post-cognition did not allow, for this was the source. He did not bother to walk along the infinite wall for there was no need. He concentrated, and the wall began to slide past at an alarming rate.

He didn't bother to concentrate on the symbols as they blurred by until he came to one particular point. He had to confirm what he was already certain of, and a moment later, the answer hovered in front of him. The symbols slowed to a stop as he reached the end of the unfurling plane of stone.

He knew from his efforts with post cognition that the Earth on which they lived, to the contrary of all they had known, had not existed for billions of years. He pushed into the wall. The Writ had many layers, and just reaching the beginning did not tell him what he needed to know.

The first layer of stone faded away and a second emerged, as if he had passed through an insubstantial curtain. Each layer concerned the makeup of a different portion of reality. Physical, metaphysical, natural law, spiritual, and several others passed by until he reached the temporal layer. This layer contained the entire history of their reality.

Here, he found precisely what he had feared. The symbols spoke of how the Writ had been created precisely twenty-eight thousand years, eleven months, twenty-one days, and thirty-eight minutes earlier. All exterior measurements of age, Surge-found or otherwise, told them that Earth was several billion years old. The Writ, though, was the absolute representation of reality. That meant that this Writ had been created specifically to hide the events of the past even from the Callers.

Osiris paused to wonder how many Callers had killed themselves attempting to do what he was doing. He fell to one knee and coughed up a gout of blood that covered his fist. He did not have long, but there was more to do. If the Writ had been created, there would be a point where its creators were present to tie the Writ's metaphysical space to physical reality.

He concentrated and the wall flew by as he pushed himself to his feet.

He placed a hand on the smooth surface as it flew past until he sensed the place where the Earth had been formed. It had taken several thousand years for the process to complete, but even that was a pace beyond all sanity. The wall slowed to a crawl. It was here that whoever had created the Writ would return to make sure the metaphysical merged with the physical world.

Instead, he found something in the record that made his hands shake in sheer blinding panic. The Writ, in forming its connection with their reality, had detected something that should not be. A creature of such vile degradation that Osiris had to control his stomach as he recoiled in pure revulsion. It came from the outside. Its only purpose was to consume.

If it were to discover their tiny blue planet, it would be the end. It could devour even the power of Callers. Worse, from what he could see of the nebulous information surrounding the creature's existence, it was seeking to consume all sentient life. How had it existed in the universe before the connection of the Writ? It took all of his will to pry his eyes away from the end of life on his world.

He continued to follow the historical record, and within minutes, he found the moment he was looking for, the moment when the Writ was bound to this reality. It came into focus. A vicious tearing pain contracted Osiris' chest. He fell to his knees, vomiting blood and bile as the life force being drawn went beyond the threshold needed to keep him vital.

The port dimension spat him out onto the sand-strewn floor of the desert outside of his current home and again, blood frothed from his mouth. Every bit of his strength went into staying awake, for if he collapsed here under the desert sun, he would not wake to see the morrow. Without what he now knew, his death would not be the only casualty of his failure to see that last small part of the puzzle.

Stumbling into the cave mouth, he took three steps and tumbled to the ground, landing half on his bedroll and half on the sandstone floor. Before passing into unconsciousness, he *burned the memory of what he had seen into his mind, repeatedly reciting the timeframe in his head. When he woke, he would find the place where the Writ had first been physically tethered to their world. He would finally explain exactly why everything they thought they knew about the history of their reality was a lie.*

Elenor emerged from Osiris' memory slightly confused, and when she realized what she had seen, panic overtook her. She shivered uncontrollably as she tried to recover from what she had seen. The Merlin's warning about not revealing everything to Helen came back to her, and she frantically tried to think of what to tell her.

Elenor decided that she couldn't lie, but she didn't have to tell her the whole truth, either. She told her only the part where Osiris found what he was looking for in the history of the Writ, but that he hadn't been able to stay long enough to observe it.

"This is not forming a good picture. We always thought that Osiris went mad from overuse of precognitive Surges. Seeing into your own future can be mentally damaging." Helen worried her thumbnail between her teeth. "But there is clearly so much more behind his actions."

"What are you saying?" Mateo asked.

"I am, not sure yet. I do not believe anything could excuse what Osiris did. His attempts to forcefully evolve humanity killed hundreds of thousands of people." Helen paused in thought and fished a small black leatherbound notebook from a pocket.

"But knowing that he was looking for something specific in the past and his willingness to spend his own life to get it do not speak to the same kind of madness he exhibited when I killed him," Helen stated.

"So what do we do now?" Elenor wondered.

"Could it have been a trick?" Helen pondered.

"¿Qué?" Mateo asked.

"At the end, he seemed quite insane. He was gibbering about the end of all things and how we would all be sorry. I wonder if it could have been an act." Helen shook her head. "I can't be sure. I remember it well, but Osiris was convincing in his madness."

"What would that mean?" Elenor asked.

"If he was only acting for my benefit, it indicates some sort of plan after his death." Helen began to chew a thumbnail in thought.

Mateo's sight ears swiveled up to Helen. "Entonces, ¿qué hacemos ahora?"

"We find the end of this thread and pull. Somehow, Osiris knew that you would be here. He will have left the rest of his story for you."

Elenor nodded. "I don't know how to find the next piece." She stood up and shook herself like a wet dog, attempting to calm the fearful shaking.

"Go through Merlin's things. They led you to this fragment, maybe they will lead you to another," Helen advised.

"¿Sabes algo más? You were there." Mateo asked.

"Only what I have told Elenor already over her training period. I should be receiving some of my own Fragments from that time in a few days," Helen said. "Go get started. I am going to finish helping Thia work up the initiator for her Writband. You're going to need all the help you can get soon."

Elenor nodded and hopped down from the couch. She tapped her tail on the flagstones of the patio and the notes of the Keymaster's March flowed from her Striker. In the middle of the yard, the doorway filled with a view of starry night through it grew from the middle of the yard. She paused for a moment when doorway fully

- ¿Qué? – What?
- Entonces, ¿qué hacemos ahora? – So, what do we do now?
- ¿Sabes algo más? – Do you know anything more?

formed. Something about the sound it made in the Chorus twinged something in her brain, but whatever connection the sound was attempting to make, it just would not come.

"What is it?"

"I'm… not sure. The sound of the door into the Hammerspace. The way it changes the Chorus here. There is something," Elenor trailed off, then shrugged. "I can't tell for sure." She hopped through the doorway and Mateo followed right on her tail. When they emerged through the darkness, they both froze. They were in an entirely different space than the workroom that they had emerged into on previous trips.

Vaulted ceilings of polished onyx marble like the night sky stretched hundreds of yards into the distance. The stone expanse was upheld by columns of black marble shot through with veins of silver. Each set of columns bracketed teak wood shelves, masterfully carved with fanciful scenes of creatures frolicking through forests never seen on earth. Each shelf was a dozen feet high and supported hundreds of books.

Just a dozen feet away, there was a collection of plush armchairs covered in deep purple velvet. Each chair was accented in white oak, with feet carved as the paws of animals. The six beautiful chairs surrounded a low stone wall with a warm glow emitting from within. The entire space was somehow lit from everywhere and nowhere. There did not seem to be any source for the lights.

Mateo stepped up next to Elenor and when she looked over, she realized that he did not cast a shadow. It was as if the light had filled the space like water.

"¡Guau!" Mateo's whispered exclamation startled a twitch from Elenor.

"It is quite something, is it not?" The Merlin's disembodied voice came from somewhere within the

• ¡Guau! – Wow!

shelves. A moment later, the remnant wandered out of
shelving, long fingered hands holding a large tome. He
was resplendent in royal purple robes with gold brocade
trim. Wide sleeves that might hide a small cornucopia
of items if they were not see through swayed in time
with the hem of his robe as he moved. The trim around
his neck was knotted, and waved in a pattern that Elenor
realized was a moment later was reminiscent of a Surge.

"Nice dress." Elenor's sardonic squeak made the
Merlin chuckle.

"I admit my younger self was a creature of his time.
Wizards were expected to wear robes in those days.
One lost all credibility without them," the remnant said
as he closed the book.

"We got the fragment. It was in Toronto." Elenor
held up the marble. The remnant peered at it for a
moment, but then shook his head.

"It is Resonance locked to you? Quite interesting.
How did Osiris know your Resonance Signature?" the
remnant wondered.

Elenor explained the memory to him and then took
the time to explain to Mateo what Helen had told her
she remembered about hunting Osiris. How they had
found his method for making Resonance Crystals and
how he had used them to create the Infected.

"I never saw any green crowns around their heads,"
Mateo said.

"After I broke the crown of the first one on Hart-
Miller Island, something changed. They started hiding
them somehow," Elenor explained.

"We never saw such things in the original Infected.
You say that after you broke it, the man returned to
normal? That should not even be possible." The
remnant turned back to the shelves and began walking.
Elenor and Mateo trotted to keep up.

"Helen thinks that because this fragment is keyed to
me, Osiris must have somehow left behind the rest of

his story for me," Elenor said. The remnant nodded. "A deduction I agree with."

"But, how do we find the rest?" Mateo pondered.

"He would have left a clue with the shard, I think," the remnant said as he walked past several shelves in a single aisle of the library.

"I watched the whole memory. There was nothing there," Elenor complained.

"Where did you find it?"

"It was inside of this black stone tablet."

"Did you break it?" the remnant asked.

Elenor shook her head. "No, I used the Ghostwalker's Etude to pull it out."

"The tablet was the likely clue."

Elenor's face pulled an extremely sharp frown. "I have to go back to Toronto? With all of those Infected?"

"Not at all. You can just make a memory fragment of your own," the remnant suggested from some unseen place amongst the shelves.

"I don't remember it that well."

"Of course you do. Alright, a lesson in the functioning of the memory. All people's memories are quite perfect. Everything you see, hear, and experience is flawlessly recorded. The issue is the interface between the consciousness and the memory. That is why Memory Fragments were created."

"So, everyone remembers everything? Like a memoria fotográfica?" Mateo asked.

"Exactly like that. The issue is not that you do not remember, it is that your conscious mind doesn't have access to those memories. I am not going to delve into the biology of the process. It does not matter. What does is that a Memory Fragment can record memories with perfect accuracy, even if you cannot consciously recall them."

"I can make a fragment that will show me what was

   • memoria fotográfica – photographic memory

on the tablet just because I saw it once?" Elenor asked.

The remnant nodded. He came out from the shelves carrying a small thick book with a blue leather cover. The remnant carried it in transparent hands to the reading area and put it down on the table.

"This book contains a number of standard Surges. Keep in mind these are note-based Surges. You know what that means?" he asked.

Elenor and Mateo both nodded. They had heard the term from Helen. It meant a drawn soundwave for a Surge that was its most basic form. To call a Surge, the base music needed to be improvised to work with the Chorus wherever you happened to be.

Elenor put her front paws on the table and looked at the Surge in the book. It was three soundwaves overlapped atop one another. In the magical way of Surges, Elenor could easily see each individual soundwave as if the others were not drawn on the same sheet. These were not drawn in a circle, but a straight line. That meant that they were not to be continuously played. They had a definite beginning and end. There was some writing above the Surge, but it was in a language that Elenor did not understand.

"What language is this?" Elenor asked. The remnant peered at it for a long moment.

"Old High German, I believe. Each is a quick explanation, but they are mostly meant for apprentices before they gain their Writband and can hear the Chorus."

Elenor studied the Surge for a moment and then tilted her head listening to the Chorus. She tapped her Striker on the floor and called the Fugue of Fragmented Memory. She concentrated on the memory of the black stone tablet. Motes of light sprang to life in the air around her head, and then a moment later, she held up her paw.

The motes streamed towards the center of her paw and gathered into a point of blinding light. She squinted her eyes, but the light was already fading. Left behind was a night black marble filled with stars.

"That was easier than I, thought, it…" Elenor's speech slurred to a stop.

"Elly?!" Mateo scurried over to her, sight ears twitching and nose snuffling.

"It's okay, she'll be okay. I couldn't catch her before she started the Surge, and by then, it was too late. I'll explain as soon as she comes to," Merlin's remnant assured.

A moment later, Elenor blinked with abnormal slowness, and then a few more times more normally. She opened her mouth to speak, but the remnant interrupted.

"Don't speak just yet. All Surges have some sort of cost. This one has a bit more of a personal cost than others. Creating a copy of a memory drains some of the electrical energy that your brain uses to function."

"That sounds really peligroso," Mateo interrupted. The remnant shook his head.

"It is not. The Surge leaves behind a small warp in reality that will draw the cost from your body's nervous system, but the transfer is a slow process. Only ever create a memory fragment when you are safe and can lie down comfortably for at least a few minutes." He reached down and plucked the marble out of Elenor's paw.

"Shouldn't we look at that?" Mateo objected. The remnant shook his head.

"Not unless you have recently learned ancient Egyptian." Elenor took a deep breath and then sighed it out.

"Alright, I think I'm fine now."

"You should be, and it's not surprising that you

 • peligroso - dangerous

missed this. It was cleverly done. The tablet," A moment later, the specter blinked and looked at Elenor.

"How did he do this thing?" the remnant wondered.

"¿Quién?" Mateo asked first, his tail lashing clearly out of his control. At least he had retracted his Striker into his Relic.

"Osiris." The remnant held out the marble to Elenor. "It is you. Here, observe your memory. You will understand."

Elenor held out her paw and the remnant dropped the marble into it. She curled her digits around the marble, closing her eyes. Watching her own memories felt slightly different. There was no sense of being outside of her body as she had previously felt when watching Osiris' memories. The only oddity she felt this time was the inability to control her actions.

She could only focus on things that were in her direct line of sight. Apparently, she had gotten her best view of the tablet when she was crouched atop the glass case prowling after the Infected in the museum.

This time, though, the tablet was different. In three locations on the tablet, she could see Surges carved into the inside of the stone. Each circular Surge pattern was a minor variation on the Da Capo Al Coda, which allowed you to teleport small objects over great distances.

"How do I know the names of the Surges?" Elenor wondered aloud. A whisper came to her ear. It was clear, but it also sounded if it was extremely far away.

"It's the Notemark. All Surges have a Notemark at the beginning. It takes some practice to sense, and see them. It is obvious you have reached the required skill."

Elenor followed his instructions. A moment of hard focus on the beginning of the Surge revealed a glowing ring of words rising to glow beneath the wave form pattern of the Surge.

 • ¿Quién? – Who?

"Whomever creates a new Surge is required to provide a name. Whenever that Surge is carved or written down, a Notemark will appear with the name of the Surge. Some were more creative with their names than others," the remnant chuckled.

Elenor uncurled her digits and the memory vanished. "The Surge only had some numbers and a direction."

"That means it was a targeted Surge. It had an anchor to work with so it didn't need exact coordinates, so the numbers are only a distance."

"The numbers weren't as big as I thought they would be."

"The distance will be in leagues. A league is ten and a half kilometers. What was the number?"

"Sixty-five point seventy-eight," Elenor recited.

"Four hundred twenty-nine miles, give or take," Mateo said, and they both looked at him.

"¿Qué? I told you I was good at math," he complained.

"Mateo, good at math is not what you just did," Elenor said.

Mateo gave a little shrug with his first pair of shoulders. "What direction?"

"Southeast." Elenor sat thinking staring at the Shard in her hand. "It has to be another museum, right?"

"Almost certainly," the remnant said.

"We need to get back. We need the Oracle."

"Elenor, Mateo, be careful. We don't have enough pieces yet to understand this whole puzzle. But I have a feeling it will have consequences beyond our sight."

Elenor nodded and Mateo waved a paw.

"How do we get back here?" Elenor asked. "When you come again, I will teach you how to get into all the spaces in this port dimension," the remnant promised.

"Soon," Elenor said.

Mateo nodded.

 • ¿Qué? – What?

"Soon." The remnant nodded.

34

"SOUNDING BOARD"

NC 17, EPOCH 19915.39

When they came out of the Hammerspace, Helen was sitting on the patio drinking a glass of lemonade. Thia wasn't far away, sitting on the grass with a large piece of thick paper on the patio stones in front of her.

Thia looked up. "You two look like you're headed somewhere."

Elenor nodded. "We need to look at the Oracle or the internet. We need to know what is exactly." She looked to Mateo.

Mateo's sight ears bobbed to one side and then the other, a roll of the eyes for him. "Four hundred twenty-nine miles to the southwest of the museum in Toronto."

"Well, there is a lot of stuff that far Southwest from Toronto," Thia replied.

Elenor unhooked her bag from around her neck and then sat back on her haunches. She found the snaps on the back of the bag by feel and flipped over the flap that held her phone. "Yeah, but I bet not too many museums." She glanced at Helen as she felt the woman's eyes on her. What the remnant had shown her came unbidden to her mind. She felt her tail lashing in irritation and stilled it, but it was too late. Helen had noticed. Interestingly, she said nothing. She merely picked up her lemonade and went into the house. Thia noted it and then looked back to Elenor.

"Alright, spill. You've been eyeing mom askance for two weeks solid. If I noticed, she noticed."

Elenor exchanged a glance with Mateo and then stared at the house. She turned around, walking towards the woods. Mateo followed, and Thia pushed herself to her feet right on their tails. They walked for a half hour to a clearing in the woods where there were signs of the training that Elenor and Mateo had been doing.

Elenor turned around and fished in the bag around her neck. A moment later, she came out with a memory fragment. She held it out between her thumb and fore digit. She said nothing and just stood there, waiting for Thia to take it. She wasn't sure she should show this to Thia, but she had held it back long enough. Thia had a right to know that something had been tampering with her mother's mind for a long time.

"What is this?" Thia asked, but Elenor just shook her head and proffered the marble again. She took the fragment and closed her fist around it. It wasn't the first time that she had used a Memory Fragment. She had used dozens when learning to call Surges. Elenor and Mateo waited, shuffling nervously as Thia viewed the memory. When her eyes crept open after a long minute, her fingers numbly dropped the fragment. She fell to her knees and tears rolled from her eyes.

"I don't know if it is true," Elenor began.

"It's true," Thia said. "You don't see everything yet. You don't have enough experience with listening to the Chorus to understand, but this memory from the Merlin is unquestionable." Thia bent down and picked up the dropped fragment. "You were right to keep it from her because I know what triggers her to do these things. I have lived with her for over a hundred years." Thia sniffed and tried to scrub the tears from her eyes with the back of a hand.

"I've only seen that power come out three times in my life, but the pattern is clear. The first two times, it was relics that could have let us look into the distant past. The last one was a journal that was supposed to have belonged to Anep Tanan Rah. He was the Osiris before the last Osiris. The journal contained a dozen Surges related to his work. Some of those Surges were for empowering normal humans with supernatural powers, but others were designed to gather information from the past."

"Así que, whatever is controlling Helen doesn't want anyone looking into the past," Mateo pondered.

Thia shrugged. "Or trying to make the masses supernaturally powerful. You need to show me the rest."

"The rest?" Elenor asked.

"The rest of what you have found. And then you need to call this Surge." Thia unfolded a piece paper and showed Elenor a very complex surge with eight notes layered over top of one another. Elenor stared at it hard for a long moment but no name rose up from beneath the waveform.

"Where is the name?"

"That is up to you," Thia said, and Elenor stared for a long moment.

"But you made it," Elenor protested.

Thia shook her head and pointed at Elenor's tan furred chest. "No, the Writ chose you for this. Without you, I would not have been able to make this Surge. It is your creation. I just helped."

Elenor looked to Mateo, but he shook his head. "I've got nothing here. I only know what you all have taught me about music. I'm still wrestling with the fact that I can play this thing." Mateo lifted his tail and shook the Striker at the end back and forth.

Elenor looked back to Thia. "I don't know."

"Well, you cannot call a new Surge without a name." Thia grinned, and Elenor's ears drew down in discomfort. "I truly hope I don't get mood ears like yours and Mateo's. You're just too adorable when teased."

Elenor bared her teeth, blades and spikes growing all over her body, vibrating threateningly like the hiss of a cat. "How about now?" she hissed, and Thia jumped

• Así que – So,

back a little.

"Augh!" Thia groaned sarcastically. "So touchy!" She sat down in the grass with a laugh. They spent a content few minutes brainstorming the name of the Surge, eventually arriving at a name they all felt was best.

"Will it happen right away, as soon as I call this?" Elenor asked.

Thia shook her head. "I have no idea. It shouldn't, because the writband should need time to work, but the Writ is more or less all powerful, so it might happen instantly."

"Alright, we'll go back to the house before I call this for you. But there were other things we wanted to bounce off of you," Elenor said.

"Alright, shoot." Thia leaned back into the grass of the clearing and pillowed her head on her hands.

"We found some other information about Osiris and what's happening with the Infected."

Thia nodded. "Mom told me about it. So far, her thoughts are that Osiris might not have been quite as insane as she originally thought, which is probably not better."

"We have something more. I think maybe he was working for something else," Elenor said.

"Something?"

Elenor took out the marble from the Royal Ontario Museum and held it out to Thia. Thia didn't take it right away.

"Why did you trust me but not Mom?"

Elenor opened her mouth, then closed it again without saying anything. She wasn't sure how to explain the situation with the Merlin.

Thia went on, "You have never seen her use that power. Where did you get the Memory Fragment?"

"I got it in the Merlin's hammerspace."

"You said you got it, not you found it."

Elenor sighed. "I couldn't tell you until you saw the bit about your mom."

"Tell me what?" Thia asked.

"There is, a, remnant in the hammerspace. It's like a ghost of Merlin from a long time ago," Elenor explained. Surprisingly, Thia's face remained entirely unphased.

"So, is it from before he became a self-absorbed nepotistic megalomaniacal piece of shit?" Thia asked blandly.

"I think so. He seems nice. He didn't try to kill me on sight. I thought you would be angry. You really seemed to hate him."

"I hated what he turned into, but mom loved him like a brother once. I think I understand him a little more, now." Thia sat up and then pushed herself to her feet. "We can talk to him later, but for now, let's see if we can piece some of this together."

Elenor and Mateo tilted their heads, ears on one side falling as the other perked up.

Thia giggled. "You two are adorable, no matter how scary you can be. I mean, we have enough information to make some guesses." Thia held out her hand for the Memory Fragment.

"I'm not sure if you will be able to see it. Your mom said only I could watch it," Elenor explained.

Thia drew back her hand. "Then I will just have to trust you to tell me everything you saw." Thia shrugged.

"I already told you the thing I was terrified about. No reason to lie now," Elenor reasoned. Then she explained all of what she had seen, even about the creature that would kill and devour every living thing on their world.

"This makes it even more likely that Osiris was not the kind of insane we thought. If Osiris wasn't just apeshit moonbat," Thia began.

"Then maybe he had a reason for doing what he did," Mateo finished for her.

Thia pointed at him. "Good reasons or not, if he is not just another madman trying to destroy the world or some other such nonsense, then we can't write him off once he is dead. If he has a true plan, that is a different thing all together."

"So, he saw that eventually some godlike creature was going to come along and eat everyone, and he, what? Decided to wreck the planet first?" Elenor postulated.

"Maybe. Maybe he thought we would be better off," Thia responded, but then shook her head. "I don't think so though. I think," Thia's eyes widened as things began to lock together in her mind. "No, it's not possible."

"What?" Mateo asked.

Thia shook as she lifted a hand and touched a finger to the marble Elenor was still holding. *Osiris discovered the extra dimensional creature stalking their reality.*

"He knew. There is more here, but this makes it clear. He knew what was coming. This thing isn't just out wandering our universe, not some naturally occurring creature. It's here, for us."

"How can you know?" Mateo asked, and Elenor nodded along, having the same question.

"It's how you phrased it. He felt like it came from the outside." Thia made air quotes around 'from the outside.' "That has a specific meaning among Callers. The outside is other dimensions. Places that are completely alien to our reality."

"When you say he knew, you mean," Mateo started, then swallowed and looked at Elenor.

"When he made the Infected, he was trying to make something to fight this monster?" Elenor's voice turned up at the end, making it a question.

Thia nodded. "Yes, but not the Infected. I think," Thia swallowed nervously and looked between Elenor and Mateo. She wasn't nervous about Mateo. He had been waiting his entire life to do something fantastical. Elenor, though, had no support. She had been ambushed by her transformation and forced to endure all that followed without any help at all. She saw the hurt, and anger in Elenor's glowing eyes as she pieced it together faster than Thia could speak.

"He knew he was making the Bearers. He knew he was turning people into monsters," Elenor finished.

Angry tears gathered at the corners of Elenor's eyes and ran down the sides of her muzzle. "He knew," she hissed in fury. She squeezed her eyes shut and a pulse of, something, passed through the air. "He knew!" Elenor's scream mutated into the shriek of a creature of such power that the entire world paused for attention. Terror beyond reason froze every animal in the forest. Squirrels tumbled from trees, and birds feel from the sky, frozen beyond their ability to reason or even act on instinct.

Thia watched, her own fear screaming for her to run, but she knew that wouldn't help. No mere mortal could outrun this.

"Elenor!" Thia tried to get her attention, but those glowing eyes fixed on nothing. She was only fury. There was room for nothing else. In that moment, Thia saw the true power hiding inside of Elenor. Those agonized eyes focused. In the tear-stained portals of boiling fire, all the loss and pain emerged. The glow intensified until her eyes were two suns burning in her skull. One blinding azure, one searing violet.

The eyes of an angry god.

Thia squeezed her eyes shut in acceptance. No prayer would save the world from the consequences of the wrongs it had done to her.

Mateo saw the danger almost too late. He dove on top of Thia, tackling her to the ground. He spread his body over the top of her and his tentacles snaked out, whipping themselves around Mateo and Thia in an obsidian cage of segmented relic stone. Blades of grass became true knives, whipping past them at speeds that boggled the mind. Mateo flattened all four ears as a roar of the world being torn apart at the seams thundered into existence. It slammed into them, threatening to tear the very fabric of reality into tattered shreds.

Trees came apart like wet carboard in the hands of a careless toddler. Roaring detonations came from each destroyed timber until there was nothing but chaos. Massive sections of earth were torn up and flung away like flotsam in a tornado as the root balls of enormous trees were torn from the ground by Elenor's rampant power. Dirt and shredded wood rained around Mateo, yet somehow, not a single piece touched Mateo's tentacles. He lifted his sight ears, but could see nothing. The sound was just too pervasive.

"Elly! ¡Para!" Mateo's bellow might as well have been a pin drop on an active battlefield, for all the chance it had of piercing that wall of absolute sound. He forced out his light webs so he could see what was happening around them and immediately wished he had not.

Complete desolation.

The wood had been swept away for hundreds of yards in all directions and pulled into a maelstrom of unstoppable devastation. Every moment that passed, dozens of trees exploded and were swept away into the furious tornado.

"I thought she couldn't control water, just in living things!" Mateo yelled.

"Plants don't die the second they are destroyed!" Thia screamed back. "Elenor! You have to stop!"

 • ¡Para! – Stop!

"Why aren't we dead?! ¡Deberíamos estar muertos!"
Mateo yelled. Elenor could be flinging them about or
ripping all the water from their bodies just as easily as
she was doing it to the forest.

"I don't know!" Thia responded.

Then, Helen flew past them in a blur of movement.
She flashed between the flying debris towards Elenor as
fast as a bullet, yet it was still too slow to achieve her
goal. Just as she got within a few feet of Elenor, her feet
came away from the ground and she was flung
backwards.

She tumbled to the ground next to Mateo. He
unfurled his tentacles and used them to drag Helen's
limp body in next to Thia. He reformed the cage. A
moment later, Helen jerked and sat up, banging her
head on the rock-hard relic stone of his tentacles.

"Fuck!" Helen groaned. "What has happened?!"

"We figured out that Osiris was trying to make
monsters! He knew, and she was so angry!" Thia said.

"He took everything from her! What were you going
to do?!"

Helen came up with a gem-cut crystal about the size
of her palm. A band of gold ringed the stone. It was
light blue in color, with flowing swirls of purple within.
"It'll calm her down!"

Mateo lifted his head and watched for a long minute.
It became quickly clear that the storm did not touch
them.

"Mateo, you'll have to get the crystal to her. I can't
do it!" Helen shouted.

Mateo shook his head. "She's not going to hurt us!"
He unfurled his tentacles, retracting them back into his
body. He turned, and, digging his claws into the torn
ground, leaned into wind generated by the swirling
objects. As he pulled himself forward, a bubble of safety
seemed to move with him. Helen stepped closer to Thia,

• ¡Deberíamos estar muertos! – We should be dead!

and just as Mateo said, the maelstrom flowed around them.

It took Mateo a full minute to push through the tremendous vortex and reach Elenor. Her eyes were squeezed shut, tears leaking from their corners, her teeth bared in a rictus of wrath. When Mateo dragged himself close enough, he put his nose against Elenor's

"Elly, está bien. We know what he took from you." Mateo didn't scream it. He was as calm as he could be with the world ending around him.

"It was my whole life, and he knew what he was doing!" Elenor's enraged sobbing cut through the roar.

"Yo sé, but you found a new one," Mateo said.

Elenor opened her eyes, and though they still glowed, it wasn't with the scorching ferocity of a thousand suns. A cacophony of wood and dirt assaulted them as the flying rubble tumbled from the sky and smashed into a perfect circle around them.

"I thought," Elenor whined and sniffed loudly, "I had this under control."

"You lost a big piece of your life and that was hard enough when it was just random," Thia comforted as she and her mother approached.

"He didn't even care who he might hurt." Elenor's furious squeak caused debris to rattle around her with threat. A few more tears leaked form her eyes, shining in the light of her glowing irises.

"What makes you think that Osiris did this?" Helen asked Thia as she turned slowly, taking in the swath of destruction Elenor had left in her wake, eyes wide with awe.

"Osiris was attempting to access the Writ, but it almost killed him to do it. But whatever he found there was important enough to keep trying. He knew he couldn't do it himself, but if he could make someone

- está bien – it's ok
- Yo sé – I know

who could," Thia postulated. It wasn't the truth. She didn't dare tell her mother the full truth until they could figure out what was happening to her and put a stop to it.

Helen began to nod uncertainly. "It makes even more sense when you consider his attempts to change the Writ as a whole," Helen agreed.

"How so?" Thia asked.

Elenor broke into the conversation. "I think I need to be alone for a bit." She turned and galloped into what was left of the forest. Mateo lifted a paw to go after her, but Thia called him back.

"I would give her a little space. She's got a lot to work out. Just be there when she's ready?" Thia proposed.

Mateo turned back and sat on his haunches. "Bien."

Helen nodded at Thia. "Back to your question. The Writ is not alive and intelligent in the way we normally judge intelligence. It does have intelligence, though, and in some ways, it is far beyond ours." Helen gestured back towards the house and began to walk towards it.

"If there is a threat to the entire planet, it will react accordingly to counter the threat. Its responses have been documented in the past, and some Callers had figured out how to trigger specific reactions from the Writ. Osiris knew this," Helen continued.

"That sounds wicked dangerous," Thia said.

Helen nodded. "Extremely so. If the Writ realizes a Caller is actively manipulating it, there are consequences. I have seen the Writ rip away a Caller's Writband for such offenses. I would much rather die than suffer that fate, and I cannot imagine any Caller who wouldn't agree."

Puzzle pieces clicked together in Mateo's thoughts. Having heard some of the other parts of the story from Elenor, the connections were now clear. His sight ears leaned drastically away from each other in a wide V, but didn't flatten. It conveyed the sense of a widening of the eyes. "Puta madre, that's why he needed the Resonance Crystals."

"You're right," Thia said. "To mask himself from the Writ."

"Así que it wouldn't be able to recognize him to pull away his power," Mateo finished for her.

Helen shook a finger at him in acknowledgement. "Of course! By passing his Surge through the crystals, it would alter the signature of the Surge." Her shaking finger slowed. "But what I still do not understand is the trigger for all of this. Something pushed him over the edge."

"Maybe we will find it in the next Fragment," Thia proposed. "But first, we need to make a monster out of me. For that, we need to help from Elenor."

"Go find her, Mateo. Thia will be along in a minute. I need to talk to her," Helen urged. Mateo nodded and trotted off into the woods, his Striker glittering a rainbow of light as it flailed behind him. Thia turned back to her mother.

"You know, you have always had a tell when you are not telling me the whole truth. You never lie to me, Thia, but when you hold back you do this." Helen pressed her lips together.

Thia opened her mouth but her mother held up her hands in a gesture of surrender. "Do not take that the wrong way. I am not asking you to tell me what is wrong, because you will do that when you feel the time is right. I just want you to know that I am not an idiot. You think there is something wrong related to me, and you think that telling me could be dangerous."

"How," Thia started, and Helen grinned at her.

"Do not let the smooth skin fool you, kid. I am

- Puta madre – Holy shit
- Así que - So

almost eighteen hundred years old. You live as long as I have, you have not just seen everything, you have seen it at least thrice. It is a little boring, honestly."

"I want to tell you," Thia frowned.

Helen shook her head. "Not yet, Thia. Trust your instincts. You will know when the time is right to fix this. I trust you, without reservation. Now go on. Help them find their way." Helen gave her a little shove in the direction Mateo had run off. "And run quick, because you cannot follow your nose like he can yet!" Helen shouted as Thia disappeared into the woods.

35

"THE LAST TIME I CRY"

NC 17, EPOCH 19915.39

Elenor sat on the banks of the South Branch of the Patapsco River and watched across the rushing water as a train rumbled by. She smelled Mateo before she could see him, so paying attention to her nose was turning out to be helpful, at least. His paws were near silent despite all of the snow and leaves. She wondered how he was doing that. She continued to watch the train go by as angry tears dribbled down either side of her muzzle.

"You know I hate crying. I never understood why other girls felt better after they cried. It just ticks me off. Am I so weak that the way I feel just gets to run my bodily functions?" The tears dripped onto her paws, and Mateo arranged his six with care before sitting down in the snow beside her. He didn't say anything right away, just sat and watched the train go by.

"My friends, before all of this, used to tell me when they cried, it made them feel better. It never makes me feel better. It just makes me feel like a failure," Elenor confessed.

"I just thought all girls cried to feel better. Figured it was just sort of baked into your DNA." Mateo had a little laugh in his voice.

"I kinda wish it was." Elenor curled her tail around her paws protectively. "It'd be nice if I could just drip a few tears and feel better."

"Maybe if you stop blaming yourself for the tears and just let yourself feel better, it could work that way for you."

"Maybe, but I don't know if I'll ever be ready for that."

"Well, I'm no therapist, but I talked to a whole lot of them after I got shot. One of the things I learned from them is that our feelings don't always make sense, even to us, but they are your feelings. Sometimes you just gotta listen to what they are telling you if you want to learn how to be yourself."

"I was hoping this would be the last time I cried, but now you're telling me my feelings are saying I'm some sort of cry baby?" Elenor grinned a sharky grin at him.

"Quizá I'm just saying that having to cry out your bad feelings isn't the worst thing to have to do."

"Oh?" Elenor looked at him her ears flattening slightly and her eyes narrowing in a predatory fashion. "So, what do you have to do to get your bad feelings out?"

Mateo's sight ears leaned one way and then the other, an eye roll, before he stood up. He padded on silent paws through the snow to a tree. He walked up the side of the tree, pausing for a second when two of his paws stuck fast to the bark. He struggled for a second to pull them lose. "Estupido spider hairs," he grumbled, and finally they released. He finished his walk up the trunk to a thick branch. Once he was halfway out on the branch, his thick rat-like tail wrapped around it several times. He flipped upside-down and hung by his tail. "This," he said.

"But you didn't always have a tail."

Mateo laughed. "No, I would hang by my legs. I went through like four therapists before I found one that actually understood why I wasn't pissed and angsty about getting shot. She helped me a lot, and she taught me that sometimes, if I just do something to make myself feel silly, it helped check all the feelings of inadequacy. The ones I had about not being able to stop those jerks from hurting anyone else." Mateo unwound his tail and dropped to the ground.

"Doesn't that hurt? Your tail is so thin." Elenor asked.

- Quizá - Maybe
- Estupido - Stupid

Mateo shook his head. "The thing is way stronger than it looks."

Elenor wiped her tears with the back of her paw. "How am I going to know when I'm finally okay with this?"

"No eres," Mateo said, his ears tilting to one side, indicating confusion.

"What?"

"You're not, Elly. You're never going to be ok with what happened to you, and you shouldn't be."

Elenor's ears fell and she stilled, looking over the water as the last train car glided past. Mateo slid his tail around her shoulders.

"You should be pissed about what was done to you. It's not about getting rid of your feelings, that's never going to happen. It's about using those feelings in a way that makes you happy. Así que, they don't eat you up inside."

"I'll try."

"Just try not to rip apart an entire forest again?" Mateo jibed.

"I'll do my best." Elenor scooted closer and put her head on his shoulder.

Footsteps came from behind and Elenor lifted her head, but Mateo's sight ears swiveled. "It's Thia."

Elenor put her head back on his shoulder. "Okay."

A minute later, Thia picked her way out of the trees and shrubbery to arrive on the bank of the river with them. She paused for a moment and then fished in her pocket. "Don't you two dare move an inch!" She was holding back a giggle. Elenor began to lift her head again. "Not an inch!" Thia hissed. She produced her phone a moment later.

"¿Qué haces?" Mateo asked.

- No eres – You're not
- Así que – So
- ¿Qué haces? – What are you doing?

"Shush, this is perfect!" Thia held up her phone and clicked a few pictures of the two of them from behind. As soon as they realized what she was doing, they scurried away from each other.

"Thia!" Elenor squeaked.

"What? I was dying of the cute you two were putting off. I had to have a picture. So many fuzzy ears!" Thia laughed, and Elenor hissed.

"Gonna have to get over it. We are cute sometimes. I mean, have you seen these things?" Mateo wiggled his sight ears and his smaller sound ears in a flutter of fur. The huge fuzzy triangles simply screamed darling cuteness.

"Fine! But I swear, if I ever see it out of that phone," Elenor growled.

Thia made a raspberry noise. "As if I'm not going to be the first one to post this when the whole world finds out about us. This is going up the second I can do it. We're gonna sell them on greeting cards and make millions!"

"Yeah, until they learn that we actually look like this." Elenor expressed every claw and spine on her entire body, opened the glowing golden eyes on her back, and peeled her lips back from the double row of murder blades filling her mouth. She crouched down, and somehow darkness seemed to gather around her.

"Well, maybe you don't show them that part." Thia tsked, and then after a moment, asked, "Are you ok, Elenor?"

All of the terrifying parts retracted into her body and the darkness fled. She sat up and her ears perked forward. Tears gathered at the corners of her eyes, but she blinked them away. There was a long pause as she stared out over the river.

"Maybe I will be," she finally said. "I'm sorry if I scared you. I don't have any excuse for what I did." Thia's face crumpled and a few tears gathered in her eyes. "Elenor, you don't need an excuse for being furious about what happened to you. Do you think that we expect you to just shrug it off? Mom only pushed you to accept this because she can't see a way to undo it." A few sympathetic tears fell from Thia's eyes. "But don't you ever think for one second that we think this was fair to you. I know she told you that she has Memory Fragments coming to help, but what she didn't tell you is that they are taking so long because the ones she demanded first are the furthest away. All the research she has ever done or collected on Writbands."

"But," Elenor said, and Thia wiped her eyes.

"She didn't want to get your hopes up, and you shouldn't, because she thinks that your band is locked into place by the Writ itself. Which means there isn't a damn thing we can do to fix it. I just want you to know that she cares a lot more than you might think. She's just never been great at showing that to others."

Elenor shook her head. "No, Thia, I mean I don't need to be fixed." Thia quirked a brow. Elenor went on. "I wasn't," Elenor paused, trying to decide how to say it. "I wasn't, _me_, when you found me."

"And you are now?" Thia asked, a little laugh in her voice.

Elenor giggled a little in agreement. "I guess I am. It was the not knowing that made this so, painful. Then when you worked that out, that he knew he was going to be causing someone all that stress. He didn't care. It just made me so…" Elenor blew out a breath. "But you are all, right. This body." Elenor lifted a paw and looked down at herself. "The magic." She lifted her Striker, rainbow light glittering through the crystals from the fading sunlight of dusk. "I'm not going to get that if I went back to my old life where I had no idea what I wanted." She stood up and turned back towards the house. "This is me, and maybe it always was. Maybe this won't be the last time I cry, but it'll be the last time I cry for what I lost, because what I got in exchange, it's pretty amazing."

36
"THREE"

It was well after midnight when Mateo noticed Thia had begun to fidget anxiously. They had spent a few hours speculating about how to help her mother. They had come to the conclusion that it was unlikely that she was being controlled by the same thing that was controlling the Infected. If whatever was controlling the Infected was controlling Helen, Thia was certain she would have noticed that. The Infected were too erratic. Helen was too controlled. That left them with few options as to how to rectify the situation.

"We should get going. I think Thia might explode if we wait one second longer to get her turned into a monster." Mateo chuckled.

Elenor concentrated on her inner power and lifted herself and Mateo just above the snow. "Climb on my back. I can't lift you like this. Your water is, a little more essential to you being alive for now," Elenor squeaked, and Thia nodded.

"How is that different for you?" Thia asked as they began to try towards the house.

"Water is still really important for us, but it doesn't need to move around our bodies like yours does. It's my guess that our blood is magic somehow. I don't really know why, I just know it somehow."

Thia opened her mouth to ask a question, but Elenor answered before she could ask it. "I only know this because of my power."

"We have to find a better way to call..."

Pain flared in Thia's chest. Her body was blasted from Elenor's back and she slammed into the ground, tumbling through the freezing snow to fetch up near the base of a huge oak tree.

Elenor released her power, allowing herself and Mateo to drop into the snow. Everything seemed to move in slow motion as Elenor spun to see Thia's body slumping limply to the ground. The thundercrack of a powerful rifle arrived a moment later, echoing through the forest.

Elenor bounded through the snow, and an instant later, she was standing protectively over Thia's prone form, every spine and claw she had standing out from her body. Mateo stood frozen, sight ears twitching back and forth. Then, they seemed to freeze pointing off to the east.

"I've got them," he said.

"We need to help Thia!" Elenor pipped, and Mateo's sight ears swiveled back to her.

"¡Ayúdala! I'll make sure there are no more shots."

Mateo leapt into the forest, his night black fur allowing him to be swallowed so completely into the darkness that only the paw prints in the snow made it believable he had been there at all. Elenor spun herself around and bent over Thia. Blood spattered the snow around her fallen form. There was a small, round hole the size of a man's thumb in the downy white front of her coat. She was not breathing.

"Damn it, what do I do?" Elenor bent and sniffed the hole. Only the smell of blood and some various internal organs came through. Nothing else was in the wound. Elenor knew beyond the shadow of a doubt that it was too late for this. Thia was already dead. Dead the moment the bullet struck. The shock must have been tremendous to have thrown her so violently from Elenor's back. She had to try, though. She slapped her Striker against a nearby sapling and the pure tone pushed away all the sounds of the world.

Elenor began to call the Mender's Lament. The mournful tones rang through the forest, but she could

 • ¡Ayúdala! – Help her!

tell that her improvisation attempting to target Thia's injury was doing no good. Nothing happened. The wound did not close. Elenor tilted her head. So focused on the Chorus was she that the second bullet seemed laughably slow moving as the sound of the Chorus warned her it was coming. She leaned her body towards the bullet and it shattered against her skin, her Relic hardening to disperse the kinetic energy of the impact.

Thia was not gone yet. Elenor could hear the sound of her lingering soul in the Chorus. She was still here, but Elenor had no idea how to get her back into her body.

The Surge to trigger Thia's transformation flashed through Elenor's mind. The Overture of Lifeshaping, they had named it. It was not at all the same Surge she had used to accelerate Mateo's transformation. During one of the final steps, this Surge pulled the Spirit from the body during the transformation. It was not dangerous, and Helen had estimated that it had happened to Elenor over a dozen times during her extended transformation. It was a way to avoid any pain during certain parts of the transformative processes. It was the only chance she had.

Another crack of thunder reached Elenor, but no bullet hit her this time. They were probably shooting at Mateo, for all the good it would do them. Elenor took a deep breath and focused only on the Chorus.

"Hang on, Thia. I've got you," Elenor whispered. She whipped her tail, and her striker cracked against a nearby tree once more. The note was so loud that it felt as if the entire world paused in respect for her Surge. The Overture of Lifeshaping began as a slow beat, almost like the beat of one's heart. Four separate notes chiming so close together that they sounded like two.

Elenor flexed muscles in her tail, tugging at her Relic to quiet notes while relaxing others to allow them to sing. Between the beat of the four notes, she wove two more, chiming high and low, off beat from one another. The last four notes slid between all that was already being played in a gliding melody that tied the rest of the notes together into a warp in reality, tying Thia to the Writ. A glowing tracery of lines scribed themselves into Thia's chest, glowing so brightly violet that it showed even through her coat.

"Please hold on, Thia," Elenor whispered as she continued calling the Overture of Lifeshaping. The light expanded until it enveloped Thia's entire body, shifting in color until it was pure gold. Just like with Mateo, the shape became slightly amorphous until it began to reshape itself into a four-legged form. At first, it looked like a big cat like a puma or a snow leopard. Then the body elongated until it was slightly more like a lizard with a long, tapering tail. The form resolved as the light began to fade.

"Thia?" Elenor asked as the light faded away, leaving behind a sleek black form. Unlike Elenor and Mateo, Thia had no fur at all. Her head was wide, supporting a similarly wide, powerful muzzle that was some combination of feline and reptile. She had a pair of horns curving back from either side of her skull above where her eyes would have been. Between the horns was a bed of what, at first, appeared to be shimmering lavender dreadlocks until they began to move.

"Next time I get hit in the heart with a high-powered rifle, you can just go ahead and let me die," Thia moaned. "Oh hell, is that my voice? Why do I sound like I'm six years old again? Why hasn't it fixed this part yet?" Her voice was not as high as Elenor's, but Thia's voice had not been as high to start. There was no question her voice had changed into something far more childlike than adult. Thia tried to get to her feet, but after a long minute of trying to get her paws beneath her, she just splayed them to either side of her body and lay there with her muzzle pressed into the snow.

"You look... too normal," Elenor said, unable to put proper words to what she was trying to say. "I mean, the lack of eyes and the worm hair are kinda creepy, but you just sort of look like a giant lizard."

Elenor walked around Thia's body. Her long body seemed to Elenor to be a combination of feline and snake, covered with hundreds if not thousands of glass smooth scales. She was sleek, and Elenor reached out to touch them, finding them beyond smooth like polished obsidian. As the scales warped to follow the curves of Thia's body, Elenor could see hints of deep purple and rose-pink iridescence in each scale.

"Thanks?" Thia mumble-squeaked.

"I'm sorry, it's just, Mateo and I look really alien. You're clearly not an earth animal, but you look a lot closer, than, we..." Elenor trailed off as almost a dozen eyes, varying in size from size of a billiard ball to a softball blinked open along the length of Thia's body. Each eye glowed with gentle violet light. There were three on her long thick neck, four more on her flank between her front leg and back, and three more on the two feet of her tail. There were two more spaced widely on her back, one in the center of her back and one just at the base of her tail. "Yeeugh, there it is. You're covered in creepy ass extra eyes."

"I don't think they're eyes?" Thia's voice turned up at the end. The sleek flow of thick digits pouring over the top of her head moved in a small wave.

"I think the... snakes on my head are my eyes." Thia very carefully tried to get to her feet. "How do you walk with these things?"

A thundercrack of sound echoed through the woods again, and Elenor growled. "Shit! Mateo is fighting. I've gotta go help him. I'll help you when I get back!" She galloped off towards the woods, and Thia groaned, slumping back into the snow.

"At least I'm not freezing," she mumbled into the snow. She paused to lick the rows of sharp triangles that had replaced her teeth. "Oh hell, do I have a forked tongue?"

"Sure do!" Elenor squeaked as she disappeared into the treeline.

"Awesome. Ow." Thia groaned and tried to remain as motionless as possible. A moment later, she decided she needed to follow them. There were questions that needed answering. Like, who was doing the shooting and how in the nine hells they had found them under the protection of the Relic her mother had set?

Thia carefully stretched her body and realized that the pain of the gunshot was completely gone. The reshaping into her new body had completely healed possibly every hurt she had ever experienced. As she reached full extension, she felt the oddest sensation she had ever experienced.

It felt for an instant as if her skin were peeling away from her body. She realized that with whatever her new type of vision was, she could see her entire body except her direct underbelly, and she sensed that was only because she was lying on it. Her scales had lifted away from her body into an almost fur-like appearance. She lifted her right front paw and ran her paw pads across the scales. They were buttery supple, like the finest leather or thin latex.

It became clear after a long moment of contemplation that she could, if desired, focus on individual scales and control them. It was much simpler to direct them all at once, though, and after a moment, they laid back down, locking into their smooth, glasslike appearance. She wondered what the purpose of that was, and if her Relic offered less protection if the scales were lifted in that fashion.

Thia lifted each paw to get a feel for how they moved. It was not quite like crawling on her hands and knees.

She wondered how Mateo had adapted so quickly to having all those extra paws. It had only taken him a few minutes to be walking around on them. She remembered Elenor walking him through some exercises. She looked off the direction that Elenor had gone. She didn't have time to learn how to walk again. She had to catch up and help.

The next sensation that came almost made her slightly ill. It was as if something inside of her body were pressing out against the skin of her back. Black, liquid appendages like Mateo's tentacles extruded from her back, extending about two feet. The two thin rods of relic stone unfolded as an opening pocket knife, and then again, until they extended to a length of 5 feet with crooked joins between each rod.

More rods extended from the joints until long fingers reached down from the rods. Membranes flowed from the rods as liquid runs from a faucet, until a pair sleek black wings like that of a bat extended from her back. Then, two ball-like structures swelled where the wings attached to her back. The two balls detached from her back and floated in perfect orbit over her shoulders. She gasped when she felt her wight fall away and she floated into the air.

"What the hell?" she squeaked. She turned her head, but there was no need. The wings were definitely not attached to her body physically, but they were somehow generating a field that kept them both connected to her and her body floating in the air. Thia went stock still. She could still feel the new wings as if they were attached to her body. Her brain gave frantic warnings that she was going to float away into space if she pushed off of anything. Tentatively, she folded her wings with the utmost care, and her paws gave off a gentle crunch as she touched down in the snow. She extended her wings again, and she immediately lifted off the ground, hovering a few inches above the snow. She moved them down in a gentle flap and she rose away from the ground, but the wings were not nearly big enough to actually be lifting her.

Multiple gunshots, much quieter than the earlier ones, rang out in the forest. Thia had no more time to learn. Either she had to just try, or wait for them to come back. She lifted her wings and flapped them hard. She shot into the sky with such speed that she was certain she had killed herself by launching herself into space. She spread her wings as wide as they would go, trying to use them as a wind break, and as soon as they reached full extension, she jarred a stop.

She had gained hundreds of feet in a couple of seconds and was looking down on the landscape rolling away from her in all directions. Lights of houses twinkled below, and in the distance, the brightness that was Baltimore flared on the horizon like a miniature sun. Of great interest to her was the way her vision seemed to narrow or expand based on where she focused. She clearly had a lot to learn about how her new body functioned. Flashes of gunshots appeared in the forest, and the green glow of one of the Infected was there as well.

Figuring out how to tilt her wings to orient her body the way she wanted to go disoriented her for a moment as her body spun into a lazy end-over-end backflip. Her wings clearly did not function entirely on the principles of flight as she knew them. When she managed to tilt them forward, her body followed the motion of the wings. She lifted them toward her head and then flapped them towards her rear. She shot towards the ground at an alarming rate.

"Shhhhiiiiiitttt!" she screeched as the ground came up at her as if she had been fired out of a canon. She tilted her head back and tried to do the same with her wings, but she did not respond nearly fast enough to pull out of the steep dive.

She saw the Infected through the trees. It was one that she did not recognize, a massive man wearing what looked like a suit of armor made out of green threads of energy. She tilted her head towards him and her body followed. She folded her wings to protect them and screamed as she smashed into him like an artillery shell.

Mateo froze when his sight ears picked up the sound of Thia's scream. Then, the sound of her whistling through the air hit his ears and he could see her clearly. She was screaming through the air at a speed that would have turned a Lamborghini green with envy. He dove behind a tree as she shot out of the sky and smashed into the Infected.

His sight ears swiveled to find Elenor, but she was standing on top of the man who had been doing all the shooting. Surprisingly, that guy was not one of the Infected. Mateo could hear his heartbeat.

"Uh help?" Thia squeaked. She had planted her paws on both of the Infected's shoulders and was attempting to hold him down. Mateo bounded towards them and the Infected twisted his shoulders mightily, throwing Thia off. She flew through the air, but just before she could slam into a tree, a pair of bat wings far too small to lift her flared behind her and she jerked to a halt. Mateo slammed a shoulder into the man before he could get completely to his feet, slamming him back to the ground.

"Es Thia?! Why can everyone else fly but me?" Mateo growled with annoyance.

"Sure is!" Elenor responded.

"How do they keep finding us?! Isn't that thing supposed to keep them away?" Mateo's annoyed shout cut through the shouting of the man struggling beneath Elenor's weight. He landed atop the Infected, black fur bristling, and drew back a paw, claws extended. He slashed at the man's chest, his claws slicing through the

 • Es – Is that

green armor in a shower of verdant sparks. The man's fist came up, but Mateo anticipated it and crouched on the man's chest. He scrunched up his body, digging the claws of his four front paws into what was left of the upper body portion of the armor. The Infected swung powerfully at his head, but Mateo just ducked beneath the swing as if he had known it was coming all along.

Thia realized that he did, in fact, know exactly what was coming. His sight ears swiveled this way and that as things moved around him. Much like her own vision, he could see everything moving around him with echolocation.

"You going to help?" Mateo quipped.

"Sorry, I'm not sure how to work this thing yet," Thia said.

"What?" Mateo's sight ears both leaned the same way, showing confusion.

"I don't know how to walk yet, dolt!" Thia hissed in embarrassment. "How did you learn to work that crazy body so fast?" she shouted in frustration.

Mateo jumped away from the huge man as he tried to throw his massive arms around Mateo in a crushing bear hug. "Well, at least go sit on that jerk that shot you so Elly can help! This freak is strong and I'm not feeling great."

Mateo swayed on his paws. Earlier in the fight, he had taken a punch to the side to discover that the behemoth man had somehow gained the same trick the other Infected with the spears had used on him. There was something broken inside of his body, and though he was fighting through the pain, jumping around so much was not making it any better.

"I'll try!" Thia took care not to tilt her wings too crazily, and finally got them angled in such a way that she was able to float over towards Elenor.

Elenor didn't wait. She hopped daintily off the man, leaving him face down in the snow. Her paws never touched the snow as her power lifted her from the ground.

"I don't think he'll get far," Elenor said as she passed.

"At least you didn't kill him," Thia said, and Elenor blanched, then paused.

"Did you think…" Elenor looked to where Mateo was dodging the Infected. Her eyes scrunched up in anger. "We'll talk about this in a second."

Elenor's face smoothed into concentration, and she spread all four feet. Her tail lifted and she pointed the spines of her Striker at the Infected. The creature froze in place, though Thia could see his muscles straining to fight against whatever Elenor was doing. Elenor spun in a blur, whipping her tail around, cracking it like a whip.

The response was instant. The Infected's body blasted away from the ground. It smashed through a tree and then launched into the sky, shrinking rapidly until it was out of sight.

"Why didn't you do that before?" Thia asked.

"I need time to concentrate. I thought your mom would have told you what I told her," Elenor complained. Thia shook her head, the purple coils between her swooping horns swaying with the movement.

Elenor bounded over to Mateo, who had laid down in the snow. He had coughed up a splatter of blood that was slightly too orange to be human. It was the color of red clay. It almost seemed to glow for a moment before the blood bubbled into an energetic froth that faded away.

Elenor put her paw on Mateo's side and focused on the power in her chest. It let her see the water flowing through Mateo, giving her an almost complete picture of his internals. She wasn't sure how she could tell that his blood was still leaking into places it shouldn't go, but she knew. Elenor tapped her Striker on a nearby tree and called the Mender's Lament. She improvised the targeting, and a moment later, the internal injuries Mateo had suffered were repaired.

"You're going to cough up a little more blood, but then you'll be fine," she assured Mateo.

"Gracias, Elly."

Elenor turned back to the man on the ground. With Thia hovering in the air just above him, he had not attempted to move. He was shaking in terror, and Elenor approached with her double row of obsidian knives she called teeth fully on display. "I would also like to know how they keep finding us."

The man's eyes locked onto her. "What the hell are you freaks?!" he screamed in terror. He was about five feet ten inches, in good shape. He was wearing winter camo fatigues that made parts of him seem to blend with the snow. It didn't hide him at all from their various forms of vision, but any regular human being would lose him quickly in the snowy forest. He had buzz cut brown hair, and was still wearing some weapons. He didn't bother going for them. Elenor and Mateo had shown him just how useless bullets were against them.

Thia folded her wings, causing her to touch down on the ground. She crouched over the man, the bed of lavender imaging coils between her horns rippling like writhing snakes. "You killed me a few minutes ago. I am the freak you are going to tell everything you know, or I'm gonna give you an intimate introduction to what that feels like." She growled, her new childlike voice somehow more terrifying than the bellow of a grizzly bear.

"I don't know anything!" the man screamed. "We were paid to do a job, that's it."

"We?" Thia prompted.

"Yeah! Kill two women with long range rifle shots. That's it! Holy shit, they told us the women might have animals with them that we would have to kill, too, but

 • Gracias - Thanks

you're fucking monsters!" the man jabbered.

Thia noticed something peeking out from beneath the man's shirt. It looked like a small glass sphere. Suddenly, she became laser focused. "Son of a bitch!" She seethed. "Elly, come here." Thia pointed at the glass sphere with the tip of a wicked black claw. "I can't pick anything up with these new paws, but can you grab that?"

Elenor pinched the small glass orb between her thumb and fore digit. When she tugged it, the glass orb proved to have a loop with a steel chain through it. Inside of the orb was what looked like an eyeball with a dimly glowing yellow iris. It spun inside the glass sphere directly toward her and she dropped it.

"Damn it, take that away from him," Thia growled.

Elenor grabbed the tiny sphere again and yanked it, snapping the thin chain.

Thia leaned over the man, her double row of razor fangs a hair's breadth from his face. "The woman!" she shrieked.

"She's supposed to be in a house on the other side of the woods, a mile south of here."

"Mom," Thia snarled. She drew back her paw, black claws extending from the thick feline toes. Elenor's paw closed around Thia's leg.

"We don't do that. He's just a human."

"Speak for yourself," Thia said, and wrenched her paw free.

Elenor was standing between Thia and the man with instantaneous speed. A moment later, Mateo was standing next to her. "I'm trying to speak for everyone who will be in our situation in the future."

"If we start killing helpless people," Mateo began, but Thia dropped her paw.

"Then no one will ever accept us."

Mateo nodded in response. "What are we going to do with him?"

"Aria of Mistaken Remembrance," Thia said. She hummed a few bars.

"Well at least I can still hum. I have no clue how to whistle with this thing." She stuck out her forked tongue.

"What the hell are you doing?" the mercenary shouted.

She just rippled her imaging coils at him and peeled back her lips in a blade-sharp smile. She began to hum the tune, all sound fading away beneath the notes. Each note was held long, and wavered hauntingly. The man's eyes went out of focus after three repetitions of the music. Thia's humming trailed off.

"He won't remember the last couple of days. Come on. He'll wake up in a few minutes. We have to find whoever is trying to kill my mother," Thia snarled, and spread her wings.

Elenor looked at her and one ear fell the other, perked in a question. Her glowing eyes focused over Thia's head then spread wide.

"What?"

Elenor waved a paw up above her head. "What's going on with your wings?"

Thia didn't turn her head. Instead, she just focused on the area behind her. Where a pair of bat-like wings hovered over her shoulders before, something entirely new floated. Hundreds of crystal blades made the rough outline of a pair of wings that seemed to bleed menace. None of the blades were of uniform shape. They seemed to be blades of every weapon and sharp tool imaginable.

Dagger blades floated next to serrated obsidian blades seemingly chipped by hand. Chef's knives and scissor halves had been puzzle-pieced together with machete blades and what appeared to be square tool blades from a lawn mower. Long, curving scythe blades framed the entire set, forming an outer cutting edge that looked sharp enough to slice reality itself.

The blades seemed to be held together by a faintly visible web of crackling violet energy. The full wingspan was only slightly broader than the bat wings had been, yet this pair seemed to somehow fill far more space than the others could have. Still far too small to carry Thia's body in any traditional sense, they, nonetheless, lifted her from the ground as she flapped them gently.

"I have no idea, but there is no time to discuss it now." Thia flapped the wings again, and shot into the air.

"No es justo that both of you can fly," Mateo grumbled, his sight ears swiveling to follow Thia's flight.

"Don't worry. We'll figure something out for you," Elenor said, and constructed the instructions in her head to lift him. Thia was already long gone, but considering her confessed lack of ability to walk, she had to catch up quickly.

- No es justo – It is so unfair

37
"A LOT OF WORK"

NC 17, EPOCH 19915.40

It had not taken much effort to find the other mercenary. The trio floated just above his position, looking down at him.

"There are no good options here," Thia whispered.

"We actually don't have to get involved," Mateo said, his sight ears swiveled as far to the left as they could face.

"What?" Thia squeaked.

Mateo pointed a paw off to the left. Thia followed where he was pointing and her new sight widened, sensory coils shifting like snakes slithering across her skull.

"Ugh, it's gonna take a while to get used to this," Thia complained, but a moment later, the snake-like strands had arranged themselves so that she could see in infrared. Then she saw what Mateo was pointing out. There were three men sweeping through the forest.

"Oh," was all Thia said before wobbling slightly in an effort to tilt her wings towards the house. She began to float forward, but Elenor and Mateo just stared at her.

Elenor put a paw over her muzzle and tried to stifle a giggle unsuccessfully. "You remember you were worried about getting mood ears like ours? Well," Elenor pointed a paw over Thia's head to her wings.

The wings had metamorphized again, but this new pair was almost comical in appearance. They appeared to have been stolen from a giant plush toy, or perhaps some sort of pool toy. They began with two disks that appeared as swirls made out of balloons. The outside of the swirl extended in a single, large, curving facsimile of a feather. Stacked below this first large "feather" were four others that curved away from the central disk. Each of the five large protrusions had a round crystal imbedded into the end. Each crystal was a different color of the rainbow save three, which were white, black, and grey. If not for Elenor's enhanced vision, she would have missed the faint purple color that rose through the black scales on Thia's cheeks and muzzle.

"Oh my dog, are you blushing?" Elenor squinted her glowing eyes at Thia. "You are!"

"You blush too. I've seen you doing it!" Thia knew it was childish the moment she said it, and she was not going to tell either of these two children that she had discovered cartoons at the age of seventy years and fallen in love with Japanese animation. There was no question that these particular wings had come from that interest, but she had no idea yet what they represented. She loved them all the same.

"No, you, haven't," Elenor sing-songed, "I have fur."

That seemed to make Thia blush even deeper, and Elenor tilted her head. Her face went from giggling to realization. "You know, I never really thought about it until now, but you don't really act like someone that is over a hundred years old."

Thia's cheeks burned with bright purple. "If you stop, I promise to tell you why later. We don't have time for this right now. We have a chance for some counter-intelligence and we can't let it go." Thia flapped her new plush-like wings and shot away towards the house.

"What was that about?" Mateo asked.

Elenor shrugged. "I'm not sure. I just noticed it for some reason. Thia told me she was born in San Francisco in 1898, but she acts and dresses, well, not dresses anymore, like she isn't much older than me." Elenor worked he way through the thoughts haltingly.

Mateo shrugged. "She said she would tell us." Elenor turned and galloped towards the house. They arrived a minute later to find Thia lying in a small crater in the snow. She had clearly not corrected her dive early enough and had slammed into the ground at speed. Elenor landed with a dainty short drop into the snow next to Thia's small depression and leaned over to look into the hole. Thia's muzzle was buried in the dirt and she was making a squeaky groaning noise.

"Ow," she pipped and then rolled over onto her back, her wings vanishing as they were reabsorbed into her relic.

"Are you alright?" Elenor asked.

"Yeah, it only hurt for a second, and I'm not even sure that was anything but my pride."

The door behind the patio slid open and Helen stepped outside, wearing little more than a light jacket and her black combat boots. "Is that my daughter lying in that crater?" Helen's grin was clear in her voice.

Thia put her paws over her head and squeaked in embarrassment. "No, just a random dragon thing. I'm not here, don't pay attention to me."

"Yeah, and I feel like I got robbed. She looks way cooler than me," Elenor complained.

"Not important right now," Thia interrupted. "We need to get more people in from our network. What we just saw is going to require some consideration."

"Kaleb just called in and said they are hiring mercenaries now. What makes you think this makes the situation more serious?" Helen didn't seem skeptical.

"Because they can." Thia said. Helen began to nod.

"No entiendo," Mateo griped.

"Hiring mercenaries says that they both have the means to do so and also that they have found a way to get in touch with such people. These Infected are vastly different than the ones Osiris created. At first, I thought they were just less destructive, but no more insane. But this speaks to a greater intelligence behind what they are doing," Helen elucidated. "Hap is on his way here with some of the guys now. I can handle his concussion and

---

    • No entiendo – I don't get it

broken arm."

Helen crouched over the crater, where Thia had not moved. Somehow, despite the absolute alien nature of Thia's new body, Helen knew something wasn't right.

"Thia, what happened to you?"

"I got what I wanted, sort of?" She let out a hiccupping little sob. There were no tears. She had no capacity for them anymore. Yet, the signs of her distress were clear. Her scales lifted until they were a carpet of tiny flags shivering in the wintery breeze. The more concrete representation of her feelings were her wings, which expressed themselves from her back, forming a disjointed framework of broken obsidian shards that outlined a wing shape that wouldn't be out of place on an owl. The framework filled with what appeared to be a lavender-tinged layer of clouds. Flashes like lightning filled the clouds, and what appeared to be rain fell from the wings around Thia's shoulders. Interestingly, the rain seemed to be falling up around her since she was lying atop her wings. It clearly wasn't real rain, as the droplets vanished a few inches from her body.

Helen climbed into the small hole and knelt next to her daughter.

"I died, Mom," Thia sobbed.

Helen reached out, and with great care around Thia's new claws, she took her daughter's paw and rolled her upright, careful not to be slapped in the face with her new wing.

"Is it going to hurt if I…" Helen held out her hands. worried about the glowing purple eyes on Thia's neck.

"No. I'm not sure what those are. yet, but they only look like eyes." Thia assured.

Helen put her arms around her daughter's neck and hugged her. "Wow, I don't think I realized how big all of you are compared to me." Thia sniffed, and then giggled. Helen continued, "Kinda glad you're not covered in razor sharp blades. Your scales are really soft."

"I'm pretty sure I can actually make them razor sharp if you are looking for something a little more, prickly." Thia snorted, and giggled a little more.

"So how are you still here?" Helen's gentle question caused Thia to turn towards Elenor.

"She saved me. We finished the Overture of Lifeshaping and Elly realized that the Overture would reattach my soul to my body. Without her, I wouldn't be here," Thia said. "I can't even cry anymore."

"Not the same way." Helen ran her hand across the curve of Thia's stormy wings and then her fingers through the wave of supple scales on her side. "But the Writ has not left you bereft of ways of expressing your sadness, and it is beautiful. Just like you."

Thia sniffed one last time and then got shakily to her paws. "Thanks, Mom. I'll be fine, in time." She wobbled her way up out of the small crater. She walked one careful step at a time to Elenor, and then rubbed her muzzle against Elenor's. "Thanks, Elly."

"My pleasure," Elenor said, a fierce blush rising beneath the fur of her face.

"I can see you blushing," she whispered in Elenor's ear, as she brushed past. "Now teach me how to operate these giant paws because we have a lot of work to do."

"Oh, you creature!" Elenor squeaked indignantly. Mateo began to chuckle. "She can see when you blush too, jerk!" Elenor hissed and stomped toward Thia. Mateo though couldn't stop laughing.

His laughing eventually trailed off and his sight ears swiveled around towards the house. "Car pulling up. Tres, cuatro, cinco voces adentro."

"Hap and the guys." Helen said.

"How do you know these guys, anyway?" Mateo

- Tres, cuatro, cinco voces adentro – Three, four, five voices inside asked.

"That is a lot of history, Kid. You can trust them."

"Ya sé eso," Mateo replied. Helen looked at him a quizzical eyebrow raised. "¿Que? Can't lie to these," Mateo said, wiggling the huge sight ears back and forth at her.

"You…" Helen started, and Mateo bobbed his head in a nod.

"Yeah, no one really thinks about the fact that I can see everything happening inside your body. It took me almost a week to realize what they were showing me."

"Heart rate, blood pressure, respiration," Helen said.

"Yep. Pretty much a perfect lie detector. I didn't tell anyone," Mateo began, but Helen shook her head.

"Because you will not use it against your friends, but it will be hard for them to trust you not to," Helen speculated, and Mateo bobbed his head again. "Listen to me, Mateo. Those two girls are all you have got, probably, for a very long time. There will be more of you in the future, but you three are looking at a long, hard road. Trust them with your secrets because they will be trusting you with theirs." She flicked one of his sight ears gently.

"Now, has Elenor taught you Mender's Lament?"
Mateo shook his head. "Aún no."

"It's time to learn, because Thia was right. It's long past time we got ahead of this, and to do that, we need Hap. We don't have time to wait for any of the other key people to get here."

"How are they going to help us? Isn't it dangerous for them to try to follow around the Infected?"

"These people know the danger. As for what they can offer us? There are three of you now, but there are almost twelve thousand people in our global network,

- Ya sé eso – Oh, I know that
- ¿Qué? – What
- Aún no – Not yet

and almost three quarters of them are former military."

"¿Cómo?"

"We have saved a lot of people from Relics over the years."

Mateo thought about it for a long moment. "Pero, even if you know all those people, that would cost a lot of money to, run." Mateo's thoughts stumbled to a stop and he looked up to Helen.

"Mateo, you can literally warp reality around you. How hard do you think it would be to quite literally make more money than you could ever need?" Helen asked as they arrived in the driveway. Grady, the only man there almost as large as Hap, was helping him from the car. He stuttered to a stop when he saw Mateo and his face went far too pale for his obvious Native American heritage. Not all of the men had met them yet.

Mateo's sight ears leaned forward in a squint of annoyance. "I'm not going to hurt you, hombre grande." He wasn't as annoyed by his new voice as the girls were, but it didn't change the fact that it still got the same first reaction from every adult.

"How old are you?"

Mateo let out a sigh and reminded himself he knew what he was getting into. "Maybe I could bite him, just un poquito?" Mateo tilted his head towards Helen and dropped an ear in question. Somehow, the man's face went a little paler, his skin becoming a ruddy grey.

"I would suggest you not judge any of the Bearers you will meet today by how they look or sound, Grady. Especially considering one of them is my daughter," Helen warned. The man swallowed and then nodded.

"Have you been listening to the Chorus?" she asked, and Mateo bobbed his head.

- ¿Como? – What?
- hombre grande – big man
- un poquito – a little

"Well, you won't have to improvise this Surge. Just call it the same way you hear it." Helen's face turned down into a frown when she summoned her striker.

She began to play.

Mateo realized not being able to call the Surge herself was painful for Helen. He whipped his tail and banged his striker on the driveway. He quickly followed her notes and did his best to memorize them. After the melody trailed off, Hap straightened and his eyes went wide with wonder.

"Thanks, Helen," Hap said.

Helen immediately shook her head, and pointed at Mateo. "Mateo called the Surge. I'm just teaching him." All of them looked at Mateo, who just shrugged.

Hap nodded to him. "I apologize, Mateo. Thank you."

"Lucas, I am sorry. I did not think you would be in any danger. I did not have the whole picture, and I still do not."

Hap shook his head. "I knew what I was gettin' into when I agreed to help you. We all did. Ya never lied ta anyone. So, how can we help?"

"By getting you all properly armed."

38

"REHOME"

Helen sat looking at the case on the large oak desk in front of her. Dozens of memory fragments were neatly arranged in dense wool padding. She did not dare pick up a single one. There was no certainty that the answers to their questions were in these memories, but there was certain to be something in them.

Thia poked her head around the door, the purple glow of her undimmed sensory coils brightening the room slightly. "Are you alright, Mom?"

"I'm concerned that what you told me is going to make me less and less useful to you all."

Thia bobbed her head and slunk into the room. It had taken over a week for her to gain any comfort with her new reptilian form. They had learned a lot about her new body in that time. The eldritch purple eyes that ran down the length of her body were not eyes at all, but rather electromagnetic emitters. They were somehow dimensionally phase shifted so they produced entirely unique waves, letting her see clearly even in electromagnetically noisy environments.

"At least until we figure out how to fix the issue," Thia said.

"Take these. You and the others can watch them." Helen closed the lid of the square mahogany box before snapping the latch shut and sliding it across the desk.

Thia's wings floated up from her back, much smaller than they had been when she had been using them for flying. They would never get much larger than six feet at full extension, but she had discovered she could make them much smaller. In their normal form, where they appeared as if stolen from a cartoon, Thia had discovered they were almost as dexterous as a pair of hands. Almost. The large "feathers" of the wings could act individually, much like fingers.

Presently, they were much smaller than normal, only slightly bigger than her hands had been when she was human. She used them to pick up the box. She turned around with greater care than seemed necessary, but she still didn't have great control over her tail.

"Thia."

Thia didn't need to turn back. Her vision allowed her to see everywhere around her. She didn't use it outside because it was extremely distracting, but inside the house, it was quite useful.

"They are going to need you to teach them to move forward. I cannot be involved with puzzling any more of this out unless you all can figure out how to alleviate the danger," Helen advised. "I will help by keeping Hap and any of the other network people alive, but they will be reporting directly to you three from now on."

"How important is what we are doing?" Thia asked, her childlike tones making her sound more vulnerable than she really felt.

Helen paused for long enough that Thia turned back and sat down in the doorway. Her sensory coils rearranged themselves so she could see using visible light, allowing her to see exactly like she had when she was human, if a little near sighted like Mateo. Finally, her mother looked up.

"I can only tell you how it feels, Thia. It feels like when I was chasing Osiris. Like if I did not stop him, our world would be broken somehow."

"We'll be quicker," Thia promised.

Helen shook her head. "You will be the best you can, Thia. No one can be more than that."

"Do you know why we don't have, powers, like Elly?"

"Runeshards. We would have called them Runeshards, though I do not know of anyone who has ever seen one."

"Because of the Runespring?" Thia's mother had taught her the rough overview of what they knew about how power flowed into their world from the Runespring. It was like a well of infinite power that caused their world to exist. It was what gave the Writ it's power.

Helen nodded. "But very few ever attempted to research anything about what powered the Writ. The Writ seems specifically designed to keep us separate from that power."

"Yeah, gaining access to absolute power doesn't seem ideal. I understand better now why you were so freaked out about Elenor's power. What do we need so much power for? Are you sure we're gonna get Runeshards of our own?"

"I am certain. Each new Bearer from now until the tenth will have access to a Runeshard."

"Until all ten Runes from the spring are active." Thia nodded.

"Correct. You are in charge now, Thia. I can only help in direct combat. You three have to figure this out. One more thing, the new place is ready." Helen then bent over her desk and began to scribble in a notebook.

"We will," Thia promised, and then turned and padded out of the room.

Thia went to the back yard where Elenor and Mateo were sparring. Elenor and Thia had both realized that while Mateo didn't seem to be as inclined to Surges as they were, he had adapted to his body far better than even Elenor, who had lived in her body for two years. He seemed to have some sort of instinct of how to move his body that they both lacked. He did still had trouble with some things, like controlling when his paws stuck to things. Still, he could take them both in a fight at the same time without much trouble.

Elenor leapt at Mateo, claws flashing towards his muzzle. He leapt off the ground, twisting his lithe, weasel-like body in the air to flip himself over. His teeth closed on the scruff of Elenor's neck. His rear four paws hit the ground and his claws dug in. He bent his entire body, increasing his leverage as he spun. His body retracted and Elenor let out a yelp as she was yanked from her paws and sent flying across the back yard. She tumbled to a stop near the edge of the woods and jumped back to her paws.

"You're not really paying attention to where your paws are going. You're taking your eyes off the target because everyone has always been slower than you," Mateo explained. Elenor bobbed her head.

"We are on our own, for the most part," Thia interjected.

"What, why?" Elenor asked.

"Because Mom figured out there is something wrong with her. She has to stay out of things until we figure out how to fix it." Thia's wings hovered next to her, holding the box of fragments between them.

Elenor face went a little slack, her ears drooping noticeably. "If she knows, are we going to be alright?"

Thia shrugged. "I don't know, Elenor. All we can do is be careful what we say around her for now."

Elenor nodded and padded back towards the house, Mateo close behind. "Are those her fragments?"

"Yes, but I think it is a lot more important for us to find the ones that Osiris left behind."

"Shouldn't we be concerned about more people showing up here to try to kill everyone?" Mateo asked. They had discovered that the eyeballs on chains the men had been wearing had been specifically designed to counter the relic Helen was using to hide them.

"No, because we won't be staying here anymore. We have a much better place to stay. It just took time to acquire it," Thia explained.

"Acquire?" Mateo asked.

Thia grinned at him. "Did you think that we were just going to save the world from a house in rural Maryland? We needed a better training ground and now we have one. All we need to finish it is for us three to call a Surge to open the port dimension."

"What Surge?" Elenor circled back.

"It is called the Ayre of the Anchored Way. We are going to create a space where we can call any Surge we want without breaking anything. So, there is going to be some improvisation."

"What kind?" Elenor wondered.

Thia grinned. "We are going to turn a dimension inside out, but first, we need to get to where we are going. Open your Hammerspace."

Elenor tapped her Striker on the stones of the patio and the Keymaster's March beat from the crystals of the instrument. A moment later, the rough stone archway into her Hammerspace grew up from the ground of the back yard. Thia hopped through the door the moment the cosmos appeared within and came back out less than a minute later without the box of her mother's memory fragments.

"Alright, let's go." Thia's wings swooped out from the Hammerspace and settled themselves hovering just a few inches off of Thia's back. Over the past two weeks, she had learned how to do a whole lot of things with those wings. They had figured out that her wings had very little to do with moving air, instead seeming to somehow generate a field that changed Thia's own effective gravity. She beat the silly cartoonish wings once and shot into the sky.

Her wings spread away from her body, floating far to either side of her. As they did, she began to drift toward the ground. After a moment, the wings catapulted forward and she shot off across the sky like an artillery shell launched from a cannon.

"Show off!" Elenor squeaked at the top of her lungs.

"She didn't say where we are going," Mateo observed.

Elenor swiped her tail and the doorway to her hammerspace sank back into the ground. Her ears perked. "It's no trouble. I can feel her no matter where she is. You too." She pulled at the power of her Runeshard floating nebulous in her chest. They lifted off the ground and floated high into the sky.

Elenor waited for her power to build in her chest as she oriented herself to follow Thia. "Hold onto your butt," she said, and they sling-shotted across the sky.

They didn't catch Thia before she made it to their destination. Elenor and Mateo touched down in a small open field between two large office buildings. Thia was standing between a brief tree line on the border of a parking lot ahead of them.

Amazingly, no one seemed to notice them despite their arrival in broad daylight. A moment later, the sound of a Relic surging against the world came to their ears. When Elenor came up to the tree line, she saw a blue sign across a street to her left. On it was a symbol that was familiar, and she squinted at the text on it. White lettering around the inside of a golden seal. The circular text came into focus, and Elenor swallowed.

"Uh, Thia, you know this is an FBI building?" Elenor squeaked.

Thia bobbed her head, her sensory coils sweeping the back of her long neck. "Sure is."

"Then why did you bring, us, here…" Elenor trailed off as Thia spread her wings. She lifted them with a quick snap so that they slapped together above her. The rainbow of tear shaped crystals imbedded in the fat tubular "feathers" of her wings blazed to life as all sounds were pushed away from them. The Arye of the Anchored Way swelled from her wings.

"You didn't say you figured out where your Striker was hiding!" Elenor protested.

"You didn't ask. I only got it yesterday. After years of practice with Mom's Striker, it still took me hours to learn how to play on these things. But what really took me by surprise was this."

Thia took a long, deep breath and a rainbow of light burst through the crevices between the banded scales on her throat and chest. It was as if her scales were vibrating in time with the Surge. Then she opened her mouth wide and breathed. A massive cone of fog exploded from Thia's mouth in a bone shaking roar. The fog was tinged deep amethyst, and seemed to sparkle as the dusk sky behind passing clouds. It spread into a wave, and then a tsunami. It washed over the entire building, consuming the entire view of the FBI office.

Elenor let out a drawn-out whisper. "Wow." The fog spread, and then thinned in the center until it was a massive window, wide as the horizon, tall as the sky. Nebulous clouds gathered at the edges of the window, the center of the space resolving until the view was clear.

It revealed an entirely different edifice. It was a structure so sleek and modern in appearance that it could not possibly be real. The building was two stories, and appeared to be constructed of massive slabs of polished obsidian. A double row of huge bay windows running the length of the building delineated the two floors. Beams framing the windows emitted a faint white glow, and Elenor realized after squinting at them that they were not emitting light. They *were* light.

"¿Por qué respira armas? <u>So</u> unfair how much cooler

- ¿Por qué respira armas? – Why does she get breath weapons?

that looks than when I call a Surge," Mateo complained.

Thia snapped her maw closed and grinned at him, whisps of smoke bleeding from the corners of her muzzle. "It does look pretty cool, but frankly I'm more jealous of how you two call Surges. Any Surge that has to have a target, I have to breath it out. You two target things just by thinking about it somehow. I have to aim."

"What do you mean?" Elenor asked.

"I'll explain later. This is our new home. It exists in a port dimension, and we co-located it with the FBI building as a sort of passive defense."

Elenor realized there were people working inside of the building. She could see them through the windows and outside of the futuristic building.

"Can we just, go in there?" Elenor asked.

Thia shook her head. "The port dimension is unstable right now. That is why I need your help. I need both of you to help me finish anchoring it."

"Así que, those people are stuck in there?" Mateo asked.

Thia nodded. "They have been in there about a year, setting things up, getting supplies sorted out."

"How?" Elenor puzzled with wonder.

Mateo's incredulous bark came atop Elenor's question. "¿Un año? How are they alive?"

"That, is complicated. It has been about a year for them, but only about a week for us. This port dimension is ancient and was created by very powerful Callers from before Osiris," Thia explained.

"Bien, pero that still doesn't explain how they got food and stuff," Mateo objected.

"We don't have time for all of this now. We have to anchor this and I can't do it alone. Ayre of the Anchored

- Así que – So
- ¿Un año? – A year
- Bien, pero – Ok, but

Way please?" Thia requested.

"Va, pero tenemos muchas preguntas," Mateo grumbled.

Elenor nodded in agreement and lifted her tail over her head like a scorpion ready to strike. "I'll go first, you can follow me." Spines lifted from her shoulders and bent with a gentle bounce before settling above them, like tiny knife-sharp wings. She swung her tail and the Striker chimed with bright sound.

"You either have to start at the same exact time or you will need to start at the beginning of the second repetition of the Ayre," Thia warned. "If you don't, it won't anchor the space. It'll create dissonance and the anchor will collapse."

Mateo's sight ears tilted forward and back somehow, conveying a blink of confusion. "That sounds, not so good."

"It would be, sub optimal." Thia's scales lifted from her body, invoking the appearance of a distressed feline for a moment. Then, she shook away the nerves and they smoothed themselves back into the perfect polished appearance she normally had.

Elenor exchanged a look with Mateo. "Ready?"

Mateo bobbed his head, and one of his tentacles came up, rolling the leaf shaped tip into a solid club with a sharp point.

Elenor called the Ayre of the Anchored Way. The long, powerful tones gave a sense of stability, and the view seemed to resolve, giving things a quality of solidity. As the second repeat came up, Mateo tapped his tentacle against his own Striker. Right on cue, he began the Surge. The view resolved once more, and the remaining veil of thin cloud cover separating them from the hammerspace was pulled back. They finished the second rendition at the same time, their Strikers trailing

- Va, pero tenemos muchas preguntas - Fine, but we have so many questions

off until the music ceased.

"Come on!" Thia shouted and ran through the massive opening into the hammerspace.

Elenor and Mateo were close on her tail, and there was brief feeling of resistance as they pushed through into the space. A few of the people working around the building looked up. Their faces crumpled into apprehension and terror as Thia, Elenor, and Mateo approached. One of the women doing some work saw them and actually shrieked in alarm. She pulled a handgun from a holster at her hip.

A tall, muscular woman with copper-colored pixie cut hair spoke from the pillared, overhung walkway at the front of the building. "Just so you know, if you shoot them with that, it's just going to irritate them."

"I assume that one of you is Thia?" the woman said.

"Hello, Marissa, how is everyone?" Thia queried.

"Supplies are getting a little low, and there have been some issues with the water intake that were really starting to worry a few of us."

"We did warn you it would get a little flakey near the end because of the dimensional instability. Should all be working now. We should be able to get out of here whenever you like." Thia waved a wing towards Elenor.

"This is Elenor. You can call her Elly," Thia said, and Elenor bobbed her head. She waved her opposite wing to Mateo. "And this is Mateo."

"Encantado de conocerte señora," Mateo said.

"Whoa, gonna have to veto the señora talk, Mateo. I'm Marissa, Mari to my friends. So, when is it, out there?"

"February the twenty-third," Thia informed.

"Amazing. According to our clocks and watches, it's January of next year already. Damien had to unhook the

• Encantado de conocerte señora – Nice to meet you,
  ma'am

computers from the clock updates from outside because they kept resetting to the same second for minutes at a time. Was screwing with everything."

"That should be fixable with a little work. How many folks are here now?"

"Twenty-eight. Only eight of us are planning on staying day to day," Marissa explained. "And whoever Helen is bringing in."

"Fifteen of the retired military guys will be staying."

"Plenty of rooms then. Come on in, Damien is waiting for you." Marissa gestured at a space on the wall of the building that looked no different than any other length. The only indication of a door was a glowing white outline, faint but distinct, eight feet by ten. A sinuous line split the wall, and the wall seemed to melt into itself, opening a door into an entry hall.

"¡Basta!" Mateo said, pausing to extend his light webs so he could examine the opening where the portion of the wall had vanished. "Is this made of relic stone?"

"Yep, whole thing can be shaped and changed unless the changes interfere with structural integrity. It'll even let ya rearrange rooms just by thinking about it. It's wild." Marissa led them through the brightly lit entryway. "Doors are actually anywhere that doesn't interfere with interior construction, as long as you have permissions to come and go."

Down a long, shining black hall with bars of soft illumination near the ceiling, they came into an enormous open space at least three hundred feet wide.

"Ground floor is mostly apartments for anyone who will be living here. There are dozens of small apartments and a few larger ones."

"Where are we going to be staying?" Elenor squeaked.

"Not down here. There are much more permanent living spaces upstairs with The Hive for all of you,"

• ¡Basta! – Whoa!

Marissa explained, leading them to a spiral stairwell that led up and down.

"What's the Hive?" Elenor asked.

A young person with long red hair braided into two long pigtails stuck their head through the opening at the top of the stairs. Their face was peppered with freckles and they had bright green eyes. Only their voice informed on what his gender might be. It was deep, and had a Gaelic brogue. "Issat dem? Da they have tha Oracle?"

"Es un hombre, o," Mateo lowered his voice to a squeaky whisper.

"I don't think Damien is an anything. I've never seen them react in the slightest to any gender label, and the way they dress will never help you either because they are just as likely to be wearing a dress and makeup as they are a pin stripped suit and alligator loafers. Damien is their own thing, just like us," Thia said.

"Yeah, D, Thia has it on her, I'm sure," Marissa answered.

"Point of fact, Elenor is carrying it for me since I have lost all ability to make myself leather gear until I figure out how to hands again." Thia held up one of her huge dragon paws, and wiggled the digits at Damien.

Damien flipped over the edge of the opening and landed on the stairs. They were wearing a hunter green knee-length jumper dress with a black undershirt and matching black leggings. Shiny green Mary Jane leather shoes that matched the dress adorned Damien's feet.

"Coom on, give it up!" Damien made a grasping gesture with their hands.

"Damien, I swear, I will bite off something you will miss if you don't slow down," Thia warned.

"Oy, wait a minute. Why do ya sound like tha?" Damien came down the stairs and froze when they saw Thia, Elenor, and Mateo. Their eyes widened to comic

• Es un hombre, o, - Is that guy, or,

widths, slowly moving from Thia, to Elenor, to Mateo and then back again.

"I," Damien paused, and then swallowed. "uh..." Sweat seemed to pop out on their forehead as if they were in a cartoon. "I,"

"I'm going to need actual sentences out of that freckled Pippi Longstocking nerd face of yours," Thia sniped.

Damien chuckled. "You three are fookin' terrifyin'. I think I almost shat out me brains just now."

"And you look like you're twelve with those braids." Thia slid up the stairs past Marissa. She ghosted past Damien and disappeared through the hole in the ceiling.

"Oy bitch, me braids are adorable!" Damien turned and ran up the stairs after her.

"Is it okay that I feel like I'm in a cartoon?" Elenor asked tentatively.

"Probably something you should get used to with Damien around. He's more than a bit of a character."

"Looks like more of a she than a he." Elenor sounded confused.

"Not like he is going to care. I say he because when I met Damien he was wearing a studded leather jacket, combat boots, and blue jeans. He had a spiked buzz cut and looked completely different than he does now."

"You are all taking this well," Mateo remarked as they came up through the floor into a massive open space.

"Everyone here has seen some real crazy shit, Mateo. You have no idea how many people Thia and her Mom have helped. Helen found me in Afghanistan about ten years ago. One of the guys in my unit had latent talent as a Caller, and activated a mystical training simulation that tried to kill the shit right out of us. Two of us didn't make it out of there. None of us would have without Helen and Thia. That's what the network is. A huge group of people the world over making sure that what happened to us doesn't happen to anyone else."

"Did he make it out?" Mateo asked.

"It was Damien. He's thirty-one now, but he was our snot nosed comms officer then. No one knew this about him until after we were all out. Helen has been keeping an eye on him ever since. He's the real deal when it comes to tech. Best there is."

One floor up, the stairwell emerged into a massive open space. In the center of the space was a wall fifty feet wide. Elenor padded off to one side and found that the space continued around the central room. It was like a squared donut running around the entire floor. Along the outer walls were soft glowing squares that appeared to be the shapes of doorways.

Five doors on the left, and when Elenor walked the other direction, there were five more glowing doors on the right. The central room appeared to have a single large door indicated on each side.

"This place is freaking huge," Elenor said.

"Coom on, you haven' seen the coolest part yet." Damien waved them towards the door to one of the central rooms. They put their hand up to the door and the panels of the wall slid away, revealing a room with creamy ivory walls, and a slate grey floor.

"Welcome, to the Hive." Damien went inside, dress swishing as he spun around to face them walking backwards. "Isn't it great?"

The room had four large black pillars at the corners. The ones at the far left and near right were placed further into the enormous room.

"Uh, sure? Kinda anti-climatic but," Mateo said, his sight ears twitching this way and that. He stepped inside and then froze in the door way. His massive sight ears swiveled towards the pillars. "¿Qué son esos…?" Mateo trailed off as he walked towards the pillar at the

---

 • ¿Qué son esos…? – What are those?

right of the door. He lifted a paw and put it against the pillar. "Hay milliones."

When the door slid closed behind them, the surface of the Pillars seemed to shiver.

"How canya even see t'em?" Damien walked a little closer and bent at the waist to peer at Mateo. "Do ya even have eyes under dere?"

"The ears are my eyes." Mateo wiggled his sight ears back and forth.

"Four ears? Dunnae tha confuse ya?"

"Nah, this pair," Mateo wiggled the smaller pair of ears. "are for hearing."

"How does tha work?"

"Getting off track, Damien," Thia prompted.

"Right, right. Da Hive." Damien held out their hand, spreading the fingers out wide. Then they made a sweeping gesture. The black surface of the four pillars burst into a riot of colors and then rippled. Millions of tiny specs floated away into the air, gathering into an enormous seething mass in the air above Damien. The pillars of the room seemed to dissipate into kaleidoscopic sand blown on an invisible wind.

Damien held their hand over their head and the cloud of multicolored snow gathered into a single completely black sphere. It filled almost all of the space between Damien's head and the fourteen foot ceilings.

"This is da Swarm. Despite seven months of studyin', I have no real idea how it wurks, but Helen tol' me it was created several thousand years ago by powerful wizards. I've been able ta make a specialized spherical interface to control the nanadots, buh there do be somethin' missin'. Each dot gets a signal from da control system, but I havan been able ta figur' out how all da signals wurk."

"I only understood about half of that. Sorry Damien, your accent is kinda hard for me," Mateo informed.

 • Hay milliones – There are millions of them

"I know. Curse ah bein' raised by screamin' Scots." Damien grinned.

"They were saying that each of these tiny grains is called a nanodot. They are used like a fully three-dimensional display for the system in here," Marissa translated.

"You were missing the Oracle Stone," Thia filled in. She gestured to Elenor.

"But wha could tha do tha I'm not already doin'?" Damien asked.

"It's a key," Thia explained. "It unlocks access to the Observers."

"Can I open my hammerspace inside of this one?" Elenor asked

Thia nodded. "The spaces are both stable now. Go ahead."

Elenor called the Keymaster's March and the door to her hammerspace opened. She was in and out in a few seconds. When she returned, she had the square leather pouch carrying the oracle stone hanging around her neck. She took it to Damien and sat down in front of him on her haunches.

"Holy shite ya really are 'uge." Damien was muscular with a somewhat wiry build that left him somewhere almost perfectly halfway between feminine, and masculine. At five feet eleven inches, Elenor's head still came up to their chest, putting her head just shy of five feet. She had never stepped on a scale since her transformation, but she guessed she topped three hundred pounds and then some.

"Was that an off handed way of calling me fat?" Elenor's eyes flashed bright with internal light and Damien edged back away from her.

"A direct way of sayin' yer a pants ruinin' experience."

Elenor giggled. "You can take it. I promise I won't bite."

Damien reached out tentatively and lifted the square satchel from around her neck. Elenor snapped her teeth, and they jumped back, holding onto the pouch.

Elenor giggled again and spun away from them. She padded back to where Thia and Mateo waited. Thia had one paw covering her muzzle as she tried not to laugh herself.

"Alright, I deserved tha," Damien said before they turned and walked a few feet further into the room. They stopped and peered at the floor for a long minute. Damien lifted their Mary Jane and then put it down with care in a very specific spot. The floor parted and two panels slid away to either side. A pedestal slid up from the floor, locking into place with an ominous thud. At the top of the pedestal was basin with a large spherical shape nestled inside. The round metal shell had wires and lights blinking inside.

Damien carefully lifted it out of the bowl. They stuck a hand into the tangle of wires and a moment later, the lights inside of the device faded away. They set it aside on the floor. With utmost care, they lifted the Oracle Stone out of the square pouch and placed it into the bowl.

The moment it settled into the bowl, the hovering cloud of sand-like grains rippled like water that a stone had been thrown into. Then they pulled together into a perfect seamless sphere fifteen feet across. Colors flowed across the grains until it became a perfect replication of the Earth.

Mateo walked closer his sight ears twitching. The light webs wrapped themselves around his ears, and he tilted his head. "Amazing, the oceans look real." A tentacle snaked forward from his back and touched the surface of the sphere. Mateo drew it back immediately. "It even feels like water."

"This, is what the Oracle Stone was originally made for. There were over a dozen of these places created some four thousand years ago. They were designed as places that Callers could both feel safe and monitor the world in real time," Thia explained. "We couldn't have it before now because it takes at least three Callers to anchor one of these to our dimension."

"How's dis data comin' in?" Damien asked, staring awestruck at the globe spinning through the air.

"One thousand and twenty-four satellite constructs in geosynchronous orbit over the earth. The only way to access their feeds is with an Oracle Stone like this one."

"I never imagined," Damien whispered.

"That people with magical powers could create technology that humans would take several thousand years to begin to replicate?" Thia's voice was a sardonic squeak that made Damien blush.

Thia held up a paw towards the globe. "Oracle, please display all Surge Anomalies worldwide. Display color code by spectral frequency."

The voice that spoke throughout the room did not seem at all computerized. "Accepted. Surge Anomalies populating." Female, soft spoken, and soothing, the voice rippled out from everywhere and nowhere.

"How do it speak English?" Damien asked.

"The same way you do," the voice answered.

Damien's eyes went wide as he stared at the crystal sphere pulsing with soft white light.

"No, it is not sentient," Thia pipped, heading off Damien's next question. "In your terms, it is a perfect natural language processing interface. Speak with her enough and you will quickly realize the truth of that."

Marissa stepped up to the floating globe and examined it minutely. Blue eyes scanned the various brightly glowing dots, some green, some purple, and some light blue. There were an alarming number of the purple dots spread across the oceans. There was a huge blue dot over the area where they were standing in Manassas Virginia. "This is how you plan to turn the ground war. There are only three of you, but with this tool, you can point us wherever we are needed to gather intel."

"Exactly," Thia affirmed.

39
"MOVE FORWARD"

"Are you sure about this?" Thia asked.

"Certain," Elenor said. She pointed a claw at the spot on the surface of the Swarm. "This is the one."

"What I don't understand is how Osiris tethered it to you specifically," Thia complained.

Elenor shrugged then pulled back her paw, revealing a light blue dot. Eight green dots surrounded it at various points. They were moving around the blue dot, circling in a random pattern.

Watching the memories that Thia's mother had given them showed that Osiris had been doing enormous amounts of research into pre- and postcognition as well as the active manipulation of the Writ.

"Well, this is going to be a joy," Thia grumbled.

"Está en la ciudad, pero I don't think it's any of the museos." Mateo tapped a claw on the dot and the globe rippled. The image on the surface changed as the billions of grains of the Swarm changed color to zoom the map up. Mateo tapped again and again until the image resolved into a perfectly clear picture of a huge house. He waved a paw and a stream of bits from the Swarm flowed out into the air next to the globe. The globe did not reduce in size, only the outer shell was needed to maintain it.

"Oracle, feed from the central server," Mateo requested. A moment later, the smaller cloud of nanodots spread themselves into a thin flat plane. Colors rippled through them for a moment and then the image of a computer screen resolved. A smaller collection of the grains formed into a flat rectangle. Letters emerged from the surface until it became a

- Está en la ciudad, pero – It's in the city, but
- museos - museums

keyboard. Mateo's tentacles emerged from his back and their leaf-shaped ends rolled until they had tiny, rounded tips. He began to use his tentacles and tail to type and interact with the screen. A moment later, a map display showed up. Mateo swept a tentacle across the surface until a map that matched what he was looking at on the Globe showed up.

Thia came through the door far across the Hive. She padded closer and then paused. "Oracle, provide overlay of central server map application to Observer display."

"Please provide assembly edge data," The Oracle requested.

"Substitute geolocation data."

"Request accepted. Reconfiguring." The thin plane Mateo had been working on disintegrated and flowed back into the globe. Then the image refreshed and all of the map data from the mapping application was overlayed on top of the real-time view of the earth.

"Okay, so how do you know all of this?"

"Years of working with the Oracle Stone. You were right, it's just some house. A really big swanky house in the Gold Coast, but still, someone's house." Thia came up and tapped a claw on the map and the image resolved even larger, showing the peaked roof of a house the size of a full city block. "Let's go." Thia turned, her tail sweeping through the globe to disperse the Swarm. The billions of nandots streamed away to form their pillars at the corners of the room. Mateo caught up a moment later.

"You know, you're going to have to explain eventually," Mateo said.

Thia let out a sigh. "I know. She's worried that after Mom, there might be something wrong with me too."

Elenor had been after Thia ever since they had moved into the Black Box, which was what they called their new home. She exited her apartment, the last one on the end to the left. "We ready to go?"

"Not quite yet. I told you I would explain about," Thia took a breath and sighed it out, "why I am the way I am."

Elenor shook her head. "You don't have to."

"We are all we've got and you have to trust me. That means I have to share this with you. I am one hundred and seventeen years old, but I know I don't act like some old lady. It's because of how the Surge my mother used to extend her life affects me," Thia explained, heading for the stairs. "For every year that I age, the aging process slows down. By my mother's calculations, from having had several dozen children over the centuries, I will likely live for thousands of years if nothing kills me."

"How does that effect," Elenor began, but Thia interrupted.

"I'm getting to it. The Surge effects everything. Including my mental development."

"Entonces, ¿qué? Have the brain chemistry of an eighteen year old?" Mateo asked. He had only sat through a dozen discussions about teenage brain chemistry between his parents.

"More like fifteen. It'll take me like a thousand years to reach full maturity. I'm gonna be fifteen for the next couple of centuries." Thia confessed.

"Wow, I'm sorry," Elenor apologized.

Thia shrugged. "Not having to keel over in eighty or a hundred years is pretty awesome, but having to fight my own brain and lose sometimes is not so fun. I'm kinda hoping that this new body will let me mature faster, but I'm not holding my breath. We are just as immortal as Mom." Thia started down the stairs, but paused when Elenor and Mateo just stood staring at her.

"What did you say?" Elenor squeaked.

 • Entonces, ¿qué? – So, you, what?

"You two didn't know? You both looked at Mateo's writband before it was finished. How could you not see?" Thia objected. Mateo's sight ears swiveled to Elenor and they exchanged a look.

"I couldn't read the entire thing at that point." Mateo lashed his tail in annoyance.

"I was paying attention to learning the Hastemaker's Cascade."

Thia sighed. "I suppose that is fair. Yes, though the more accurate term is timeless. We will not age past physical maturity. I'm not sure true immortality is possible, but considering how difficult it is to damage us, we are pretty close." Thia started down the stairs again, and this time they followed.

"Not sure how to feel about that," Mateo said.

"I wouldn't expect you to be sure," Thia said as they came out onto the ground floor. This floor was a bustle of activity as twenty-odd people worked at various tasks, building furniture, work benches, and installing computer systems. Everyone froze when the trio stepped off the stairwell.

"When are you all going to stop staring at us like we're going to chew off your foot when you aren't looking?" Thia pipped. Mateo chuckled.

"Come on, Thia, can't expect them to get used to living with actual nightmare creatures in a few days," Elenor comforted.

"It's just because you're not cuddly like us!" Mateo teased. Thia fluffed up her scales until it looked like she was covered in a shiny coat of tiny pillows.

"Bring it on, furball. I'm plenty cuddly," Thia retorted.

A younger man with teak skin, kind brown eyes, and a square face came over from where he had been working at a table full of medical supplies. His name was Elisha, and he was a medical doctor that they had saved when he had been working with Doctors without

Borders. He was one of the rare few people with inborn Caller talents, and he had run into a very dangerous relic. He had accidentally activated the ten-foot-tall statue designed to protect a Caller's reliquary.

"I'm sorry about that. You three are very striking, that's all," he offered.

"Uh-huh. Don't butter me up, Eli," Thia grunted. Eli frowned and opened his mouth, but she spoke over him. "How much do you have left to do?"

"A few hours. Just making sure that the operating room is sterilized, and that one of the adjoining apartments is reset as bedrest and another as triage and emergency."

Marissa joined them as they made their way towards the west exit. "Do you really think we are going to need a surgeon and team here twenty-four seven?" Marissa adjusted the holster she clearly wasn't used to wearing anymore.

Thia didn't turn her head, there was no need. Her sensory coils showed her the look of skepticism on Marissa's face as clearly as any eye. "Listen to me, Marissa. The teleportation anchors we made you will be literally the only thing that will save your lives if you are attacked by the Infected. You fight only if there is no other choice."

Marissa swallowed. "Alright, so why are we going out there at all if it is so dangerous?"

"If I had my way, you wouldn't be, but I'm pretty sure my mother told you what was at stake here. We can't be everywhere, and the Oracle can only tell us where they are, not what they are doing." Thia stopped at the door that led outside the Black Box. "Now get to it, already. We have to go get a missing piece of this puzzle."

"Are ye three gonnae be allrigh'?" Damien's concern was sincere, and they were likely the only one. The three had spent a lot of time with Damien over the last few days as they worked together to get modern computer systems working in conjunction with the Oracle.

"Who knows? Life is dangerous, Damien," Thia said, and then she padded away as Damien looked on with concern.

"How do we get back out of here without anyone seeing us?" Mateo asked.

"The Black Box uses teleportation anchors to get back outside. Just use the Percept's Rest to keep people from seeing you." Thia crashed her wings together above her and the pure chime flowed into the Sonnet. She stepped onto the purple stone disk that stood at the edge of the wall of misty clouds that bordered the realm.

"Wonder what happens if you walk into those?" Mateo asked the question Elenor had been thinking.

"No clue. Ask Thia?" Elenor squeaked, and then jumped onto the purple stone, vanishing. Mateo followed a moment later.

When they appeared in the field outside of the FBI building, it was a busy afternoon. People were streaming out of the building, but none of them saw Thia, Elenor, and Mateo as they lifted into the sky.

"How far away is it?" Elenor asked.

"About six hundred miles," Mateo informed.

"So, about an hour," Elenor said.

"I can get us there much faster," Thia suggested.

"So can I, but your mom said if we went too fast, it would draw attention."

"If we go fast enough, it won't matter." Thia had been practicing and had learned that her wings were mostly for aesthetics, only acting as a way to direct her flight since her ability to fly had very little to do with aeronautics. "So how fast can you really go?"

Elenor shook her head. "I've never gone as fast as I can. I don't know how fast I can make myself go."

"Time to find out." Thia's wings began to shift shape. The puffy, cloud-like swirl that provided the central point to the balloon-like feathers melted away into a sleek framework of night-black bones. A moment later, a thin membrane spread over and between the bones as the feathers of her normal wings were drawn into the transformation. Her wings folded as if flexing away cramps, and then she snapped them open. Sleek, batlike wings spread into a twelve-foot wingspan that was still far too small to truly carry her large form.

"I wonder why you have wings. They are way too small to actually carry you, I think?" Elenor remembered watching a video explaining how a bird's wingspan was proportional to their body size, and their hollow bones helped to make it easier for them to fly by reducing weight. Thia was slightly smaller than Elenor, but that wasn't saying much, as Thia likely still tipped the scales as well over three hundred pounds.

"They do actually help me steer most of the time. I don't need them, but it takes a lot less concentration to use the air." They had quickly learned that the same manipulation of gravitational forces that allowed her to fly kept her wings attached as well. A tether of force ran between them and her body.

Elenor wished for a long moment that her vision was more like Thia's or Mateo's. She had to turn slightly and open one of the eyes on her back to see the flow of energy as it gathered around Thia. Two long purple tethers ran from the wings to Thia's back, lengthening as they spread away from her. They moved forward away from her until the threads attaching them to her back were stretched thin, and almost twenty-five feet long. Then, a purple circle gathered between the wings. Thia shot forward through the circle, and her wings snapped into place on her back, folded backwards so they wouldn't drag. When she hit the circle, her body turned into a streak and a massive boom sounded as she reached supersonic speeds.

"Esto no es justo," Mateo grumbled.

"Come on." Elenor laughed and closed the eye on her back. She was at least happy that opening the eyes on her back no longer made her instantly dizzy.

"We're never going to catch her," Mateo said.

"Wanna bet?" Elenor pointed her tail at him and then whipped it forward. Mateo shot away so fast that all of his ears plastered to his skull and he felt like his fur might peel off of his body. He began to slow, and then Elenor shot past him, screeching with laugher. Then he had to plaster his ears to his head to protect them from the sonic boom as they screamed across the sky.

After a long roaring moment, Mateo learned he could not extend his light webs to see anything visually with so much wind roaring past him. Thankfully, just after the second boom from reaching supersonic speeds, Mateo felt a change in the air as Elenor began to call a simple two note surge. The Melody of Static Breath hardened the air around them to reduce the drag and make the ride more comfortable. They did indeed catch up with Thia, after the first five minutes.

"How fast are we going?" Mateo shouted, his voice shrill with the volume.

Elenor changed her Melody, and suddenly the wind seemed to fade into a low buzzing sound.

"I don't know how fast we are going, but you can probably figure it out, Mr. Math. Just gotta figure out how far we go and how long it takes."

"Five hundred and eighty-one miles from Manassas to Chicago, as the crow flies."

"How do you do that?" Thia asked.

Mateo shrugged his first pair of shoulders. "I've always been able to remember almost everything I read. It doesn't work for everything, though, just stuff I read."

 • Esto no es justo – That is so unfair,

With Elenor Surging a shield of pressurized air around them, even moving at hundreds of miles per hour, the ride was fairly smooth and quiet.

"So, what do you think will be in the next fragment?" Elenor squeaked.

"I don't think Osiris ever found what he was looking for. I think my mother killed him before he reached it," Thia replied.

"So, what's the point of this?" Mateo asked.

"He was vague about how he accessed the Writ. We assume that when we create a resonance with the Chorus, energy is released from the Writ to alter reality. But what he said, fueling his Surge with his own life energy, we need to know more if we want to find out what he left behind."

"He left how he did it in the last fragments?" Mateo asked.

"That's what I think," Thia responded.

Elenor flipped down the pack around her neck and poked at the cell phone within. "We're almost to Fort Wayne." She hooked her bag back around her neck. "We should go lower!"

"We have to be careful moving at these speeds. The bow wave behind us could be pretty destructive if we go too low."

"How fast are we going?" Mateo wondered aloud again. "Fort Wayne. Four hundred and twenty-nine miles." Mateo mumbled inaudibly for a long moment. "Seventeen hundred miles an hour? Are you two insane?!" Mateo yelled.

"We can go faster!" Thia cried.

"Shouldn't we be generating heat going this fast?! This is past Mach Two," Mateo objected.

"Not with Static Breath going around us. We should slow down before we get too close or we'll overshoot and we don't want to get too close to any of the airports," Thia explained. Fort Wayne was only a blur as they passed, heading straight towards Chicago.

"Land in the lake, but we need to slow down. If we hit the lake at this speed, someone will definitely notice," Thia laughed, and spun herself in a barrel roll.

"Yeah, not to mention it would hurt like hell," Mateo said.

"Tuck in your skirt, Nancy," Thia teased as she tilted her wings, angling her towards the lake. When they came to the edge, she flared her wings and her speed fell off to a slow glide. Elenor followed her lead. They came down to the surface of the water and headed for the shore.

As they got closer to the shore and slowed to a less mind-destroying speed, Elenor ceased her Surge and snapped her striker against the spines on her shoulders. She began to play the Percept's Rest, hiding them from anyone seeing them coming into the city. Elenor waved her paw, bringing Thia into the power of her Runeshard and Thia dropped to run along the top of the water with them.

"¿Así que, qué es el plan?" They both looked at Thia.

"Why am I in charge?" Thia grumbled.

"You've been blowing shit up and stealing things from powerful jokers with your mother for a hundred years?" Mateo explained.

"Fine. Elenor, you get into the house to get the Fragment. Mateo and I will run interference with the Infected. Don't expect we'll be able to handle all eight, though. We have to assume they all know how to actually hurt us so holding back would be kind of stupid."

"Alright, alright. I've heard it from both of you already. I won't hesitate, but I'm gonna look for ways to break those magical bands they're supposed to have. If Elly can change that one guy back, maybe we can do it

• ¿Así que, qué es el plan? – So, what is the plan?

too," Mateo asserted.

"You can, but I don't know where they are hiding those crown things," Elenor said.

They came up onto the shore and the Chicago skyline rolled out to the horizon, the sun silhouetting the city before them. The Gold Coast was one of the most beautiful city neighborhoods Elenor had ever seen, but the money that had to go into building such a place had to be beyond all reality. Elenor and Mateo shook water out of their Fur.

"So, how do we get their attention?" Mateo asked. Elenor headed down the beach to the north.

Thia tilted her head one way and then the other. Her sensory coils rippled like a pit of writhing snakes. "I've got an idea. Stand back by the shore. This will feel strange if you're standing in it. This is the Whisper of Levying Aide. It is something only Callers can sense. It used to be used as a call for help."

Thia spread her feet and crouched down. She lifted her wings. They were still in the shape of a bat's wings, which was odd. Usually, they reverted to their cartoonish shape as soon as her mood changed to anything calmer than excited. The bones between her wings flashed with light when they slammed together. She hadn't been able to explain how she controlled her striker. Her wings didn't really have muscles to flex to act as dampers, so none of them were really sure how they worked.

A melody so soft that even Mateo could barely hear it began to play. The bones of her wings began to shimmer with light that bubbled up, soon fizzing away as her chest lit up with bands of light between the armadillo-like scales. Her chest expanded as she drew in a breath and breathed out a massive cone of mist. This was not like the clouds she had breathed onto the FBI building. This was a diffuse mist, bubbling like the froth at the top of a soda. It was bright blue-white, like the cool glow of a distant star.

It streamed from her mouth in a bar six inches thick. It smashed into the sand a few yards away, creating a small crater as it gathered in to a sphere. The sphere swelled until it was the size of compact car, then the size of a two-story house, and then the size of an apartment building. It exploded apart into a tidal wave of mist that flowed into the streets of Chicago.

"What will that do?" Mateo asked when the stream finally petered out.

"It's a distress call only for Callers, but all of the Infected should feel it too. They should be coming," Thia said.

"Bien, so what are we going to do to fight them?" Mateo asked.

"We can't kill them, but we can damn sure try. Just be ready to move when they show up and attack."

"You know I can't fly or anything like you and Elly, right?" Mateo complained.

Thia blew a raspberry, her bright purple forked tongue fluttering out of her muzzle. "Oh, please. You make lighting look slow. Now stop whining and just get ready," Thia prodded.

"¡Va!" Mateo chuckled. He arranged his six paws until he was sitting comfortably on his haunches.

"Still not sure how you work with those extra paws," Thia said, before she flapped her wings, lifting into the air.

"Ni idea, it just makes sense to me."

"Wish there was some place to hide. It's not quite dark enough for the night to hide me," Thia complained, then zipped into the sky to hover a couple of hundred feet above him.

- Bien – Okay
- ¡Va! – Fine!
- Ni idea – No idea

Mateo twitched his sight ears from side to side, a roll of his eyes. He didn't have to wait long for the Infected to emerge from the streets of Chicago and make their way toward the beach. Mateo finished counting at six.

40

"UNCOVER"

Elenor crouched at the side of the highway running parallel to the lake shore. She stepped out of the beach sand onto a concrete beach as she moved north along the shore of Lake Michigan. She considered how best to make her way into the city. Flight was probably the easiest way to avoid most of the cameras she could see, but until night truly set in, flying through the sky might be a poor choice to keep from being noticed. She could use the Percept's Rest, but Thia had warned her after their trip to Toronto that the Surge could be dangerous to use in a big city.

The more people effected by the Percept's Rest, the more power it would take to sustain it. Thia had revealed that they had only scratched the surface of how Surges could function. They could control the strength of a Surge by making certain alterations to increase their Resonance. This could keep them from getting too fatigued by calling too many Surges. It also meant that if they were not careful, their Surge could be too powerful and cause deadly issues to normal humans. It was why she had been so exhausted after Toronto and even during the battle in the church. She hadn't been adjusting the power of the Surge so the cost was manageable.

"Screw it," Elenor said she clanged her striker against the post of a street sign and began to play. The sounds of the city faded as the first note rang bright and clear. She flexed her tail, damping the note while she counted in her head. She released it and the note sang again, informing the world of the strength of the Resonance. Then she continued the Percept's Rest. Elenor watched the traffic zoom by on many lanes of Lake Shore Drive before diving into a gap between cars. She bounded between them, no one seeing her as she passed. Then realized she was barreling towards a large group of people walking on the sidewalk.

There are so many. She gathered her legs beneath her and soared over the sidewalk. She stuck to the side of the building on the other side like a thrown bowl of Jello. It was the most ungraceful she had felt since her transformation, and she realized she had been focusing far too much of her attention on the Surge.

Feeling stupid, she scrambled up the side and then around the corner of the building. Sprinting to the west up Burton Place, she leapt from buildings of sculpted white stone to facades of brownstone houses and then to bright clean red brick. The leap from one side of the street to the other was long and she had to use a burst from her Runeshard to carry her.

She had to pause for a moment to look at address numbers, and then she was running again. The strain of playing the Percept's Rest was starting to tire her, and when she got to the address she was looking for, she walked up to the roof and ceased the Surge. The moment the Surge fell away, she felt something slam into her side.

The spear of putrid light shattered against her relic, but the power was delivered to her insides. Immediately, she began to cough, and blue blood spilled, bubbling out onto the rooftop.

The Infected she had fought in the Church landed on the rooftop across from her. Elenor narrowed her eyes. She had had enough. Enough of everything. Enough of not knowing what she was facing. Enough of being completely out of control of her own life. Enough of these things hunting her for reasons unknown.

"Enough," Elenor whispered. The Infected did not reply. She only drew back her fist, clutching a spear of veridian light. Elenor took one perfect step to her left, and the spear smashed into the rooftop, blasting away green shingles and leaving a hole in the roof. She flew towards the Infected. The petite muscular woman spread her legs and raised her fists.

Elenor called on the power of her Runeshard reflexively, flinging her body to the left. She planted her front left paw and spun herself like a top. Confusion bloomed on the woman's face as Elenor's tail whipped around with a crack, smashing into the Infected's skull. Surprisingly, it did not sheer straight through. Some unseen barrier intervened.

The Infected was spiked violently face-first into the roof. She smashed through it as if it were wet paper. Elenor did not hesitate. She jumped through the hole and crashed claws first into the back of the Infected. The internal floor seemed to be sturdier than the roof, as they smashed into it at speed but did not burst through.

Tiles shattered as she landed with all of her weight on top of the Infected. She heard bones snap and the woman let out a grunt of pain. She tried to roll and throw an elbow at Elenor, but Elenor just jumped off her back. The woman sprang up, but it was already far too late. Elenor had been given plenty of time to construct a new instruction set for her Runeshard. She lifted her paw and the Infected rose from the ground.

She spun lazily, and when Elenor saw her eyes, she realized the Infected was terrified of her. She didn't understand for a moment. After speaking with the man she had saved, she thought that whatever was controlling them would make them fearless. She had never thought to ask the man if he had been afraid.

"I don't want to hurt you," Elenor said.

"All evidence to the contrary," the woman spat. The coils of light around her arm spooled out into a spear.

Elenor spread the digits of her front paw and the woman's arms were yanked out to the sides, preventing her from throwing or thrusting the spear. Elenor tapped her Striker on the tile floor. She played the Requiem of

Shattered Resonance. The green light surrounding the woman's limbs burst apart as the disrupting notes smashed her Resonance to pieces. That was when Elenor saw that odd line of green light she had seen in Toronto.

"Let me go, monster!" the woman screamed.

Elenor crept closer to the woman and tried to ignore her screeching as she listened to the Chorus. The sound that the fading thread made in the flow of the Chorus was so familiar. It had a muffled echoing reverberation as if... Elenor's eyes spread wide glowing with realization, "As if it is coming from somewhere else!" Elenor squeaked. "That's how you're doing it! You have the crown hidden in a hammerspace!"

Elenor snarled and whipped her paw back and forth. The woman's movement violently tracked Elenor's paw and she smashed off of the walls and floor, leaving behind dents in the plaster. The floor titles shattered, revealing the stone floor below. Bones shattered and Elenor grimaced at the sound of the woman's grunts. When she let out a scream of pain, Elenor paused. They had never done that before.

She raised the woman and looked at her face. She had no cuts and no bruises, but her nose had clearly been broken. She was grimacing in pain and her eyes were filled with terror. She opened her mouth to speak, but then her face stilled and her pupils drew down to burning pinpoints of poisonous light. Then they widened again and the woman gritted her teeth, beginning to struggle.

Elenor stared stupidly for a moment before she began to put it together. "It can't control all of you at once. You're still human underneath."

The woman froze.

"So, why are you helping it? Do you know what it is here to do?" Elenor asked. She knew from Osiris'

Fragment that the creature was there to devour every living thing on the planet.

"Like we have a choice! It tells us that if we don't kill you, it will kill our families! It's always watching!" The Infected hissed in fury.

Elenor shook her head. "I can help you if you take that crown out where I can destroy it."

"What crown are you talking about?" the woman snarled. She tried to form another spear, but it was shattered by the Requiem the instant it took shape.

"I will help you, but not right now." Elenor made a gesture as if she were throwing something over her shoulder. The woman, dragged by all of the water in her body, shot through the hole they had made in the roof. She streaked through the night sky to the west. She wouldn't land until she was well outside of the city.

Elenor sagged as the effort of holding onto the Runeshard for so long hit her. She wished she understood how to make it easier to use. If she could use it at will for as long as she wanted, defeating the Infected might become trivial. She could just hold one of them for as long as they needed to figure out how to get their crowns out of the hammerspace. She shook her head and tested her body for any pains. Their bodies did have some rapid regeneration, but certain kinds of damage needed to be healed to keep them from bleeding out internally. She didn't feel any further pain. She stretched and trotted into the house to find the Fragment.

The room she had landed in seemed like some sort of storage space with stacks of boxes and pieces of furniture covered in old drop cloths. She found the door after a moment of searching through the massive room and carefully popped it open. She paused, taking deep breaths trying to scent if there was anyone in the house. She hadn't paid nearly enough attention to her nose as she should have over the years, but she did know how to tell when scents were old and when they were fresh. There were no fresh scents in the hallway.

Elenor crept out into the hallway and followed it to the left, where she could see a stairwell. There were no lights on, but she didn't need them. Though all the colors were muted, everything was clearly defined in her vision. She slunk down the stairs, careful to keep her tail up and still so as to prevent her striker from hitting anything. She paused at the landing on the next floor, opening the eyes on her back.

Rolling them one way and then the other, she scanned the house for any indication of the Fragment. She didn't see anything right away so she closed her eyes and decided to sniff around the entire house to make sure it was empty. She assumed no one was home or someone would have come running when they smashed through the roof like a wrecking ball.

For a moment, Elenor felt bad. She hadn't much thought about how many laws she had broken since her Transformation. There really hadn't been time, but there had definitely been few choices for her. She shook her head. Thia and Mateo were fighting for her.

It took a little more searching to find her way down to the second floor. Elenor felt less badly as she realized just how lavish the house was decorated and furnished. Whoever lived in this place did not want for money. Considering how much marble and gilt she could see, they didn't want for anything. That was likely why they owned a piece that Osiris would have marked to receive the Memory Fragment. A quick scan of the second floor revealed a flickering white glow, barely visible, on the western side of the building.

The central stairwell lead off into a hallway with wood-paneled walls polished to complete perfection. Even in the darkness, she could the see the polish of the brass handles and display cabinets. She followed the hallway until it opened onto a large room with a fireplace at one end. There were leather chairs and a large carved oak desk at one end of the room. To the left, between two windows, was a pedestal with a weathered black bust atop of it. Much of the painted enamel had worn away over the centuries, but there was enough left that with the gilded headdress, it was distinctly Egyptian in style. The left-hand eye had a slight shimmer to it, the telltale sign that she was looking at the fragment.

Elenor ceased the Requiem and began to surge the Ghostwalker's Etude. She altered the plodding melody until both she and the Fragment shared the same incorporeality. Then she swiped her paw through the display, extracting the Fragment. She stared at the cosmos shining inside.

"We should probably sit down. We have a lot to talk about."

Elenor nearly jumped from her skin, every blade on her body springing out with a speed born of reflex. She spun around violently and the noticed a man sitting in one of two plush leather armchairs.

"What the actual hell?!" Elenor shrieked.

"Oh, simmer down. I am not truly here. I have been dead for," the man paused. His chin length hair was slicked back and his white robe was crisp, leaving one side of a muscular chest bare. Elenor crept around the chair and deep amber eyes fixed on her. He had golden tanned skin and a bright smile on his face. "Well, you are certainly a sight to behold, young Bearer."

"Who are you?" Elenor asked.

"I am the Osiris, and we have some things to talk about."

Elenor slunk back away from him and bared her teeth. "This is all your fault!" Elenor hissed.

"Not all, but yes, much of it is. Please sit. This is going to be extremely unproductive if you remain angry throughout the entire conversation. I promise I will give you ample time at the conclusion to curse me if necessary."

Elenor rolled her glowing eyes and then slid around the chair he gestured to. She got between the chair and him, continuing to face him. Never taking her eyes off the man, she pushed the chair with her back until it slid around to face him. She kept pushing armchair until it was a good eight feet away, close enough that talking would not be a shouting match, but far enough away to give her room to move.

Elenor pulled herself up into the chair and curled herself into a comfortable position, putting her head on her paws. "Talk."

The Osiris nodded. "Before I can give you access to this Memory Fragment, I feel that I need to apologize."

"Because you turned me into a monster and ruined my life?" Elenor snapped.

"No, Elenor, because if I am right, the loss of your humanity will be the least of the horrific experiences you will endure."

Tears gathered in Elenor's eyes. "Did you just leave this message to gloat, then? Seems like a pretty shitty cliché," she growled.

"I will not apologize for what I did, because that would mean I wouldn't do the same thing again. I was not insane when I made the choice that set all of this in motion. That does not mean I do not realize how unfair it is to you and others like you." Osiris steepled his fingers before his face, his mouth a grim line.

"Don't patronize me. There is no moral high road for this!" Elenor squeaked. "You deserve everything you got."

To her surprise, Osiris nodded. "I am not here to take a moral high road, Elenor. If there is any equity in this universe, whatever was left of my soul will suffer every horror I visited upon the world for us to reach this point. Even if what I did was the only choice I could make, that is not justification for the suffering it caused. There is no defense for what I did. Only necessity."

"You think I'm going to feel sorry for you after this?" Elenor asked.

"I should fucking hope not. I killed millions of people in my attempt to reach this point. For that alone, I should be hated and damned." Osiris brought them back to the topic at hand.

"This message is here because I left a mystery behind that I was unable to uncover fully before the Iðunn tracked me down. I suspect I was dead within hours of making this Fragment. I refuse to unlock the memory until I am sure you are the right one to see it, because you will be the only person ever to see it first-hand. To leave a Fragment this heavy with a piece of my mind means it will only work once. So, let us get down to brass tacks, as they say. You saw there was one more piece I couldn't see in my visitation to the Writ in the last fragment?"

Elenor nodded. "How do you know who I am, anyway?"

"Not important. We have very little time to work with and I have questions that need answers. Is the Iðunn still alive?"

"Yes, she's the one who has been teaching me how to call Surges."

"That is both good and bad news." Osiris shook his head. "No time now. Are there more Bearers like you?" Orisis asked.

"Yes, two more, but they don't have powers like mine yet."

"What do you mean by powers like yours?" Orisis asked, though by the way he said it, the tone told Elenor that he already knew the answer.

"Powers from the Runespring. Helen called them Runeshards."

"Then it is as I expected. There should be seven more to come, at the least. But," he paused for a long moment and then pointed at Elenor's chest with two fingers. "You said she has been teaching you to Surge. Do you have a Writband, then?"

Elenor nodded and hummed the Surgecaller's Revelation. Her Writband glowed brightly through her fur, revealing all three twisted rings.

"Such, power," he whispered as he stared at the band until the glow faded. "Better than nothing, I suppose. Now the hard part. Why are you here, Elenor?"

Elenor stared at him for a long silent moment, all breath frozen in her chest as two years of anger found a long-sought outlet. "Because of you!" she shrieked. "Because you didn't give a shit about what happened to anyone in the future and you made us into monsters! I should tear you apart!" She realized that her claws and spines had not torn the chair to pieces, and she looked down at it. "What the hell?"

"It is a Fragment. Nothing here is tangible to the observer. You are the observer."

"Arh!" Elenor roared in frustration. In the middle, it mutated into a true roar that would have made a lion cower in fear.

The Osiris looked startled, his eyes widened in something that was almost fear. "I feel I am quite glad that I am not actually here. Also, you have not answered my question. Why are you here?"

"Why the hell do you think I am here?" Elenor screeched in fury. "Because I just want to be me again! It's better now, I have friends, but it's just us three. There is a whole world of shitty people out there who would love nothing more than to kill us just because we look like monsters to them. That is your fault!" Elenor shouted, her fury flashing in her glowing, mismatched eyes.

Osiris shook his head. "That's why you are angry, not why you are here."

Elenor narrowed her eyes, still fuming with anger. She turned around in the chair until she curled herself into a comfortable swirl on the rust-colored leather cushion. Osiris raised a brow in question and Elenor bared razor teeth at him. "I'm here because I want to know what in the hell has happened to me and where this is going. Even if I am stuck like this, I can't really live any sort of life if these Infected things are running around the world for the rest of my life."

Osiris' eyes fixed on her. "What if you are a monster for the rest of your life?"

Elenor shrugged, her ears drooping a little as pensiveness rose in her eyes. "That's what I used to think." Elenor put her head down on her paws again and closed her glaring eyes. "Do you know that it took almost a year for someone to see me after I ran away from home?"

Osiris shook his head, but said nothing. It was not the time for speaking. If he wanted the answers, it was the time to listen.

"I didn't know, then, that I was protected. I spent that whole year hiding, terrified. Terrified, look at me. I thought about it all the time - what a monster I was." Elenor sighed and lifted her head, looking down at her paws. They were so close to being the thick-fingered hands of a human and yet so far from her own human hands.

"I didn't realize it at the time, but I stopped thinking I was a monster that night." She folded her paws again and rested her chin on them. "Because as easily as I could have killed someone by accident with my relic, I would never have done what that cop did on purpose. He shot me just because I looked like I could be scary. Just because he <u>thought</u> I was a monster. He didn't even try to understand, just took out his gun and pulled the trigger." Elenor turned her glowing eyes up to Osiris, haunted with the memories of terror.

"I'm not a monster, no matter what I look like. It's people like you that are monsters. You didn't care what this would do to me. You didn't care how long it would take me to understand. You only cared for whatever you wanted." Elenor's quiet malice was righteous and unyielding. She thought she hated this man, but having met him, she knew that hate wasn't required to know he was the kind of person that she needed to protect other people from.

Osiris watched her, his eyes searching for something that he knew was there. Then he closed them before they could brim with tears. "And by the slimmest hair of margins, we have a chance," he whispered, and Elenor perked her ears forward.

"As I said, I will not ever think of forgiveness for what I have done. Atonement, perhaps, but not forgiveness. Even if I am proven right, it does not justify what I had to do. Still, I must ask. If that goal was to prevent something even worse than what I did, could you understand?"

"I don't know if I am ready to understand something like that," Elenor confessed.

Osiris' eyes searched her face again and this time, found what they were looking for. Then his eyes moved to his steepled fingers and he let out a contented sigh. "You are likely the best I could have hoped for. Honest, at least. A little less emotional fragility would be useful, but it is not as if you have no reason for it."

"Hey, fuck you, buddy. I'm not fragile," Elenor squeaked angrily, and Osiris grinned.

"Perhaps you are not as you seem," he suggested and she shrugged.

"The fragment will relent to you. We have perhaps a few more minutes. The lensing effect of this memory is wearing thin."

"Lensing effect?" Elenor wondered.

"This has been happening at the speed of thought, which means it is taking far less time than it feels like it is taking. Still, if you do not leave soon, it'll start to take a lot more time. I have one more thing to tell you. About the Miasma," Osiris said. When Elenor dropped a single ear with puzzlement, Osiris went on.

"The Miasma, the Surge that the Iðunn uses to erase things from existence. More importantly, what allows her to call on it."

Elenor sat up with interest now. "Do you know how to fix it?" she asked.

Osiris shook his head. "I never made it that far. I can offer you only this. You cannot counter the Miasma with a Surge. There is no way to hear what it does to the Chorus, and so, if she attacks you with it, you must use your Runeshard." The Osiris rested hands in his lap and then looked down at them. "When you encounter the Writ, have a care. It will not allow you into its port dimension easily."

He looked up at her and gave a pained smile. "Lastly, you can help the Iðunn. Her Writband holds the secret to what controls her, but I do not know of anyone who has ever gotten a look at the Writband of someone who enforced the laws of the Writ. Most people did not even realize there was a problem."

He began to hum. Five notes, intricately intertwined, issued forth from the Osiris. Elenor heard the name of the Surge in the calling. It was called the Direction of Greatest Need. When he ceased, he let out a breath as if laying down a heavy burden. "You will need to call that Surge to go further. I don't know where or when you will need it, but you will need it." The Osiris returned his hands to the arms of the chair. He didn't push himself up, though, he just sat, staring into the fire.

Just as she was about to get up to leave, he spoke again. "I'm sorry that you have had to take advice from me. If I had any other better way of passing information on to you so far into the future, I promise you I would have used it. I assure you this is the last time you will ever have to endure my presence."

Elenor did not feel anything for him. He was directly responsible for what had happened to her and anyone else that came after her. She stood up and stretched on the chair, arching her back like a scalded cat. She hopped down to the floor, but paused next to his chair. "I don't know if this is going to get back to the real you, wherever you are, but…" Elenor paused and took a deep breath.

"I still think you're a pretty shitty person for what you did to me, but I would be lying if I said I didn't understand hard choices." Elenor walked away from the chairs and the world around her flickered. The fire blazing in the hearth vanished, along with Osiris. The room returned to its previous weary, empty feel, as if no one had been there in living memory.

No more than the slightest sound pricking her ears warned her as a massive force slammed into her spine.

41

"Dragon"

Mateo showed no fear, standing at the edge of the beach where concrete met sand. He wanted them to chase him into the sand, where being on six paws would give him a slight advantage. He watched with some curiosity as they wove between cars on the highway. The cars moved around them as if they could see them, but there were no horns, no stopping. It was as if they somehow moved reality around them so they could stalk across the street unabated.

The figures were of varying sizes. One was clearly the giant from Toronto, a man well over six and a half feet, covered from head to toe in glowing green threads that closely resembled muscle fiber. Another was just as clearly the tiny girl from outside of his apartment. She had several large geometric shapes floating around her in spirals of green light.

The others were all just as strange. One of them was even shorter than the girl, with their limbs covered and enlarged by wires of green energy. They were like the limbs of a massive cat with huge claws. This allowed the Infected to walk on all fours with a strange gait that seemed like it should be ungainly. Still, somehow, they were smooth, with predatory movements.

Mateo was not afraid of these people. This was his trap, not their ambush. He backed away slowly to draw them in until he reached a large rock placed onto the beach as décor.

"Where is the fragment?" the beastial looking one on all fours shouted.

"Long gone," Mateo said. His need to look up and see where Thia was itching at him. He forced it down so as not to give her away.

"Well, at least we still have you."

"You sure do." Mateo grinned as the last one got close enough. He whipped his tail around, his Striker smashing into the rock with a deafening chime. Immediately, the Requiem of Shattered Resonance flowed from his striker and the power of the Infected burst apart into motes of poisonous light that faded into the night.

With perfect timing, a thunderous boom came from above and Thia arrived in a blast of distorted gravity. Her wings slammed together in front of her, activating her Striker. She flared them, initiating a transformation into a pair of wings composed of a tangle of obsidian blades. They dripped with glowing purple energy, like they were sluiced in alien blood. Several of the blades in the tangle glowed with rainbow of light and Thia breathed in, her chest expanding as the cracks between her scales filled with an ominous blue glow.

Thia breathed out with a roar horrendously louder than any that Mateo had previously heard. The noise was so pervasive that Mateo's vision went white and he folded his sight ears down against his head. A bar of blue-white fire exploded from Thia's mouth, so hot that Mateo leapt back as his fur started to smoke from twenty paces away. Thia yanked her head back and forth, the bar of fire snaking through the small crowd of infected. It sheared through everything it touched.

The Infected in front, who had dropped to hands and knees when her power had been shattered, was hit first. Her entire head vanished in an explosion of white fire, her body collapsing in a twitching tangle of spastic agitation. Arms and legs went spinning away from bodies as the fire streaked through them. The sand beneath them boiled instantly to glass as the grains were flash heated to thousands of degrees.

When the bar of obliterating fire tapered off, Mateo could only stare at the destruction the breath weapon had caused. He didn't know how to call the Surge she had used, but he definitely wanted to. He ceased his Surge as he felt the fatigue of continuing to play it wash over him. Helen had told them over time, they would be able to Surge for longer. It couldn't come soon enough for him.

Thia did as they had agreed, beating her comically small wings down to launch herself back into the sky. Their plan had been simple. Thia would menace them from the sky after her initial attack while Mateo did the rest.

Mateo launched himself, paws churning the sand as he ran into the fray. Of the three left standing, the one in the middle was the worst off. They had lost an arm. It was a younger man with chin-length black hair and almond-shaped eyes. To Mateo's surprise, he dodged back out of the way as he went by. Mateo landed and immediately threw himself to the left. He swung around the Infected in the middle.

This time, it was the second largest of the three. The man was not as huge as the giant they had fought in Toronto, but he was well-muscled and holding two brightly glowing green mauls. Had they been made of steel, the hammers were far too big to be able to be wielded by an average human. This man twirled them as if they were weightless.

He interposed one of the glowing hammers between Mateo and himself, trying to hold Mateo at bay. Mateo whipped one of his tentacles through the air. It flattened until a wicked arc of scalpel-sharp obsidian smashed into the hammer. It sheared through the green light with little resistance, causing a shower of blinding green sparks. The second hammer caught him in the shoulder, knocking him away and delivering a punch to the inside of his chest. Mateo felt something tear inside, but he kept moving.

Stupid! He chided himself for leaping around like that without all of his blades to protect him. He tumbled through the sand, fetching up to a stop against a concrete curb. An enormous webwork of green threads wove itself around Mateo and snapped tightly against his body, binding him into a tight cocoon. He felt it straining to pull even tighter against his hardened bones, and skin.

It could not possibly penetrate his relic, but through the tight weave of threads, Mateo could see the other two Infected charging at him. He concentrated on sharpening the edges of his tentacles, but he knew he wouldn't be fast enough.

"Hold your breath!" Thia's screech came just before a vociferous chime from her Striker rent the air. He did not recognize the Surge she called this time either, but there was no time to try to listen. The roar of her breath burst out into the world. Mateo drew in as deep a breath as he could.

He could hold his breath for hours with that much warning. A cloud of choaking gas enveloped him. It was impossible for him to tell what color it was without his light webs extended, and he did not care to push them out because it became quickly apparent that what Thia had breathed out was some stripe of acid.

The Infected actually began to scream as their bodies broke down under the onslaught of Thia's breath. They began to melt as she blurred past and pulled back up into the sky. The bindings holding Mateo fuzzed into bubbling light and faded away. He scrambled to his paws and galloped out of the cloud and blew out through his nose to clear any gas lingering that he might have involuntarily inhaled.

"Well, that was the most horrifying thing I've ever seen. Thanks for the nightmares!" he shouted at Thia, his boyish voice almost, but not quite cracking with strain. Then he began to cough and safety orange blood spat from his muzzle into the sand.

"They were gonna kill you and they shrug off regular fire a little too readily for me to trust it to stop them. It takes me a while to recover from using the Dragon's Heartsong so I couldn't use dragon breath again." Thia dropped to the ground next to him, her sensory coils rippling until the correct set was exposed. Glowing lavender eyes winked open on her neck, and then on her flanks, back, and tail. In a moment, she was leaning closer to him.

"It looks like you are healing on the inside." She reported and then looked toward the city. "She still isn't back."

Mateo realized the likely reason. "There were only six here."

"She can handle two on her own."

Mateo nodded. "But maybe we should catch up with her," he urged, and Thia nodded. As they trotted towards the highway, he looked back over his shoulder and slowed to a walk. "Should we do something to clean that up?"

"Nah! By the time anyone gets here, the Infected will be gone. All that will be left is the glass. They'll think it was a lightning strike or something," Thia squeaked back, and Mateo sped up again to catch up with her.

Mateo was continually amazed by the power of his new body. With so many people watching, they each had to maintain their own Surge, the Percept's Rest blanketing the entire highway. Mateo leapt between cars without any trouble at all. The dashed into the picturesque Gold Coast neighborhood.

"Do you really think they got her?" Mateo worried.

Thia shook her head. "I doubt it. She's not invincible, but her Runeshard is absurdly powerful."

Instead of dodging between people, Mateo leapt onto the side of one of the office buildings and scrambled along the wall. Thia beat her wings, lifting into the air next to him.

"Eso es tan injusto," Mateo complained.

"For someone who can walk on walls, see through walls, and tell when people are lying, you sure do bitch a lot about not being able to fly," Thia snarked, and then beat her wings and shot down the street.

"Show off!" Mateo yelped, and then he put his head down and stretched out into his run. It didn't take long to make it the few blocks to the address they had seen on the Oracle Stone. The house they had found was one luckless moment away from a 911 call. Smoke poured from several windows and there were holes torn in the exterior stonework as if a wrecking ball had smashed through various parts of the building. Whatever had caused the ruinous wounds in the building was still in progress, as roaring crashes echoed from within the massive white-stone mansion.

Thia banked around and came to hover just outside of the house, where Mateo was standing on one of the exterior walls that remained intact. "Go in the bottom, I'll drop in from the roof, and we meet half way."

Just as they were about to run inside, a thunderous crash echoed down the empty streets. White stone exploded from the side of the mansion as a body tumbled through one of the massive columns. Chaotic rubble rained into the street around the tumbling body. Elenor's claws dug into the pavement and she skidded to a stop. Blue blood dripped from her muzzle and striated across her bared teeth.

The thing that slammed into the sidewalk a moment later, shattering the concrete as if it were glass, was not at all like the other Infected. It seemed to be a withered husk of a person. The threads of magic that had previously been used as weapons and armor seemed to be woven through this body. There were no eyes, only

 • Eso es tan injusto – This is so unfair

empty pools of poisonous green energy. There was no way to tell if it was a man or a woman. It had no build, almost as if a skeleton had skin stretched over its bones before being infused with a web of magical threads. Mateo started forward, but Elenor shrieked.

"Stay back! It's different than the others. I can't get ahold of it with my Runeshard. It's got no water or blood inside of it."

Elenor crouched and then bolted across the street in a blur so fast that even Mateo's Echolocation had trouble keeping up. A sound barrier shattering boom echoed down the street and Elenor appeared in front of the creature. It lifted a hand, a point, blinding radiance forming in its palm, but then Elenor was just gone.

She appeared behind the creature and spun herself like a top. Hundreds of spines grew from her tail, and she whipped it into the creature's back. The spines pierced the glowing mummy half a hundred times lifting it from its feet. A split second later the spines vanished releasing the creature. The blow blasted the thing from its feet, bowing its back from the sheer force. It streaked across the street and smashed through the façade of a brick and stone building across Burton Place.

Mateo cringed as he heard further booms. She had hit the Infected with such force that it seemed even several buildings were insufficient to impede its tumbling body.

Elenor stood panting on the side walk, blue blood effervescing into bubbling azure light as it gathered on the sidewalk below her muzzle. Her ears drooped and all of her spines flexed as if made of rubber.

"I don't," she took a deeper breath, coughed flecks of spittle and blood, "think I can kill that thing on my own." She looked ready to collapse from the effort she had expended.

"What the hell is it?" Mateo wondered.

"It's like a mummy with those threads woven

through it to move it like a puppet." Elenor hung her head and panted heavily. Mateo trotted over to her and lifted one of his sight ears towards her.

"There is so much damage," Mateo whispered.

"I'll be fine. I just needed a breather to make healing instructions for my Runeshard, but I'm almost spent."

He realized she was right as he watched the torn organs and tissues inside of her begin to mend themselves. The magic of her Runeshard was knitting together rent flesh and regenerating missing blood. The sound of crashing stone assaulted them. Mateo turned his sight ears towards the enormous hole through the building. He could see the creature moving as the sounds bounced around the buildings.

"It's coming back," he informed, and then noticed the Surge being called by Thia. His ears leaned away from one another drastically, in an eye widening gesture. She was facing towards Elenor and the Surge she was calling was intricate, all ten notes going into the playing.

A moment later, as the music flowed, Mateo was able to pick out the name of the tune from the calling signature. The Lullaby of Shaded Rest. It sounded like something that would put someone to sleep, but he could tell by the complexity of the tune that it was far more than that. Then, Thia's chest was expanding a misty seafoam glow, drifting between the banded dragon scales on her chest. She breathed out almost gently, compared to the normal roar that came with her breath weapons. Verdant mist flooded the street, swirling in eddies around Elenor and Mateo. When Thia closed her maw, whisps of the mist leaked from her nostrils and the corners of her muzzle.

"Take a deep breath of the mist," she ordered.

Elenor and Mateo exchanged a look through the shifting clouds of mist. They both shrugged and breathed deeply, taking in as much of the mist as they could. The moment both of them stopped breathing in, the mist vanished as if it had never existed.

Elenor held her breath for a long moment, but nothing happened. She took a step towards Thia and opened her mouth to speak. Before she could utter a single breath, she felt her insides burn with comforting warmth. It filled her, and she let out a startled breath as all of the fatigue that had been weighing on her a moment before drifted away as if it had been taken with the vanished mist. She felt as ready, hale, and rested as she had ever been in her life. "What was that?"

"Something I've wanted to try for fifty years. The Lullaby restores all of your vitality. It's a good night's sleep and a good meal all at once. You can't use it again until you get those things for real, though, so use it well." Thia turned towards the churning rubble that blocked their view of this new Infected monstrosity.

"We don't have a lot of time. The rest of them will pull themselves back together soon," Mateo observed.

"We could just run. You have the Fragment?" Thia suggested.

Elenor nodded. "But I don't want to leave this thing in the city. It doesn't avoid people like the others. It smashed through buildings, cars, and probably people to get here."

"There is only so much we can do about it. We can't kill it," Thia protested.

"Do you know how to break open a hammerspace?" Elenor asked.

"Do we have time for this?" Mateo asked nervously.

"No," Thia affirmed.

At the same time, Elenor spoke. "Yes! Because we can stop them."

"Alright, I'll stall. You two figure it out," Mateo said before darting across the street towards the zombie creature that was pulling itself from the rubble.

Elenor watched as he swung wide and then galloped down the street past the creature. As he went past, one of his tentacles whipped around the creature's neck and yanked it from its feet. Mateo ran for all he was worth, dragging the creature behind him.

"What are you talking about?" Thia demanded.

"Each one of them has a tether to a hammerspace. I noticed it in Toronto but I didn't know what it was. It took until tonight for it to click," Elenor explained. The sound of police sirens began to echo from the corridors of the Chicago streets.

"Look, what you're asking for isn't easy. Port Dimensions are keyed to the Resonance of the person. There are ways to break in, especially to ones that aren't anchored to anything but the person, but it's tough." Thia's sensory coils rippled nervously as she watched the fight between Mateo and the Infected.

"Thia, he can take care of himself. Tell me what I have to do!" Elenor snapped her back to the conversation.

"You can't do it like this. You need to be able to listen to their Resonance without all this noise." Thia snarled, feeling helpless.

"Augh!" Elenor snarled squeakily. "Fine, but we have to get that thing the hell out of here."

Thia stared as Mateo smashed the creature against stone buildings and steel light poles. It struggled with the tentacle wrapped around its neck. It was somehow protected from the cutting edges of Mateo's tentacles, or its head would have surely come off by now.

"Alright, count to 30 and then get it up into the air. I'll get it out of the city and into the lake." Thia didn't wait for a response. She beat her blade-tangled wings with a spray of violet energy, and vanished into the sky.

Elenor started counting in her head. Mateo went flying past her. Before he got too far, she held up a paw and grabbed ahold of the water in his body. He froze, and she pulled him down next to her. The Infected creature pulled itself from the rubble of what used to be another mansion-like home. There was the sound of someone screaming inside of the building and Elenor desperately wanted to go to help. To help, though, she needed to get the creature up into the air. She reached fifteen in her head.

"We need to get it up into the air!" Mateo nodded in response. "I'll get it to you. Use your tentacles to throw it up." Elenor said, and like Thia, she didn't wait for a response. She called up the power of her Runeshard and bolted down the street towards the emerging creature. She didn't quite reach supersonic speeds, but she made it to the creature in less than a second.

Stopping just before the shattered rubble of the house, Elenor whipped herself around and smashed her tail into a collection of rubble. Dozens of stones pelted into the crater, smashing into the thing and knocking it back. Elenor stood her ground, and the creature came roaring out of the remains of the shattered building.

It ran towards her, smashing chunks of rubble out of its path like an enraged Abrams tank. Before it reached her, it skidded to a halt and raised a hand. A brilliant point of light gathered in its palm. Elenor turned slightly and brought her tail around until the thick appendage was interposed between her body and the Infected. The dozens of blades created an impenetrable webwork of shielding.

A beam of gangrenous light shot from the creature's hand. Instead of shattering against the hardened spines of Elenor's tail, the beam split refracted hundreds of times by the mirror polished spines. The beams cut into the broken rubble and still standing walls of the house. Several of them shot back towards the creature. Caught unaware, it was unable to dodge, and light beams carved through the desiccated flesh.

Clearly, it had a similar effect to the other Infected because the beams delivered some form of kinetic payload, blasting the creature back through the detritus, smashing one of the remaining walls of the house to bits.

"Get ready!" Elenor squeaked and then streaked away down the street.

Mateo braced himself, his ears up and forward focused. The creature emerged from the corner of the street. The moment it was clear of the building, Elenor came back towards Mateo in a blur of speed. Still intact windows shattered as her bow wave blasted the street around her. It somehow sensed her coming, but it was far too late. It attempted to leap out to the left. Elenor adjusted just slightly and her shoulder slammed square into the middle of its spine.

Bones crumbled under the force of the hit, causing a ripping crackle like someone had punched a bag of dry pasta with a battering ram. The Infected was blasted towards Mateo at funny car speeds.

Mateo was ready. His tentacles wrapped around the creature's throat as it flew past and snapped taut as he mentally hauled back on them through his relic. He whipped the creature around, smashing it off of three buildings, and then with a shout of effort, he whipped his tentacles towards the sky, launching the creature into the air.

It reached the apex of its flight just as Elenor hit thirty in her head. The sound hit Elenor like a physical thing as Thia dove out of the sky. What few windows that remained intact exploded from overpressure. Parked cars rocked up from the ground before slamming back down. She swooped almost to the pavement and then streaked up towards the Infected.

At the last possible instant, her wings vanished into her Relic. She coiled her long body into a tight ball and smashed into the Infected. The cacophonous boom echoed through the city, launching away the Infected as if it had been fired from a rail gun.

Thia dropped like a stone as if she had been knocked unconscious, but as she fell, her wings unfurled from her

Relic in what Elenor thought of as their normal shape –
two cartoonish swirled clouds with five huge swooping
balloon-like feathers emerging from each. They
stretched to either side and she slowed to a stop,
hovering only a few feet off the pavement.

The sirens were growing alarming in their closeness,
and Elenor dashed to Thia.

"Are you alright?"

"It was the best thing I could think to do. I think I'm
okay, but I'm exhausted after all those Surges," Thia
sighed.

"Can you fly?" Mateo was standing statue still, his
sight ears twitching and swiveling.

"Nah, I'm totally spent. I either find a nice place to
hide, or you can carry me?" Thia's voice turned up at the
end making it a question.

Elenor nodded. "After that last Surge, I feel pretty
great. Let's get out of here." Elenor concentrated on her
Runeshard and all three of them lifted into the air.

"Wait!" The voice was one that Elenor recognized.
The Infected she had thrown towards the edge of the
city. They spun in the air towards the voice.

The woman was haggard and her clothes showed the
rips and tears of her rough landing outside of Chicago.
She must have sprinted the entire way to get back.

"Did you mean it?" she shouted.

Elenor just bobbed her head in recognition.

The Infected's face crumpled, but she did not cry.
"Thank you!" she shouted. Elenor waved a paw as she
directed them up and out of the city.

"Realmente eres un dragón," Mateo said, looking at Thia
with a little awe. She began to blush, purple rushing
into her shining black cheeks.

Thia giggled. "I always thought it would be so cool
to breath fire like a Dragon. I guess the Writ took that
into consideration."

• Realmente eres un dragon – You really are a dragon

42
"THE BIG PICTURE"

Only Mateo had the energy to function over the next five days. When Elenor had briefly woken up, she told them about the mummified creature's attack on her after her talk with Osiris. She had eaten eight hamburgers with all the trimmings and then immediately disappeared back into her apartment to sleep. Thia had managed to pry herself from her bed after the third day and had spent many hours staring at the fragment Elenor had recovered as if it held the secrets of the universe.

"You already said it won't work for you. Why do you keep starring at it?" Mateo asked.

"Just thinking about the big picture. It doesn't make any sense. We already know about the, whatever it is, out there looking for us," Thia began, and Mateo nodded along.

"But he told Elenor that there was something more, so that means the thing out to kill and eat us, what?" Mateo pondered. He folded himself to the floor, arranging his six legs beneath himself until he looked like an enormous cat loaf, his long, glimmering tail wrapping around his paws.

"What indeed. At this point, we have to assume, with the research we knew Osiris was doing, that he was specifically trying to trigger the Writ to create more powerful Callers."

"To fight this monstruo from the Outside?" Mateo guessed.

"That's what I thought, and it's what Mom thought too, but now…" Thia trailed off, staring at the marble.

"What else could there be?"

  • monstruo - monster

"...that could be worse than that?" Elenor finished for him as the door to the Hive slid open. "Let's find out." Elenor sat down next to them, reached out to the small bowl on the table where they had put the fragment, and closed her paw around the marble. She willed the memory from the Fragment.

NC 17, EPOCH 18418.182

He had spent weeks pouring over the memory of the Writ, trying to pull free even the barest splinter more than what he saw before he collapsed. Now the Iðunn had found his trail and there was no more time for him to tug at the end of the thread. He had known that this moment would come when he began and that eventually, he would have to leave it to the Callers who would come after. Still, there was the thread to leave behind. He squeezed the Fragment in his fist.

"See what I saw," he whispered.

Osiris lay on the cool lack of a floor in the infinite void of the port dimension the Writ had generated for their encounter. Blood trickled from the corner of his mouth as he tried to make his eyes focus on the preternatural symbols etched into the endless stone wall. The symbols expanded until he was seeing two almost humans.

Their odd clothing was somewhere directly between feminine and masculine, with nary a seam or fastening to be seen on the colorful garments. One was dressed all in shades of blue, the other in shades of green. The clothing was skin tight, covering them from neck to toes. The upper body of each outfit was pastel light, though it bled to a darker color at the gloves that covered their hands. The only decoration on each outfit was at the waist. The figure in blue wore a skirt that hung almost to their knees. Organic patterns glowed on its surface, giving the impression of flowering vines. Decorations that appeared to be memory Fragments were sprinkled across the skirt, somehow attached the center of flowers made of folded ribbon. The figure in green wore a shorter skirt that stopped at the top of their thighs, geometric patterns glowing in white on its fabric.

A carved square archway made seemingly of pure gold framed the scene. Facets cut in the gold made it seem as if it were a gem made of metal. The center of the arch was filled with a cosmos of stars. At the top of the archway was the last thing that Osiris was able to focus on, a symbol at the apex of the door. The symbol was an odd swirl, like a symbolic whirlpool contained within a circle. The swirling lines extended past the bounds of the circle, almost hypnotic in the look of it. Osiris had seen the symbol before, but he couldn't place it as he released the Surge that kept him inside of the Writ's port dimension.

NC I7, EPOCH 19915.58

Elenor gasped as she emerged from the memories of the Fragment. Unlike other Fragments, this one burst into a tiny pile of dust the moment Elenor was finished viewing it. The magical matrix that caused the Fragment to exist could no longer withstand the tremendous amount of energy it contained.

Elenor immediately lowered herself to the floor of the Hive and tapped her Striker against the floor. She began to play Fugue of Fragmented Memory, and, after the Fugue trailed off, she had a hard time thinking for a few long seconds. She blinked away the aftermath.

"I don't know what I am supposed to get out of this." Elenor gave them a quick explanation of what had happened in the memory. When she got to the part about the symbol above the door, Thia's sensory coils rippled so violently that Elenor could tell Thia was feeling sick, even though they were still figuring out what all of her and Mateo's expressions meant.

"Let me see," Thia squeaked. She opened her mouth, not wanting to wait for her wings to reshape themselves into makeshift hands. Elenor shrugged and dropped her memory fragment in. She had one fleeting thought about what happened when any of them ate something. She knew from experience that she could hold something in her mouth without it burning up as long as she didn't try to swallow it.

When Thia's sensory coils shuffled again, she spit the Fragment into the middle of her huge feline paw. She held it out to Elenor, who lifted her head to give Thia access to the bag around her neck. Thia dropped the Fragment into the bag.

"I," Thia stammered, "That symbol." Thia's sensory coils dimmed from their purple glow until they were almost transparent. "I need to speak to my mother, but,"

"No podemos. What is it, Thia?" Mateo asked.

"That symbol is the universal mark for the Runespring. The only time I have ever heard my mother speak of that symbol," Thia paused to swallow, "she said it was an abomination that she wished she could have destroyed. But more than that, what were those people doing there? To be there at the binding of the Writ to the world, tampering with the process, I can't imagine how it's possible."

"Gonna need more than that," Mateo said.

"Seventeen hundred years ago, when Mom had just become The Iðunn, she was told a rumor about a laboratory where Callers were attempting to decipher a way to bypass the Writ and access the Runespring directly. They attempted things like extra-dimensional tunneling, and apparently, they connected tunnels to other places with, things." The glow of Thia's sensory coils brightened as she calmed with the telling of the story.

"Mother said that when they found the place, the creatures living inside were almost impossible to kill. Knowing what we know now, that makes the proposition of having to go there… unfortunate."

"And what about the second part?" Elenor asked.

"Well, it would take a lot of power to tamper with the

 • No Podemos – We can't

Writ as it was being made, and I can't imagine any good that could come from tampering with the foundation of a local reality."

"Do you know how to get to the place your mother talked about?" Mateo asked, sight ears swiveling as he listened to everyone moving around them inside of the Black Box. He stood up.

"We need to get downstairs. Someone just teleported in and they're in trouble." Mateo dashed towards the featureless wall of the Hive. He waved his tail at the wall in a gesture of command and a door opened. He dashed through and headed for the stairwell.

"He really hasn't adapted to the building yet, has he?" Thia said. She swiped her paw across the floor and a hole opened up in the polished grey material. They jumped through to the next level, just beating Mateo to a scene of carnage.

One of the three-man surveillance teams was on the floor. One of the three, a middle-aged woman with night black skin, was screaming as she clutched at the stump of her leg. It had been sheared off just below the knee. Elias was standing over the three, calmly inspecting them despite the screaming. A large man with milk-white skin and freckles dusted across his face came barreling out of an opening in the wall with a stretcher on wheels. His scrubs already had some blood on the chest and legs. He had clearly checked the injured before running for the stretcher. Hux was his last name, and no one seemed to know his first.

As soon as Hux appeared, Eli went into motion. "Deacon is in the most danger right now. Get him on the stretcher,"

Hux took something off the stretcher and tossed it to Elias, who caught it and knelt next to Shandy. Hux then loaded Deacon, a thirty-something man with bronze skin and brush-cut black hair, onto the stretcher, and Elenor followed behind. Thia noted as Hux lifted

Deacon onto the stretcher that there was a sucking hole the size of a quarter in Deacon's chest. Hux pushed the stretcher back into the door that led to the living quarters. They had set up their makeshift hospital in the first three apartments on the right.

Elias wrapped a black nylon strap around Shandy's leg as a tourniquet and pulled tight. Shandy gritted her teeth and groaned as the bleeding finally quit.

"I know it hurts, but you're going to be fine, Shandy."

Elias took a small flashlight from his pocket and spun himself on the floor, heedless of the blood his sneakers slid through as he moved. "Look at me, Marcus," Eli said, and he shined the pen light into the last man's eyes. "Grade one concussion."

"I'll take care of that," Thia squeaked. "Shandy, we'll fix you up good as new. Eli, morphine for the pain, low dose. She won't have to deal with it for long."

The doctor nodded and rushed off. He was back in a moment. He carefully administered the shot into Shandy's arm, and after a breathless minute, Shandy was able to relax. Her eyes fixed on Thia.

"Came back with us." Shandy passed into unconsciousness.

Thia's sensory coils shuffled nervously and she crouched, her wings expanding from her back into the tangle of dripping blades. Eli backed away from her.

"We are not alone," Thia hissed as she shuffled her sensory coils so that she could pick up her unique electromagnetic signature. The eyes along her body opened, and Thia received a clear picture of everything happening within a hundred feet of her.

"Mateo, go with Eli. He has to help Elenor with Deacon," Thia ordered, and Mateo bobbed his head.

"Ándale, Doc," Mateo said, and ushered Eli away.

 • Ándale – Come on

Thia kept her emitters open, her sensory coils rippling with awareness. She stretched her wings, tapping them together behind her. The Mender's Lament flowed from Thia's striker, and she tried to keep her attention on her surroundings as she took the breath required to push out the Surge. Thia breathed out a cool, blue mist that flowed over the two people. She did not watch as Shandy's leg grew back, as it was rather nauseating to watch bone, flesh, and skin reform.

"Marcus, what happened to you?" Thia asked as the blue mist was absorbed into the two in front of her. Marcus blinked brown eyes stupidly.

"We were following that group of three Infected that showed in upstate New York. They were trying to dig up something there and we were trying to get a look. We didn't get too close, though, but they weren't actually digging anything up. They were waiting for us." Marcus shook his head and blinked his eyes clear. "It was an ambush. They were trying to get in here."

Thia crouched even lower, her sensory coils rippling madly to shift the correct coils to the top of the nest. She needed both visual light and infrared. She tried to focus everywhere at once. The infrared overlaid on top of her normal, humanlike vision helped her see the people who were supposed to be there, but it was less helpful than she was hoping. She could see the heat ghosts of people through the walls but not the visual detail to tell who those people were.

She needed to trade places with Mateo for this. Her sensory coils had almost all the same capabilities as his sight ears, but she couldn't pick up completely mechanical energy. He would be able to hear the person with no heartbeat. Thia reared up and put her paws against the wall of the building. The deep matte black walls rippled as if a stone had been thrown into a still pond in the night. Bars of shimmering red light emerged from the middle of every wall. They gave off a soft glow to let everyone in the building know to be on alert, but not to distract.

"Marcus, guard Shandy until she wakes up. You see anything that isn't one of us, kill it."

Thia turned and bolted for the operating room. The building responded instantly to her desires and the doors slid open, revealing a shining black hallway with white rectangles perfectly spaced on either side of the wall serving as doors. The first three on the right had open spaces inside of them. She skidded to a stop in the door, a tableau of horror inside.

The operating theater that Eli had constructed within was in a shambles. If one ignored the center of the room, everything seemed fine. Medical cabinets and equipment neatly lined the walls of the garage-sized room. The enormous operating table had been flipped over, nearly sheared in half, and pushed to one side of the room. Deacon lay on the floor in a puddle of his own blood.

Elenor was crouching protectively over the man, her fangs bared in challenge. Her tail was arched over her back like a scorpion ready to strike. Opposite her and the door was the Infected. She was surrounded by a tangled web of green threads that seemed to emerge from her body. In front of her was Eli. His body was bound by wire-thin green threads at the neck, ankles, and wrists. The threat was clear. They did not want a headless doctor in their future.

Thia's sensory coils rippled in their nest atop her head as she searched for Mateo. It took her only a moment to spot him. He had gotten behind the Infected by sliding his lithe mustelid body between the web-like threads. His mouth was open wide, hovering just behind the Infected's head. She could tell by his posture that biting off a person's head was not appealing to him. She didn't think it would stop him if it came to it, though. Something about him, though, was odd. It was almost as if the Percept's Rest was being played even though his Striker was quiet. Had he discovered some new talent like the eyes on Elenor's back?

Thia took one extra second to perform a quick inspection of Deacon, the emitters along her body pulsing with violet light to give her a better view of him. She froze. Deacon wasn't breathing. He had no heartbeat. Her head crept back in the direction of the infected.

"You're going to let my friend go," Thia hissed. The dripping amethyst glow around her wings intensified with her fury. She noticed that Eli's eyes were locked on her. He gave her the barest of nods. He was telling her not to save him if it meant stopping this thing.

Elenor stood over Deacon's, body her spines trembling with the threat of a rattlesnake. Her eyes blazed so bright that Thia thought that if she still had eyes, the glow would have struck her blind. She couldn't use her Runeshard because it wouldn't stop the Infected from thinking, which would still be enough to get Eli killed.

Thia watched Mateo more closely. She could tell he was struggling with the decision to kill the Infected. For the first time, she blessed the change in her ability to see. Without human eyes, there was no way to see where she was focusing her vision. Still, it wouldn't be long before the Infected felt Mateo hovering behind her. He would lose the element of surprise.

There was something wrong with the entire situation that Thia did not understand. They couldn't kill the Infected yet, but one of them coming here on their own made no sense. *What could it accomplish?* Even if it killed the humans here, it had no chance against all three Bearers. It didn't matter. It had killed Deacon with its interference. She had not known him well, but that was hardly relevant. He was one of her mother's people, and therefore, one of hers.

Mateo's sight ears swiveled slightly towards Elenor. She shook her head and then rolled her eyes around, focusing on all the threads. Mateo's sight ears dipped forward in a blink, but then he pulled back, his tentacles silently extruding from his body.

He carefully wove them, along with his long tail, through the threads, just out of sight of the Infected. Then, the appendages flattened until edges gleaming with menace emerged. They only needed a single split second of inattention to pull Eli out.

Thia did not even nod. She just flexed her muscles as if she were about to bob her head. Mateo would see it. She just hoped that Elenor would be ready to yank Eli out. Mateo's tentacles flashed in a murderous blur. A storm of green sparks erupted as the threads were slashed apart in a single move. An arm spun away from the infected when it intersected one of the threads holding Eli and Mateo's tentacle.

Elenor made a pulling gesture with her paw and Eli was yanked away across the room so violently that Thia worried that she had broken the man as a child might smash a doll against the floor. Clearly, though, the Infected had been prepared for this, because she ignored her lost arm. More threads spooled out from her in bisecting arcs towards Eli's back. Elenor's striker smashed into the floor and she roared in fury. The sonorous notes that poured from her Striker warped the world in a way that Thia never thought possible.

The world vanished.

They were suddenly standing in a blank white void with no sense of what was up, what was down, or even what was real. Eli had not made the journey with them, so Elenor had somehow excluded him. Thia tried to listen to identify the Surge, and a moment later, she was able to visualize the waveform. The mark that rose up from the Surge when she focused on it said only The Silence.

Elenor stalked forward, shoulders rolling like a big cat as she loomed over the fallen Infected.

"This will stop," Elenor snarled.

The music seemed to warp and flow into a completely different song as it continued unabated. The Infected threw a fist at Elenor but she batted it aside. Then made a gesture with her paw. Her Runeshard activated, slamming the Infected to whatever passed as the floor inside this terrifying desolation.

Thia felt her sensory coils still in what she knew was sheer unabated surprise. Elenor was calling two surges at the same time, and she had no idea how it was even possible. Thia was certain Elenor didn't know how she was doing it, either.

Stark against the background of white was the one remaining thread that her Surge had not blown away. The only Surge on the Infected that was a fixed warp in reality. The anchor to her hammerspace. Elenor hooked a claw around the thread, and after a long moment of holding, it the notes of her surge reformed yet again. Verdant bubbles of light fizzed from the emerald thread and then Elenor yanked her claw through it.

The thread exploded.

Green sparks, far too great in volume to have been released from that one Surge, sprayed around Elenor. Fine emerald sand bled from the air, streaming to several points around the Infected's head to form into a crown of brutal jade shards, three times the diameter of the Infected's skull. Thorns sprang from the crown, piercing the head in multiple places. They passed through the skin and bone, fuzzing to incorporeality where they entered the physical material. The Infected's eyes tracked every tiny move Elenor made.

Elenor waved Mateo and Thia forward. "This is what I saw before." Elenor somehow knew the spikes passing through the flesh of the Infected were not actually incorporeal, even though they appeared to be so. They were somehow integrated with the brain tissue within, allowing remote control of the person within the crown.

"How did you break it?" Mateo asked.

"The same way you just did with her threads."

Elenor hooked her claws around the crown and began to pull. This time, there was no struggle like she had felt on the island. She simply braced herself, flexed her entire body, and drew her claws with unerring determination through the crown.

This time, the explosion of light and power when the crown shattered did not seem nearly as overpowering as it had before. Elenor tumbled ass over tea kettle before coming to rest a few feet away. Her eyes wandered for a moment, slightly dazed, before she focused on the woman left behind.

She was, beyond all reason, undamaged from the experience, though she responded not at all when Thia retracted her claws to shake the woman.

"¿Está muerta?" Mateo asked.

"You'd know better than we would."

"I can't see anything. No heartbeat, no breathing," he replied, his sight ears swiveled toward the woman, sound ears twitching.

"That's how the last guy looked," Elenor informed. She padded closer and bent her neck to sniff at the woman's body. "She doesn't smell dead."

"The Black Box will record everything so we can just leave her here until she wakes up. The building will notify Damien." Thia folded the tangle of blades and they shrank into her relic until they vanished. "Until then, we apparently have to go attempt to get eaten by extra dimensional things."

 • ¿Está muerta? – Is she dead?

43

"LAST CHANCE"

NC 17, EPOCH 19915.60

After two days of discussion and discourse, the three Bearers had concluded that they needed confirmation from Helen about where they needed to go, if not what they needed to do. The possibility of triggering the Miasma in Helen was too dangerous for anything more than getting a direction.

"I can't tell you everything and I still need your advice," Thia complained. Her mother just grinned at her. The apartment in the Black Box her mother had taken up residence in was spartan in appearance, with only the most basic, but comfortable, furniture in each room. They sat in two comfortable chairs with a walnut coffee table between them. Thia had curled herself into a coil and sat with her gleaming muzzle on her paws. Helen cupped a mug of hot cocoa between her hands. The rest of the living room was bare except for a large television on one wall.

"It is not so fun as you thought it would be to be in charge?" Helen teased.

"Hey, I didn't ask for this," Thia grumbled. "Can you at least tell me what The Silence is?"

Helen eyes widened. It was slight, but it was there. With her sensory coils, Thia couldn't miss it. "That," Helen paused for a long moment as she seemed to think something through. She took a sip of her cocoa, "is only a legend. It can't…" Helen trailed off, her eyes shifting back and forth as they only did when she was deep in thought.

"Are you certain? Could you see the wave of the Surge?" Helen asked.

Thia shook her head. "I couldn't see the complete wave, but the Notemark was The Silence, without a doubt. Parts of the wave seemed to just be missing,"

Thia explained. The look on her mother's face told Thia she might not answer. Thia's sensory coils rippled with agitation. Helen held up her hands in a placating gesture.

"I'll tell you what you want to know, but that Surge," Helen shook her head. "The Silence is among a number of Surges that are only theories. We have anecdotal evidence that they exist, but no real proof. You cannot be taught such Surges. They have no note base. They must be learned by instinct alone and I've never known anyone capable of that."

"The Runespring mark." Thia said, and her mother sat forward immediately.

"To open that place is to invite death into our world."

"We have no other choice. It is where the puzzle leads."

"Were it not for what you just told me, I would say that no one could reopen that door. The last Indra killed himself sealing that portal specifically so it could never be reopened."

Thia nodded, then circled back. "Why is she so special? I don't think I am jealous. I got everything I've always wanted." Thia lifted a gleaming, scaled paw. "Even my new body is amazing, but I don't understand why Elenor learns everything we can't."

Helen chuckled. "I do not think she does so much as she has a large head start in her development. I know Mateo has the same worries, but I do believe that you both still have some growth that has not happened yet."

"That makes sense. Mateo did just develop the ability to divert attention from himself without a Surge," Thia said.

Helen nodded in response before her eyes hardened with certainty. "The anchor to the Wound can be found beneath Aleppo Citadel in Syria. One of the anchor endpoints outside can take you to Tbilisi, which is a few hundred miles from Aleppo, in what is now the country of Georgia." Helen produced the information as if she had read it only moments before. It was one of the things that she would never forget.

"The Wound?" Thia queried.

"It is just what we called it. The tunnels that they unwittingly opened were like wounds on our reality." Thia bobbed her head and climbed down out of the chair. "Thia."

Thia turned back, sitting down. With her mother sitting down, this put her almost eye to eye with the woman she had looked up to all her life.

"If you open that place, you must kill every single thing within. This is not like the Infected. The things in that place are not from this reality and they see us only as enemies. Our reality will not properly adhere to them. They would kill in an unstoppable frenzy for centuries, if not longer," Helen warned.

"Are you sure?"

Helen's eyes, hard as granite, fixed on Thia's sensory coils. "Certain, for me. Efforts were made to attempt to return the creatures to their own worlds. They did not go well. That said, you three are more powerful than all of us who assaulted that place put together. You can do as you wish."

Thia paused for a moment as she thought long and hard. "Tell me what you are waiting to tell me. What you have been waiting to tell me since we found Elenor."

"I am a little surprised you noticed that in all the other mental issues I have displayed." Helen's somber voice made Thia feel wary.

"A hundred years is a long time to live with someone," Thia affirmed.

"I suppose it is. I will tell you, but if you noticed enough to realize I had something to tell you, you noticed enough to know what it is."

Thia nodded quietly. She understood why her mother wanted what she didn't say. The aforementioned mental issues were part of that concern, but there was so much more. A thousand years of watching people age and die when she remained precisely twenty-eight years old, which was the point at which she stopped aging as a Caller.

Even Callers died of old age. It took them three or four centuries and they never really aged physically, but it still happened. Her mother, though, was immortal. She had seen a need to carry forward the knowledge of Callers and so she had constructed a Surge that would remove all biological aging. What she had not counted on was that she would be unable to turn it off. She had assumed when the Bearers appeared and connections with the Writ were once again available, her own powers would be reinstated. While they had not been able to find Elenor, her mother had known the instant Elenor had begun her transformation. Her power had never returned.

Finally, Thia replied. "You want to die."

Helen let out a laugh. "Oh, do not make it sound so grim. Yes, I hope to go on from this life to whatever comes next, as we all should eventually do. But, I suspect that even once my Surge is broken, it will take at least a hundred years for my life to run down, and that is a very conservative estimate. I will likely live much longer. You will not be rid of me anytime soon."

"Alright." Thia still seemed troubled somehow.

"What is it?" Helen prompted.

"I just have uncertain feelings about this. Not just because of what you told me about that laboratory. It's why I had to come and talk to you even if it's dangerous. I wish I could tell you everything we found about Osiris. I wish we could get your opinions. This feels like some sort of last chance," Thia lamented.

"Thia, you haven't needed my opinions for decades. Despite your developmental hiccups, you are well beyond any training I could give you, and well past experienced by any human standard. Trust your instincts."

Thia sighed, then headed for the door.

"Three weeks on your own and you suddenly forget how to give your mother a hug?"

Thia grinned and turned around. Her scales lifted away from her body until she had the fluffed appearance similar to a fresh groomed poodle.

"Hey, I figured you'd be worried about the sharp pointy bits."

"Worth it."

When Thia emerged from her mother's apartment, Elenor and Mateo were waiting both tense with apprehension.

"It's fine. I was careful, and she told me what we need."

Thia walked towards the Hive in the middle of the building. When the doors opened, they revealed Damien and Marissa working separately to connect everyone in their network to the central communications system Damien had been developing. The globe they had been using had been reduced in size by half to allow the swarm to form many other displays, constantly updating Damien with information about their operations across the world. The incidence of Infected was becoming dangerously high, and they all knew that if something was not done soon, the entire world would know about the magical creatures hiding amongst the populace.

"Have you had any luck teaching Mateo how to call The Silence?" Thia asked, and Elenor shook her head. They had been trying nonstop for two days, but even if he played a note perfect recitation of what Elenor played, it did not function for him.

"You can stop. Mom says that Surge is impossible to teach. You either learn it by instinct or you can't, which checks out, considering how odd it sounds when I listen to you call it," Thia explained. She held up a paw and waved it back and forth minutely until the Swarm recognized her a second later. Then she swung it to spin the globe until Europe and the Middle East were facing them. She pointed a claw to a city in the country of Georgia.

"This is where we are going to come out if we take the northbound gate to the Middle East. Tblisi is about five hundred miles from Aleppo, Syria, which is where we need to go to get to The Wound."

"Five hundred fifty-nine miles," Mateo said, and Thia rippled her sensory coils in annoyance.

"How do you do that? That is not just memory," Elenor accused.

"It was, at first, but now I don't know. I just know where every place is, and how far apart everything is." Mateo shrugged.

"Honestly, it makes sense. It's an extension of your mundane abilities," Thia theorized.

Elenor made a tsk sound. "Wish what I got was like that. Feel like I'm some prototype before all the bugs got worked out. Stupid glowing eyes, stupid extra eyes that I can barely use because they might turn someone to stone."

"Least you have eyes instead of a nest of snakes on your skull," Thia grumbled.

"I think I'd skip the eyes to be able to see all around me like you or Mateo."

"You should just open those eyes on your back and keep them open until you get used to them," Mateo advised.

"I tried that once. I lasted an entire week trying to use them before I fell off a building from vertigo. I'll take a pass on that." Elenor shook her head, ears flopping, in an attempt to shake out the memory of that awful experience.

"Back to the topic, I think we should go at night. From what we can see, there is some construction activity happening daily which would mean we would have to use Surges to get inside."

Thia made a grasping gesture with her paw in the direction of the floating globe and then pulled her paw towards herself. The globe rippled, and the image resolved into a view from the top down, from about ten meters above the tallest building. The buildings atop the large earthen mound seemed badly damaged and broken down, though some were pristine. People moved about it like ants.

"How do we get down to the lab? It has to be pretty far below the surface if no one in a city that big has found it," Elenor wondered.

"We should be able to use the Ghostwalker's Etude to get down to where we need to go," Thia theorized, but Elenor shook her head.

"I'm worried. Did your Mom tell you anything else?"

"A little. She said that the Wound is filled with murderous creatures from other dimensions, and that we should probably go in there with the intention of killing everything we see because it will certainly try to kill us."

"Could they be like the Infected?" Elenor asked, but Thia shook her head immediately.

"Mom said that we could try to communicate with them if we wanted to, but they had tried that before. I gather it ended with some Callers being devoured."

"Does that mean we are going to have to exterminate everything in the place before we can go looking for whatever pocket dimension we need to figure all of this out?" Mateo asked.

"Seems that way." Thia made a waving gesture with a paw and the swarm flowed away, separating into black columns at the corners of the room.

Elenor's eyes fixed on the floor between her paws. "Are we ready for this?"

"Claro que no, but if we want to have any chance of our planet not becoming a buffet for some eldritch horror, we have to be the bigger monsters," Mateo joked.

Thia put a paw on Elenor's shoulder, slowing her to a stop. "If working with my mother has taught me anything, it's that you're never ready. Being ready and being capable are two different things. We are capable."

- Claro que no – Of course not

44

"WORLDS WITHIN"

Elenor's glowing eyes roved the perfectly square cave that contained the entrance to The Wound. She stood upside-down and opened the shimmering golden eyes on her back. The sound of the Chorus told her that there was something odd about the floor, but there was so much mystical noise coming from The Wound that she couldn't be sure about what she was hearing.

The floor of the cave lit up with a webwork of light. Each line of the web vibrated with subtle menace. The very nature of reality had been warped here by the overwhelming power needed to forge traps that would last.

"What do you see down there?" The voice came from a small collection of the microscopic machines that made up the swarm, feeding sound directly through her ear bones.

"They left surprises. I think we can shut them off, but as far as I can tell, they stop at the door, so if we can get it open…" Elenor startled when she saw intense glowing green lines around the outside of the door. She took a deep breath, realizing it was only some sort of magical writing. "There is some weird writing around the door that I can't read. Just make sure when you come through, you don't drop to the floor."

The sound of the Ghostwalker's Etude warped the Chorus as Mateo and Thia floated down through the ceiling of the cave. Mateo had flipped himself upside down. He immediately ceased his Surge and slapped his paws against the ceiling, where they stuck without trouble. Thia merely unfolded her wings and hovered. She peered at the glowing green text.

"This is old. Older than human civilization." She floated closer, her sensory coils rippling to better absorb the energy given off by the warp in reality that formed the text.

"Can you read it?" Mateo asked. The scribbles were similar to cuneiform, but the shapes were more flowing and organic.

Thia nodded. "Yes, but this is older than the form of Nyceric that my mother taught me."

"Nyceric?" Elenor asked.

"The first language ever created on earth. It was made by Callers." Thia studied the flowing symbols for a long moment. "It's a warning." Then Thia began to read. "Seek not within to carry away more than what you see this day. Deep within these hidden halls lie secrets that will end all dawns. For though this world be made for sacrifice, all others will live to see new light."

"That doesn't seem like something people sealing up the door would carve into it," Mateo theorized.

"No, it does not," Thia said skeptically. "Damien, can you hear me?" The tiny machines tucked into her ear canal were linked back to the swarm by what scientists would have likely referred to as quantum entanglement.

"Loud and clear. Wha' da ye need?"

"Can you see what I am seeing?"

"Aye."

"Good. Go get my mother."

"She told us not to." Marissa's voice seemed a little further away, but that was likely because she was standing at the globe, away from her terminal. She hated the thing following her around.

Thia's sensory coils lifted from her head, rippling madly. "I am about to walk into what is likely an insane hellpit. I swear, if I hear one more word of backtalk right now, when I claw my way out of this hole, I will bite off something you will miss," Thia snapped testily.

Vague sounds of footsteps leaving and then returning filled their ears for a moment. "You know this is dangerous?" Helen warned.

"Yeah, I don't want you to risk anything, I just need to know. Did you carve this?" Thia gestured with a paw at the writing.

"Thia, that is not The Wound."

"What do you mean?"

"That entryway is not made of stone. Illuminate the area so you can see better, then brush away the dust." Helen's voice held a level of concern that Thia had never heard before.

Thia floated across the room and tentatively reached out a paw. She rubbed her paw pads against the surface of the arch and the dust rose. It was smooth, and freezing cold to the touch.

The soft chime of Mateo's striker against the ceiling pushed away all the other sounds and the birdlike notes of the Dawn Song filled the cave. An orb of bright daylight the size of a basketball filled the larger part of the cave with light. As soon as the light came up, Elenor's eyes glowed with the intensity of sunlight. The arch, though, seemed to shiver, and the entire thing glittered with golden reflections.

"That is not gold." Helen's voice was a whisper in their ears. "It can't be. It doesn't exist."

"What is it?" Thia asked, but she was sure she already knew. She had seen the description in one of her mother's notebooks. With the light, she could see the facets and crystalline structure of the golden material.

"It is Purestone. It, is not supposed to exist. It is the foundation the universe is built upon. Check their coordinates." The last was clearly spoken to someone else in the room.

"Swarm reports eleven hundred meters below the Citadel at Aleppo."

"You should not go in there," Helen advised.

"What does the Purestone mean?"

Helen hesitated. She was in uncharted territory, supported only by rumors, and legends. At least they had had some anecdotal evidence of the existence of Surges like The Silence. Those little pieces of absolute power at least had been known. To see Purestone, though, there was nothing there but myth.

"I do not know what it means, Thia. Purestone is a myth, even to Callers. There is no knowing what it means that the entrance to the Wound has become Purestone. I can give you no advice, daughter, only guesses, and precious few of those." Thia herd footsteps. Helen had turned away from the terminal.

"You can't stay," she said.

"Not for this. It is far too dangerous for me to stay involved. I will make two guesses. First, do not expect Surges to work in there. That gate is pure reality. It will not bend to Surges. It is a part of the power the Writ is built upon. You will only be able to depend on the power of your Runeshards and your bodies. Second, if you die in there, I cannot be sure as to what will happen to you. That place could be completely detached from this reality. A reality unto itself. Be careful." Then her footsteps receded, leaving them on their own.

"What did she mean?" Mateo whispered.

"We don't have time to discuss it now. Cliff notes is that you have a soul, and it does go on after death. She's telling us that if we go inside and die, she doesn't know what will happen to our souls." Thia lifted a paw towards the circular golden plate set into the center of the massive Purestone doors.

"This seems a little too risky," Elenor worried.

"If you have a better way to get to the bottom of this, I am all ears," Thia replied, gesturing to the tiny ear holes inside of the gentle curl of her horns.

"We have to do it. This has gotten way bigger than us. Look at what that says." Mateo gestured with his tail at the inscription around the door.

"More important than what it says, how did it get there? If this is Purestone, we couldn't hurt it even with magic." Thia slashed at it. Claws so sharp they could cut through steel and stone scraped against the golden material, leaving behind not even the barest scratch in its mirrored surface. Much like the relic stone of their bodies, it seemed utterly immutable.

Mateo walked up the wall to more closely examine what appeared to be a carved inscription. He leaned close, his sight ears pricked forward. He clicked his tongue and his ears twitched.

"It's not actually cut into the stone." The web of transparent threads extended from his ears and wrapped themselves around the edges. "It's just sort of stuck here." Mateo crawled back down to the floor.

"If this is supposed to be the end of the trail, why doesn't it feel like that?" Elenor asked.

Thia shook her head. "Because we are just finishing the puzzle. We have no idea what the whole picture will be." She put her paw against the plate, and pushed. A sinuous line split the center of the plate and the two doors jolted apart as if a mechanism under pressure released. They made no sound as they slid to either side, opening onto a recognizable expanse of a cosmos seen from afar.

Thia raised a paw and put it up to the opening tentatively, only to find it stopped by an invisible barrier. "What did Osiris say about going into the hammerspace where the Writ was located?"

"He said he had to use his own life force to get through the barrier, and it kept draining him once he was inside," Elenor recited.

Thia pushed a little harder, and her paw went through. The air inside was cool, but not unpleasantly so. "I think it was because he didn't have a Runeshard to protect him."

Mateo's ears tilted far to the right in skepticism. "Neither do we?"

"Yes, we do. We just haven't figured it out like Elenor has yet," Thia said.

"We don't have time to figure it out now." Mateo swiveled his ears to examine the massive square cave. "I get the feeling if we don't get in there soon, the Infected are going to find a way down here."

Thia nodded and then pushed through the barrier into the cosmos, her tail vanishing with an odd tiny pop of sound, similar to a loud drop of water.

"She's insane," Elenor grumped.

"Sure is, but at least she isn't boring." Mateo turned and leapt through the door, resulting in the same ridiculous water drop sound. Elenor rolled her eyes and jumped after him.

A bright flash of light dazzled Elenor as she emerged from the portal. She blinked the afterimage away and then her eyes went wide as she was assaulted by the view. The inside of the portal was not at all what she had expected. There were no blank institutional halls, no creatures from beyond reality rushing at them as Helen had warned. Nor were the walls made of enormous blocks of purestone as she half expected. No, this seemed much worse.

Everywhere she looked, desolate wastelands stretched to the horizon. Grey hills rolled away from them into the distance. The landscape was littered with burned foliage, and smoke rose in wavering pillars into a sky darkened by rainclouds on the verge of downpour. A massive structure loomed in the distance.

Elenor couldn't be sure from this distance, but she thought the base of the structure was at least a mile wide, and it stretched into the sky at least fifty stories. It was a trapezoidal building, tapering as it grew into the sky, but the top leveled off without reaching a point. It was made almost exclusively of charcoal grey stone. Spaced at even intervals in place of windows were enormous plates of Purestone.

"Madre de dios ¿Qué diablos es esa?" Mateo asked. All three of them drew in a sharp breath when bursts of verdant light appeared randomly from various parts of the structure.

"It's a testing ground," Thia hissed, her blade wings emerging from her back, dripping with violet energy.

"How did the Infected get in?" Mateo wondered.

"I'm not sure that they did. The gate wouldn't admit them like it did for us. Look up there." Elenor pointed with her tail up at the sky. Mateo could see nothing right away, and Thia was similarly blind to what Elenor could see with the Gorgon eyes in her back. It took them only a moment to adjust.

A ripple of Thia's sensory coils and Mateo's light webs allowed them to see it. A glimmering emerald fissure in the sky, torn directly from reality itself.

"How is that possible?" Thia wondered.

"Remember what Osiris saw in the Writ. It comes from outside of our reality. Maybe it can break even something as powerful as whatever the Writ is built on top of," Mateo proposed.

"Then is it here already?" Elenor worried.

"I don't think so. Something with that much power wouldn't send its minions. It would just destroy everything it could. We need to get in there, find the Writ, and figure out what we're missing." Thia lifted off the ground.

"There are so many, and you guys can't Surge The Silence."

"There is no time, Elly. This is what we came here for. It's our only shot." Mateo followed Thia, and Elenor

• Madre de dios ¿Qué diablos es esa? – Mother of god, what the hell is that?

ran after them a moment later. They wove their way through the bombed-out landscape towards the massive building.

"Do we even have a plan?" Elenor asked as they galloped into the shadow of the massive, ancient pyramid.

"What I said *is* the plan! We don't know enough to make a better one!" Thia shouted.

"We should split up," Mateo suggested.

"Why?" Elenor's concern was clear in her voice. "If we run into too many Infected all at once..."

Mateo shook his head. "We are all strong enough to tear through the Infected. We just have to do it. If we split up, we can find what we need faster."

"We can't communicate with the outside world in here, but we can still talk to each other. The Swarm pieces we have here are still entangled," Thia advised.

Elenor slowed to a stop as the senses of her Runeshard warned her of something. There were not enough sources of living water within to account for all of the emerald glows within the pyramid.

"There are more of those mummy things inside. They are a lot stronger than the other Infected. It's like they are made of," Elenor paused, not sure how to describe it. Magic was not a word that they used. Helen had explained that magic was a blanket term for things people didn't understand. "Resonance?" Elenor's squeak turned up at the end, making it a question.

Thia, and Mateo circled back to her a moment later.

"Elly, we will be fine. We knew this would be dangerous," Mateo said, and Thia nodded her agreement.

Tears welled up in Elenor's glowing eyes. "I just," she sniffed, and then sighed out. "I don't want to be alone again. So be careful."

"You too," Thia said, and then drifted up away from them before blasting towards the roof of the pyramid in a burst of lavender illumination.

"Middle or bottom?" Mateo asked.

"I'll take the bottom. Want a ride up to the middle?"

Mateo bobbed his head. Elenor paused to construct instructions in her head and then lifted her paw. Mateo lifted a few inches off the ground. Elenor made a throwing motion with her paw, and Mateo zipped away in a blur of motion towards the pyramid. She waited long enough to control his landing, and as soon as he was safely down, she ran for the bottom.

As Elenor got closer, she realized she didn't know how to get inside the building. Clearly, there was a way in as the Infected had made it inside, but she saw no openings. Massive panels of charcoal grey stone interrupted by glittering golden squares that were somewhere between crystal and metal gave an impression of impenetrability. When she was about a hundred feet away from the wall, she felt a pressure in her chest. It faded, and a rectangle faded away in the wall of stone. Through the opening, she saw only dim illumination. Then she was leaping through to be blinded by a wall of snowy blank void. She blinked away the blinding whiteness and her mouth fell open with astonishment.

A bare two feet ahead, the world fell away into a sheer granite cliff. Far below, a pristine river carved the land in twain. On her left was a dense rainforest, brilliantly lit by a moon so massive it felt as if it might fall from the sky and crush the world. Enormous trees swayed in an unfelt breeze, their foliage in every color of the rainbow. It was unlike any forest she had ever seen on earth.

To the right of the river was also wild forest, but this forest was evergreen and covered in the snow of a deep winter. The blanket of white shimmered with refracted moonlight, giving off opaline shades of lavender, rose, and azure. It did not matter which side she chose; she would be intruding upon a landscape so pure it strained the boundaries of her very imagination. It was on this perfect snow that she now stood.

Elenor turned back to see the blinding white rectangle that had led her into this pristine fairy tale shrinking until it vanished, leaving only the perfect division of beauty behind.

"This construction needs be brief lest it is exposed to the Otherthing."

Elenor spun, snow flying as her tail whipped through the downy blanket to face the source of the voice. Pushing through the snowy evergreens was an absolutely bizarre figure. It seemed to be barely corporeal, as Elenor could see all the way through the four-legged creature. Still, it disturbed the bushes as it passed through them. It was hard to look at, made entirely of curving organic lines as if it had been forged from thick rods of golden metal by some godlike blacksmith. The rest of its form was filled out by glowing golden panels, like blown amber glass set between the framework of golden rods.

It reminded her of a big cat, and its eyes were two orbs of golden glass with no pupils whatsoever. It was impossible to tell where the thing was focused. More disturbing, though, was that she knew it had not been there a moment before. It glowed in her night sight like a golden beacon. Should could not possibly have missed it. It spoke again.

"This construction has been provided to inform the First Bearer that the Third Bearer was both correct and incorrect." The mouth did not move. It only opened and the voice issued forth from within.

Elenor just stared, mouth gaping open as the creature aped life at her. After far too long, she shook herself free of her paralysis. "What does that mean?"

"This construction has limited ability to inform you. This construction is only able to deliver this message.

The oversight did not wish for this to prove a testing ground for thee, Bearers. The Otherthing interfered, and this," the creature gestured a metal paw around to the environment, "stopgap measure was necessary to ensure patency of this reality. Surge restoration has been authorized. Undo the puppets of the Otherthing and ye three Bearers may make the Gateway at thy meeting. Begin thy hunt here. So sayeth the Overseer."

The creature gestured a paw to the pristine landscape once again. Then, the cat constructed of flowing metal bars faded away as if it had never been there. Only the disturbed snow showed its passing.

"It just keeps getting weirder," Elenor mumbled to herself. She waited another long minute to see if anything else would sneak up on her, the golden eyes on her back open and scanning her surroundings. Elenor focused on her Runeshard and lifted out of the snow. Padding atop the air itself, Elenor stepped over the edge of the cliff and followed the creature's advice.

Mateo found himself in what at first seemed like a massive, empty space. Then, high walls of rough stone resolved themselves in his vision. He walked closer to one of the walls, but the distance seemed on the scale of giants. When he reached the wall, he found pure artwork.

The wall was carved with whorls that formed confusing geometric patterns reminiscent of some Incan designs Mateo had read about. Unlike Incan designs, there was no pictorial themes, only the geometrics.

Mateo clicked his tongue, resolving the image of the landscape, and boggled at the scale. Even as massive as the building had seemed from the outside, there was no way it could contain what his sight ears were telling him. The passageway he was in was hundreds of feet wide. It took long seconds before the image of the building around him resolved. Even once it did, he could tell that his vision was not reaching the outside wall of whatever building he was in. It cut off midway through several rooms.

It was not quite a maze. It was more like someone had constructed a building in such a way that it would be confusing to anyone trying to make their way through. It was not much trouble for Mateo, but for anyone who relied purely on eyesight he could tell it would be very confusing. The scale worried him, though. *How far can I walk in this gigantic space before I reach the end?*

He spent many minutes scanning his surroundings, and it became clear that he was not alone. Within range of his sight ears, he could see at least two other people. One was clearly one of the mummified creatures, as not only did it lack a heartbeat, but the sounds of its movement made it fuzzy in his echolocation. Its body crackled and rasped in ways that a living body never would.

Mateo could not see far enough to see the way out of where he was, but some of a pattern emerged. At the edge of his vision, there was what looked like a stairwell the size of a cliff. He put his front paws up onto the wall and then crawled up onto it. He was always wary of climbing on some new surface, but his paws had not failed to cling when he wanted them to yet.

After a moment, he skittered down the hallway wall, angling himself towards the ceiling, which was more than two hundred feet above him. Less than five minutes, later voices reached his ears. The vibrations of the voices resolved the image.

"How do we know we can trust the voice? Look what it did to us." The first voice was deep and unfamiliar to Mateo. The second voice, though, Mateo recognized as the beastlike woman from Chicago.

"Why do you care? It gave us power! Look at what we can do." The woman snarled.

"Because I want my kids back." The voice seemed on the verge of violence, and Mateo focused his sight ears on the approaching duo.

He finally reached the ceiling, and he ran towards the pair. Elenor had explained what she had done to cut free the infectious crown of the infected they had caught in the Black Box. Neither he nor Thia had been able to replicate the feat, but he hoped that in the heat of the moment. he would be able to learn what she had done.

He reached the end of the massive hall, and turned right, into the ceiling of a stairwell. The stairs were like tiny cliffs, each one at least eight feet high. It took him almost a minute to climb to the next floor up. Oddly, he got a sense that this stairwell did not take him to the next floor in the tower. He knew on a subconscious level that this entire maze was one floor, and if he managed to move through to another floor of the tower, it would be a completely different landscape from this one.

The feeling of knowing something so strongly that he had no real way to know was eerie, and he shivered a little. It did not stop him as he slipped around the corner at the top of the massive stairwell. He froze there, and he could feel his body somehow gathering the shadows, darkening his fur until he was nigh invisible against the stone. Even the brighter colors in his fur seemed to wash themselves out until he blended in with his background. He waited for them to pass, but they paused at the head of the massive stairwell.

"What's with this place? Did we get shrunk or something?" the man asked. His deep voice bounced off the walls drawing, a perfect picture of the two Infected for Mateo's sight ears.

He crept down the wall, his claws retracted in perfect silence. He drew close to the two figures, razor jaws parting as he crouched into a prowling slink.

Twenty feet.

Mateo terminated his breathing. He had no need.

Ten feet.

The two Infected froze still as statues as their instincts told them they were being stalked. Mateo could see the hairs standing out from their arms. He slowed to a crawl so slow that he was barely moving at all.

Five feet.

The Infected turned with the strained sluggishness of those gripped in the unyielding fist of terror. Though they looked straight at him, their eyes passed with no glimmer of recognition.

"Did you feel that?" the male of the pair asked, and woman wearing energy shaped into the body of a massive wolf bobbed her head.

"We are not alone."

"Nothing here now." The male continued to turn.

"No, it is here. We just can't see it," the woman responded from within her animalistic construct. For a long moment, the eyes of her wolf construct focused directly on Mateo, and he was certain she would pierce whatever magic kept him hidden. Then the head of the beast moved on.

Mateo considered attacking then, while he still had surprise on his side. Just as he was about to leap onto the pair, a thunderous detonation echoed down the grand hallways of the enormous fortress.

Mateo's instincts kept him frozen like any good predator. The Infected, though, whipped around and bolted towards the explosion. As soon as they weren't watching him, he bolted after them. Whatever that noise had been, he could use the distraction to take out the Infected more easily.

After a quarter mile, the hall they were in ended in a
T. Smaller explosions rumbled from the left-hand fork,
and the Infected ran that way. Mateo's sight ears,
though, told a different story. The vibrations originated
from directly ahead of him. If he was any judge, they
were almost a mile off, still, but the powerful sounds
allowed his sight ears to map out what lie ahead. The
right fork would get him to the whatever battle had
begun faster. He hesitated.

Mateo knew they were here to find a way to visit the
Writ. They were not really sure how to find the way in,
but they were fairly certain that the Infected were
between them and it. The explosions worried him,
though. What if it was Thia or Elly fighting, or perhaps
even worse, what if the Infected had found the entrance
and were trying to batter their way inside. He walked
up the wall to the ceiling and then peeked around the
corner to the right-hand path. When he saw nothing, he
turned the corner and sprang down the path.

Thia's sensory coils curled in an approximation of
blinking. Whatever had happened when stepping
through the portal had blinded her in every single
electromagnetic spectrum. For a moment, she was
helpless. Thankfully, nothing sprang upon her as her
senses returned. Her sensory coils stilled as her
surroundings became clear. She goggled at what lay
before her. This was not some floor of a building, even
one as massive as the pyramid she had flown into. This
was a world. The alien landscape stole her breath.

Fingers of charcoal stone grew from the land into
massive ribcages of razor blade protrusions. Canyons
formed by long-vanished rivers stretched across the land
as if some planet sized creature had raked claws across

the world. In the distance, rising into the sky between the crystalline spires, was a mountain that dwarfed anything Thia had ever seen on Earth. Gleaming flows of sulfurous violet lava spiderwebbed the slopes. Spews of amethyst lava issued forth from the peak.

From her vantage at the top of a massive spire of black rock, she could see several green flares of light moving in the chasms of the chilling landscape. She wasn't sure what to do next. They could tear the Infected to pieces, but they would just come back from it. Only Elenor could change them back into humans permanently. She watched the lights moving for long minutes. Maybe, she could learn how to do what Elenor did. It was a Surge. If one Caller could play it, another should be able to as well.

She took a deep breath and unfurled her wings. The cartoonish clouds with long balloon feathers spread, and her paws came off the ground. "We aren't here to kill them, we are here to find the Writ," she reminded herself.

Pausing for a long moment, she considered how she might go about doing that. She had no reference for what she had walked into. Was this the entire inside of the pyramid, or was each floor an entrance to a new reality? How big was this place? The mountain appeared to be at least a hundred miles away, but without knowing how big it actually was, there was no way to know for sure. If that was the case, she could spend a lifetime in here searching and never find what she was looking for. At first, she tried to listen to the Chorus, but if there was something like that here, she wasn't certain what she was listening to.

She stood frozen, her sensory coils rippling, expose certain ones, allowing her to shift through several spectrums of vision before stopping with the coils exposed that allowed her to see Surges as they warped reality. Unlike the general sound of the Chorus, these coils seemed to absorb certain bands of energy generated when a Surge was Called. The four Infected wandering the alien landscape showed up like beacons in the grey, lifeless world this spectrum of her vision showed her.

There was nothing that indicated an Anchor in this vision of horror. She lashed her tail in thought, but could not come up with a better way to find what she was looking for. She considered for a moment just attempting to blast her way down to the next floor, but if this was some sort of collection of port dimensions, that might not work at all. She could just hit the edge of the port dimension and run into the recirculation fog. If she went into the fog, it could spit her out at any other point on the inside of the hammerspace.

Thia shook her head. There was no point in just sitting around. She beat her wings once, launching herself into the night black sky. Thia decided a preemptive strike was best. It would let her search for a while without worrying about having to fight them. Thia drew back her wings and slammed them together in front of her. The chime of her Striker resonated through the sky.

She drew in a breath and felt the burning fire within. It rose up her throat as she Surged the Dragon's Heartsong. Instead of releasing it in one long blast, though, she kept her mouth shut, forcing it to gather within. She swept her wings back and blasted towards the nearest Infected.

She gave no warning as she rushed towards the Infected. No sound came through the Dragon's Heartsong as the Infected came into sight. She opened her mouth and spat an incandescent white sphere the size of baseball at it. The creature spun, raising a sphere of energy of its own, but it stood no chance. The sphere of blazing white fire hit the creature and exploded to the size of a compact car. The creature evaporated in cleansing fire.

Thia repeated the attack twice more before she felt the drain. Clearly, the way she had originally used it in Chicago wasn't nearly as efficient as what she was doing now. Thia shot towards the last creature, gathering herself for one last blast. She realized her mistake too late. Not all the Infected were the same. The last one was one of the mummified creatures. As she neared, a lash of Emerald energy whipped between two of the needle spires and wrapped around her throat.

She back-winged reflexively and jarred to a halt. The creature was powerful. Thia opened her emitters and shuffled her coils until her image of the world snapped into sharp relief. The thing had anchored itself to the rocks to try to pull her from the sky. She tilted herself down and released the blast of dragon fire at the creature, but it yanked itself to one side, allowing it to pass harmlessly.

"You will be the first morsel of the feast!" The creature's voice grated unnaturally, a facsimile of human speech. Another lash of energy spiked into her unprotected stomach. She felt something break inside of her, but the pain was small, not life threatening. When she attempted to strike her wings together to Surge the Requiem of Shattered Resonance, more tendrils cinched around them, holding them apart. Thia focused on her power over her own gravity, trying to rip herself free of the creature's hold.

Stone shattered as she grunted with the strain as the tendrils wrapped around her pulled tight. If they snapped now, the resulting backlash would tear apart everything they hit. Still, Thia was pulled inexorably towards the creature. Another lash struck the side of her head and pain lanced through her entire body, a minor concussion blooming from the internal strike.

Thia fought through the blinding pain in her head. She could sense that there was something she was not seeing. Something about her power that was just beyond her reach. Another whip came at her head, and she lifted a paw. The line of emerald light wrapped around her paw and then yanked her leg taut.

What was that feeling in her head? Thia roared in frustration as more ropes secured her other limbs, leaving her as a pinata for the Infected. It was right there, so obvious, like the sound of music on the other side of a wall. She could hear the notes, but not understand how they were being played without seeing the source. A blinding verdant light appeared to the left of her head.

The wall broke.

Time froze as knowledge filled Thia's mind. With stark certainty, she gained a basic understanding of the function of her Runeshard. She had been using a small piece of the power to fly the entire time. It was a portion of Space, the power that governed the rules of the universe, a piece of control over one of the powers that drove the engine of their reality.

Gravity.

In the space between her wings, she was the absolute master of gravity itself.

With speed that defied all laws, her wings shrank out of the hold of the Infected's lashings. They blurred in front of her, and a dot of blinding amethyst energy the size of a grain of sand exploded to life in the space between them. It was a point of absolute mass, the power at the center of a black hole, and it ripped the lash of energy to pieces.

The pair of wings, no larger than a pair of hands, spun around her tethered by her will alone. They twisted in a blur until each line of power holding her had been shattered. Thia began to fall, but her wings settled behind her once again, sweeping away from her and stretching to their full size. The appendages grew slightly larger, transmuting until a collection of obsidian blades of every description dripped behind her in a suspension of liquid light.

"I will not let whatever controls you touch this world."

With her Runeshard now fully under her control, she understood just how dangerous the situation was. It was something that Elenor would not have understood. She had not been trained in the powers of a Caller for over a century. Her mother had been right, there was no question. The Writ had given them the powers of the Runespring to balance something so much worse than they had ever imagined. It was not just the thing from the outside. That did not require this kind of absolute power. She could destroy a planet with the power she held.

Elenor was not one iota weaker, she just did not yet understand how to utilize the power she held. If anything, she might even be more powerful than Thia. Thia shook her head and brought her mind back to the battle. This thing was no challenge anymore, and they had far more important things to deal with.

Thia beat her wings down, throwing herself hundreds of feet into the air. Then, with a mental push, they blurred away from her, leaving her in freefall. They smashed through spires of stone, causing a coruscation of falling rock to slam down around the Infected. Lashes of light smashed falling boulders to pieces, giving her wings a perfect opening.

They slid into place on either side of the Infected. The impetus of her will pressed another singularity into existence. The mass she had created compressed everything so violently that hundreds of feet of stone were obliterated in a perfect sphere. When she released the gravity, the explosion was the loudest sound that

Thia had ever heard, and she reflected that she may have overdone it.

Her wings shot out of the emerging mushroom cloud to resettle behind her, stabilizing her in flight. When the dust began to settle, she could see a perfectly circular hole as if it had been scooped out of the ground by a melon baller the size of an aircraft carrier. Through the hole Thia could see, someplace else. Had she broken through to the floor below? The scale of the room boggled her mind. Her sensory coils allowed her a sense of the size of the room by how long it took for it to resolve. At over a mile wide, it had to be part of the largest structure ever to exist on the earth. The massive walls were charcoal-colored stone and had the impressions of strange carvings.

It had the appearance of a maze. With hundreds of thousands of square spires of varying heights packing the room, it appeared like some sort of pixelated landscape stolen from Q*Bert. Thia shrugged. "Might as well get on with it before some other madness pops out at me," Thia squeaked and beat her wings, throwing herself down through the gap.

45

"BIRTHED FROM THE OTHER"

NC 17, EPOCH 19915.61

Elenor ran through the blinding snow. The Chorus in this place sounded somehow artificial to her, and she realized it was because this world she had entered was, itself, artificial. It did not seem to hinder her playing of the Percept's Rest.

She skidded a halt and opened her gorgon eyes. She closed her normal ones and flicked the power-filled golden orbs around the beautiful dreamscape. She could tell that the building she had entered was a container for these artificially made worlds.

She couldn't see through all of them, but she could see a dozen worlds stacked on top of this one. Only a few of them contained Infected, and from what her gorgon eyes could tell her, there were no other Anchors. She realized that there wouldn't be. The creature had told her that they wouldn't be able to get to the Writ until the Infected were beaten.

Elenor watched the green lights moving in the gold-tinged vision of her gorgon eyes. Unfortunately, it didn't show her how to move between the pocket worlds. Some of the green lights were much brighter than others, and those, she thought, were likely the corpses the creature had Infected.

What she now knew, though, was that their original vague impression of a plan was no longer viable. She hoped that the creature had visited Thia and Mateo. When she had carefully touched the earbud nestled deep into her musteline ears, there had been no response. Her course of action was clear. She had to find them before they could move forward. She had to hope that going up through the other "floors" would eventually lead her to Mateo and Thia.

An emerald glimmer appeared in the corner of her gorgon sight and she dropped flat in pure reflex. An enormous scythe ripped through the evergreens surrounding her like a razor through rice paper. She snapped her gorgon eyes closed and immediately threw herself forward.

She was sprayed with an explosion of dirt and pebbles as the scythe slammed into the spot she had just occupied. She ceased the Percept's Rest, realizing she had let herself rest in the snow. Her butt print, so clear in the white powder, had given her away.

She spun herself to face the absolutely bizarre tiny figure holding the enormous scythe. This Infected had wrapped themselves entirely from head to toe in the green surge energy they generated. The outer suit of overlapping threads gave them the appearance of a Halloween scarecrow. Elenor shuddered as the thing's ball-shaped head split at the middle into a maw of jagged fangs. It screeched at her and lunged forward, swinging its massive weapon.

Elenor, though, simply backed away through the trees as the scythe whacked branches from evergreen trees on either side of her. She lifted above the snow and swung herself out of sight through the canopy of snow-covered branches as the Infected burst through, screeching an insane battle cry.

"Too late now," Elenor's high, child-like voice echoed between the trees.

The Infected whipped its construct back and forth, trying to locate the source of Elenor's voice, but it was no use. Elenor considered her options. She floated to the ground and watched the shimmering figure in the trees. There had been more than one, and she didn't want to leave herself exposed. Elenor slapped her Striker against the trunk of an oak tree, and then, after a moment, she tilted her head to focus on the Chorus and began to Surge.

The world began to fade to white and, while the trees were still visible, Elenor followed her instincts. She ran in a wide circle, her paws silent on the air until she was behind the Infected.

It impacted her side with unbelievable force, throwing her through the air. She slammed into a massive oak tree, her spines slicing it to pieces as she tumbled to a stop, the tree toppling away from her.

The next sound she heard terrified her more than anything. Her Surge, only halfway through the first repetition, aborted. The world exploded with light and sound so violent that all sense of the physical world was obliterated. When she blinked the tears from her eyes, everything around her was broken.

The interrupted Surge had disjointed the flow of reality into something so twisted that it almost forced Elenor to vomit. Trees had been bisected and their upper portions were floating in the air, twisted into ribbons of bark and branches as if they were stretched taffy. Yet somehow, she knew that they were still whole. The ground flowed about with every step, as if she were walking on a filled waterbed the size of a planet.

Then, in a flash of confusion and pain, the world snapped back together. Elenor became violently ill as she was shoved back into the flow of reality. She puked up a stream of black molten ash that sprayed across the ground. It melted grass, stone, wood, and dirt into an acidic soup with a temperature near the surface of the sun. White light spiderwebbed the ichorous blackness, pulsing with threat.

Some instinct told her that she had to consume what she had just expelled. It was matter in the process of transmutation to pure mystical essence. Still, she knew without any doubt that if she did not swallow that burning soup back down, it would result in an explosion as powerful as any nuclear weapon.

With frantic abandon, she scrabbled over to the burning black pool, stared at it for only a moment, and plunged her muzzle into the vile looking goop. To her disbelief, it tasted like she had opened her mouth on a summer day and warm sunlight hit her tongue. It didn't taste good or foul. It was only the feeling on her tongue. When the white cracks of light began to pulse more violently, Elenor choked it down faster. She had to get it back into her stomach so her body could absorb the energy being released.

She caught movement out of the corner of her eye a moment too late. The scythe slammed into her side, blasting force into her internal organs. She just managed to keep from being ill again, clenching her jaw over a groan of pain as she tumbled to a stop once more.

None of that mattered to her as her eyes locked onto the last few mouthfuls of bile pulsing with warning energy. She crawled toward it, but a pair of bare feet appeared in her way.

"You have to let me finish," Elenor begged.

The mummified corpse did not respond. It only held out its hands, forming huge hammer of blinding green energy.

Elenor stared up at her death in the eyes of the creature, the green pinpoints of the eyes of the thing controlling the corpse. She had promised her friends she would be more careful with her power, but the rage she had felt in the woods rose inside of her. It howled into her as the hammer came down. The hammer slammed into the trunk of a tree bending like rubber under the force of Elenor's Runeshard.

Elenor's voice became a roar, barely supporting human language. "No further!" The entire world seemed to lean away from the volume of her roar.

This rage, though, was different than before. Elenor did not simply lash out without control. Her focus was pure. She would not let these pitiful adversaries stand in her way. She would not be afraid of her own power anymore. In that moment, she knew that her friends had been right. She had not been chosen at random, and if she wanted to enjoy her life, she couldn't simply ride along. She had to take control.

Through the power of her Runeshard, she could feel the water moving through every living thing around her. The trees, the grass beneath the snow, even the withered Infected had some water in its desiccated form, though she could feel it was dead and beyond her power. With the clarity of an epiphany, she understood.

Living water meant water that had been infused with the mystical energies that were required for life. It did not have to stay within the living thing to fall under her power. Elenor reached into the trees around her and drew forth the water. She did not need to kill the trees to get what she needed. From each, she took a small bit, no more than a mouthful. It started as a single drop hovering in front of her. Then it swelled to the size of a basketball, then a garbage dumpster. She made her intent clear to her power, and the water exploded apart into tens of thousands of drops, hovering in a cloud around her.

Each drop was held together by the absolute control of her Runeshard. The scythe smashed into the drops of water and halted as a bullet bounces off an armored vehicle. Elenor turned only her burning eyes to the Infected, and in the clear, cold squeak of her normal voice, she denied, "No, further." She turned, the drops of living water following her movement. They began to spin around her, slowly at first, turning aside the scythe as she stalked toward the Infected.

"You will not take one single step more against me and my friends."

Crystaline teardrops became a blur of motion as the cloud of living water spun around Elenor. Elenor lifted a paw into the cloud and the impenetrable barrier moved away from her. It returned the moment she dropped her paw. Elenor bobbed her head, satisfied that the barrier would continue even without her attention. The construct with the scythe backed away, the body posture of the suit reacting to its wearer's terror.

She walked undeterred to the remaining bit of what she had vomited and ate the last few burning mouthfuls. She shivered at the thought of what she had just done, but when the scythe skittered off her shield of water drops a second time, she turned and glared at the Infected.

A terrified feminine voice issued from the scarecrow creature. Clearly the Otherthing, as the golden cat creature had called it, had lost control of one of its puppets. "What are you?"

Elenor's voice fell off to a whisper so fierce it could have sliced steel.

"I am the end."

Elenor lifted her tail and carefully, she extended the crystalline rainbow of spines into the swirling drops of water. The chime rang and she called The Silence. At the first chime, the wasted corpse turned and ran.

Elenor let it go. She could do nothing for that thing. This girl, however, she could help. Elenor saw that she was just a young girl of no more than fifteen as the Scarecrow construct vanished. Maybe closer to twelve. What must the Otherthing have threatened the girl with to get her to do this?

Long brown hair fell to the middle of her back. A single pink streak the width of two fingers was dyed into it. Save for the pale grey skin, she was cute, with a heart-shaped face and a button nose. Her glowing green eyes darted back and forth nervously as she tried to watch the whole whirling cloud around Elenor at once.

Elenor began to realize the importance of several things she had been doing for some time with respect to her Runeshard. One was that her mind would construct instructions for the power based on physical gestures if the instructions were simple enough. She used that power now, waving her paw to sweep a gap into the swirling barrier of living water.

"I don't want to hurt you," Elenor pipped.

The girl's eyes froze, locked onto Elenor's face. When it was not strained into a hiss of fury, Elenor's childlike tones were disarming. The world had fully faded away into the white void. The scythe the girl had been gripping in her right fist shattered into motes of green light as power of the Otherthing was subverted.

Tears welled in the young girl's eyes. "I can't, be me, anymore," she sobbed. "I killed my little sister. I couldn't stop."

Elenor held back her own tears because that was not what this girl needed. "You didn't do that. The thing controlling you did that."

"My, parents, won't, know that!" she shouted in broken hiccupping sobs.

"Then I will make them understand."

The thread connecting the girl to the port dimension hiding her Crown emerged. Elenor paused for a moment, head tilted, listening to what small part of the Chorus still existed in this space. Then she reached up with a claw and snapped the thread. The Crown filtered from the aether to form around the girl's head.

"You are going to sleep now. I promise you'll be safe and fine when you wake up. It can't hurt you anymore." Elenor would help this girl even if it killed her.

"How can I trust anything you say?" the girl sniffled.

"You can't, but unfortunately, I don't have time right now to do more than this."

Elenor lifted a paw and pointed two digits toward the crown. Drops of living water flowed forward forming a thick bubble around the crown. Spines surged from the interior of the bubble. The Crown exploded. Though the bubble expanded it contained the explosion.. Elenor sat for a moment, staring at the girl's unconscious body. She hadn't even asked her name. It didn't matter, she had to help. She wasn't sure when she had decided that, but it was evident to her that she would never be able to stand by and do nothing, even if everyone saw her as a monster.

She thought about what to do with the living water she was holding. She could feel the spiritual energy draining out of it, and soon it would be just water again. Using some carefully crafted mental instructions, she returned the water to the trees she had taken it from.

She wondered why the corpse had run off. Unlike the humans who had been Infected while still alive, she knew there was no fear involved. It was controlled completely by the Otherthing.

Mateo quickly located the Infected again within the mazelike world he had entered. He had seen Thia jump down from the ceiling and disappear into spires of stone filling the room, but since the Infected were headed straight for her, he thought it best to simply follow them.

He couldn't imagine what she had done to open such a massive hole between the floors. Stranger still was how she had moved so far so quickly. She had gone into the pyramid at the top. That meant she should be many floors away from him. Did she blast her way through all of them? Had she gotten her Runeshard working? It didn't really matter. She was here now.

He paused in his sideways skitter along one of the pillars as a thought hit him. He had tried the tiny device nestled into his ear before, but now that they were in the same space, it might work. He rolled one of the spades of his tentacles until it came to a dull point the size of a finger and carefully touched the device in his ear.

"Thia, can you hear me?" he whispered. Damien had said they picked up sounds by vibrations, not the volume of the sound, so they would pick up even a whisper. A moment later, the device gave a soft crackle.

"Yes, Mateo, are you alright?"

"Sí por ahora."

"I haven't been able to find anything like an Anchor that would get us to the Writ. I did figure out my Runeshard. If the comm is working again, you must be in here with me?"

"I saw you jump down from the ceiling a few minutes ago. I was chasing two Infected that were headed for you."

"No response from Elly, so she must still be further down," Thia postulated. "I saw a few Infected when I dropped in."

"Do we have to fight them?" Mateo crawled up higher onto one of the spires to make sure he didn't lose sight of the Infected he had been trailing.

"Not if we find what we need without them getting the way."

Mateo's sight ears twigged to the bright tack, tack, tack of footsteps on stone, and he skittered to the top of one of the square spires. A moment of concentration later, the image resolved into one of the husks of a human being. The sound was that of its bare heel bone striking the stone where the flesh had been stripped away. Mateo shivered in disgust.

This thing could not be helped. Mateo crept down the side of the Pillar, his tentacles mutating into blade-thin whips. He wished he understood how the instincts he had gained in his transformation actually functioned. He couldn't explain why he could move so well compared to Elly and Thia. He had tried to tell them

• Sí por ahora – Yeah for now

that they just had to listen to their instincts. Still, he knew without any effort just when the creature was about to turn and see him. He knew just how to move so it wouldn't see him.

He pounced.

The Infected spun at the last possible second, somehow sensing him. Instead of being buried into its back, they slammed into its bony shoulder. Even the glancing blow was enough to bring the arm close to destruction. It hung uselessly. Mateo tumbled awkwardly to the left, his tentacles lashing out to scrape through the stone, yanking him to a halt.

He jumped back from a pair of spinning triangular blades made of emerald energy. They buried themselves in the stone. Mateo was peppered with stone chips when the two blades exploded, spending their kinetic force into the wall. Mateo rolled to his left, regaining his feet and then threw himself further that way.

The Infected was surrounded by dozens of triangular blades that whipped around it, attempting to slam into Mateo. His tentacles slashed though the flying blades one after another, throwing off showers of poisonous sparks. He backed away until he neared the shadows in the corner of two pillars. When he slipped close enough, his instincts informed him how to blend in with the shadows. The blades froze, the Infected having lost him in the final shower of bubbling sparks. Mateo stood frozen, waiting for five deep breaths as the Infected turned away from him.

His tentacles lashed forward. To his surprise, the Infected once again sensed the movement. This time, it was too late. Spinning verdant blades swung between his tentacle and the Infected. The tentacle never even slowed, slashing through the energy and the Infected's neck in a single deadly arc of relic stone.

Mateo emerged from the shadows. He wasted no time slicing the remainder of the creature's body into dozens of smaller pieces. This thing was dead and he didn't think it needed a head to attack him. He extended the light webs around his sight ears so he could tell for certain when the green glow faded away.

It would not be enough, he knew. He could still see the faded jade thread waving away from the dissected body like a flag declaring the creature's return. Mateo leapt onto one of the spires and scurried up the side.

"Mateo, are you alright?" The voice in his ear almost made him lose his footing on the wall.

"Yeah, just ran into one of those stupid zombie things. I'm not hurt yet. Since searching from top to bottom looks like it isn't going to work the way we thought, we should meet up."

"Agreed." A second later, Thia launched into the air above the mazelike structure in a burst of pale lavender light. He saw her spinning, looking for him. Mateo wasn't sure what to do as his body almost perfectly matched the stone. He tried waving, but she didn't see him at first.

Mateo tapped his Striker against the stone and Surged the Dawn Song. A small orb of sunlight flashed into existence next to him. Thia spotted him a second later and swooped down to land next to him. He ceased the Dawn Song, rubber necking around with his sight ears swiveling madly to make sure nothing had seen his light.

"We need to find Elenor," Mateo said. His sight ears twitched, and for once, he was actually listening to the Chorus with his sound ears. "Because for some reason, it looks like all the Infected are trying to get together in one big group."

Thia's sensory coils rippled until those sensitive to warping of reality were visible. "This isn't like any other port dimension I have ever seen. It's like there are no dimensional divides. This entire place should be collapsing but it isn't. It makes no sense."

"None of this makes any sense to me. Pero do we just blast our way down floors?"

"I don't think that's necessary."

"Así que, about that giant hole you made?" Mateo pointed with one of his tentacles at the massive gap in the roof of this world.

"That, was not my fault!" Thia protested. "I had just gotten the stupid instruction manual for my Runeshard crammed into my head. What do you want from me?" Thia grumbled, her squeaky voice ruining the anger.

"Pues, not putting a hole in the world would be awesome." Mateo chuckled.

"Anyway, there is a way to travel between port dimensions. I'm sure of it."

They saw it at the same time and bolted away from each other. A blazing jade sphere landed where they had been standing, exploding like a fragmentation grenade. Stone chips sprayed them as the top of the spire blew apart.

"¡Hijo de puta!" Mateo shouted.

Thia burst into giggles as she swept her wings forward, shooting back away from the explosion.

"What are you laughing about?" Mateo leapt back out of the way of another blast as the Infected focused on him.

"Cursing in your five-year-old voice is ridiculous!"

"Oh, like you have anything to talk about, Little Miss Duck Squeak." They both knew they needed the banter, if anything because of the danger of the situation. Even for them, explosions were terrifying.

Each explosion fuzzed Mateo's vision as the loud noise momentarily washed away his sight like a bright

- Pero - But
- Así que – So
  Pues - Well
- ¡Hijo de puta! – Son of a bitch!

flash of light. Unlike when he was human, his echolocation adjusted instantly, and the reverberations from the explosions actually made his surroundings clearer. Clear enough to realize that not all of the Infected were gathering on the floors below.

"¡Viene más!" Mateo shouted up to Thia.

"Great! Screw this, let's get the hell out of here!" Thia yelped. Her wings swirled out away from her body until they were swinging in a wide circle with Thia and Mateo at the center. Suddenly, Mateo felt all the weight of his body slough away and he floated into the air.

Then he drew closer to Thia, and her wings floated to either side of them. From this vantage, Mateo could see that the outsized maze stretched away for miles into the distance, far beyond the point where his sight ears could no longer see. Something else drew his attention.

Every sound clattered off the walls of the maze, resolving the image in his echolocation. Mateo had gotten used to how his sight functioned without the use of his light webs. Without sound, he was effectively blind. Yet, as the image of the maze below faded, leaving him in darkness, he could see the pieces of something forming in the flashes of sound.

"Thia, I need a big sound. I need to see the whole maze!" Mateo's excited shout cut through the sounds of wind rushing by as Thia flew them over the walls of the maze-like landscape.

"Alright, let me take us down."

"No, I need to see the whole thing from up here."

"We're gonna fall for a second. I'll catch us," Thia said, and then they were falling as Thia's wings shot away from them. "Get ready!" she shouted. Then her wings drew together until they were touching, with a circular space between them. A tiny spark of lavender light gathered, and then it vanished. An ear shattering pop rang out, as though a firecracker the size of a dump

• ¡Viene más! – More coming!

truck had exploded. The wave of sound blanketed the maze and the image resolved.

To Mateo's amazement, the sound echoing off of the square spires formed a clear picture in his vision. Not the spires, but the sound itself. To Mateo's echolocation, it was like an image had been drawn in light. Pulses of sound echoing off the stone filled in the image as Mateo watched until he had the whole picture.

Just as it started to fade, it all came together in a final burst of light. At the bottom of the picture that formed in his mind was three tiny outlines sitting side by side by side, seen from behind. The one in the middle had two pairs of ears, one large triangular set and a smaller, curved pair, and three long tentacles in stylized curves surrounding their body.

The figure on the left had numerous porcupine-like spines jutting out from their body with a thicker tail also covered in spines. Very clearly, there were two large eyes open and staring at him from their back.

The figure on the right had tiny stylized wings, a long lizard-like tail, and two curving horns with a bed of stylized snakes between them.

There was no doubt who the figures were. They were sitting before a massive tunnel that looked crystalline in nature. In the center of the tunnel was a sea of stars, just as in any other anchor. Behind the archway loomed an absolutely massive waterfall. Clouds of mist billowed for what seemed like miles on either side of the tunnel. Between the tunnel and the waterfall, the most amazing feature of the image drew his attention. A gargantuan swirling vortex the size of a skyscraper seemed to be holding the archway in its grip, as if threatening to devour it.

There was no question that the image was meant for him to see. Only someone with his ability with echolocation could see this thing, and only with Thia's or Elenor's help could he have possibly seen it.

Just when he was about to turn away to speak with Thia, the sound bounced off of the outer edge of the maze and a ring of symbols encircled the image. It was so bright that there could be no doubt that somehow the sound had been amplified. Miles of enormous cuneiform characters enfolded the image. He could not read it, but he knew how he could share it with Thia. One part of it, though, was as clear to him as a shouted curse.

"We need to find Elly. We can't get through without all three of us," Mateo affirmed.

"We are certainly going to need her to deal with whatever, THAT, is." Thia pointed with her tail as her wings swirled around them, stabilizing their flight.

Above them, crouching on the lip of the massive hole, was a lizard-like creature. It was easily the size of a half dozen greyhound busses duct taped together. Made up of hundreds of withered corpses bound together by the mystical energy of the Infected, it had a shape that was something like an alligator, yet nothing like the actual animal, in that parts of it made no sense.

The limbs of corpses waved insanely from the enormous legs and tail with no purpose. Upon the wedge-shaped head, where the eyes should have been, dozens of desiccated skulls stuck up out of the rope-like threads of energy.

"How did they move between the floors?" Mateo wondered.

Thia swept a paw around, pausing to point to several spots where glowing emerald gaps dotted the landscape around the massive maze. "They are tearing apart the dimensional fabric of this dimension. What did you see?"

"I can't explain, and there is more Nyceric that I can't read. Can you hold me up while I Surge the Fugue of Fragmented Memory?"

"Do it quick, because I'm pretty sure that thing is going to try to kill the shit right out of us!"

The creature roared, and then a colossal sphere of emerald light grew in its maw. A beam of light thick enough to fill a train tunnel split the air with thunder that would drown out a tsunami. Mateo felt them lurch violently to the left as the beam seared the air. Were he still human, he felt the heat would have cooked him alive. It slammed into the stone walls of the maze and carved a hole miles deep into the rock. Earth-shattering sounds of stone slabs the size buildings crashed to the ground.

"Hustle up, I can't dodge this thing forever!" Thia urged.

Mateo closed his eyes and slapped his striker against one of his blade-hard tentacles. The sweet chime of his striker pushed away even the thundering sounds of falling stone. He called the Fugue of Fragmented Memory. He focused his attention on the Surge as he remembered the image in full. He made sure to make tiny alterations to the Surge to cause the Fragment to appear in his mouth, so he could be sure he wouldn't drop it.

"O'a, Ah go' it!" he tried to shout around the fragment in his mouth.

"Oh, fuck me!" Thia shrieked, and Mateo almost blacked out from the force against his body from the burst of gravity that threw them towards the maze below. "Hold on to your ass!"

Mateo felt an odd weightlessness come over his body, then his whole body shook violently as they crashed into and through one of the massive spires. That was when Mateo was able to get a handle on the flashing images picked up by his echolocation. The gargantuan creature had jumped down through the hole on top of them. Thia had created a bubble of altered gravity around them to protect them from the impact. Still, they had been buried in an avalanche of broken rubble.

"We're fine for a second," Thia whispered. "It lost us in the rubble. Did you see it cut a hole down through the next couple of floors with that blast?"

Mateo nodded, knowing she would be able to see him with her sensory coils. He shook his head a little, trying to clear the aftermath of surging the Fugue. He said nothing, still holding the memory fragment in his mouth.

"Maybe we can use it to get closer to Elenor." Mateo carefully spit the memory fragment into one of the spades of his tentacles once the rumbling faded away. "You need to see this. There is more of that picture language in it that I can't read." He curled the fragment in his tentacle to make sure he didn't lose it. "¿Cómo en el infierno are we supposed to fight that thing?"

"First, we need to figure out how to get past that thing without getting flash fried!" Thia hissed.

- ¿Cómo en el infierno – How the hell

46

"THE WAY TO ANSWERS"

NC 17, EPOCH 19915.62

Elenor's golden eyes shifted nervously, roving around the forest and then up to the places above. Some of the Infected were still in place moving around through the different dimensions, but the most powerful signatures, the ones from the corpses, had disappeared. The girl she had rescued had not woken up, but that was not odd.

After a long, few minutes spent listening to the Chorus, she managed to open her hammerspace and place the girl inside. She found it strange that the remnant of Merlin was nowhere to be found, even when she called for him. Her time spent quietly observing the Chorus had also tipped her about how she could move between the different floors of the pyramid.

Echoing from the opposite end of the valley was a discordant mixture of sound. The space above was grinding against the one she was stood in in that direction. That was where she was headed now. Still, there were at least twenty other Infected to be dealt with above her. Probably more, if there were more dimensions than she could see between her, Mateo, and Thia.

The Chorus changed. The sounds of the world around her jittered as a needle skipping on a scratched record. The sound was so abrasive that Elenor folded her ears and immediately shoved away the sound of the Chorus.

"What the hell?" she squeaked, but the Chorus did not lie. Before she had shoved it away, the picture was clear. It was as if all of the Infected had been somehow overlapped into a single space, warping reality so violently that the Chorus just became a clatter of conflicting sounds.

There was no more time to waste. Whatever had happened had concentrated almost all the power of the Infected in one spot. That could not possibly be good. Elenor lifted herself with her Runeshard and shot towards the opposite end of the valley. As much as she wanted to help free all of the Infected, she couldn't possibly take the time to do it.

Elenor reached the other end of the valley in just a few minutes. What she found was a swirling portal of bubbling rainbow light. What amazed her about it was that she couldn't see it from a distance. It did not appear until she was standing right in front of it. If she had not spent so much time listening to the Chorus, she would have never found the portal. She leapt through the portal into another vista of otherworldly beauty.

Elenor stood on a small island no more than a few hundred feet wide. Around her, plant life exploded with a full rainbow of colors. Clearly alien, many of the plants had wild gradients of color shot through their petals and leaves. The trees were similar to palms, with tall trunks free of branches until the canopy. Unlike palms, a wide canopy of branches with thousands of tiny leaves spread around them in a woven rainbow carpet, extending almost a hundred feet in diameter.

None of that was what had captured Elenor's unwavering attention. Ten scant feet away, the land fell into a bottomless sky. Clouds passed by beneath the island, which floated weightlessly across the summer heavens. Her eyes tracked across the endless blue to find other islands floating in pairs. Each of the islands moved in low gravity hops, in perfect unison one above the other. Improbably connecting each of the island pairs was a waterfall that flowed in the wrong direction, against what Elenor felt was the pull of gravity. The water roared up from the bottom island to arc onto the top island. Frothing clouds of mist emerged from the bottom one, where the water shot up into the air to flow across the upper island, vanishing out of her sight.

"This is so unfair. Coolest shit I'm ever going to see and I have to go running through it like I'm on fire," Elenor groused. She closed her eyes and tilted her head, listening to the Chorus. She quickly discovered there was no way to tell where the portal to the next floor up would be. She was standing too close to the lower floor's portal. She would have to move away so she could hear both.

She carefully turned her back to the edge of the island and opened her gorgon eyes. A quick scan around showed her several sources of the emerald energy that indicated the Infection by the Otherthing. She snapped her gorgon eyes closed and lept off the side of the island. She had to find her friends.

Mateo crept towards the edge of the tear through the reality they inhabited. Thia had folded her wings away and was following in Mateo's every paw step. She had no trouble admitting that Mateo was far stealthier than she and Elenor put together. He had taken them on a circuitous route, circling around the freakish kaiju creature rampaging through the port dimension. They had almost been hit by the creature's beams of raw energy three times, but each time, Mateo had pulled them away at the last second.

It took almost an hour for Thia to realize what was happening. She had thought that her sensory coils were a more advanced version of his echolocation. Indeed, in some ways, her view of most of the electromagnetic spectrum worked much like his echolocation. However, in a situation like this, the mechanical vibrations that Mateo picked up with his sight ears were much more informative. The vibrations passed around corners and through many objects more readily than most of the electromagnetic spectrum she could perceive.

"What the hell is that thing? How can it produce all of this energy without tiring out?" Mateo whispered.

"With a creature from another dimension like the thing controlling the Infected, we have no idea what the limitations might be," Thia whispered back. "We can beat it, though. I just need Elenor's help."

"I wish I could help more." Mateo froze and then scrambled through a twisting pile of rubble that he could barely squeeze through. Thia was hot on his heels, and a moment later, a roar of sound ripped through the debris where they had been. Mateo skidded to a halt the moment the blast tapered off.

"Go back!" Mateo shrieked over the sound of tumbling stone. "That blast ripped through to the next floor. Stay right on my tail!"

Mateo folded his lithe body back the way he came and darted past Thia. He forged a path, darting between falling slabs of stone as the world seemed to crash down around them. After a long moment, Thia began to catch up as her sensory coils were able to follow the rubble falling nearby. She dodged between two slabs of stone, but her tail was smashed between them, causing her to stumble.

She yanked her tail free, but it was too late. To her gape-mawed amazement, Mateo slid himself between every bit of falling rubble and appeared at her side. His tentacles flashed, slicing dozens of pieces of stone apart. It gave her just enough time to get up and get moving again.

"How in the hell did you do that?" Thia stared at him in wonder as she ran through the falling rubble.

"You two don't listen to your instincts enough. We got them for a reason. They'll tell you how to do things if you just listen," Mateo explained as he wove them through the destroyed landscape.

Thia realized that he was right. While her sensory coils allowed her to see almost everything nearby, including all of the gaps, Mateo didn't seem to pause to judge whether they could fit. He simply twisted and turned as if there were signposts to tell him with unerring precision where they had to go. He shot every gap and paused only occasionally to peer back at Thia. She realized that he was judging her size, because several times, he turned aside from an opening between cross-laid slabs that she didn't think she would have fit through.

Mateo skidded to a halt with a large square gap ahead that had formed from a slab of stone wedged between two other slabs. Mateo eyed the top slab warily.

"There's nothing holding that in place but friction." Mateo's sight ears twitched wildly. "And there's about a half mile of open ground between us and the gap down to the next floor. I think I can get myself through without that thing seeing me, but not you."

"Then we'll just have to get there so fast it doesn't have time to stop us." Thia expressed her wings, allowing the silly cartoon things to float up from her back. She had kept them very small, no larger than a pair of human hands. Then they floated forward until they were hanging in the gap over open ground.

"When you jump between them, they will accelerate you. It's not going to be safe and I'll have to catch us at the gap, so brace yourself. This is probably going to hurt."

Mateo said nothing. He just turned and bolted for the gap. There was no time for hesitation. They needed to get somewhere the thing wouldn't be able to follow right away so they could review what he had seen. A sphere of lavender light swirled between her wings, which had now grown to their full five feet of height.

Mateo jumped through and shot away fast as a sniper's bullet. Thia jumped through a moment later and her wings blurred past her on a burst of gravitational force. They arrived well ahead of her, creating another swirling field of gravity between them. The light had nothing to do with the forces involved. Rather, it showed where the field of warped gravity began and ended.

Mateo jolted to a halt and then immediately fell through the slice in reality acting as a doorway into the next port dimension. A shiver ran down his spine and he let loose a clicking formed by tightening the muscles in his throat. The sound resolved the image he could see through the slice in the world. The creature had seen them, and while he had made it through the gap, Thia was still dropping through.

"Thia!" Mateo screamed in warning, but he could tell that Thia had already realized the danger. There was just nothing more that could be done. Thia fell through the gap, but there was nothing between her and the gathering strike of the massive creature.

Nothing, except for her wings, which spread wide. For a single moment, Mateo felt terror. A point of lavender light so bright that he could feel it even without his lightwebs gathered between the wings.

A roar of sound so thunderous that it shook both pocket dimensions overtook the world. Mateo was certain all four of his ear drums would burst from the pressure as hundreds of millions of tons of stone were ripped through the gap. They smashed together before Thia and vanished into the point of light as they were crushed and compressed beyond the limits of mortal imagination.

He felt himself rising against the pull of gravity from below as the tiny point gained mass equivalent to that of a small planet. The beam of light blasted through the hole in reality, causing the air to scream in anguish as everything was burned off. The beam struck the point of mass between Thia's wings. For a moment, it seemed as if it would burn through whatever Thia had done, but more stone continued to pour through the hole crushed into the singularity Thia had created.

The beam split.

Smashed against the irresistible mass of a small planet, there was no way the beam could possibly penetrate. The energy blasted away to either side, slamming into the landscape below. It carved two furrows, thousands of feet long, in the darkened landscape below before it cut off.

Then they were falling towards the ground.

Mateo's eyes widened as he realized several things at once. The first was that Thia was unconscious. Her wings were falling away from her, and her body spiraled toward the ground just as out of control as he was. The second was the landscape below.

He sounded his click again and then extended his lightwebs. The transparent filaments wrapped around his ears, letting him see the distance to the ground. It took a full eight seconds for the landscape below to resolve in his echolocation. The depth only added to his visual perception of the breathtaking desert below.

Pearlescent lavender sand shimmered, bathed in the light of a moon so bright it could almost be mistaken for the sun. Chatoyant rainbow glimmers floated in waves across the sea of sand. The beauty was so sharp that had Mateo still been possessed of eyes, they would have gathered tears.

Circular craters dotted the landscape. Unlike the meteoric disasters of the surface of the moon, these were almost artistic in their organization. They gave the appearance of being carefully sculpted by a master. The bowl of each crater held a tracery of lines that were at once geometric and organic.

His wonder lasted only a few scant moments before the reality set in. He realized they were reaching terminal velocity and Thia showed no sign of waking up. He was fairly sure they could survive the fall, considering how well their Relics absorbed external impact. That was not the issue. Mateo could see the creature forcing its maw through the slash they had fallen through. Their constant rate of descent made them an easy target. He had maybe ten seconds to figure out how to fly.

He had been amazed to learn that flight was not a power that any Surge could offer them. Surges altered local reality, and flight altered one's physical location so quickly that it was impossible to maintain flight, leaving him only one possibility available.

They had made very little headway on finding out what Runeshard power he had access to. The only thing they had been able to discern was that it was similar to Elenor's, in that he was able to control something inside of living things. He suspected that was part of why his instincts had become so sharp. He could feel something inside of the living things around him. Unlike Elenor, he could not feel things inside of plants as well as people, which indicated it was something other than her abilities with water. He tried to feel it now. He folded back all four of his ears, blocking out as much of the sound of rushing wind as he could.

Forty seconds to impact.

He concentrated on the vague feelings he got from Thia. He could feel the warmth in the center of his chest that Elenor always described. He had been able to feel it for weeks, but now, he felt it giving off tiny shivers as it picked up some energy given off by Thia's body.

Thirty seconds to impact.

He couldn't understand what within Thia's body was giving off the energetic noise that his Runeshard was picking up on. He could feel an almost identical low-level vibration coming from his own, so it was certainly something they shared.

Twenty seconds to impact.

Mateo forced himself to put the ground rushing up at them and the creature behind them out of his mind. He struggled to understand how to grab ahold of things with his Runeshard. Elenor had told him that he had to put together instructions for it in his head. He knew they had to be specific. He needed to understand what he was trying to grab ahold of in himself, Thia, and others. He focused all of his attention onto that hum of power in his chest. Where was it coming from?

Fifteen seconds.

The image in his mind resolved. Something that was spread throughout both of their bodies, but not at the surface. Something hard and strong, but still somewhat flexible. It snapped into perfect clarity under the strain of his reckless focus. Her skeleton. The pulse was coming from her bones and his.

Ten seconds.

Mateo turned in the air, feeling the power of the Infected gathering behind him. The sphere of energy in its maw was nearing the size it had been the last time he had seen it fire.

Eight seconds.

Mateo unraveled the mystery of his Runeshard, and at last, knowledge rushed into his mind. With frantic abandon, he flung instructions at it, grabbing ahold of both of their skeletons and launching them in a sideways arch.

The redwood trunk-sized bar of energy seared past them, just missing Thia. It cut a burning line into the violet landscape, leaving behind a glowing trench that appeared to be molten glass.

The mental strain of so much knowledge caused him to lose his grip on the power of his Runeshard. He and Thia tumbled through the air for the last twenty feet.

He slammed face-first into the sand. Thia, at least, had a softer landing than he had, flopping on her belly and throwing up a small cloud of sand as she tumbled. The impact had not been painful, only stunning. He groaned and flexed his body until he flipped onto his paws. There was no time to think about any aches he might feel. He scrambled across the lavender sand to check on Thia. Sand churned as he darted across it. He skidded to a halt next to Thia's motionless body.

The ground shook beneath him as he was leaning over to try to listen to Thia's insides. He turned shakily, and his ears fell in pure shock. It took only a single split second for him to realize what had happened. The mass of stone that Thia had super-compressed had been held in place by the power of her Runeshard for just over a minute before it had faded. It had to weigh millions of tons, all of which plummeted several thousand feet to the desert floor. The shockwave was so vast that it carried a tidal wave of lilac sand that rushed towards him at highway speeds.

"Fuck a duck," Mateo whispered as his muzzle tracked toward the briming rim of overflowing sand. He turned and dove on top of Thia to protect her. At the last moment, he realized he could feel parts of the sand as if it were alive, just like his living skeleton. The sand smashed into his back.

Elenor raced towards the edge of the island. As soon as she had started to jump from island to island, the Infected had come for her. She had thought before that the Otherthing that controlled them could only control so many. Otherwise, why were she able to talk to any of them? But now, not a single one of the seven Infected leaping from island to island behind her were aware. Their eyes were pinpoints of vomitous light, and they did not speak or respond to any of her shouting.

She had thought about just flying to the exit to the next pocket dimension, but she could feel the massive power gathering somewhere above. Then, the dimension itself had shaken, almost causing her to fall into the sky. She had felt the resonance of another Runeshard being used. She wasn't sure how she knew what the vibration in her chest meant, she just did. That meant she would need to save all the power she could, because whatever her friends had found, it didn't feel like they were strong enough to beat it alone.

Elenor raced through the brilliant flora, wishing she could just stop to gawp at the vista of utter beauty she was smashing through. There was just no time. She pushed herself to run faster towards the waterfall. She had discovered that there were currents in gravity between the islands that she could ride, but they only started for the upper islands.

At first, she had jumped from the bottom island to the top one. Then, she had stepped onto a shifting rock and fallen into one of the waterfalls. It had carried her to the top island, where she had managed to paddle her way out of the water. Whatever carried these islands through the sky ran in a sort of current underneath, and then up the back side of the island, keeping the second one in the air. If she jumped off of the top island, the current that kept them aloft would launch her toward the next in the chain.

Elenor came upon a crystal pool of azure water frothing with mist. She leapt into the water and paddled toward the waterfall. As soon she got into the current, it began to carry her toward the top. She closed her eyes against the water, but then opened the eyes on her back.

Not a moment too soon. One of the Infected she had seen before was standing on the banks of the pool below. It was the girl from Chicago, the one that Elenor had said she would help if she could. It was clear that she was not in control, and she hefted a javelin of light.

Anger welled up in Elenor. She did not want to waste any of her strength, but the moment she had nodded to the woman trapped inside of this Infected flashed through her mind. That nod was a promise that Elenor wouldn't break.

She couldn't be careless, though, so she let herself be carried to the top of the waterfall. If she stopped to engage the woman, the rest of the Infected in here would catch up to her. She couldn't fight them all, even if she caught them all in The Silence. Instead, she sat at the top of the waterfall and carefully constructed a set of Instructions for her Runeshard. She had to take a risk if she wanted to save the girl. To be sure none of the other Infected could interfere, she would have to shove them all off the island at once with a burst of power. It meant she might have to fight more than one at the same time, but she would just have to endure long enough to catch them all in the blast. Instructions set, she crept to the edge of the upper island.

"Shit!" she squeaked, and jumped back. The stone lip of the island exploded. A spear of light slashed through the stone, just missing her muzzle. It had come from off to the right. The woman had jumped into the waterfall. Elenor snarled, "I will not let you have her!"

She leapt from the rim of the island. Another spear of light burst from the Infected's hand. Elenor twisted her body, bubbling emerald sparks bursting as her spines slashed through the Infected's attack. She crashed into the woman, driving her out of the waterfall and down towards the lower island.

Falling toward the island, she sensed the approach of another of the Infected. She shoved off of the woman, throwing her toward the ground with bone-breaking force. A basketball-sized sphere of jade light with dozens of blades emerging from the surface blurred between them. Elenor hit the ground and immediately flung herself into a roll. Another bladed sphere slammed into the ground where she had been a moment before.

There was no time to be gentle. Retracting the spines on her tail, she dashed past the woman and curled it around the Infected's neck just as the woman began to rise. It was clear that she had several broken bones, including a leg that was twisted absurdly, to the point that the bones were pressing against the skin.

Elenor dashed into the overgrowth, dragging the flailing woman behind her. Three more Infected landed on the island and began to tear apart the pristine forest. She couldn't risk continuing to fight the woman she was trying to save. She ran onto one side of the island and then skirted toward the back of it, to one side of the waterfall.

Spinning with a brutal snap, she yanked the woman by her neck and slammed her into a boulder near the backside of the pool. Bones snapped, and the sickening hollow thud of her skull being staved in jarred the space. Elenor unwound her tail from the woman's throat and then slapped her striker against the boulder.

The Keymaster's March floated through the air and the gateway to her hammerspace pushed itself up from the ground. The moment the blackened window blazing with the stars of a distant cosmos appeared, she lifted the infected and threw her through the gate. The gateway dove back into the ground just in time for the remaining three Infected to arrive on the Island. Trees toppled in a continuous roar as they tore their way across the island looking for Elenor.

They did not have to look for long. Backing up, Elenor used her Runeshard to launch herself up onto the top island of the pair. The moment she crested its lip, a massive maul flew towards her head. She twisted her head just enough that the massive sledge smashed into the spines on her shoulder. It exploded into a shower of sparks, blinding her.

Elenor tumbled to the ground, furiously blinking. Before she could bring the world back into focus, something struck her in the side, the force pounding her insides. She howled in pain as a second impact blasted her across the pebble-strewn riverbank.

Her scream cut off as frothing blue blood filled her mouth, spilling out between clenched teeth. She leaped away from the river, but stumbled as something inside of her gave away. A third blow struck the side of her head and the world fuzzed to incomprehension.

Elenor realized that if she didn't do something to keep herself conscious, she was going to die. Bending all of her will to the task, she whipped her tail around her Striker, crashing it into the spines on her shoulders. The notes of the Requiem of Shattered Resonance rippled across the space.

She knew she couldn't keep it up. Her mind was too fuzzy to maintain her focus. She just needed to keep herself awake and alive long enough for the rest of the Infected to be close enough. There were five on the island, and the sixth was close.

Elenor stumbled to her feet and pushed herself towards the back of the island. She made it two steps before she lost her balance. She collapsed and began to crawl as the Requiem faded with her failing concentration. Muscles tore in her right hindleg as a tiny wrecking ball of emerald light smashed into it.

With the last of her strength, Elenor expressed every blade and spine, curling herself into a ball. She just had to hold together long enough. Blows shattered against her spines as the Infected tried to force their way past her defenses to reach her body. Tears leaked from her eyes as blows rained down on her spines. Some of the force got through, bruising her body from every angle. She gasped, and blackness invaded the corners of her vision.

The sixth Infected arrived.

Her Runeshard responded.

"I, win," Elenor gasped as she fell to one side. Each of the Infected was gripped by the power of her Runeshard. The blast threw them away with such force that they vanished into the limitless sky. One of the nearby islands shattered when the irresistible power of her Runeshard brutally forced the body of the Infected through the bedrock of the island in a thunderclap of cracking stone.

Elenor sneezed, bubbling blue blood effervescing into light as it sprayed across the ground. "Augh, I hate my life," she whined. She still wasn't sure how to heal anything complicated with her Runeshard, so she spent long minutes in a cycle of spitting up blood and then catching her breath before the pounding in her head subsided enough for her to surge the Mender's Lament to pull together her broken insides

Elenor jumped from the island and launched towards the next one in the chain. Several more jumps brought her to the island with the grinding sound of the portal. She squeezed her eyes closed and jumped through the swirling rainbow of frothing light.

Rapid blinking cleared the dazzle from her eyes, revealing a landscape barren, yet still possessed of limitless allure. Dunes rolled in gentle waves as far as she could see. The sand refracted the moonlight into a prismatic sheen that rolled in waves of light that traced the rolling sands. She could see from her vantage point that as the land sloped away, there were numerous craters of varying sizes that had been scooped from the land as if it were a desert shaped by the hand of a master pâtissier.

The sound slammed into her as a physical thing, bowling her over backwards. She landed on her back slightly dazed and wondering just what the hell had happened. It wasn't something heard, because much like the reaction of their Striker, this sound overwhelmed every other sound of the world.

Then she saw the tear in the sky and the head of the gargantuan creature trying to claw its way into the port dimension. Considering how far away the thing was, it had to be at least the size of a small office building, or maybe even a large one.

"Is that a fucking Kaiju?" Elenor squeaked in complete disbelief. "We have to beat that thing?!" Elenor flipped onto her paws and stomped in a circle in fury. "This is bullshit!" she shrieked, and then looked up at the creature again. It seemed to be searching for something, its head swinging back and forth. It then pulled back and vanished. Elenor didn't think it would give up so easily. It would be back, and by then, she had to find her friends and be ready to fight it. Elenor reached out with the senses given to her by her Runeshard, and after a single terror filled moment, she felt the weak signature of her friends living water.

Elenor tilted her head and listened to the Chorus. Unlike the worlds she had run through before, the Chorus here had an unmistakable pattern threaded through it. There were other portals that went to the other port dimensions, but here in this space, there was something else. It sounded similar to the other portals, but this one was muted somehow. It was as if the sound were coming through a thick wall of stone. She could hear it, but just barely. The portal to the Writ was here, and to reach it, they had to banish all of the Infected before they could open it. This was the way to get the answers they needed.

Elenor galloped down the dune toward her friends. She would have those answers, but she could only do it with their help.

47

"THE END"

Thousands of pounds of sand foiled Mateo's efforts to force himself up. Thia made an uncomfortable groan beneath him.

"Wha' happen'?" she mumbled.

"That rock you made to block the blast fell nine thousand, four hundred and twenty-eight feet, eleven inches and made a fucking tidal wave of sand that we are under," Mateo grumbled.

"I'm sorry, Mateo. I couldn't think of anything else to do."

"No, está bien. I just don't know how to get us out of here safely. I used my Runeshard at the last second to make a tiny bubble in the sand around our heads, but we are still buried. Can you get us out?"

"I don't think I can. My wings are buried about a hundred feet away, and if I try to do anything to pull the sand away, I could pull us into it too." There was a short pause, and he felt her struggling below him unsuccessfully. "Wait, you used your Runeshard?"

"Sí." Mateo shifted, but if he moved much more, he might cave in the space around their heads.

"What's it do?"

"Well, I know what you meant by having a bunch of stuff shoved into your head, now. It works sort of like Elly's, except it lets me control stone of a certain density inside of living bodies."

"So, you can pick me up by my skeleton?"

"Yep, the minerals in bones and our relics are in range, but it has to be alive? I don't get it all yet."

"Then you can't use it to get us out of here?" Thia asked. Mateo shook his head a little, but stopped when

- está bien – It's Okay
- Sí - Yes

sand shifted around him.

"I can feel some of this, but I don't think I can move enough to get us out." Mateo clicked, trying to get a better picture of what was around them, but the sound only traveled about twenty feet before it dissipated, leaving him no idea of how far down they were. "We have to find a way out of here or we're going to run out of air really quick." With their odd metabolisms, they could go hours without air, but they would need to breath eventually.

"I think Elenor will find us pretty soon. I can," Mateo paused as he tried to decide what his senses were telling him, "feel her, I guess? She is here."

"Mateo, do you know how far down we are?" Thia asked, her voice small, more childlike than Mateo had ever heard it. He had never heard fear in Thia's voice before.

"I don't, but it's more than twenty feet. I'm worried if I make a click loud enough to see further, it'll shift the sand."

"We can't wait for Elenor. It could take her hours to dig us out. I can drag my wings to us and then use them to blast our way out."

"Sounds like we might get crushed even more than we are if you do that," Mateo suggested. Thia had begun panting. "¿Eres claustrofóbico?"

"A little. It's not great, but I can deal for now. If we don't get out of here soon, I might have a serious freakout." Thia took a deep breath, then let it out slowly.

Mateo could feel parts of the sand above and around them. He couldn't lift all of it, but they only needed a hole big enough to get them out. He began to construct a set of instructions in his mind. If he could just get enough sand gathered above him, he could use it to push the rest.

 • ¿Eres claustrofóbico? – Are you claustrophobic?

"Hold your breath. We're going to get buried."

"Mateo?" Thia's voice shook a little.

"Trust me?"

Thia took a long breath and then let it out. Then he felt her nodding.

Mateo set his Runeshard into motion. Their bubble collapsed around them, shutting off all air and sound. For a long moment, Mateo almost lost his concentration, but he forced away his fear and waited for the sand to shift. The warm thrum in his chest pulsed, and he knew the living sand had gathered around him. Mateo flexed his paws, the only part of him he could move.

The sand pushed away from them in all directions, opening a gap. Thia let out a gasp and scrambled out from underneath him.

"Alright, get close to me." Mateo rolled over onto his back and pushed all six of his paws towards the ceiling of their small cave, as if he were on some sort of alien bench press at the gym. The ceiling of the cave deformed, pushing out away from them in a cone a few feet wider than the tiny cave. Mateo wanted to make sure that the tunnel was wide enough that even if there was some collapse, it wouldn't immediately bury them.

Once he was sure the sand would hold, he snapped his legs to full extension in one jerky motion. A circle of sand five paces wide pushed up through the rest like an artillery shell fired from a battleship cannon. When the plug of sand blasted from the hole to reveal the sky above, they could see that they had been about a hundred feet below the surface. Mateo flopped, panting, onto his side.

"We have to go before this collapses," Thia urged.

"Yo, solo, necesito," Mateo blew out a breath. Using his Runeshard was way more difficult than he had imagined. Elenor and Thia made it look so easy.

 • Yo, solo, necesito – I, just, need

"Necesito un segundo para respirar."

"You take much more than a second and we're going to get buried again. It's already unstable." Thia shoved her paws against his side, trying to roll him onto his paws.

"Thia, I literally can't. I feel like my chest is going to explode."

"Hey are you guys all right?!" The shouted squeak came with a darkening of the hole as someone leaned over the edge between them and the blinding moon.

"Pull us out! This is gonna collapse soon!" Thia shouted up.

Both Mateo and Thia were lifted out of the hole. A blurring moment later, they shot out of the hole and then settled gently to the ground next to Elenor. Then they were both laying on their backs with Elenor on top of them. Her legs were wrapped around their necks, hugging them with such force that if they needed to breathe, it would have been a problem.

"No more freaking splitting up. I almost got beaten to death searching this damn place!" Elenor sobbed. "And what the hell did you two do? Did you wake up four-legged Godzilla or something?" Elenor's words tumbled over one another, and finally, Mateo shoved her off of him.

"We didn't do anything!" he grumbled. "Those mummy things all smashed themselves together like a corpse transformer and made that thing, and it almost killed us. Twice!" he growled, sitting on his four rear paws, using his front paws to dust himself off.

Elenor noticed Mateo had begun shaking as if trying to contain laugher. "Mateo?"

Mateo spread his legs, crouched down, and shook his entire body like a dog throwing off water. Pounds of lavender sand flew from his fur into a massive cloud

- Necesito un segundo para respirar – I need a second to breath

that floated away. He walked out of the cloud, sneezed, and flattened his massive ears in displeasure.

"I was really trying not to do that. I feel like a dog."

"Creepiest dog monster in the history of the universe," Thia mumbled.

"What's so bad about being like a dog?" Elenor asked.

"Porque," Mateo paused, then frowned. "¿Estás bien?."

"We're avoiding the topic." Thia stared fixedly across the desert.

"Yeah, because there is no fucking way we can kill that thing," Elenor growled.

"We can do it," Mateo affirmed.

A beam of jade light cut through the sky and slammed into the sand several miles away. Clouds of sand were blasted into the air. When the dust settled, there was a pulsing line of molten glass. Even at that distance, the bar of light was bright enough to leave a flashing purple bar swimming in Elenor's vision.

"Did you see that thing? It's the size of a freaking sky scraper. How long do we have before it finds its way down here?" Elenor seemed a bit panicked, and Mateo sat on his four hind paws, making a calming gesture with his forepaws.

"Elly, we've got your back. All the way. We have our own Runeshards under control now, we can help. We can do it."

Elenor took a deep breath, let it out, took another, and then bobbed her head.

"We should find a way to the next floor down. We still have to find the way to get into the Writ," Thia said.

Elenor shook her head. "No, the entrance is here. If you listen to the Chorus, you can hear it." Elenor turned and pointed a claw toward the horizon of the space.

- Porque – Because
- ¿Estás bien? – You're right

"Pero there are no waterfalls here?" Mateo said.

Their attention focused on him. It was harder to tell with Thia, but he could feel her focus.

"Ah, sí! Así que, before the mega lizard up there tried to kill us to death, I saw something on the last floor." Mateo extended one of his tentacles. The spade end of it unfolded, revealing a memory fragment. The tiny marble filled with shining stars winked at them. "I think what I saw is a puzzle."

Elenor held out her paw, and Mateo dropped the fragment into it. It took her only a moment of holding it before she blinked away the vision and then held it out toward Thia. Thia took it carefully in her teeth, and then held it in her mouth.

She didn't seem to be adjusting well to using her wings as her hands. They worked just as well as any human hands, but for some reason, she avoided using them for that. She seemed to prefer to hold things in her mouth whenever fine manipulation was not an absolute necessity. While they all produced minimal saliva and the fragment wouldn't get coated in drool, it was still an oddity to Elenor and Mateo.

Mateo held out one of his tentacles, and Thia spat the memory fragment into the cupped spade. "I don't know what it means. It says, 'Let go thy fearful tether. Thy Spring become the key, the lock, the door.'"

Another commuter train-width beam of green energy slashed down from the sky, smashing into the sand and throwing up a cloud that superheated so quickly that it began to rain drops of molten glass. A massive piece of the sky shattered, dissolving into glittering showers of bubbling sparks the size of watermelons. Bursting through the falling shower of light was the creature. It appeared to have grown even larger, and none of them had any misconceptions that it would be killed in the

- Pero – But
- Ah, sí! Así que – Oh right! So

fall. If they wanted this thing destroyed, they would have to do it themselves.

"I'm not sure how to deal with that thing," Thia squeaked.

Elenor padded forward, leaving stark pawprints in the sand. Her eyes were locked on the creature, glowing like two stars in a sky of shining brown fur. "The same way we beat the other Infected. The tether that ties it to the hammerspace holds the Crown." Elenor held out her right front paw and curled the digits until she was pointing a single one directly at the creature. Her claw moved with unerring precision, exactly following its movement. Elenor's ears twitched, and then twitched again as she tried to adjust them to better hear the Chorus.

"It's there. I can hear the echoes, just not the whole thing."

Thia tilted her head towards the creature, and after a long moment, she shook it. "I can't hear it. There's so much noise coming off of that thing. But I trust you. I'm not sure we can crack open something that big, though."

Elenor took a deep breath. "We have to stop that thing before we can get into the hammerspace with the Writ."

"¿Qué? How do you know that?" Mateo demanded.

"When I came in there was a, thing, like a giant cat robot made of the Purestone we saw coming in." Elenor quickly explained what the creature had told her.

"Pero, what about the rest of the Infected?" Mateo asked with some concern.

"The last of them that I saw went nuts. I think the Otherthing, that's what the cat monster called it, lost control of them. I have a couple trapped in my hammerspace. Well, only one is still Infected," Elenor

- ¿Qué? – What?
- Pero – But

said.

"We can't really fight that thing, can we?" Thia asked.

"Thia, I think fighting things like that is what we were made for," Mateo said.

"Can you surge The Silence for something that big if we can get to its tether?" Thia asked.

"Only one way to find out." Elenor lifted into the air. She held out her paws and made a gesture like she was lifting something into the sky. "There are thousands of little animals living in the sand. That's what's giving off all the," Elenor paused, not sure how to describe what she was feeling, "life energy?" For hundreds of feet all around, drops of water lifted out of the ground and into the air. They rushed towards Elenor, gathering into spheres of water the size of bowling balls. There were dozens of them bobbing in the air around her.

"Amazing!" Thia exclaimed.

"I learned some things about my Runeshard. We can talk more about it later. Mateo, what does yours do?"

"I can control stone that is… alive? Like bones inside of living people."

"Then it is similar to mine. The stone should pick up, well, life, just from living things handling it and living near it. That's how you moved all that sand. The animals living in the sand give it… life?" Elenor explained what she had learned.

"Then I should be able to…" Mateo sat back on his four hind paws and held out his forepaws in front of him. He sat there for a long moment.

"Mine doesn't work like that. I can control gravity in the space between my wings," Thia said

Elenor shrugged. "Do you have any sort of plan?"

"You're asking me?" Thia complained. Mateo and Elenor shrugged simultaneously.

"I mean, I sort of figured an old fart like you would at least have some ideas." Mateo's grin was full of teeth.

His ears folded down, indicating he wasn't really looking at anything, but rather, concentrating.

"Augh! Jerk!" Thia grumbled. Her wings unfolded behind her in their leathery, draconic form, and she lifted from the ground. With a grunt, Mateo lifted his front paws and the sand rumbled with ominous foreshadowing. Pushing their way up from the sand, spheres of lavender stone began to orbit Mateo.

"I can feel, something. Like they are leaking something," Mateo mumbled. Elenor opened her mouth, but then he kept speaking. "I wonder if I…" He grasped the digits of his paws. He couldn't make a fist like he had when he was human, but the stone orbs began to give off a pulsing, glittering shimmer of soft white light. "Puta madre, I did it."

"What did you do?" Elenor peered at the stones. She didn't understand why her eyes worked quite the way they did. The eyes on her back let her see anomalies in reality, viewing places where the Chorus had been forcefully altered, what she thought of as seeing magic. That always seemed redundant once she was able to listen to the Chorus. Her normal eyes, she had realized, could cycle through various parts of the light spectrum, both visible and invisible.

Elenor had asked Helen if all she was seeing was light, why did she see rainbows around Helen and other callers. Helen had explained that their Writbands had given them the power to interact with reality directly. That power was what made their bodies give off various wavelengths of invisible light. She wasn't sure why it looked like a rainbow to Elenor. What Elenor saw around the spheres was not the same as the rainbow around a caller, but it had many similarities.

"The energy was leaking out. I was just trying to make it stop leaking out so I," Mateo paused, trying to figure out the words, "twisted it? I don't know how to

• Puta madre – Holy shit

explain. It won't last forever. It's still leaking out, just a lot slower."

"This is fascinating, and I truly mean that, but we might want to pay attention to raging murder beast flopping around over there?!" Thia hissed the last part of the sentence through gritted teeth.

"Might be a good idea not to be on a clock? Because when the energy runs out of the stuff we are controlling, we can't control it anymore." Elenor coached patience.

Thia hissed in frustration. She pointed the tip of her tail towards the monster. "Hope you two can study on the fly, because it spotted us. Move!"

Elenor and Mateo whipped their heads around to lock onto the Infected. It had opened its mouth and an enormous sphere of poisonous light was gathering there. Thia zipped away into the air, and Elenor followed a moment later. She turned right where Thia had flown left, making it impossible for the creature to aim at them both.

It took Mateo a moment longer to lift into the air and begin to run across the sky. He wasn't as fast as Elenor and Thia, making him the target for the creature's attack. He thought for a single uncharitable moment that they had abandoned him. Then he saw a brown blur shooting towards the creature from his right.

Elenor made a gesture, and the orbs of shimmering water spun together in front of her until the orb was the size of a boulder. Then it shot forward, the speed so great that it was only a blur. With a thundercrack, the glittering sphere smashed into the side of the creature's head.

The creature's head turned sharply, almost to the point that Mateo would have thought the neck had been broken. The blast of light shot off into the distance, ripping a burning line of seared glass across the desert.

The Infected reacted more quickly than Mateo thought possible. A redwood tree-thick foreleg whipped up, bashing Elenor out of the sky. With his lightwebs out, he was relieved to see that there was no discharge from the blow like there had been with the other infected. Still concerned, as the impact alone might have been enough to injure, he ran towards the cloud of sand rising from where Elenor had been driven to the ground. "Elly!"

There was a grit of teeth in the squeaky shout that rose from the cloud. "I'll be fine in a second. Help Thia!" He heard Elenor cough, but did his best to ignore his worries. This was a fight for their lives. They were going to get hurt.

As he ran towards the creature, he saw Thia lifting into the air with something that terrified him. She stood atop a sphere of stone the approximate dimensions of a dump truck. He could feel the pull of the stone's gravity. It was clearly the gravitationally compressed mass she had created to block the Infected's attack. If she dropped that thing from any height more than a foot, it would, like as not, create the same sort of tidal wave of sand it had before, albeit a less violent one. The creature was stomping towards Elenor, and Mateo wasn't sure what to do. He realized he had to trust her. She said she would be fine, and she would. He galloped towards Thia at speed.

"What are you doing with that?" he shouted as he got closer to her.

"I'm going to use it as a weapon, unless you have a better way of hurting that thing!" Thia shouted back.

Mateo paused, watching her rise higher into the air. He wasn't sure what he could do. He never felt like he was creative, except when he was in front of his drawing table. Then he realized he had everything he needed. It was all right there on that table.

He hadn't come up with any heroes that had power to move the earth yet, but he knew the tricks of so many. Tricks that lived in the imagination of that kid from so long ago who didn't want to join a gang. Sitting in the palace of comic book stacks that littered his room had filled him with memories of what his heroes had done with powers like these. He wondered at Elenor, though. Where was she getting her inspiration? She seemed to have taken to her power over living water as if she had been born to it. She had admitted that she hadn't used it almost at all, even though she had access to it for two years. How was she so good at manipulating it?

He shook himself to bring himself back to the moment, and concentrated on the stone he was holding domain over. The dozen stones the size of basketballs had begun to float in a swirling pattern around him like particles orbiting a nucleus. A boom brought his sight ears up twitching towards the monster as the resonating sound outlined the landscape. Thia had smashed the mass-heavy sphere into the spine of the creature, pinning it to the ground. To his immediate dismay, the creature's massive legs flexed, and though the strain was clear, it lifted itself against the mass of the stone sphere.

Mateo concentrated on his spheres and the stone flattened under his will, until each sphere was a disk, slightly thicker in the middle and thinned towards the edge. The edge of each disk began to gleam with keen polish. He set them orbiting him and then ran towards the fight.

The moment Mateo was close enough Thia shot towards him. She kept her voice down. "Help Elenor keep this thing off of me. I don't think it can dislodge that sphere as deep as I have driven it. It can lift it, but just barely, and if it rolls over, it will have to tear itself free before it will be able to move at all. I can tear it open, but I'm not practiced enough yet to do it fast! Buy me time!"

"¡Va!"

Mateo waved the stone blades forward, and they

• ¡Va! – Alright!

began to spin in elliptical arcs until they were a blurring blender of blades moving at speeds that caused air to churn and run off from them. The spinning blades slammed into front right leg of the creature and began to tear it apart. It stumbled, but still managed to catch itself with more speed than it had produced before its head whipped around. It released a blast of light far less powerful than the ones it had emitted before. Mateo had no chance to dodge, but before the beam of light smashed him from the air, a blob of water appeared before him as if by teleportation. The beam exploded into a kaleidoscope of light, splitting around the blob of water.

"Keep up!" Elenor squeaked with bizarre enthusiasm as she shot past him, collecting her sphere of water. Was she having fun? It seemed so out of place to Mateo that it took him a moment to process it. She had been so fearful when they had first met. When had she broken past that wall? He shook off the mental dissonance and decided he would just be happy that she had.

"¡Listo!" He gestured with a paw, and half of the stone-bladed discs that were shearing away the leg of the creature pulled away. He directed them towards the creature's other foreleg and then galloped out of the way of another blast of light.

He noticed Thia's wings dancing around the creature's head in whirling circular arcs. Bubbling violet light fizzed off of her wings, dissipating into the air almost as fast as it fell away.

Thia watched as Mateo and Elenor harassed the creature. For a long moment, she had been concerned that Mateo wasn't ready for something this huge. He

---

* ¡Listo! – Got it!

had hesitated and was almost blasted by the creature. Then Elenor had said something to him and he seemed to pull himself together. She would have to ask them later what Elenor had said.

Thia refocused herself. She had nearly reached the height necessary to start her plan. What she was about to do was dangerous. It would, without a doubt, kill her if she was still human. Even as a Bearer, she wasn't sure she'd survive. Slamming into the ground at terminal velocity might or might not be absorbed by her relic. Still, if she stood still on the ground, the Infected would focus on her, and she could not do what she needed to with her Runeshard without concentration.

The world fell away as her wings shot towards the Infected. She dropped into freefall. This was the limitation of her Runeshard. She could only control the gravity in the area between her wings. If she used it as a weapon, she could not use it to keep her aloft. And so, she fell. She picked up speed as she focused all of her will on generating the most powerful and compact gravitic anomaly she could manage.

Something inside of the creature drew her attention. It was as if a light bulb had been lit inside of the Infected's torso. She shivered as all of the heads acting as the creature's eyes began to scream in an overlapping babble of jagged insanity. A bubble of venomous energy blasted into existence around the creature. It shoved away all of their attacks, and even the sphere of super-compressed stone was launched from the creature's back. The power of that dome shoved back against her wings, throwing off her working as they spun away from the creature. She called them back with all haste, but before they reached her, the dome of sickly energy expanded.

To double its size.

The power pushed against Thia's senses as if it were a physical thing being pressed into her brain.

Triple.

The dome filled a huge amount of the space, engulfing miles worth of sand. Thia realized that it was going to explode and take everything with it. She grunted with effort, and with a thought, a gravitic ring appeared between her wings as she fell towards the ground.

She had no time to spare. In the glare of the impossible amount of power, she could see Elenor and Mateo. They had huddled together behind shields formed from the elements controlled by their Runeshards.

Thia blasted through the ring, being ejected with a boom of sound as she reached speeds that made sound seem sluggish. As fast as she was moving, her wings shot past her in a streak to arrive just behind the others' position. A bubble of warped gravity caught her and decelerated her to land lightly behind them. She gestured her wings forward and they slammed together behind Elenor's and Mateo's constructs, acting as a third shield. The supermassive stone she had created earlier would have worked better, but there was no time.

The bubble exploded.

The sound was not sound. It was a physical force that slammed into their shields and deafened all three of them. Mateo, especially, couched down, and though his sight ears seemed fine, bubbling orange blood trickled from the smaller pair of sound ears he used for simple hearing.

Then the true blast wave hit. All three Bearers tumbled into one another as their shields were pushed back. Each knew without any doubt that they could not bother with attempting to control the tumble of their bodies. The force of the explosion was so massive that if they lost focus for one second, their shields would shatter and they would be obliterated.

Then the second explosion came. They tumbled across the ground and the shield of water Elenor was holding showed dozens of cracks. Thia had no idea what to do, but then she saw Elenor catch herself, digging her claws into the sand. She still slid, but she had gained her feet.

Thia and Mateo stared in abject terror as Elenor's power swelled against the assault of the Infected. Water began to flow up from the desert in huge torrents, as if the ocean had been pulled from the sand. The cracks in the water shield bled away until it was one homogenous plane. From the knowledge that had been forced into their minds, they knew one day they would have power like this, but not this day. Living water gathered into hundreds of thousands of spheres in their around her, like rain suspended in flight.

Elenor took a single step forward.

The burning light of the Infected bent around her shield as she moved ahead against the tide of power.

Another step.

The force fell away from Thia and Mateo, letting them stand as the wave of force flowed around them, splitting against the shield of water.

"No Further!" Elenor's roar filled the world with such volume that it overpowered even the thunderous roar of the Infected's explosive power. The entire world paused at that roar, and even the monster, more powerful than all the Callers the world had ever known, could not stand against the power of the Bearer.

Elenor stared at certain blinding death as raw, reality warping power pulsed from the Infected monster. Time and again, they had attacked Elenor and her friends. It had Infected other humans and then forced them along through methods so noxious in their efficiency that Elenor felt sick just thinking about it. Now it was going to kill them to prepare the way for it to kill and devour everything on their planet. Elenor could feel the weakening flicker of the Bearer's magic inside of her chest and knew she couldn't hold the shield any longer.

What more could she do? She could feel her limits as her power pushed back against the monster. Tumbling behind her shield from the sheer force of the repetitive blasts coming from the Infected, Elenor's hope dwindled until there was nothing left but the knowledge that she was not enough. Mateo and Thia were cowering behind her as they tried to hold back the tide.

Let go thy fearful tether.

The words of the puzzle echoed inside of her head. It was the thing she had been struggling against since the power had bloomed in her chest and knowledge spread in her mind. Why had she been given such absolute power? She had known from the first just how much power her Runeshard had given her, even when she had not known what it was. It was too much for any one person to have. Why her?

She had promised herself she wasn't going to be afraid of her powers anymore. She would help people with it. It would be good. Now she realized that even that affirmation was not quite the right one.

Let go thy fearful tether.

She had been chosen because she was afraid. Because she didn't think anyone should have the kind of power she had been handed. But in the face of the Otherthing's puppet, she knew that without power like this, everything she loved would be taken from her. Their world would wink from existence as if it had never been. There would be no one left.

Let go thy fearful tether.

She needed her fear to make her think well before using her Runeshard. She needed it for what that fear could become. Respect.

The tether snapped.

Potential burst.

"No Further!"

The admonition that she had used earlier came back to her, and she let it out in a roar to shatter the world. With her mind, she constructed instructions for her Runeshard and the magic swirling inside of her surged out in torrents that she thought might burn her alive. It reached into the land, touching the hundreds of thousands of small animals burrowing below the lilac sand. Just as she had before, she pulled water from all of the living things beneath the sand, but this time, she did not restrain the power. It spread for miles around her, pulling bits of living water from every single creature until a torrent as wide as a city block burst from the sand, streaming towards Elenor.

Elenor made her shield larger, giving them more breathing room. Mateo's stone shield separated back into six spheres, drifting back to orbit around him. Thia's wings followed, and then the sounds went away as Thia clapped her wings, activating her Striker. She called the Mender's Lament, refreshing them all. The tune changed and melted away into the Requiem of Shattered Resonance. Despite the fact that it could not overpower what the Infected was doing, it did push back the ear destroying sound.

Thia's sensory coils stilled in a stare as she watched Elenor collect enough water to fill a small lake. Her body tremored as she took in the sheer universe-shattering power that Elenor held. Then she focused past Elenor.

"It's going to tear apart the entire hammerspace!" Thia snarled.

"No, it isn't." Elenor held up a paw. At the gesture, the flood of living water shaped itself into a sphere of such utter mass that it pressed against Thia's gravitational senses. "We have to let go of the fear of using our Runeshards and master their power. Respect, not fear!" She made a wide, arcing gesture. A portion of the water streamed away from the sphere, shaping itself into a scythe-like half-moon, tapering to edges that shined with menace.

"Because this thing is just a puppet compared to what is coming, and if we are going to beat that, we have to be better! We can't be afraid of ourselves!"

Elenor whipped her paw forward and the blade shot away in a blur. They couldn't see where it landed, but a split second later, the blasts of nauseating light cut off and a rumbling boom sounded.

"Can you do it?" Elenor squeaked. Her shield flowed into a stream, rejoining the sphere of water that she had gathered, and then she streaked away back towards the sky scraper-sized Infected.

Thia and Mateo turned to each other. Neither of them wanted to admit just how much getting access to their Runeshards had terrified them. After seeing what Elenor could do, they had been apprehensive at best about gaining access to that kind of power. Until this moment, they had simply ignored the implications, using the current situation as their armor against the truth. Now they were forced to consider the truth that Elenor had been living with since her transformation. She had done it all on her own. If they were not careful, it would be so very easy to become the monsters that people would judge them to be.

"She needs our help," Mateo said.

"We could kill everyone, everything we care about," Thia worried.

Mateo shook himself. "We could." He bobbed his head in acknowledgement. Thia opened her mouth, but Mateo went on. "But, if we don't do this, we could be doing the same thing. I would rather know."

"Know what?"

"That my best wasn't enough. If I don't try, that's the same as letting it happen. I'd rather know my best wasn't enough than that I didn't try at all."

Mateo turned his sight ears towards the Infected and then the rest of his long body followed. He lifted into the air and then ran across the sky. Streams of sand poured up from the desert, gathering around Mateo until he was surrounded by a dozen stone spheres, then fifty, then hundreds. It was clear he had found his inspiration in what Elenor had said.

Thia watched him go only for a moment before she made her own decision. She wasn't sure she could overcome her fear like that. It was so much for one person to shoulder. Concentrating on her Runeshard, she floated into the air, her wings mutating into what she thought of as their nightmare shape, dozens of rough relic stone blades suspended in dripping violet light.

Maybe she couldn't do what they had done, but one thing she did know is that she would never leave her friends to fight something like this without her help.

The fight between the Infected and Elenor was surrounded by a churning cloud of violet dust. One of the creature's legs had been nearly sheared off, but the gap was closing up in a cascade of bubbling green light.

As Thia approached, Mateo joined the fight. Dozens of spheres of pulsing stone smashed into and through the creature's hind legs. Bodies and the emerald energy conduits holding them together were torn to pieces, and the creature stumbled. It swung a massive foreleg and Mateo was forced to recall his spheres to defend himself. Even then, he and his mass of stone spheres were driven across the sky like a boulder sized bullet.

Thia took his place. She ceased surging the Requiem of Shattered Resonance. In a single motion, she beat her wings down, throwing her into the sky and activating her Striker once again. She called the Dragon's Heartsong. Diving towards the creature, she inhaled all of the breath she could, expanding her chest. Ethereal azure light filled the spaces between the banded scales on her chest.

She shot between the creature's fore and hind legs, turning her body on its side, the leg-thick shaft of blinding fire bursting from her jaws. It sliced through one of its hind legs like a shark through calm seas. Her jaws snapped shut in startled horror when she saw the Infected's stomach descending towards her at dreadful speed.

She dove. Shoving her wings in front of her, a gravitic anomaly formed between them. It shot her forward in a boom of shattering sound. There was no time to correct, and she smashed into the sand. She tucked her body into a ball, tumbling across the sand, Even her relic could not fully absorb the impact, and she felt something break inside of her. She was miles away when her body finally ground to a halt in a trench of disturbed sand.

The boom of the Infected falling onto its side caught up with her a moment later. Thia tried to push herself to her feet, but blood filled her maw and she coughed the frothing purple stuff onto the sand, which drank it greedily. The emerald light washing across her face caused her to peel her eyes open.

The Infected was on its side, maw agape as a sphere of energy gathered between its jaws. Its aim was a direct path to Thia. And then Elenor was there, between her and the Infected, her water gathered into a pyramid shape with the point towards the Infected. The pyramid was the rough size of a city bus, and it blasted away toward that orb of energy with all the power of a falling meteor.

It smashed through the orb and did not stop until the Infected's head exploded from the force of the impact. Desiccated bodies rained from the sky, tumbling to the ground around the body of the massive Infected in a torrent of putrid green sparks.

Thia looked up to see Elenor crouching over her.

"You alright?" Elenor trilled.

"I will be."

Mateo pushed himself out of the small crater his body had dug into the sand just in time to see the Infected's head explode. He gaped as the bodies rained down, but he could tell that wasn't going to be enough to stop it. The creature seemed stunned, but it had not fallen. Focusing on his Runeshard, Mateo floated into the air again and pushed himself towards the creature.

The hundreds of orbs of living stone around him flowed together until they formed a spear two hundred feet tall and twenty feet wide. It tapered to a wicked point, and Mateo gained speed. Stones continued to pour themselves into the construct until it had a massive conical shape. He came within a hundred yards of the infected before he drew to a stop. He lifted his forepaws, standing on both rear sets of hind paws, suspended only by his power. He took a pose as if he were holding up the gargantuan stone shape. Then he snapped the entire upper third of his body forward, every muscle straining with the effort of launching the weapon.

The cone of stone blasted forward, shattering the air with a boom of sound. By the time it hit the Infected, it was traveling at the speed of a railgun bullet. It smashed into the side of the Infected with an earth-shattering roar. The beast was knocked from its remaining three paws onto its side. When it struck the ground, a thundering boom echoed through the world.

Thia pushed herself to her paws, watching in awe as Mateo smashed the Infected to the ground.

"Thia you have to go help him! I need to call The Silence!"

Thia coughed up another gout of violet blood. Whatever had been damaged inside of her wasn't healing properly on its own.

"I, can't, something, broken," she gasped out.

Elenor looked back at her, her eyes widening in alarm. "Thia?" Elenor scrambled back towards her, her Striker held up as if to call a Surge. She skidded to a halt in front of Thia.

Thia shook her head. "Already, used, Lament."

Elenor stood frozen, watching Thia.

"Go!" Thia hissed. "There is…" She vomited another small blob of purple blood.

"Shut up!" Elenor snarled. She smashed her Striker against her spines and began to call The Silence. She closed her eyes, gritted her teeth, and then she trusted her mind to do what any Caller's mind should be able to. Call a Surge without really paying attention. Helen had told her that after some time, she would reach that point, but she had never been able to do it. Now there was no other way. She let go of her focus on the playing of the Striker and held herself in absolute stillness. The next note played, then the next, and then the next.

Carefully, Elenor focused on her Runeshard. She touched Thia's side and felt the flow of the water

through her body. She traced the blood until she found
the broken place next to Thia's heart. Her heart did not
beat, which was not abnormal. Their systems did not
work like a human's. When they were injured, it
seemed there was some instinctual reaction that caused
their hearts to beat as slowly as possible to keep from
causing more damage through blood loss.

Something had slammed her insides together, broken
one of the arteries around her heart, and punched a hole
into her trachea. Elenor slowly, carefully constructed
instructions for her Runeshard on how to shape the
water in Thia's body to hold together her insides so her
body could heal properly.

"Look out!" Thia shouted, bubbling violet blood
running down her muzzle.

Elenor didn't move. Water flowed, and a wall of it
formed between them and the Infected. A massive
boulder smashed into wall and shattered. Then The
Silence took hold and the entire world faded away to a
blind white world.

"Why hasn't it done that thing with the bubble
again?" Thia asked.

"If you watch the energy moving through it, it needs
its whole body in one piece to do that."

The Silence continued to play, and Mateo lifted into
the air carried by his Runeshard. "Do whatever you
have to do. It's struggling damn hard to get off that
spike!"

"Blow the spike apart to rip it open. I need to see
inside of it," Elenor said when Mateo settled down next
to them.

Elenor lifted into the air and shot off towards the
Infected.

"¿Estás bien?" Mateo whispered.

Thia bobbed her head. "I think I hit the ground
around twice the speed of sound."

• ¿Estás bien? – Are you all right?

Mateo cringed. He saw Elenor wave and did as she asked. The enormous cone of stone ripped apart, tearing its way through the Infected and leaving an enormous hole in the creature. It began to move, but the sound of The Silence changed. A tree trunk-sized tether of energy emerged from the air above the creature, then traced itself back to the monster. Elenor floated away as it threw up its forelegs at Elenor in desperation.

With a sudden movement, the fore leg of the creature detached, flying towards Elenor. It disintegrated into a wave of Infected bodies that crashed over her.

"¡Carajo!" Mateo yelled. He flew towards the conflict, but before he could make it even a hundred yards, water streamed into the pile of writhing bodies. Arcs of water formed into blades, slashing bodies and smashing flows of Infected energy.

Elenor lifted into the air, every hair on her body bristling, her spines vibrating with menace. Her body tilted in the air until she was almost vertical, and she held one of her front paws over her head. Living water streamed up from below, swirling into a helical twist of dozens of glowing rings. It grew until each of the rings mutated into spinning blades. She threw her hand forward, and the blades blasted away in a roar of wind, each the size of a Boeing 747's wing.

The blades cleaved away each of the massive creature's limbs like a scalpel through skin. It slammed back to the ground. Then Thia appeared above the creature. In their inattention, she had found time to retrieve the stone she had created earlier and now rode atop it.

"Cut it!" she trilled at the top of her lungs.

Mateo waved a paw as Elenor's blades harried the creature to make sure it did not pull itself back together. The stone under his control gathered, and with a crackling sound, it solidified into a blade of stone fifty

* ¡Carajo! – Damn it!

feet wide, glittering sharp as shattered glass. He launched the blade, and it crashed into the Tether, slicing through it with so little resistance that the blade cut a swath through what remained of the creature before grinding to a stop in the sand beyond.

The crown that emerged was a wide band of emerald crystal, twenty-five feet tall and hundreds of feet in diameter. Unlike the others that she had seen, this crown did not have spikes piercing the creature. Instead, thousands of wires arched down, piercing into the body in uniform lines along the limbs, down the spine, and over the tail. All parts were connected. It was truly like a puppet master's controller.

Thia did not waste a single split second. As soon as the crown appeared, a ring of purple light appeared between the supermassive sphere of stone.

Mateo's sight ears leaned away from each other in expression equivalent to widened eyes. His normal ears laid down in pure astonishment. "This is the part where we run," Mateo squeaked, then turned and bolted away from the creature. He and Elenor streaked across the sky, shattering the sound barrier in their desperation to escape.

The stone sphere hit the gravitic anomaly and then surged forward as a ball fired from a canon. Thia was right behind the orb. Her wings jerked to face toward the hole in the ceiling of the world, and she passed through them at the same moment the sphere struck the vast jade crown. The explosion of the Infected construct washed away the world.

48
"DOOR, LOCK, AND KEY"

"The city of Aleppo has suffered a massive localized earthquake. Estimates indicate a non-terrestrial source, as the area was limited to only a few miles around the city. GSN Monitors indicate that the earthquake was roughly equivalent to a nine point nine," the news reporter, unseen on a screen that showed the destruction at Aleppo, announced in grave tones. Hundreds of pillars of smoke rose from the city as hundreds of fires had broken out, but that was the smallest part of the absolute destruction the earthquake had wrought. The demolition was so thorough that the city may as well have been razed to the ground.

"Viewer discretion is advised as the following images are graphic." Footage from a number of drones followed. It was clear that there were almost no survivors. Bloodied limbs emerged from the debris as if the dead were begging for rescue. Marissa and Damien stood in the Hive, staring in abject horror at the various projections of the swarm as dozens of news networks reported the earthquake.

"'Oly shite, did we do 'his?" Damien whispered.

"Not we. Only gods could do something like this, Damien."

"Dey aren' gods," Damien replied.

"Are you sure?" Marissa whispered.

Damien stared at the projections and shook his head. "Not anymore."

The doors to the Hive melted, and Helen stepped inside. If her face was a thunderstorm, it would have been the apocalypse. "What did they do?!" she roared, but Marissa could see that Helen was pale and sweating.

"Helen, what's wrong?" Marissa's apprehension was palpable. She had known Helen for over twenty years and had never seen the woman pale with panic.

Helen pulled down the collar of her sweater to reveal the top of her chest. There was nothing but milk white skin between her breasts. "My Writband is gone."

Elenor spit out lavender sand and shifted her body. She was clearly buried in the sand, but not enough to actually need to be pulled free. She flexed all four legs and pushed herself up. There was enough sand that she was certain that had she still been human, she couldn't have lifted it.

Now, it was no trouble at all. She shook herself, throwing a cloud of sand out of her brown fur, leaving behind a powdery lilac coating that made her appear to be a frosted grape donut monster. A moment later, the sand to her right exploded away from Mateo as he shoved himself up and out of it. He shook himself, but oddly, all of the sand fell out of his fur as if he were made of Teflon. As if it had no grip on him. They exchanged a look.

"Thia!" they both shrilled at the same time. They both looked around, but no further eruptions from the sand showed her location.

"Up here!" Thia shouted down from the sky as she floated towards the ground. Her scales rippled as she shook herself in relief.

"How come you didn't get blasted out of the air?" Mateo asked.

"I shot up into the next hammerspace up. The blast singed my scales a little, but I'm fine. You don't want to go back over there… you'll smell it soon."

"Already can." Mateo stuck out his bright orange tongue in a disgusted expression, his sight ears folded down the back of his head as if he were squeezing his eyes closed.

"We have to go. There isn't any time to screw around now." Thia's forked purple tongue snaked over her teeth nervously and she spun in a slow circle. "Do you know where we have to go?" she asked, and then finished her spin to look at Elenor.

Elenor tilted her head and listened closely to the Chorus. She closed her eyes, and her body began a gentle swaying as if following a long passage of looping music.

"It's here," she whispered. With deliberate care, Elenor began to shuffle her paws to turn her body. Finally, she stopped. She lifted her tail and pointed off in the direction opposite the sinking sun.

"Considering the position of the sun, that's east. At least we don't have to pass that mess we made," Thia said. Each of the Bearers lifted into the air and orientated themselves in the direction Elenor had indicated.

"How far?" Mateo asked.

"Far. It's faint. I would guess a hundred miles if that wasn't impossible," Elenor said.

"It's very possible. This is a pocket dimension. This desert could theoretically be the size of the earth, or bigger," Thia informed. They fled the setting sun, picking up speed in an attempt to reach the port dimension as quickly as possible. Less than ten minutes later, they came upon a new, impossible sight.

Drifting to the desert floor, they landed in front of yet another marvel beyond the human imagination. All three of them gawked, maws agape, as the vista before them filled their hearts and minds with wonder. Extending into the distance to the left and right, a collection of mountainous blocks rose thousands of feet

into the sky. The blocks were made of a pearly white
stone that appeared to be polished to a mirror shine.
The polishing was the verisimilar result of the endless
falls of lavender sand that flowed over the edge of the
blocks in a perfect silica-based facsimile of a waterfall.

The three of them sat and watched in rapt attention
as the sandfall made almost no sound. A gentle
susurrus of moving air was all they could hear as
hundreds of millions of pounds of sand crashed into the
desert floor with each passing moment. Yet there was
no buildup of sand at the base of the waterfall, even
though the cloud of dust thrown up by the falling grains
made it clear that they were striking something at the
base.

In the center of the sandfall was a Purestone tube at
least five hundred feet across. At first, they thought it
was a tunnel. Thia called the Dawn Song and sent a
sphere of burning light into it. Within a hundred feet,
they found that the sandfall was rushing by at the back
of the tube.

"Are we supposed to walk through?" Mateo
wondered.

"Maybe you could keep the sand off of us, but if there
is just a giant white wall at the back," Thia started.

"It's not alive. The sand here doesn't have any life in
it. I can use what I have to…" Mateo trailed off as he
looked at the gargantuan tube of stone.

"What is it?" Elenor asked.

"La foto from up above." Mateo's voice was distant
as he tried to decipher the meaning of what he had seen.
His ears twitched left to Elenor. "The key." Then his
ears swung towards Thia. "The door."

"What?" Thia asked.

"You two both saw my memory. Look at how we are
sitting. Just like the image,." Mateo pointed his tail at
Elenor, then himself, and then at Thia. "The key, the

 • La foto – That picture

lock, the door."

"But what does that mean?" Thia wondered.

Mateo shrugged. "I'unno, I just noticed that we are lined up just like what we saw up there." He pointed up to the broken sky with the tip of his leaf spade tail. "Could something have known we would do this?"

"Seeing the future is very complicated, but it can be done sometimes. It all depends on what you are trying to see. My mother says that it can drive people mad," Thia warned.

"It's about our Runeshards somehow?" Elly asked.

"I think so, but I'm not sure what we are supposed to do," Thia replied.

"In the picture, there is a big swirling vortex the tunnel is going into. There isn't anything like that here," Mateo said.

"There was also a star portal in that picture, not sand," Thia pointed out.

"Right, but we have to open those portals once we make them." Elenor posed and then tapped her Striker against the spines on her shoulders. She tilted her head, listening to the Chorus, then began to play the Keymaster's March. Two full repetitions of the melody passed and there was no reaction. Elenor ceased her Surge and stared.

"No, remember what the message said. 'Let go thy fearful tether.' You figured that out, Elly. That it was about using our Runeshards, and so is this," Mateo affirmed.

"Okay, if I am the door, then I have to go first. You can't have a lock to put a key into without having a door first." Thia tilted her head up to the huge tunnel, her sensory coils writhing into a new position atop her head. As she moved them, the new position caused the coils moved to the bottom of the nest to go dormant. Those on top came active, changing how she saw the world.

Listening to the Chorus was one way to understand the shape of reality around them. However, there were others, and her sensory coils gave her one more. Surges changed the flow of reality, worked with it to bring about effects that people thought of as magic. But magic was not a force of its own, it was simply a word that people used when they did not understand how something worked. Thia's perceptions allowed her to understand things about the world in ways she had never been able to in the past, and without it, she would have never seen the message circling the Purestone tunnel. "Can you two see that?"

Elenor seemed to understand without further prompting, turning around and sitting down. She closed her eyes, opening the gorgon eyes on her back. She blinked them a little as their odd double cruciform pupils adjusted to the light. They went wide. "Whoa, there is more Nyceric around the tunnel,"

Mateo made a loud clicking sound, drawing both Elenor and Thia's attention.

"What was that?" Elenor asked.

"Es..." Mateo twisted his sight ears away, leaning them in a way that somehow communicated sheepishness. "I learned how to do it a few weeks ago. The pulse of sound makes it easier to see without my light webs. I'm learning more about how my sight ears work. They don't just pick up all the sounds if I don't want them to."

"That's not just sound," Thia said. "That click has a low power electromagnetic pulse attached to it." Thia considered it for a moment. "You haven't had trouble seeing yet, even when we were moving faster than sound. That's how you are doing it, even without your light webs out. Your ears have three sensory organs attached, not just two."

"Interesting as that is, did you see a message?" Elenor

• Es - Its

asked.

"Sure did. Memory Fragments?" Mateo asked. Thia and Elenor both bobbed their heads.

A moment later, they were all holding memory fragments. Thia held her wings, which had reverted to their childlike cloud form. They had shrunk to the size of a pair of large cartoonish hands. Elenor and Mateo deposited their newly made fragments onto the balloon-like swirling cloud acting as the palm of the wing. The smooth puffy feathers curled like fingers around the fragments.

The violet glow of Thia's sensory coils dimmed almost to full dormancy, indicating she had closed her eyes. As she viewed each fragment, her muzzle scrunched in further dismay. "I don't understand. We should be able to see them all, but these all show different parts of one message." Thia's sensory coils brightened to show she had opened her eyes. Mateo and Elenor exchanged a glance, but then just waited.

"They read," Thia's long serpentine tail curved around to point at herself, "Part the curtain of thy reality," she swung her tail to point towards Mateo, "and anchor thy world in purest stone." Her tail moved to Elenor. "Pour life into the path of stars and seek thy goal beyond thy boundaries."

"That, doesn't mean anything?" Mateo speculated, but Thia's sensory coils stilled in contemplation.

"No, it does, but probably not to either of you. You're both so young, and there is so much you have to learn. Even I haven't had time to confirm everything my mother taught me. What I do know is that what science thinks of as laws are not as set in stone as they seem to think they are."

"What does that have to do with this?" Elenor asked.

"One of the parts of the Keymaster's March and the Ayre of the Anchored Way is that they use a relatively low-powered gravitic anomaly to force open spaces between the threads of the fabric of reality."

Thia padded forward, putting herself between them and the sandfall. "I don't know how I'm supposed to do this," Thia said shakily. "What if…" Thia shook her head. Elenor had been right. They were just people, and it wasn't fair to ask them to take so much responsibility. She felt Elenor's paw on her back, between her shoulders.

"Didn't you tell me I got picked for a reason?" Elenor asked.

"But I didn't get picked," Thia said. "We triggered my transformation."

"Sure we did, but we definitely didn't give you the power of your Runeshard. You were picked just like we were. You're just as worthy as any of us," Elenor assured.

"After a hundred years of training, I think that's an understatement." Mateo said. "We trust you. You're the best one for this."

Thia took a deep breath and her sensory coils shifted with nervous energy. "I'm just guessing, you both know that, right?"

"We know. Just do your best, because that's all we're going to be doing," Elenor urged.

"Alright, here goes nothing." Thia's wings swung wide and shot along the huge tunnel until they disappeared into the falling sand.

"Hold your breath, because if I screw this up, we probably aren't going to have time to notice we're dead," Thia said.

A bright lavender glow filled the tunnel. The sphere of light grew until it became a ring with a void in the center so deep that it seemed to draw in the light of the ring surrounding it.

"Here it comes," Thia said. In the blink of an eye, the ring of purple light expanded to twice its size.

The pull of gravity became tremendous, pulling all three of the Bearers slowly towards the entrance to the tunnel. Streams of violet sand streamed up from the desert floor and into the void from the sandfall. They dug their claws into the sand, slowing their forward momentum but not stopping it.

"Thia!" Mateo shouted.

"Just hang on. It'll stabilize in a second! I can feel it!"

The ring grew to triple its size. The streams of sand turned into torrents that flowed into a vortex pattern swirling around the central node of absolute emptiness. It was not simply black, it was something much deeper.

The vortex exploded to ten times its size, capable of consuming the entire tunnel twice over. It appeared just as Mateo had seen it in the image. Just as Thia had said the pull tapered off, and Thia let out a breath. "Okay, it's stable. Any idea what to do now?"

The grinding sound of turning stone rumbled through the ground around them, and they all stared as the tunnel began to spin. "Are you," Elenor started, but Thia shook her head.

"Anchor your world in purest stone," Mateo said, and his tail waved in a near perfect circle, symbolically tracing the mouth of the tunnel. "It's Purestone. It isn't alive, but maybe I could…" Mateo held up one of his front paws. He spread the toes of the paw and two dozen spheres of stone shot forward. His sight ears folded back, closing off his sight so he could bend his full concentration onto what he was doing. The spheres burst apart into a stream of sand that expanded until it was a perfect circle the same size as the opening of the tunnel.

Mateo grunted, his paw flattening out and his body flexing as if he were pushing against a wall. Finally, he blew out a breath and relaxed.

"I guess I can't just shove it into place, but that has to be it, right? The Purestone has to be the lock," Mateo said.

"No, no. The Purestone isn't the lock. Your Runeshard is the lock," Elenor said. "I think you need to make the missing Purestone."

"¡¿Qué?! How am I supposed to do that? ¡Estás loca!" Mateo spat in exasperation.

"She's not crazy, well, not that kind of crazy. I think it's like you said. Door, lock, key." Thia pointed with her tail at herself, Mateo, and Elenor in order.

"Okay, okay. Let me..."

Mateo drew back the ring of sand with a mental command and formed it back into spheres of stone floating around him. He floated into the air and drew closer to the slowly rotating tunnel of Purestone. He put his paw against the smooth, crystalline surface of golden stone. The stone slid against his paw, and though he could not touch it with his magic, through his Runeshard, he could feel the stone.

"I'll try."

The stone spheres blew apart like dust in the wind. Living stone streamed into the space between the tunnel and Thia's gravitic anomaly. It formed into a ring exactly matching the tunnel in size and dimension. With slow care, Mateo filled in the space. The sound of grinding stone intensified. Soon, it was so loud that the roar of grinding stone blotted out all other sound.

Elenor tried to shout over the sound to tell Mateo to stop, that something was wrong. She might as well have screamed into the vacuum of space for all the good it did.

The stone ring that Mateo had built began to glow. First, at the edge where it met the Purestone tunnel. The glow slowly crept across the entirety of the band of

- ¡¿Qué?! – What?!
- ¡Estás loca! – You're crazy!

stone. Bubbles of golden light began to fizz from the place where stone met stone.

An explosion of golden sparks blasted around the tunnel, ejecting Mateo from the spot where he hovered it. The tunnel ground to a halt. He cannonballed towards the desert floor, but jerked to a halt just before he hit. Drops of orange fell to the sand as Mateo lowered himself to the desert floor. A gentle glow rose from the blood streaming from Mateo's nose and sound ears.

"That was harder than I thought." He lowered himself to the sand and blew more fizzing orange blood out of his nose. Elenor skidded to a halt next to Mateo. She slapped her Striker against the spines on her shoulders, but no sound rang out from the instrument at the end of her tail.

"Oh no, the Chorus. It's gone," Elenor said.

"The Anchor is built, Elenor. Can't you feel it? We aren't in our reality anymore."

"I'll be fine, Elly. It's just some burst blood vessels. I strained too hard. My ears are already feeling better," Mateo assured.

Elenor shook her head. "You idiot." She looked at him with fond eyes and lifted her right paw. Her Runeshard pulsed as she used it to mentally feel her way through Mateo's body. Once she could feel the broken blood vessels, she instructed her power to pull them back together.

He had been right, there was nothing putting him in real danger. He would have healed just fine on his own, but he shouldn't be in pain if she could fix it. When the bubbling sparks of golden light finally faded from within the tunnel, the entire end ad been filled with a stone disc. At the center of the disk was a spot of emptiness, revealing the center of Thia's vortex.

They padded into the tunnel, which turned out to be much longer than it had seemed from the outside. It was twice as long as it was wide, stretching their walk to the back of the tunnel to a few minutes. The massive disc filling the back of the tunnel was lit by subtle dots of light that filled the walls like distant stars. Geometric patterns scrawled across the surface of the disc, surrounding dozens of holes bored into the surface. These did not go all the way through the disc. Carved indentations flowed across it like a maze connecting various groups of the holes.

"I think it is safe to say that Mateo has succeeded in creating the lock."

"But, I didn't." Mateo tilted his head. "Well, I did, the shapes in the stone just felt right."

"My turn, I guess." Elenor padded forward and reached toward the stone disc with her right paw. Thia and Mateo both examined the disc as well. Mateo made a clicking sound, soft in comparison to his earlier echolocation pops.

"If it's a lock, does it turn?" Elenor asked.

"How could we turn it? Es muy grande," Mateo wondered.

The moment Elenor's paw touched the cool violet stone, light ignited in the carvings. The open spaces outside of the carved outlines of the maze filled with nebula clouds sparkling with rainbows of light. Each cloud was peppered with a coruscation of brighter points. Elenor watched the clouds. She noticed that Thia and Mateo were similarly enraptured.

"So if my power is the key, what do I do with the water?" Elenor asked.

Thia noticed that Elenor had lost at least a few of her spheres of water. "Why are you losing water?"

"Because it has to have some sort of energy in it for me to control it. I can't explain it right because I don't understand. Whatever got shoved in my head tells me that the water has to be alive," Elenor said. Mateo

• Es muy grande – It's so huge

bobbed his head in agreement.

"Why don't you do what Mateo did?" Thia asked.

"Because I'm not sure what he did."

"*I'm* not sure what I did." Mateo's sight ears had not turned from the disc. "It's a maze, but there are a bunch of exits. They all go to those holes, but can't you just, fill the whole thing?"

"I don't think so." Thia pointed her tail in slow succession at several of the holes drilled into the disk. The ones that were close enough to point to. Each one was blocked off by a small vertical wall in the carving of the maze.

"You mean I have to solve the maze with my water?" Elenor lifted her head and looked back and forth. There were thousands of holes and paths through the maze. Maybe tens of thousands.

"I don't think it's that simple. I had to feel my way through making that vortex. I had to keep adding new instructions to what I was doing or the whole thing would have collapsed," Thia explained.

"Mismo. I didn't know at first that would happen when I started filling in the space between the Purestone tunnel and Thia's vortex," Mateo affirmed.

Elenor looked up at the maze, took a deep breath, and then traced her paw down to the only entrance point to the relatively tiny canals of the maze. The remaining orbs of water elongated and joined into a spiraling stream that piled up near the entrance to the maze like snaggled spaghetti. It streamed into the entrance to the maze and began to fill the tiny canals of the lock.

Her first attempt, she tried to simply fill all the holes as the water passed through the channels of the lock. By the time one quarter of the maze was filled with living water, she had an inkling the lock would not open.. The nebulas floating across the surface of the lock began to

 • Mismo - Same

dim, and with each of the small pits filled with water, the stars dimmed further until they were almost imperceptible. More importantly, she could feel some sort of feedback through her Runeshard.

It was like the harder she pushed the water through the maze with the intention of just filling the entire thing, the more difficult it became to go further. Near the halfway point, Elenor became certain what she was doing would not work.

"This isn't the right way. I can feel it. Something is pushing back against me." Elenor withdrew the water from the maze with a wave of her paw.

"Pour life into the path of stars," Mateo repeated, and Elenor looked back up at the massive disc blocking their way. He pointed at the nebulas floating across the surface of the disc with the tip of one of his tentacles, then another and another.

"But they don't make a path. They're just floating everywhere," Thia said.

Elenor's eyes followed the clouds of stars as they floated through the corridors created by the channels carved into the stone. Her eyes fixed on one of the small pits. One of the tiny nebulas swirled around it, and as it trailed away, a small cloud of sparkling cosmic dust was left behind for a moment before it faded. Of most interest, though, was that the cloud of stars was left behind around one of the tiny wells that was blocked off by a wall.

"Is it a trick?" Elenor wondered.

"What do you mean?" Mateo asked.

"Watch the star clouds, they leave behind something when they swirl around certain," Elenor paused as one of the clouds began to swirl around a well, "Right there!" She pointed excitedly with the tip of her tail.

"But they are only the blocked off ones," Thia said.

"Maybe…" Elenor backed up away from the wall until she could see the entire thing. With deliberate care,

Elenor watched and tracked every single tiny well in the door that was blocked off. Instructions came together in her mind, and the stream of water floating in the air around her reshaped itself. Breaking apart into hundreds of tiny spheres of water, they then reshaped themselves into what looked like hundreds of tiny icicles. Elenor gestured forward, and the rods of glowing water shot forward, sliding into place, each one slotted into one of the tiny wells behind a wall in the maze.

"Which way do I turn it?" Elenor asked. Mateo shrugged his front shoulders.

"Counter clockwise, against the swirl of the vortex. When the Ayre of the Anchored Way is played, it creates an instability in the fabric of reality. The Keymaster's March then creates a counter force to stabilize portals through that fabric," Thia theorized.

Elenor made a gesture to her left, and the grinding sound of stone against stone stirred echoes throughout the tunnel. With a loud click, the maze changed. The tiny walls vanished and Mateo let out a whoop.

The spears of water were pushed out of the wall as stone filled in the pits she had used to turn it. This left a far less difficult maze behind, having only a few dozen exit wells and proper paths. Elenor quickly filled them with water. When the pattern was filled, it looked rather like a lotus blossom.

Elenor turned the stone again, and with a final click, the door split along the lines of water. The stone irised away, opening onto a doorway filled with a starry cosmos.

"We did it!" Thia squeaked. Her wings zoomed in from the tunnel behind them and settled in on her back.

They all looked at each other. Despite all of them not actually having eyes, the look exchanged bolstered them all. All three of them jumped through the portal together.

49

"ANSWERS"

Stepping through the portal felt like no other portal they had gone through before. It felt like they had stepped into a space so disconnected from their own reality that they might never return home.

The place they emerged into was an infinite white void, similar to what the world looked like when Elenor had surged the The Silence. A moment later, though, the white faded to black, and streaks of light shone all around them as if they were standing inside a night sky painted with shooting stars.

Elenor looked down and discovered that, while she knew they had not been standing on anything a moment before, now they were standing upon a polished grey granite floor with golden veins shooting through it.

"Welcome to the Runespring. You have gained my attention." They all spun to find the creature that Elenor had encountered upon first entering the pyramid. A felinesque body the size of a tiger constructed of a lattice of thick golden bars. Panels of transparent golden light filled in the honeycomb of spaces along the entire body. Golden orbs of Purestone, tracked them as eyes as the creature padded across the polished stone.

"You sound much better than you did earlier," Elenor said.

The voice that issued from the muzzle of the golden feline was deep, melodic, and enunciated with such precision that it stood out as completely artificial. "That construct, while identical in appearance to this construct, did not have my full attention placed upon it."

"You're the Writ," Thia whispered.

"Yes and no. I am Overseer, and I have a great deal to reveal to you, but first, there is another who needs to explain themselves to one of you." The golden feline bobbed its head behind them. A small bubble of golden light appeared, and then with a pop of sound, a large orange and cream tabby cat appeared out of thin air.

"Whot in tha' bloody 'ell?!" The voice that issued forth from the cat had a slight accent, Scottish, or perhaps Irish. High enough to be feminine, low enough to be masculine, the voice was a balm to the ears. Elenor would not have tried to guess at the cat's sex if she didn't know for certain the cat was female.

"'ow in the nine 'ells am I, in, a," her words began trailing off as the fur on her back and neck stood in recognition, "body?" She drew out the word until her tiny feline mouth made an 'O' of utter astonishment.

"Bottlecaps?" Elenor stared, eyes wide, at the small orange and cream shape.

The cat, back still toward them, turned its head in a creaky motion filled with apprehension. Its wide green eyes spread even wider when she saw Thia and Mateo flanking Elenor.

"Familiar, the time for secrets has passed. Deliver explanations to the Waterbearer," the Writ's physical construct spoke again. Its words, precise enunciation with sharpness enough to slice stone, left no room for argument. The cat would explain itself or face consequences most dire.

If the cat's eyes had gone wide at the sight of Elenor and her friends, they seemed in danger of rolling free from their sockets upon spotting the Writ's construct. The cat hurried over, and in an odd gesture, it prostrated itself before the construct.

"This humble servant apologizes. It is beyond my ability to share the details you request." The cat's accent was still there, but the cadence of her speech was different. She shook with terror.

The construct's golden eyes bore into the cat before it. It made no response to the cat's protest. Instead, it tapped a glowing golden claw on the stone in front of the cat. A pulse of golden light expanded from the tapping claw, passing through the cat then vanishing before it could reach Elenor, Thia, and Mateo.

The glow of the construct's eyes intensified as it stared into the cat. After a long count of thirty, the creature spoke again. "You will share your deceit, Familiar."

There came a pop of sound. It pervaded the space with such overwhelming completion that it pressed down against everything in the space as if it meant to crush the entire universe. Yet there was no pain, and it faded as quickly as it had come. The trembling cat bobbed its head.

"This humble one serves," the cat said. Then she pushed herself to her paws, turned, and hurried to Elenor.

"Elenor, Thia, Mateo, my name is Areti, and I am, was, the Merlin's familiar."

"Areti is a Greek name, but you're, Irish?" Thia observed.

Areti bobbed her head. "Aye, Irish, but the Merlin was originally a Greek. He fancied the name, and I rather fancy it myself." She looked back over her shoulder toward the construct and shivered.

"T'ppears I 'ave some things ta share with ya." Areti paused for a moment. Then she spoke again, her accent a scant remnant of what it had been a moment earlier. "I'm sorry, my accent gets worse when I am nervous."

"Why didn't you tell me?" Elenor asked. The cat had lived with her for over a year. It had never spoken once.

"There are two reasons for that. The first was that I couldn't. This is not my original body. I was controlling the cat through a Surge, because," the cat let out a little sigh. "I wasn't actually in a living body. There are a few things I have kept from you, and," Areti paused, eyes going wide again as she spun around back to the Writ.

"The Resonance Stone!" Areti exclaimed.

The construct shook its head. "The extradimensional anomaly maintained by the stone of which you speak has been fully tethered to the power of the Waterbearer. The stone is no longer required."

"Then I am free," Areti mused, "but without my familiar bond, I'll just die. After all this time, there is nothing to tether me to this world."

"Familiar, you may choose to accept the contract of your previous master. No more stalling. Explain thyself."

"Yes, yes, I apologize, Overseer."

Areti turned back to Elenor. "I have a few things to tell you that I couldn't before, because I was under a Surge preventing me from speaking about it. You need to know that I am not blameless. I accepted the Surge, knowing that it might prevent me from speaking when I should have. I trusted the Merlin enough to do that, but I feel that some fault lies with me."

"What do you mean?" Elenor lowered herself into a sitting position, watching Areti with thorough care.

"I know that you know Osiris did not want to do many of the things he did. He felt they were necessary," Areti said, and Thia nodded in response. "Well, once the Merlin discovered what had driven Osiris to kill all of those people, he came to the conclusion that Osiris may have been right."

"So, the Merlin knew too? He could have stopped this from happening to us?" Elenor's anger was plain.

Areti shook her head. "By the time he figured it out, he couldn't stop it, but he could have warned people. We argued for almost a decade before he convinced me that it would do very little good to warn anyone. Especially since we wouldn't be able to change what was going to happen to them."

"But it would have! At least I would have understood!" Elenor shouted, her teeth bared. "That doesn't explain why he tried to kill me!"

"Elenor, the Merlin was not trying to kill you." The cat sat back on her haunches and made a calming gesture with her forepaws. "Please calm down. I'm not defending what he did and I do not agree with his methods. I'm simply telling you the truth."

Elenor took a calming breath and blew it out. "Fine, tell me."

"I have three things to tell you, and looking at the looming expression of the Overseer, I hope you will let me tell you all three before you jump down my throat again."

Elenor bobbed her head.

"Just remember, I couldn't tell you some of these things because there was a magic binding me against telling you." Areti's ears were back, her expression nervous.

"First, the Resonance Crystals. There are still numerous Resonance Crystals in the world that you need to find and break. The way Osiris made those crystals tortures the souls of the familiars trapped within. They have been in torture for over a millennium. They need to be freed. The Merlin left those crystals in place to make sure the Chorus would be stable until there were Bearers." Areti waited, breath held, while all three Bearers stared at her. The next question that came was not one that she expected.

"You said 'the way Osiris made those crystals.' That indicates that there is another way," Thia said.

"You don't need to know that. No one ever needs to know that." Areti seemed a little frightened that Thia had caught the slip.

"Why not?" Elenor asked.

"Because it is too dangerous for anyone to know. Please leave it at that." Areti's expression changed for just a moment, and if it had not been for two years of living with only animalistic facial expressions of her own, Elenor would not have caught it. It was fear.

"You, that's why you asked the," Elenor searched for the word Areti had used, "Overseer, about a crystal. You were surprised you were in a body when you got here. You were in one of the crystals."

Areti's ears fell and she let out a tiny sigh. "Well, at least you are intelligent enough to see the danger."

Thia spoke then. "Resonance Crystals can be made without murdering Callers and their Familiars, but there is still a cost. Everything has a cost."

Areti nodded. "If we agree to be used in the creation of a Resonance Crystal, our confinement in the stone is painless. But, we cannot free ourselves, and our Crystals can be used by any Caller to expand their resonance." Her tense body and bristling fur gave away the truth.

"Like you were," Mateo guessed.

"Like I was."

Elenor gaped. "The Merlin trapped you inside of a crystal for fifteen hundred years?" Elenor hissed, a little outraged.

Areti shook her head. "No, Elenor, I agreed to help. It just wasn't a fulfilling existence, and I would never ever want to go back to it again. I don't want any familiar to ever experience it. Especially if it is someone careless. We are aware inside of the crystal, but we can't communicate with anyone outside except for the Caller who created our crystal."

"So, how did you communicate with us?" Thia asked.

"The Merlin was not careless."

"Could have fooled me," Elenor grumbled, and Areti gave her a narrow eyed look.

"I told you he was not trying to kill you," Areti said.

"And you lied to me that you hadn't spoken with him in hundreds of years," Elenor squeaked.

"This is the second thing I have to tell you. I did not lie to you. It was the argument that made us stop speaking. He was hellbent on the idea that anyone who went through what you did would not trust us enough to be persuaded to fight the Infected and whatever else Osiris foresaw. I assume he decided to push you into a vulnerable position where you would have no choice but to fight them. Great way to build trust, the jackass," Areti quipped.

"Why were you ever his familiar?" Mateo asked.

"That's not any of your business," Areti snapped back, and Mateo's sight ears leaned back away from the hissing feline. Then he leaned forward, a mouth full of razors bared.

"You know I can bite off your entire tiny body?" The cat rolled her eyes at him. "Oh, big tough monster boy picking on a tiny cat," she snarked, and then went on. "Last thing, and probably the most important." Areti took as deep a breath as she could manage.

"The Merlin kept something from the Iðunn. Something that I wanted to tell you so badly, but he was terrified to tell because it could have backfired horribly. He discovered, without a doubt, what was controlling your mother, and even how to fix it. The problem was the approach, because the problem was," Areti turned her eyes towards the Overseer.

"The problem was with the Writ of your world." The Overseer's over-precise tones cut through everything with such power that the three bearers and the cat all froze for a disrupting second. Then, all four of them had to spread their paws and shake off the pause.

"Apologies, do continue, Areti. I assure you, you are safe. My attention is upon this world."

"The Merlin found out at least a small part of what Osiris had been searching for. He was certain that our Writ had been tampered with by an outside force bent on destroying all knowledge of the past. If he'd had the time, he was certain he could have." Areti squeezed her eyes shut, took a deep breath, and let it out.

"He could have, but terror stayed his hand." The Overseer padded across the stone and put its massive paw on Areti's back, almost engulfing the tabby cat. "That is not your fault, Familiar. As you well know, fear, uncertainty, hesitation, these are not the way of those with the strength to wield the magic of the Callers. That was a failure of the Merlin."

"Areti," Elenor corrected. The Overseer tilted its head at her.

Areti began to respond, but the Overseer patted her back, silencing her. Then the feline construct bobbed its head at Elenor. "You are quite right, Waterbearer, Elenor. None of you are so simple a thing that you should ever be summed up with anything less appropriate than your chosen name."

"Gracias for telling us all of that," Mateo said, "but there was something you said earlier. What is the contract of your previous master?"

Areti looked up at Elenor. "When you accepted the inheritance the Merlin offered you, you became my bonded master. The Overseer was pointing out that if I wish to stay, I can accept your bond and become your familiar. Familiars live as long as their masters, and longer, if their bonds are passed."

The Overseer spoke, interrupting the explanation. "It is unfortunate that time is short, and you do not have time to decide this now. Areti, I will tether thy soul to this plane for a short time. I must insist that the Bearers see what they came here for."

The Overseer made an expansive gesture with its paw. A wall of grey stone ten feet high and extending into infinite distance to the left and right appeared. Then the wall began to fly past them with such speed that it turned into a streak of light as if it were a long

 • Gracias - Thanks

exposure photo of a car passing in the night.

"Elenor, Mateo, and Thia, I must give my apologies. It is the responsibility of the Overseer to maintain the balance of a universe, and in that task, I have allowed a momentary failure that has mutated into a monumental miscarriage. Now, I must ask for your assistance to correct this error, as I cannot reach you where you are without such assistance." The Overseer curled its toes into a semblance of a fist and the wall halted. They had reached the beginning.

"But, aren't you everywhere?" Thia asked. Obviously, she understood some things about the Overseer that the rest of them did not.

The Overseer bobbed its head. "Yes, and no. Even I have some small limits to the power I have been given. Those limits have been exploited in this place. If I were to transition my full attention to the space containing your world, it would collapse and your world would cease. I will show you the beginning and hope that you can reach the end."

"Before we look at that, why do all of this? The pyramid? The door?" Thia asked. "If you were just going to show us what we wanted, why not get us here as fast as possible?"

The Overseer bobbed its head. "The creature you face is not of this reality, and it could corrupt the foundations of all things if it were given access to do so. It was far too close, and I needed to be certain that only the Bearers could transition to this space. Do you have any other questions?"

"Thousands, but we can ask them later if there's time," Elenor said. Mateo and Thia nodded in agreement.

"I apologize, Overseer. Please show us," Thia squeaked.

The Overseer pointed a paw up to the wall and a layer of stone vanished to reveal a second wall, then a third, a fourth. "This is the bridge between physical and metaphysical. Here you will see what Osiris searched for." All four of them padded across the granite and put their paws up on the wall. Everything changed.

NC IO EPOCH 0.0

"What have we done?" The figure seemed human, but the way they were dressed was unlike anything Elenor had ever seen. She looked around and realized that while Mateo, Areti, and Thia were nearby, they seemed frozen. Apparently, viewing this was only meant for one.

Elenor realized that she was standing in the void of space, yet was unaffected by what should have been devastating vacuum. That made sense as she was just viewing the past, but it didn't explain how the two figures were doing the same. How they were talking was also a mystery, but she figured she could ask the Overseer for the answer when this was done.

Both figures were dressed in outfits that covered them from neck to toes. They fit tight to the skin like a onesie made of spandex. One in bright royal blue, the other in deep forest green. The only incongruity to the painted-on fit was a skirt around the waist of each figure. The figure in blue had a skirt that was longer, reaching almost to their knees. The skirt had hair-thin lines of golden light curling across it like vines, and along the vines were outlines of beautiful rose-like flowers. The figure turned, showing a feminine silhouette with small breasts beneath fabric perfectly fit to contain them.

She had been the first to speak. The other figure wore a green outfit, and Elenor was not sure she could call them male. Their figure was masculine with powerful muscles beneath the painted-on fabric. Yet despite the lack of breasts, their lithe figure and long black hair gave them a distinct androgynous look. Their voice sounded as masculine as their muscles looked when they spoke.

"We have saved our people," he spoke. He turned away, and behind them was the Purestone archway that Elenor and her friends had used to enter the dimension where they found the Pyramid.

"At what cost, Eritri?" the blue figure said.

At that moment, something flickered behind the figures. The image, which vanished immediately, was so massive it filled Elenor's vision. Then it snapped into resolve. Elenor had to turn her head to see space around the entirety of the Earth. Their entire planet blinked into existence. The green figure pointed at the planet, and the archway of Purestone shot away towards the surface of the world.

"What other choice do we have? The creature has devoured billions of lives, Antamae! It must be stopped!"

"By allowing it to devour billions more?" Antamae hugged herself, rubbing her azure gloved hands against her biceps.

"This Earth is not our Earth. It is not anyone's Earth. We created it outside of any reality specifically to contain the Netherspawn. It will not remain here free of chains unless it is fed. It cannot be killed, it cannot be banished. This is the only choice. It is us," the figure in green gestured toward themselves, "or them." It pointed to the newly formed planet.

"I am aware of the situation. That does not mean I must enjoy it," Antamae said coldly.

"Do you think I enjoy this?" Eritri shouted into the void.

"I don't know what to think of you. This solution borders on chaos, Eritri. Intentionally breaking a Writ? Forcing a world outside of the purview of an Overseer? Even for timeless ones like ourselves, there will be consequences, Eritri." Antamae turned her back on the figure in green.

"If you are so terrified of breaking the rules, why did you help me?"

"Because that is the one thing we agree on. At present, it is a choice between this and death, but I will continue to search for a better way. Replicating our world and allowing it to be devoured over and over by the Netherspawn is not the way." Antamae stepped away from Eritri and vanished.

NC ??, EPOCH ?.?

Elenor gasped and coughed as she emerged from the memory. Thia, Mateo, and Areti all were standing, paws spread, shaking with the transition between realities.

"How many?" Elenor hissed. The Overseer watched her passively for a long moment, as if it understood her by her appearance alone.

"Seven," the Overseer stated. Thia looked up, and Mateo's ears arranged themselves in a posture of confusion. One massive sight ear up, the other laid back.

"How many what," Mateo paused as the realization of what she had been asking came to him. "Siete?"

"This is the seventh iteration of their replication. Past iterations have all been devoured by the Otherthing. That's what the old Callers referred to as the Netherspawn."

The Overseer looked back towards the wall. "There is one last piece that you must see."

"Seven." Thia whimpered. She couldn't process what she had learned. "Seven, Earths, full of people? Billions, of people, gone?"

"Yes," the Overseer answered, not realizing that Thia already knew the answer.

"How?" Tears of loss left tracks in the fur of Elenor's face for those unfathomable nameless dead.

"How?" the Overseer asked, though it was clear that its precise enunciation was a request for clarity.

"How, just how!" Elenor howled. "How could they do that? How is it possible? How is it allowed? Just how?!" Elenor snarled in despair laced with fury.

The Overseer seemed lost at the flood of questions and anger.

"How, are we supposed to stop that?" Mateo asked.

The Overseer turned to him and it dropped its jaw in a reassuring grin filled with sharp golden teeth. "You are the Shardbearers. Even the power of the Otherthing shrinks before that of a Runeshard well wielded."

The Overseer waited patiently for the four figures to process some of their grief. When Elenor looked up, muzzle stained with tears, it was prepared for her question.

"You said there was more," Elenor piped.

"There is but one more sorrow to view, and perhaps if you do not understand once it is done, I will explain." The Overseer gestured to a new section of the wall. This piece was somewhere in the middle, though none of them had noticed the wall moving to arrive at its new position. "Prepare."

NC 11, EPOCH 0.0

Once again, Thia stood in the vacuum of Space, but this time, only the figure in green stood in front of the archway of shimmering golden Purestone. Eritri stood, his hands behind him, left wrist gripped in his right. It was not long before the figure in blue stepped into view, as if appearing through a door that Thia could not see.

"You dare call me to this place again, Eritri? I know what you have done. The Spires of Resonant Harmony? Did you think I would not see from where they draw their power? Did you think I would help you begin this cycle of death and horror again?" Antamae hissed out the last words.

"I dare? As if there is another choice. The spires are an attempt to gain positive outcomes from this negative situation. I am attempting to right the balance of our reality."

"You are using the resonance of the Netherspawn to gain power! That resonance is chaos manifest. You are not balancing our realm. You are furthering chaos," Antamae pronounced.

"Do not be a fool, Antamae. We can harness this power to ensure that when the next Netherspawn appears, we can simply banish it." Eritri turned back to the golden arch.

"Eritri, I will not be a part of this any further. There is only the choice we agreed upon. Banish this port dimension and the Netherspawn with it. It is weakened and will return

to the Void." Antamae turned away from Eritri and began to walk away.

The pure tone at the beginning of a Surge rang through the space. Antame froze as if she were a statue.

"I cannot let you do that, Antamae." Eritri turned back. Hanging from the spread fingers of his left hand was a glowing crystal ring swinging from a glowing crystal chain. It vibrated with the notes of a Surge.

"It took me over a thousand years to construct this artifact. I knew you would betray me one day. All you have ever cared for is the so-called balance. You have never served our people." Eritri drew a dagger with a blade so black it could only be relic stone. "Good bye, old friend."

A pop of sound so pervasive that it might have been the finger snap of a god smashed the notes of the paralytic surge.

The crystal ring exploded.

Antamae rose to her full height. "Did you think that trinket could contain me? A thousand years to buy you ten seconds. You should talk less, and act more."

"I had hoped to save you from having to take your power by force." Eritri shook the crystal dust from his hand as he stepped back into a defensive posture, dagger held in a high guard.

Antamae held up her left hand, and with her right index finger, she flicked the bangle around her left wrist. The sound vibrating from the bangle felt as if it would shake all of reality would shake apart. The sound itself somehow condensed into a sphere vibrating above Antamae's palm. "If you wish to take my resonance, come and claim it."

Thia noticed that Eritri was doing something with his free hand. His fingers flew, seemingly tapping his own palm, but Thia could see there was some sort of device strapped around his wrist. He was playing a surge!

It was over in an instant. Antamae made her move. The sphere above her palm pulsed with the threat of every hive of venomous insects in all of the universe packed into the tiny space. She leapt back away from Eritri, and Thia's breath caught.

A black cloud of mist rose into a wall behind Antamae and she burst through it. The sphere of absolute sound exploded when it struck Eritri's shoulder as he dove to the left. Thia watched, breath held in horror as somehow, the sphere of sound unfolded into what appeared to be millions of lines of compressed air razors.

Yet, it was more than that. Eritri screamed as his arm evaporated. Skin, muscle, blood, and bone were shredded until there was nothing left at all. Somehow, Thia knew that even atoms did not survive that Surge.

Antamae, though, was far worse. The black miasma clung to her body as it disintegrated. Yet, she smiled through the agony.

"Even when you win, I still win."

Eritri rushed forward, attempting to shove his relic stone dagger into her chest. With the last of her life, she flicked a finger against her bracelet again and her body vanished into vapor.

"No!" Eritri shouted. The dagger fell from nerveless fingers as he fell to his knees. He narrowed his eyes at the cloud of drifting dust that had been Antamae. "You have only doomed another to be my accomplice," he whispered in fury.

NC ??, EPOCH ?.?

"He did it," Thia whispered. "He knew what he was doing. Such greed."

The Overseer nodded. "You understand."

"I don't," Elenor said.

"Well, let me spell it out for you. When the, Otherthing, feeds on the earth in this port dimension, it gives off massive amounts of Resonance, disrupting this small reality. When that happens, this pocket dimension gives off immeasurable energies that can be used to call impossibly powerful Surges. He's collecting it for his own purposes. He is killing billions of people, over and over, for his own gain." Thia growled, but her anger was not for Elenor. Her sensory coils rustled, and her face was turned directly towards the Overseer.

"As unbelievable as his greed is, it's even worse than what we have just seen, isn't it?" Thia asked, and the Overseer bobbed its head.

"He planned it from the start. When they figured out how to trap that thing in this pocket dimension, he already knew what he would do. Otherwise, why prepare things he might need to kill Antamae? Will he be punished, as the Writ punishes Callers who try to take power that isn't theirs?" Thia asked.

"That is the wrong question," the Overseer said.

Elenor and Mateo had simply laid down with Areti between them. The cat had not spoken a single word, and the way her whiskers and ears had fallen, she might not ever speak again.

Elenor felt broken inside again. She had only wanted to know why she had become a creature out of nightmares. Then she wanted to learn so she could just get some normalcy back. Then she had learned so that she could keep herself and her friends safe from the real monsters.

But now, this thing, god, whatever it was, expected her to be some kind of hero. Was that who she was? It hadn't been easy for her. It had hurt. She had almost died, more than once. She hadn't killed anyone yet, but she knew that she had been lucky. If she kept going down this path, killing would likely not be the most difficult thing she would have to do.

"Is that why you gave us our powers? You needed heros?" Elenor asked.

"No. I have no use for heroes." The creature spat the word heroes with some disdain. "Heroes are fools who will sacrifice too much to gain too little. I require warriors and predators who will achieve the goal. There can be no Hero's Sacrifice in this. Heroes believe they can save everyone, and that if they cannot, they should give themselves to try because they cannot accept that sometimes losses are inevitable. I need more than

Heroes. I need those who would wield powers that even gods hold in reverence. Those like you."

The Overseer looked each of them over, assessing, judging. Elenor had no idea if she could be something like that.

Mateo rose from where he had been lying and padded to Thia. The Overseer was paying attention to Elenor. Thia and Areti were whispering quietly. He got the sense it didn't matter how much they whispered. The Overseer was something else. Perhaps an omnipotent force. Perhaps even a god. So, he asked.

"What do we know about this thing?" he whispered, his voice becoming a raspy squeak at such low volumes.

It was Areti who answered him. "The Overseer is a legend. The Merlin, and many other Callers, had theories about the functions of the universe. They theorized that the Writ had some kind of intelligence backing it. That it protected the balance of reality. They thought that if the mystical balance of the world was interfered with to a great enough extent, an Overseer would appear to correct the imbalance. Seems they were right."

"Entonces, ¿es un dios?" Mateo asked.

Areti shook her head. "Not a god, not like you think at least. If I am guessing right, and it is a guess, it has that kind of power, but it also has rules about how it is allowed to use it."

Mateo looked back to the Overseer, his sight ears swiveling to focus directly on the creature of gold and light. "Así que, is that it? That's all we are good for? Fighting, and fighting until we win?" Mateo asked, a little angry. "We aren't supposed to help people, or save people?"

The Overseer stared at him for a moment, and Mateo felt the power of the creature settling on him. He

• Entonces, ¿es un dios? – So, it is a god?
• Así que - So

squared his shoulders and stood, unbent by the creature's power. He had faced death in his life, and he wouldn't be cowed by this thing.

"A poor assumption, Mateo. I do not expect you to simply pass when those who need your help can be helped. You each were chosen with simple criteria in mind. You will not misuse your power for your own greed. You have the potential to develop a mind that will remain collected no matter the pressures of your task. And perhaps most importantly, you can learn how to choose your battles."

The Overseer's gaze lingered on each of the Shardbearers until it seemed to be certain of something. "I do not expect it to be easy for you to know when you must lose something to gain something greater. However, that is the potential you were chosen to discover. You can be heroic without the suicidal drive of a hero."

Thia had continued her quiet conversation with Areti until she stood up. "Mateo still has a point, though. Is that all we are here for? To fight?"

The Overseer shook its feline head. "No, as I have stated. More is needed, but you have already proven the capacity for thinking beyond that which is obvious." It turned toward the wall displaying all of the history, knowledge, and function of their reality. "We are almost out of time and there is less existential information that I must pass on. I know you are all still processing what you have learned. I would offer you more time if it were possible, but it is not. You still have questions. Please ask them."

Elenor was the first to speak. "Why do we look like this? Couldn't we have been just as powerful and still looked human? You can do anything, can't you?"

The Overseer nodded. "This is a complex question, but I will attempt to summarize. Even my attention cannot be everywhere at once, and so, the Writs of any given world have their own kind of intelligence derived from my own. Your forms were chosen by that intelligence for their predatory potential, mystical abilities, defensive adaptations, and your ability to interact with the world. One of the weapons of a predator is fear, so your chosen forms were creatures that induced fear by the sheer potency of their otherness.

To be clear, even if the intelligence available to the Writ had chosen a human-like form, you still would not have been human any longer. The human form is far too fragile to sustain the mystical energies of your increased power as Callers, to say nothing of a Runeshard."

Elenor scoffed. "Well, it sucks at picking things that actually work right. These stupid eyes on my back are impossible to deal with."

"As I said, the intelligence here is limited in its ability to make choices. The process that reshaped your bodies used some of your own fears, knowledge, and preferences to shape bodies that would be comfortable and utilitarian. Unfortunately, since your transformative process was the first, it was also the least refined." The Overseer's face shaped a tiny, quiet smile onto the golden muzzle. The only expression of emotion they had seen on its face so far.

"That being said, in this place, I can offer you a single chance to refine your bodily functionality into something that you can more easily utilize. I can offer the same chance to each of you. Next question." The Overseer watched them expectantly.

"Why us?" Elenor asked.

The Overseer took a long moment staring at the Writ wall before it responded. "I mentioned the main reasons, but it is my thought that you mean, isn't there anyone else better?"

Elenor nodded in response. The Overseer shook its feline head the ruff of golden threads acting as fur around its face rustling with faintly musical chimes.

"No, because there was one criterion I did not mention. Only those with the predisposition to being Callers could be chosen. While any creature with a soul can become a Caller, very few have the predisposition." The Overseer turned to Thia as she opened her mouth. She didn't get to speak.

"But my family doesn't know anything about this stuff?" Elenor wondered.

"No, but it is a predilection of the Spirit, not genetics, of which I speak. When that is added to the criteria I have already exposed, you are quite rare indeed," the Overseer said, and Elenor looked down at her paws, losing herself in thought.

"What is the Miasma?" Thia asked.

The Overseer nodded. "The Miasma is an ancient and powerful Surge, like The Silence. It is one of the absolute powers of destruction. However, what you refer to is something more. Eritri tampered with your Writ so that when some Callers were given their Writbands, they would be infested with a magic to protect against the inhabitants of this reality learning their situation. If the magic in question came into contact with something that appeared as if it might reveal the truth, the Caller would be forced to Surge the Miasma to destroy the offending material."

"Can you, fix it?" Thia asked hesitantly.

"It has already been done. The Writ of your world now functions in balance as it should. There will be some side effects, but they should be minimal, considering how many Callers with active Writbands there are on your world." The Overseer glanced back at the wall. "Time proceeds, continue with speed."

"I thought that was only one now," Thia said.

"Technically two. Areti still has an active Writband or she would not be able to speak. However, she did not carry the corruption," the Overseer replied.

"And the side effects?" Thia asked.

"Writbands will need to be re-instantiated. Note also that anyone who gains a Writband at this point will experience a transformation similar to your own. Energetic requirements for Calling now exceed the threshold of tolerance for the human form. At minimum, all Callers will receive relic skin reinforcement like your own and internal modulation for energetic endurance."

Elenor spoke next, but her subdued squeak would have been imperceptible to any with ears less sharp than her current company. "Is this what I'm supposed to do?"

The Overseer turned to her and its eyes softened. "That, is not for anyone to decide but you. I can change many things in this reality, Elenor, but nothing, not god nor Otherthing, human nor monster, Caller nor Overseer can ever change what you decide for yourself. Will is the immutable benefit of life, and it is more powerful than any force in creation. It can be beaten down, but to think it can be broken is the most heinous of lies. Do, what you feel is right for you."

"That doesn't really help," Elenor said.

The Overseer did something then that startled them all. The creature of gold and light let out a booming laugh. It lasted for a long moment until it noticed all of them staring at it in astonished terror. "What? Did you think I was just some analytical machine? One cannot understand the balance without the emotions of the living."

They continued to stare at the Overseer. "We, didn't," Mateo started but he trailed off unsure what he had been about to say. The Overseer let out another little growling chuckle. It turned back to the wall.

"Unfortunately, we are out of time. They are near to the surface, and if you do not go soon, there will not be enough time to stop them," The Overseer said, and turned back to the Shardbearers.

"Quién?" Mateo asked.

"The Infected. They were all drawn here by the call of the Otherthing. Many were made from the recently dead, but there were some dozens that can still be saved if you are willing."

"We are, but we need Elenor. She's the only one who can play The Silence," Thia said, and the Overseer responded with a shake of the head.

"Not right now. When you unmade the Thaumalgam,"

Mateo's yelp interrupted the Overseer. "¡Espere! You have seen that thing before?! No, you have seen it enough times that it has a name?!" Mateo sputtered in shriek of insanity.

The Overseer rolled its golden eyes and went on without responding. "You temporarily cut off the Otherthing from all of its puppets. If you hurry, you can strike at their tethers without needing to reveal them."

Elenor stood up and turned away from the wall. "We have to help!"

"There is a little time still. There are some things I must tell you before our time here is done, and I fear you will all need some time to process what you have learned once you have taken care of these Infected." The Overseer made a calming gesture with one of its massive golden paws.

"You understand now, your world is a copy that is meant only for the Otherthing to devour. You think that the Infected are something that Osiris created, but they are not," the Overseer said, and Thia continued for it, her sensory coils rustling with excitement, giving the impression of eyes darting back and forth in furious thought.

"He tapped the power of the Otherthing, didn't he? Did he do it on purpose?" Thia wondered.

- Quién? – Who?
- ¡Espere! – Wait!

The Overseer nodded in response, but paused when Elenor spoke. "Your mom said they studied the Writ to see how it would react to certain things," Elenor squeaked, and the Overseer gestured her on with a paw. "So, without your attention here, the Writ only reacts in specific ways. I bet it has a specific way to react to stuff like what the Otherthing does," Elenor finished.

"Yes. Creatures from the Void, which have many names, are always forces meant to unbalance our reality. The Writ, left without supervision, took the predictable measure of releasing the power of the Runespring to restore balance. A measure with which I agree." The Overseer looked up when everything shook around them.

"That is not a good sign," the Overseer said.

"There are but three things I yet have time to tell. First, the Otherthing will be back, but there is some time before it reestablishes the connection you have broken. Remember, it is powerful, but it is not of this reality. This is your world." The Overseer did not seem nervous, but it was hurried.

"Second, you will not be able to stop it from escaping this pocket reality. You have power enough to defeat it, but it will not stand and fight when it returns. By drawing my attention to this place, you have shown it the way to freedom. It will escape back to the reality that birthed this dimension. When it does, the mad Caller Eritri will attempt to seal off the dimension to prevent its escape. You must be ready when he does. You will only have one chance to lock open the way. Eritri will not come himself, but he will send others through. You will know when it happens. When it does, you must find them and kill them. Their connection to the complete reality will lock open the way back. Then I can assist further." The space shook again, and the wall of stone that held the Writ began to dissolve.

"Third, you are not alone. There are ten Fundaments that feed the Runespring. The ten magics that make all realities what they are. There will be ten Runeshards. Before this is finished, they will need your help, and you will need theirs." The golden panels of light filling out the Overseer's form flickered. It gestured them closer with a golden paw.

"This is the last of my power I can inject into this reality without risking collapse. This," it reached out and carefully touched a claw to Elenor's chest. Her Writband lit up beneath her fur with golden light. All three bands pulsed, the inner band, the middle band, and then the outer band before the sound waves faded. "will give each of you the opportunity," the claw touched Thia's Writband, which pulsed in the same golden pattern. "to make some minor adjustments to your bodies."

The claw touched Mateo's Writband, pulse, pulse, pulse. "I strongly suggest you consider making these adjustments only minor. While the transformative process was flawed, it was flawed only in small ways. These are bodies that are fit to your personalities, given predatory impetus." The Overseer gestured with its paw and a golden rimmed portal filled with stars appeared not far away.

"One last thing. When you leave here, you have to choose if you will reveal yourselves to the world or try to fight in secret. Peril lies in both directions, be prepared." The Overseer flickered, then vanished.

They all stood there, staring at the spot where it had been for a long moment.

A tiny voice broke the silence. "T'anks for nothin'! 'ow am I supposed ta ge' back home?!" Areti yowled into the silence.

50
"THE BEGINNING COMES AT THE END"

Stumbling onto the streets of Aleppo, the four figures blurred by dust stood frozen in confounded silence.

"It did not look like this when we came in," Elenor stated as her eyes roved over the destruction.

"Thanks for that stunning report, Capitán Obvio," Mateo sniped, his sight ears twitching. "Did we do this?"

"I don't know. Let's get to higher ground. There are a lot of hurt people in this and we need to figure out if we can help them," Thia said.

Elenor tapped her tail against the paving stones and began to play the Ghostwalker's Etude. She altered the Surge to include her friends, and then bobbed into the air. Thia and Mateo followed her into the sky with alacrity. They found themselves to the south of the Citadel, or at least what was left of it. Not one stone was standing atop another.

"If we can help them?" Mateo said.

"If, Mateo. If we help, in broad daylight, there is no question the entire world will know about us. You heard what the Overseer said. This is clearly what they meant," Thia said.

"Thia!" The voice that squawked in Thia's ear made her jump. "Are you alright?!"

"Helen, could you please stop yelling. Sensitive ears here!" Mateo hissed.

"Right, sorry, are you three all right? What happened?"

The smoke and dust cleared as they gained enough altitude that the entire city came into view. They all stared in stunned silence.

 • Capitán Obvio – Captain Obvious

"My first guess, would be, a lot," Areti whispered, feline eyes wide with shock.

Spread below them was a city laid waste. From this height, it appeared as if a toddler had shaken a basket full of plastic Lego bricks into a sandbox, leaving behind a chaotic wasteland of nothing that even remotely appeared to be a city. Stones barely peaked from the sand. That was the appearance of the entire city. There were no buildings, only rubble. People hurried through the streets as they attempted to find sanctuary or assistance. Wails of pain and terror could be heard from nearly all directions.

"Mom, what happened to Aleppo?" Thia asked.

"There was a massive earthquake while you were in the pocket dimension. There isn't much left."

"We have to help these people," Mateo said again, but Thia held up a paw, her mouth falling open. Then she pointed a claw out towards the city. Across the city, dozens of pulses of green light were appearing in the rubble.

"I think we have bigger problems to deal with. If what the Overseer said is right, then we have to stop that before we can help anyone," Thia said.

"Thia, what is happening there?" Helen asked though the comm unit.

"Mom, we," she took a breath, "we're going to have to discuss this later, because right now, if we don't stop what's happening here, there are going to be a lot more casualties."

"What's happening there?" Helen asked again.

"From the looks of it, there are about a hundred out of control Infected about to tear apart everything that is left in this entire city," Elenor filled in. There was a long pause on the line.

"Then you're going to need our help." There was a commotion through the line. "Tell me one thing, did you find what we needed to know?"

"We got what we came for. Now we have a lot more questions to answer," Thia replied.

In a surprise to everyone, Helen just chortled. "So the beginning comes at the end. This has been a mystery for fifteen hundred years. You really should have expected that."

Thia rubbed a paw over her muzzle. "Can you please provide us with support?"

"Damien is working on it now. One more question," Helen said.

"Yes?"

All levity fell from Helen's tone and her voice came through the comms like a lead brick through a plate glass window. "What, did you do, to my Writband?"

"Can we focus?" Mateo asked, ignoring Helen's question. A tremendous explosion sounded from the north, and they all spun in that direction. A dome of emerald energy covered a small part of the city.

"We need to go. Areti, can you help, or do we need to get you somewhere safe?" Thia asked.

"I can help if Elenor takes my bond, if not, I am just an exceedingly cute cat," Areti said.

"Exceedingly cute?" Elenor looked skeptical.

"The cutest. You always said so, every time I brought in a new bottle cap. Speaking of which, we need to fetch my collection."

Elenor sighed. "I would really like to discuss what that involves. I'll keep her with me," Elenor said, and Areti nodded. She floated closer to Elenor, and they began to descend towards a nearby verdant glow.

"Observer imagery is coming in now." Helen spoke into the comm. "We will let you know where to find each Infected so you three can stay out of sight as much as possible."

"Are you three ready?" Thia asked. Mateo nodded, and Elenor joined him a moment later. "Let's get this done."

www.ingramcontent.com/pod-product-compliance
Lightning Source LLC
Chambersburg PA
CBHW011510010826
48973CB00014B/2804